Hayward's Revenge

· THE ELDERS BOOK THREE ·

Cailyn Lloyd

Hayward's Revenge

© 2021 Land of Oz LLC

All rights reserved. No part of this book may be reproduced or transmitted in any form or by any means, electronic or mechanical, including photocopying, recording, or by any information and retrieval system, without permission in writing from the copyright holder.

This is a work of fiction. Names, characters, places and incidents either are the product of the author's imagination or are used fictitiously, and any resemblance to any actual persons, living or dead, events, or locales is entirely coincidental.

ISBN-13: 978-0-578-83233-3

Cover design: Rose Miller

For Katie, Ryan, Sarah, and Jesse
Just this once, Kato, you're not last

One

The loud roar of a car engine spooked Leah MacKenzie. An odd sound, it burrowed into her sleepy brain. She lived in a quiet neighborhood and people there didn't drive fast. Usually, lawn mowers and snow blowers were the only sounds that disturbed the peace.

Leah was homeschooled, but on this warm, beautiful day, Mom had sent her outside for some fresh air. Leah had fallen asleep on the front lawn in the shade of an oak ablaze with bright fall colors. She felt a little groggy, still half asleep. Lying on a blanket with her dolls and an ornate wooden dollhouse, she had been dreaming about a doll wedding. The sound of that roaring engine washed over her like a murky shadow, a bad feeling.

A warning.

Her eyes flew open.

Focusing on an approaching car, she sensed something dark. Something within the car or maybe even the car itself. She stood, grabbed her dolls, and glanced at the shelter of the garage but sensed she had no time. The engine revved and metal scraped as the car bounced over the edge of the driveway. Leah dashed behind the tree and pressed her back against the thick trunk as the car careened across the yard and crashed into the old oak with a horrendous screech of twisting metal and breaking glass. The tree and the ground beneath her feet shuddered with the impact and nearly knocked Leah off her feet.

For a few seconds, there was silence other than the faint hiss of steam. The air smelled like burnt plastic.

Leah peeked toward the house just as Mom flew out the front door, looking about frantically, yelling, "Leah! Leah!"

Several neighbors rushed out onto their lawns wearing shocked expressions. Mr. Spencer was talking on a phone and pointing with a serious face.

As Leah stepped out from behind the tree, her mother grabbed her into her arms. "Thank God you're okay."

"I'm okay, Mom. We should check the car, though."

They inched toward a twisted mess of metal barely recognizable as a car, the steering wheel pointing uselessly through the broken windshield toward the sky.

Mom held her hand and clenched it tighter as they approached. Leah knew she was nervous about what they would find—blood and guts, or something worse—but the driver's seat was empty.

Indeed, the car was empty. No driver nearby, just the crushed remains of her dollhouse. Still in shock, Leah started to cry. That antique house had once belonged to Grandma Laura. It was her last connection to a woman she loved dearly and who was now gone. Sadness washed over her.

And then fear. That car had been aimed at her.

Moments later, she heard sirens.

Two

Dana MacKenzie sat at the kitchen table, fretting silently.
Her kitchen was a mix of old and new: black stainless steel appliances, refinished oak cabinetry, quartz countertops, ceramic flooring patterned in a mix of brown and sage, the table reclaimed pine with a thick distressed top.

Watching Leah eating her bedtime snack—chocolate frozen yogurt—Dana tried to control the jumble of thoughts and fears rushing at her.

The wrecked car had been towed away after being reported stolen earlier in the day. The police had canvassed the neighborhood and learned nothing. They suspected the driver had jumped out just before impact, but Dana didn't believe it and sensed they didn't either. None of the neighbors actually saw anyone flee. The accident was inexplicable. A minor incident in the minds of the police, she feared, and an event soon forgotten in the face of more pressing matters.

Dana feared a darker possibility. Two years ago, her parents had been killed in Wisconsin, part of a twisted, improbable story involving a strange old Englishman named Kenric Shepherd, a mysterious, dangerous presence in the house, and a series of events that led to a devastating explosion.

Afterward, Dana concluded that her mother and Shepherd had stared down something evil in the house, the nature of which she could scarcely imagine. No need to. She believed that dark episode had ended when the house was destroyed, the remnants consumed by fire. Whatever they faced that night had died along with her parents and Shepherd. Believing that story implicitly was the only way Dana could live without fear, without looking over her shoulder every moment of the day.

The first crack in the story appeared when another Englishman, Lachlan Hayward, came to visit last year. A longtime acquaintance of Shepherd's, he claimed to be investigating the death of his friend. He asked questions about the house in Wisconsin and they talked for a while. He had promised to follow up with her, but she never heard from him again. Leah had, though...

"Can I sleep in your room tonight?" Leah licked the spoon clean.

Dana nodded. "Of course. Shower first."

Leah whined, "Mom. No, not tonight!"

Dana rolled her eyes. They had this battle before every shower. "Not open to discussion. Go!"

"I knew you'd say that." Leah glared for a moment and skulked off.

Dana heard the shower start a minute later.

The other reason she feared a darker explanation was Leah herself.

Just five, Leah was tall for her age with long blonde hair like her grandmother. She was highly intelligent and read at a fourth-grade level. She was even better at math—one reason she was homeschooled. The other was her keen perception.

Her advanced mental capabilities emerged more than a year ago, first as an avid desire to read, and then as a rapidly expanding vocabulary.

Incidental to that, it was soon clear Leah had inherited a gift from her grandmother. It had many names. The sixth sense. ESP. Second sight. Laura MacKenzie had been a reluctant psychic, but Leah seemed content to embrace it.

They were visiting Uncle Nate when Dana first realized it. He had lost his wallet. Leah, cute as could be, told him she had a dream. She dreamt the wallet was in his sofa. And it was.

Dana knew instantly what that insight meant. After a period of denial, she searched the internet and discovered a veritable trove of material on raising a psychic or *gifted* child. Who knew? It was rather intuitive, all about giving children the room to develop their skills naturally. Encouraging them, but also helping them avoid sensory overload with their feelings. Dana became a convert and supported her, fighting an ingrained bias against the paranormal.

Still, as Leah grew and her gift became more evident, Dana felt less and less up to the task.

Lachlan Hayward was also psychic, and he established a connection with Leah during his visit. A month later, Leah had a dream in which Lachlan warned they were in some inexplicable danger, that they should move. He had been silent since.

At the time, Dana didn't take the warning seriously. It was only a dream, and Leah didn't seem overly worried about the message. And she had sensed no immediate threat.

Dana felt one now, and so did Leah.

"Will you dry my hair?"

Leah stood at the doorway with a towel wrapped around her head.

"Yes, let's go." Sometimes, the mundane aspects of motherhood kept her from becoming too introspective over the challenges of her life with Leah and her special gifts.

An hour later, with Leah safely in bed, Dana paced on the flagstone patio behind their home—a beautiful, century-old Craftsman house with slate-blue siding and white trim in Naperville, Illinois—sipping wine.

A danger existed, but what could she do?

She had no one to call, no one to confide in. She wasn't psychic like Leah, and yet, Dana knew she was in danger, that her safe story had come unraveled. That whatever killed her parents had just paid them a visit, driving a stolen car.

Assume the worst and plan accordingly, she decided.

A runaway car was a difficult threat to anticipate or fend off. They had been lucky this time. The solution was obvious.

They needed to leave the house for a while.

Without second-guessing herself, Dana grabbed her laptop and searched for a house online. Within ten minutes, she had bookmarked five promising furnished rentals where they could stay until she felt certain of their safety again. She would schedule tours in the morning. By tomorrow night, they would be somewhere else—whatever it took to ensure Leah's safety.

While Dana wasn't Leah's birth mother, she had fully embraced the role.

Leah was her late brother's child, and the resemblance was striking. At times, she saw Jacob in her expressions and mannerisms, and she found it both sad and warming. They had been close, and her deep grief remained, only partly assuaged by having his daughter to love and care for.

Leah had lived with her grandparents, Lucas and Laura MacKenzie, until they died in the explosion at the house. Dana had then taken Leah in and adopted her. Being her mother and guardian was a full-time job. She remained single, too busy to worry about dating.

Though Dana prayed the business in Wisconsin was over with, she had prepared as if it wasn't. She bought a gun, a Beretta M9. Obtained a concealed carry permit and practiced at a range weekly. She earned her second-degree black belt in Taekwondo. Carried a Taser, pepper spray, and a knife. Dana had become very proficient in self-defense and was determined that Leah would live a life free of the fears Dana had lived with for the past two years.

Dana poured another glass of wine, then field stripped and cleaned her gun. She walked a perimeter of the backyard, the Beretta in hand. The area was fenced, so she checked for breaches and scanned the ground for footprints. Satisfied the yard was secure, Dana locked the house and armed the alarm system for the first time this week. She had been getting careless lately.

After changing into pajamas, Dana slipped the Beretta into her nightstand and set the Taser next to the lamp, though they seemed inadequate against something that could send rogue vehicles after them. She slid into bed and stared at Leah for a minute—a beautiful and angelic child in repose—easing stray hairs away from her face. Dana put a protective arm around her and tried to relax, waiting for sleep to come.

★ ★ ★

Leah awoke in a dark room.

She took a moment to orient herself. Pressed against her mother, her faint scent was pleasant, reassuring. Within that cocoon of warmth and familiar smells, Leah felt safe, protected. Mom was asleep, breathing lightly, but Leah felt turmoil in her dreams. She couldn't see the dreams but sensed her mood, and the mood was troubled.

Leah felt troubled too.

Leah couldn't stop thinking about the car and knew it had been sent to hurt her. The police said the driver had probably run away, but Leah knew that wasn't true. No one was driving the car. She'd seen the empty driver's seat with her own eyes, but the police ignored her story. She was just a kid. What could she know?

More than they realized.

She had a special ability. She knew when Mom was sad and why. She had dreams and occasionally saw things before they happened. Sometimes, she could hear other people's thoughts—not exact words but impressions of what they were thinking and feeling.

At first, she assumed it was normal, that everyone was like her. Until she found Uncle Nate's wallet.

Mom quietly freaked out. She was alarmed for some reason and Leah felt bad, felt that she had done something wrong just because she found the wallet. Leah tried to turn the sensations off but didn't know how.

Slowly, Mom relaxed. Then she bought a book called *Your Psychic Child*.

Most importantly, she stopped treating Leah like a misfit. Encouraged her to talk about it and share her feelings and dreams when she had them. Bought Leah books about special kids like *Matilda* and *The Third Eye,* a story about a girl with ESP.

Then Lachlan came to visit.

They had met only once, but Leah felt a strong and immediate connection with him. They shared the same special ability—the only person she had ever met who was like her. They could talk without speaking and have conversations in their heads. Until then, she had sometimes felt alone, even with Mom close by. She was different in a way that Mom didn't fully understand. Lachlan understood.

After that first meeting, he spoke to her in a dream, and warned her their house wasn't safe.

While the dream was upsetting, Leah didn't feel any immediate sense of danger. Mom seemed to trust her feeling on the issue.

Besides, Lachlan had sounded confused, had said he was asleep in a hospital and couldn't wake up. Leah didn't understand. If someone fell asleep in a hospital and didn't wake up, weren't they dead? Since then, she hadn't heard from Lachlan and felt no risk in the house.

Until now.

That car had been after her, driven by some mysterious thing Lachlan called the darkness. Leah just knew it. But she had no idea what to do next.

Then she realized: if he could talk to her, she could talk to him. But how?

Leah closed her eyes and pictured the person she remembered. A vivid image, a man with a kind face and a full head of white hair. She held the image front and center and sent out a thought: *Lachlan, I need to talk to you.*

She repeated the message for several minutes in her head, then tried speaking the words aloud.

Nothing happened.

Of course not. She had no idea what she was doing. She would talk to Mom tomorrow and ask her to find Lachlan. He would have the answers to her questions.

Mom wouldn't like it, though. Whenever the subject of the old house in Wisconsin came up, she grew quiet and had sad thoughts.

Finally, she decided to sleep on it, rolling over and snuggling into Mom.

Then, as clear as a bell, she heard Lachlan speak. *Leah! How are you?* At first, she didn't realize the voice was in her head.

"Lachlan!" She spoke quite loudly, but Mom didn't stir.

She wondered how she should proceed. Talk? Just think the words? Finally, she thought, *I'm okay, but someone tried to hurt me today.*

At the house?

Yes.

I was afraid of that.

She could picture him talking, though he looked thinner than she remembered. Was that possible? To see him now? She wondered where he was.

Can you come here?

No. I'm still asleep. Do you understand what a coma is?

No.

I'm asleep and I can't wake up. His voice was fading, growing quieter as he spoke. *I need help. I need Fynn.*

What's Fynn?

A friend. He can help me.

Can't you talk to him?

No, he's too far away. I need you to call him on the phone. He slowly recited a string of numbers.

Leah pictured the numbers in her head in bright colors. Now they were memorized.

Can you repeat it?

She did.

The voice in her head grew fainter. *I'm at Elmwood Rehabilitation Center in Auburn. Will you remember that?*

Leah repeated the name.

In a faint whisper, he said, *Very good.*

One more thing. Remember these words. Repeat them to Fynn.

He spoke a string of words. They made no sense to Leah, but she would remember them phonetically. She had a very good memory. She repeated them.

Perfect, Leah!

Mom stirred and rolled over, looking at her through one sleepy eye. "What are you doing?"

"What?"

"You were whispering. I thought you were talking in your sleep."

Had she been talking aloud? "I was talking to Lachlan."

Mom suddenly sat bolt upright, a worried look on her face. "What? How?"

"In my head."

Mom brushed her dark hair from her face and eyed Leah with an expression somewhere between concern and anger. "What does he want?"

"He needs help waking up."

"What?"

Mom looked dazed and anxious now. Leah wished she had been quieter. This talk would have been easier in the morning. "He's still asleep. In a coma."

"How can he talk to you then?"

"I don't know." Leah shook her head, still confused by the question herself.

"He wants help from you?"

"He wants me to call a friend of his."

"I don't want you involved, sweetie." Mom knitted her brow in worry.

"I think I already am. So does Lachlan." The strange, dark sensation she felt earlier in the day returned.

"Damn it!"

"Mom!"

"Oops." Mom covered her mouth, pretending shock. Leah giggled. Mom looked silly.

Mom leaned over and turned on her bedside lamp. "I guess I'm done sleeping for the night."

"So, what are we going to do?"

"We're not taking any chances with your safety. Tomorrow, we're going to rent a house for a month or two until we figure this out."

"We should call his friend right away," Leah said.

"It can wait until we get situated somewhere else. Did you write the number down?"

"No." Leah recited the long string of numbers.

"Whoa, slow down." Dana grabbed a pen and a piece of paper from the nightstand. "Tell me again, please."

Leah repeated the number, then said, "I'm tired, Mom. Can we go to sleep now?"

"You can sleep. I'm going to make some coffee."

Mom got up. Leah rolled over, exhausted, feeling sad that she had upset her mother again.

She called to Lachlan one more time but received no answer.

Drifting off to sleep, a black cloud lurked at the edges of her consciousness.

A sign of trouble ahead.

Three

Kiera O'Donnell stared at the bouncing road ahead.

Black asphalt. Yellow lines. A stunning array of trees ablaze with reds, golds, and yellows lining each side. Trying to maintain the singular frame of mind needed to finish, she controlled her breathing and paced her stride, her footfalls thumping in her head. Others ran ahead of her. More runners followed behind.

Sunny and sixty, it was a perfect day to run.

Still, she was sweaty and exhausted, and her left knee felt tricky. Less than three miles remained to the finish line of the Kettle Moraine Fall Marathon, her first full marathon in two years, a course that wound through utterly beautiful countryside in eastern Wisconsin.

Kiera focused on the goal, not the fatigue, or the searing pain in her quads and hamstrings, her aching feet, her chafed thighs. Someone ahead fell and was slow to get up. Kiera feared falling as well and being unable to continue. Quitting in sight of the finish line. The guy stood and walked a few steps. Kiera gave him a light pat on the back as she passed.

"Good job, you got it." If only she felt as bright as she sounded.

She passed the sign at the Miller's Crossing city limits. A different feeling overtook Kiera as she passed vacant lots and stretches of new construction, reminders of the tornado last year that destroyed half the town. A bittersweet feeling really. At the tremendous sense of loss she felt personally and for the town itself. Still, people were rebuilding, businesses returning. They had almost finished the new bank. Dozens of houses had been rebuilt. Some of their favorite haunts that had been closed for months had opened again. These stray thoughts kept creeping in, interfering with her concentration.

She refocused on the road, the runners ahead, the people lining the course. Man, she was tired, so tired that knowing only a mile or so remained failed to spur her on. Every bone, every muscle in her body ached. Why was she doing this? Though with the marathon almost over, it was a strange time for second thoughts.

Oh, yeah. The marathon was part of a "personal rebuilding effort" after a particularly shitty year. Running, dating again, writing, all efforts to put her life back on track. She was running, so that was good, but her writing languished and dating was a nightmare. Men in their forties didn't want to date women in their forties. They were chasing the cute twenty-somethings. Instead, she was besieged with messages from men in their sixties, and while she recognized some hypocrisy in her decision, she had no intention of dating any guy old enough to be her dad.

Concentrate, Kiera. Run.

Then she saw Martin Road ahead and the corner where Quinlan's Tavern used to stand. Once a thriving business, she and Josh had built it from scratch. Now, it was something of a metaphor for her messed up life. The tornado had destroyed the tavern and Josh had walked out on her in anger. The sight of that empty lot threw her breathing and pacing. It felt like a stab wound to the heart. Kiera thought she was ready to face it after avoiding this spot for months. She stared straight ahead and tried to ignore it.

Running past the lot, her right foot landed in a dip in the road, her ankle twisted, and Kiera went sprawling. She hit hard and felt the road tear her knee; she lay there for a moment, forcing back tears. Her ankle throbbed, the same ankle she broke fifteen months ago in a bad landing from a skydive.

Damn it!

Perversely, lying there felt good. She could stay down, but Kiera refused to yield to defeat.

She rolled and stood, slowly bringing weight to bear on the ankle. It hurt like hell, but it held. She took a step, then another, working up to an excruciating but manageable hobble.

Passing runners patted her on the back and encouraged her on. People lining the road cheered the runners on; cheered her on. Looking ahead, Kiera saw the last curve on the course as she ran northeast on Main St. It was under half a mile to the bridge crossing the Milwaukee River and the finish line.

A mental sigh of relief. She had this!

She saw Willow Monroe, wearing a forest green maxi-wrap and a wide brim sun hat, waving. She and Willow had been friends since childhood. A flower child and new age fruitcake, she was a genuinely sweet soul who dabbled in Tarot, palmistry, and numerology. None of it helped her in the relationship department. Willow went through boyfriends like some women went through purses. She looked stunning in a way Kiera never would with wavy blonde hair and a dewy complexion that was perfect. Though Willow was forty-four, she looked ten years younger.

Fighting back tears of pain, Kiera limped until she crossed the line with a bloody knee and throbbing ankle.

She did it!

Willow ran over and gave her a big hug, saving her from collapse. "Awesome, sweetie! Just awesome!"

"Thanks," she murmured with a pained exhalation.

Willow handed her a Powerade. "How's the ankle? I saw you go down."

"Bad. I need drugs."

"How about chardonnay?"

"That'll do—for now."

★ ★ ★

Kiera iced and wrapped her ankle and then showered.

After the run, Kiera was craving carbs, and a big plate of pasta was exactly what she needed. They went to dinner at a lovely new Italian restaurant in town. Bartola's had a cozy Italian feel, and being a Saturday night, it was crowded. Luckily, they had made a reservation the night before. The waiter, tall and hot, wearing a crisp white shirt, a black bow tie, and black dress pants, led them to a small table with a white linen tablecloth, a candle, and roses in a centerpiece. After handing them menus and taking an order for two Sonoma Cutrer chardonnays, he disappeared into the kitchen.

"He's rather yummy," Willow said with a naughty grin.

Kiera waved her off. "Go for it. I'm off men."

"Will you get over Josh already?"

Kiera crossed her arms. "I can't. And you aren't dating anyone either."

"That's just me. I'm not sitting around moping and feeling sorry for myself," Willow said smugly.

"Am not."

"Are too."

"Really?" Kiera said. "Aren't we a little old for this?"

"I'm serious. The marathon was a good start, but you need to get a job or do something meaningful." Willow adopted a motherly expression.

"I am." Kiera dropped her napkin in her lap. "I'm writing a book."

"So you say. I haven't seen a page yet."

"Hey! I've been taking classes and working with an editor who says I'm not completely hopeless."

"Whatever."

"And what have you been doing?" Kiera poked Willow's arm with a finger.

"I've been busy. I picked up a ton of new clients after that magazine article in August."

The waiter returned with their glasses of wine and took their order, a seafood fettuccine for Kiera and shrimp scampi for Willow. He did have a lovely basso voice and a nice ass, she noted as he walked away.

"I'll have a draft of the book ready in a week. Wanna read it for me?" Kiera said—though she would only have something ready if she wrote like hell.

"Of course I do. You didn't make me look too crazy, did you?"

"Not too much." Kiera smirked. Crazy enough, but it was entirely accurate. "Your name won't be Willow in the book anyway."

Willow suddenly frowned and put her fingers to her temple with a wince.

"Headache?"

Eyes still closed, Willow shook her head.

"What?"

Willow held up a finger with a dramatic flourish. She was prone to drama. Kiera sat, patiently waiting for this scene to play out.

Finally, Willow shook her head, appeared to be in a daze.

"Are you okay?"

"I don't know. I just had the weirdest feeling. Like I was in the cavern again and the darkness was nearby."

Kiera felt a queasy sensation rising at the mention of the cavern. Her therapist said she had PTSD. She couldn't bear to relive any of those moments.

"Flashback?"

"No. It was like it just slid beneath us."

She couldn't even contemplate a return to that insanity, especially the final day when they faced off against—?

She didn't know. Their friend Lachlan had called it the *darkness*, a preternatural entity that had been attracted to a cavern beneath the city. They had defeated it, but not before dozens of people were killed and half the town destroyed. Lachlan still lay in a coma in nearby Auburn.

They sat silent for a minute until the dark moment passed and their dinners arrived.

"Have you visited Lachlan this week?" Willow asked.

"No, I haven't. Training and all that. Wanna go tomorrow?"

"Sure. I've been going every other day lately, anyway."

"Why?"

Willow looked at her earnestly. "I know what they say, but I sense some activity underneath that supposed vegetative state crap. I think he's trying to wake up. I'm being supportive."

"Your faith is admirable, but how can you be supportive?"

"I don't know. I just am. I talk to him and send him good vibes."

Kiera admired her loyalty. Lachlan had been in a persistent vegetative state for a year, after suffering a head injury in the cavern last year.

The neurologist said a recovery was unlikely, doctor-speak for *it's not happening*.

As if reading her mind, which she did with unnerving frequency, Willow said, "He's coming back. Mark my words."

Kiera did and a small shiver passed down her spine. She felt a great affection for the man, but the last time he showed up, chaos had ensued.

Four

Dana stared at the strange house.

Sadness washed over her. She loved the Craftsman home where she had lived for the past four years. To be pushed out—even for a month or two—was upsetting, especially since she didn't know who or what had targeted Leah.

A generic ranch-style in Elgin, about twenty-five miles from home, it was brown outside and white inside. The furnishings were dull but adequate. Dana felt like a guest here, though she had been lucky to grab the house so quickly.

The temporary relocation was sad and inconvenient but not really an issue otherwise. Leah was her primary focus to the exclusion of almost all else. Home-schooling simplified Leah's education, but she had good friends in the old neighborhood. For her, that part would be hard, but against her safety, it was a small sacrifice.

Money wasn't an issue either. She had inherited several million dollars from her parents' estate, money that sat languishing in a brokerage account. Dana had hardly touched it. Didn't want it, but she would have to tap into it—again, for Leah's safety.

The constant vigilance left little time for a personal life. She hadn't dated in ages—though she recognized events at the house in Wisconsin had traumatized her and wasn't ready to date. Dana had been working toward a Master's degree in Psychology but had let that slide, too. In truth, she had become a near recluse since her parents died.

Uncle Nate had helped them move their luggage and some boxes of personal effects earlier, but he had gone home and she felt adrift and melancholy on her own.

By six, the sun was setting, and they had settled in. Dana had stowed their clothes. Leah had set up her room and put her toys in a closet, but she had been very quiet. She was upset by the move, too.

The warm fall weather lingered, and Dana sat, drinking a beer on a deck behind the house, a poor and inadequate replacement for her beautiful patio.

She wanted to go home, and Dana was convinced that the quickest way to do so was to wake Lachlan. He would know what they needed to do. Perhaps he and his friend could fix things. He was the key. She just knew it.

To do that, she needed to call his friend, Fynn. Until now, getting out of the house had taken priority over making the call.

As if reading her mind, Leah stepped outside holding Dana's phone. She dropped it into Dana's hand with the doe-eyed expression that often allowed her to get away with murder. Leah said, "It's time."

"Okay." Dana felt tired and frazzled, her eyes dry and sore. Still, it was just a phone call.

Leah had programmed the number into the phone. Dana punched the contact, and after a long pause, the number rang.

"Speaker, please," Leah said.

Dana clicked it to speaker just as a voice with a thick, vaguely Irish accent spoke. "Good morning."

Good morning? Where was this man? Dana said, "Mr. Fynn?"

"Just Fynn, ma'am. How may I help you?"

Dana hesitated, leery about involving another person. She had already decided to direct this Fynn character to Lachlan's facility and keep Leah out of it—if she could.

Leah jumped in. "I talked to your friend, Lachlan. He needs your help."

"You spoke to Lachlan? How old are you?" he asked with a good-natured tone.

Leah put a hand on her hip. "Five. How old are you?"

"A good deal older, my dear. Who am I speaking with?"

"Leah MacKenzie. And my mom."

"Very good, Leah. Tell me, what did Lachlan say?"

Leah closed her eyes, seemed to be searching for the exact words of Lachlan's message, though her memory was impeccable. To Dana, the message sounded like a jumble of nonsense.

Then Leah spoke. *"Oaft shayal airal moaneg, anays willon, wraetch ondrayohgon."*

A long silence followed.

"Oh dear. Why didn't Lachlan call?"

"He's asleep. In a coma," Leah said.

"And you spoke to him while he was asleep?"

"Yes."

"Curiouser and curiouser."

Leah gushed, "That's my favorite book ever!"

"You have good taste, young lady."

Finally Fynn said, "I shall come at once then. Please tell me where you are."

Dana hesitated and then said, "Just a minute. I have no clue who you are—I'm not just handing out my address to anyone."

"I quite understand."

"I'll give you Lachlan's address."

"I should like to meet you both first. I haven't the foggiest what this is about. I haven't spoken to Lachlan in some time. If he is in a coma, he won't be able to tell me much. Your daughter seems to have the most direct connection with him."

"I'm not comfortable with you meeting my daughter."

"Sorry?"

"You heard me. I don't know a thing about you and an attempt was just made on her life."

"Oh my. Sorry to hear that," Fynn said. "I wish to point out that you called me. I don't know you. If Lachlan talked to your daughter and asked for help, he wouldn't send someone to hurt her."

That rang true, Dana decided. Still, she would take every precaution.

"Fair enough. But let me warn you. For a number of reasons, I take my daughter's security very seriously. When you arrive, I will be armed. I will search you and then—if I decide you're okay—you can meet Leah. If not—"

"Understood and acceptable."

After Dana gave him the address, he said, "I'll leave first thing tomorrow. Still, it will be at least three days before I arrive."

"Three days? Where are you?"

"A remote village about two hundred kilometers outside Ulan Bator, Mongolia."

"Three days then."

Dana tapped the red icon and pulled Leah close. Leah hugged her tight. No words were necessary. They knew they had just opened a door to a rabbit hole and that things would soon change again. They were MacKenzies and had been in danger all their lives even if they hadn't known it. They could have run but they had made a decision to stay and stick it out, for better or worse.

Back to the mundane. "Snack time, sweetie."

Afterward, Leah went to bed and Dana let her read for thirty minutes before shutting the light off.

When Leah had fallen asleep, Dana unlocked the kitchen drawer secured with a new lock and pulled out her Beretta M9, slipped into a dark coat, and walked a circuit of the yard. Returning indoors, she checked all the locks, then stowed the gun for the night. She didn't want it in the bedroom since Leah was sleeping with her. She kept the Taser and pepper spray closer at hand in the nightstand.

Feeling secure for the night, Dana poured a glass of wine, suspecting sleep would be long in coming.

Contemplated the present.

The car. This strange house. Lachlan in a coma. Shepherd dead. It felt grim.

But now, some guy named Fynn was coming. She hoped to hell he had answers that would end this nightmare, once and for all.

★ ★ ★

Leah lay in the strange bed, tossing and turning.

Some nights her sleep was deep and dreamless. When she dreamt, she remembered little in the morning—except when her dreams were haunted by a scary old house where she and Grandma once lived. Most were snatches of memory intertwined with impressions of a shadowy monster that lived in the basement. Leah felt sad whenever she saw Grandma in her dreams, alive and smiling. Even now, she missed her almost every minute of every day.

Leah trembled in fear when she dreamt of the thing in the basement, but it wasn't a real monster. It looked more like a cloud, a black storm cloud, that forever changed shape as it moved around in tunnels, caves, and fissures underground that led away from the scary house. While she dreamt, she couldn't escape it. The dark cloud was always the pursuer, chasing Leah—who searched for safe places everywhere but never quite found shelter. It was exhausting, hours of running, trying to escape, never caught, but never out of danger either.

Now the dark cloud had come for her during the day, driving the car that crashed in their yard.

It would be back. She would have to be very careful now.

Tonight, oddly, the cloud was floating away in her dream and she was the pursuer.

She still felt afraid. The dark cloud, or *darkness* as Lachlan called it, was up to no good. Perhaps this was a chance to spy on it, find a way to make it go away forever. She felt no fear of the tight spaces in the rocks, though; felt as light as a feather. This was important, like a secret mission. Soon, it would chase her again. That was what it did. She needed to be ready.

Hours passed as she chased it down in the rock, floating on a tide of air or an invisible magic carpet, she didn't really know. It was a dream and dreams seldom made sense.

Near morning—at least she thought it was morning because it had grown lighter—she left the caves and tunnels and floated in the sky over water. Nearby, on a high point of rock, she saw a tall lighthouse.

The dark cloud had come to rest right beneath it, and she sensed it planned to stay for a while. It was resting or sleeping, recharging like a phone. There were turning lines in a big circle overhead. They also flowed through the lighthouse and into the ground. Leah had no clue what they were.

She didn't recognize the place, but she would never forget the vivid pictures in her mind: the deep blue water, the black rock, the beacon of the lighthouse like a living eye, watching and waiting.

Leah woke with a start, but it was still dark, the room pitch black—oh, the new house. Mom snored lightly.

The dream lingered and she thought about waking Mom, telling her about it, but her sleep seemed to be peaceful. Better to let her rest.

Leah rolled over, snuggled against Mom's back, and fell asleep.

When she woke again, the room was filled with sunshine, the lighthouse just a hazy, fading memory. Try as she might, she couldn't pull it out of the fog.

Leah quit trying.

It probably wasn't important, anyway.

Five

Kiera and Willow rode in silence.

Saving their chit-chat for Lachlan, they were driving through the Kettle Moraine in Kiera's RAV4. The fall colors were brilliant, the sky deep blue, fluffy cumulus drifting overhead like grazing sheep.

At the edge of Auburn, Kiera pulled into a parking spot behind the Elmwood Rehabilitation Center. The name was disingenuous. Few people were actually rehabilitated and sent home. It was a nursing home, a place to warehouse the terminally ill. Most of the residents died there. As a result, Kiera felt a sense of melancholy every time she visited Lachlan.

The day was cool, the wind raw as they stepped out of the vehicle. Indoors, the facility smelled like a place that housed people, sanitary with superficial perfumes masking the underlying smells of adult diapers and base odors of metabolism and disease. A depressing aura of decline and death.

Lachlan had a bright suite at the south end of the facility, a sterile white space except for the plants they had brought in to confer some life and color to the room. The floor nurse waved from her station and said, "Afternoon, ladies."

Lachlan lay on his back, eyes closed, white hair and moustache well-trimmed, his face wearing a grey pallor and sunken expression despite his normally strong features. He could be asleep, but the truth was darker. He had been in a coma for a year. While there were no visible tubes or IVs, Kiera knew he had a permanent G-tube for nutrition and fluids.

Willow took his hand and closed her eyes. This had become routine during their visits, Willow trying to forge a psychic connection with Lachlan. Thus far, she had been unsuccessful. Nevertheless, Willow felt certain he remained lucid somewhere within.

They took chairs on each side of the bed and launched into casual conversation about their day, the weather, whatever came to mind. Kiera hoped he heard their conversation on some level, that it comforted him, but she couldn't know for sure.

Despite the grim diagnosis, Kiera and Willow tried to stay optimistic about his future. Lachlan was unique. They both owed him their lives. As long as he still drew breath, they would be here for him.

Having exhausted their idle chatter, Willow pulled a Tarot deck from her bag and wheeled the tray table over, positioning it across Lachlan and the bed. She shuffled the cards for a minute; excessively, Kiera thought, but she knew better than to say so.

"What are you doing?"

"I'm doing a read on him," Willow replied. "I'm hoping for a sign."

"Tarot cards? Doesn't he have to choose them?"

"I'll let him guide my hand."

That sounded suitably vague, Kiera thought, knowing Willow would draw the most favorable conclusions from the reading. Still, she had a deep respect for Willow after the events last year in the cavern. Even the staunchest skeptic would have been convinced of her psychic powers that day. There were things and forces in the world that couldn't be explained by conventional or scientific examination, a particularly bitter pill to swallow with her scientific background.

Still, Tarot seemed like a superstitious throwback more than legitimate psychic tool. It had been little use to them in the cavern.

Willow laid the deck on the table and set his hand on it for a moment. Still holding his hand, she spread the cards in line, face down. Then she drew six cards and pushed the others aside. Willow laid the chosen cards, face down, in what Kiera knew to be a universal six-card spread.

Willow took a deep breath and turned the first card on the left.

The Hermit. An old man with a staff and a lantern.

"Very appropriate. This is how he feels about himself." Willow spoke quietly, reverently. "He feels lonely at this time, a period of introspection, obviously. He's still there, struggling to find answers. They will come. This is a time for rest and recuperation."

Kiera did a mental eye roll. What else could you say about a man in a coma?

"Okay. Next, what he needs most at this moment." Willow flipped the card.

Strength. A woman standing and petting a lion.

"Oh, awesome! I don't think I need to explain that card at all."

Kiera looked out the window. She didn't see how this was helpful. She held her tongue to humor her friend.

"Now, this card represents his fears." She tapped the next card and turned it over.

The Tower.

It was a fearsome-looking card, ominous and foreboding: a tall stone tower, a bolt of lightning striking the structure as flames leapt from the windows. Kiera had no idea what it meant. Before she could ask, Willow reached for the next card and said, "And the things in his favor."

The Chariot. A rider in a chariot with two Egyptian lions in the foreground.

Willow visibly relaxed as her shoulders fell. "A good card. He has a great internal drive. Not a quitter. The Chariot signifies victory in conflict. He will succeed. He will wake up."

Kiera struggled against the futility of this exercise. While she wanted it to be true, it seemed Willow was reading the best into every good card and ignoring the bad. Confirmation bias. Isn't that what they called it?

"Now critically, the factors against him." She hesitated, then tipped the card over.

The Tower.

Willow sucked her breath in sharply.

What the hell? Kiera looked at Willow. "Are there two of those?"

"No. Unless I somehow mixed up my decks, and I don't think I did." She picked the two cards up and examined them.

They looked identical to Kiera. "Are they the same?"

Willow nodded and exhaled loudly. She grabbed the cards she had set aside and flipped them over, but the rest of the deck looked perfectly normal. "Something's wrong. This isn't possible. Someone's trying to tell me something."

"You're kidding, right?" Kiera suddenly felt her heart palpitate. This had gone from a casual visit to something eerie.

They both eyed the last card. Willow flashed Kiera a nervous look and flipped it over.

The Tower!

Willow went pale. "That's impossible!"

Kiera felt icy fingertips sliding down her spine.

For a moment, neither spoke.

Then Lachlan's arm twitched and his hand struck the underside of the table.

Willow yelped and Kiera muttered, "Holy shit!" as they both jumped.

Examining the three tower cards in a useless gesture, Willow shook her head, a befuddled look on her face.

"Willow, what's going on?" Kiera felt genuine alarm.

Willow shook her head and shrugged. "I wish I knew."

"What does the Tower mean?" Kiera tapped the card.

"Change, upheaval, destruction, chaos. It's one of the most feared cards in the deck." Willow stared into space. "This was a normal deck when I left the house."

Almost afraid to ask, Kiera said, "What does the final card signify?"

"The likely outcome." Willow looked pensive.

"I've tried to connect with Lachlan for the last year and I've had no luck at all. Lachlan hasn't moved in a year. Damn it!" Spoken as if she was talking to herself. Willow swept the cards from the table and they scattered all over the room in a creepy game of twenty-two-card pickup.

Kiera felt a sinking sensation in her gut, illogically afraid that the Tower cards were some sort of message. "What's going on?"

"There's only one explanation. Remember my feeling the other day?"

Kiera nodded.

I think it's starting all over again." Willow looked up. "I think Lachlan just sent us a warning."

Six

Zoie Andolino drifted just offshore.

Casting a line, she was having miserable luck. This spot, at the northern tip of Door County, had been hot for smallmouth bass a couple of days ago, but now it was dead. The day itself was cool and damp, the sky monotone grey, the boat rocking gently as waves lapped at the hull.

A half mile south, the Porte des Morts bluff rose straight up from the water, crowned by a lighthouse of the same name. One of the many lighthouses dotting the Lake Michigan shoreline, Zoie knew the history of every lighthouse in Door County. This one—a tall limestone tower with a keeper's house—was perhaps the most beautiful and held special meaning for her.

Zoie's father had fished Lake Michigan and the Bay for a living and, from the moment she could hold a rod, she fished too.

When she was six, they went out on a Sunday morning for a couple hours in the smaller boat. Dad had always considered a couple of hours on the Bay worth more spiritually than an hour in church. They were fishing in the Porte des Morts strait when a sudden storm blew up.

In minutes, the rain and wind were like a hurricane. While he was trying to cover the boat with the canvas cover, they got turned around and he lost his bearings. He had no gear, not even a compass. All his navigation gear was on the big boat and he didn't take a phone on the lake. It seldom worked and he didn't like them anyway.

She knew he was afraid they would blow away from shore and out onto the big lake.

Suddenly, he stopped and pointed. He swore he saw the Porte des Morts lighthouse flash even though it had been shut down years before. Based on that sighting, he found the way back to shore. From then on, she believed the lighthouse to be special—haunted—believed that some spirit had saved them that day. The event had also fueled a fascination with ghosts and the paranormal. So much so she started a local ghost hunting group, the Door County Paranormal Society.

As legend had it, the Porte des Morts lighthouse was reputedly home to vengeful spirits ready to torment anyone foolish enough to try to get inside. Indeed, some of those spirits had lured unsuspecting sailors to their deaths. Other stories told of dead Potawatomi warriors lurking within, ghosts still angry that Europeans had taken their lands.

Zoie believed none of that nonsense, but she wasn't a skeptic. Far from it.

As an active ghost hunter, she had long prayed something spooky would happen at the lighthouse. She had fished these waters for years, day and night, three seasons of the year and had never seen a thing. It was a lighthouse on a rock, unchanging and ageless. No auras or weird lights, no manifestations, no rattling chains. She felt nothing near it. She had been involved in many exciting ghost hunts with the Paranormal Society and always felt a vibe. Always. Here, she felt nothing even though her dad saw it flash all those years ago.

So, no one could have been more startled than Zoie when the lighthouse flashed.

Once. Vividly.

It was freaky. With a heavy stratus deck obscuring the sun, the day a dull fall-grey, it wasn't a reflection nor sun glint. She looked around to see if anyone else had been watching, but she was alone on the water. The rocky beach farther up was empty as well.

Zoie stared at the lighthouse for five minutes, but it remained dark. She scarcely believed that she had seen the flash, but it had burned a negative image onto her retina. As much as she believed in the paranormal, she was also a fan of science and rationality, and there was no reasonable explanation for the flash.

The lighthouse had been deactivated in the '50s, but the Coast Guard owned the property and maintained the tower and the keeper's house. A number of decommissioned lighthouses had been sold and converted to private homes over the years, but there was no sign of activity beyond basic maintenance. The property was secured against intruders and vandals with a tall chain link fence topped by barbed wire. The shoreline, a sheer wall of rock, rose sixty feet straight up. It was virtually impossible to land a boat there.

Still, the lighthouse had a rich reputation that stemmed from its location overlooking Death's Door, the adjacent strait that had been colorfully named by the French. They in turn took the name from the local Native Americans. Porte des Morts, literally the Door of Death, was one of the most infamous passages in Lake Michigan ship lore and had been the site of hundreds of shipwrecks over the years. Before Europeans arrived, the Native Americans told stories of warriors killed by the rocks, dangerous currents, and the treacherous waves in the strait. Door County took its name from the passage.

There were rumors the fence was electrified and the property booby-trapped with explosives, but Zoie assumed those tales had arisen from local gossips with nothing better to do. Nevertheless, the property had remained undisturbed and the local kids evidently stayed away because of those stories—though up here at the tip of Door County, there weren't many teenage kids anyway. And despite the paranormal legends that long predated the rumors about the fence and hidden snares, the lighthouse rarely attracted the curious.

So, now what?

She couldn't let it go. Zoie pulled the boat in for a closer look, but there had been no changes to the grounds. It remained overgrown with wild grasses, bushes, saplings, and tall Colorado and blue spruce trees.

She couldn't imagine what the flash meant but given the history of the strait and the lighthouse, she would bring it up at the next meeting of the group on Friday.

Another twenty minutes spent staring at the lighthouse were fruitless. She turned the boat and headed for the landing.

Zoie trailered the boat and drove to the main lighthouse entrance on Hwy 42. The front gate and the door to the keeper's house were visibly padlocked. There were no vehicles parked there. No *For Sale* sign. No evidence anyone had visited the grounds in months. A shame, really. The lighthouse and keeper's house were beautiful and picturesque, strong and immutable like the limestone they stood upon.

She snapped a dozen pics and hopped into Dad's F-150, headed for home.

Zoie could still picture the flash in her mind. Vividly. She hadn't imagined it.

Nope.

But she wanted proof for the group. She would set up a wildlife camera in the woods outside the fence to capture the next flash.

Tingling with excitement, Zoie needed no proof herself.

She was already convinced the Porte des Morts lighthouse was haunted and the ghost had just woken up.

Seven

The doorbell rang.

Dana blew out a sigh of relief.

Fynn had arrived. She had been on edge for three days waiting to meet the mysterious Fynn, nervous and thrilled in equal measure that his arrival might mark the beginning of an end to their problems. Or would it? Lachlan had appeared and promised to keep her informed. She never heard from him again—beyond the enigmatic message he sent to Leah. Would Fynn just disappear too?

Besides, between Lachlan and Shepherd, not much good had happened. What would be different now?

Dana checked her bearing in the mirror. Her expression firm and serious, she looked like a cop wearing a gun in a belly band holster worn over her clothing, leaving it clearly visible.

She opened the door to a tall gawky man of indeterminate middle-age, wearing a tam. With thick mousy brown hair flecked with grey and equally thick moustache, he looked classically British.

"Miss Dana MacKenzie?" His accent had a lilt—from Ireland perhaps—more pronounced than when they spoke on the phone.

"Yes. Fynn?"

He tipped his hat. "Ma'am."

"Please turn around."

He turned and put his arms out, perhaps anticipating the light pat-down she gave him.

"Please come in." Dana stepped aside and directed him a toward recliner in the living room.

He tipped his hat. "I respect a capable woman. I assume the security is related to the message from Lachlan?"

Dana nodded. "Cup of tea?"

"Love one if it's convenient." He sat and fiddled with his phone as Dana walked to the kitchen and put a kettle on. She wasn't a big tea drinker, but she assumed Fynn would be, as were most of the English and Irish people she had met.

Minutes later, she carried a tray with tea, hot water, cups, milk, and sugar into the living room and set it down on the coffee table.

"How was your trip?"

"Arduous. I'm still making the adjustment from Mongolian time."

"Understood. I'll be blunt. I see no good reason to give you access to my daughter."

Fynn stared into space, as if he were listening for something. He might have been in a trance. What was he doing? Dana was about to snap her fingers when Leah walked into the room and said, "He's okay, Mom."

"Did he tell you that?"

Leah smiled and her eyes lit up. "Sort of. He's like me."

Dana now felt dumb. The capabilities Leah possessed were difficult enough to comprehend. With two of them in the room, evidently communicating, she felt like a Neanderthal.

Fynn and Leah held eye contact for a minute. Then he said, "Lovely. Now I have some idea what's going on. Your daughter is quite remarkable—as I'm sure you know."

"I do."

Fynn leaned forward and prepared his tea with a dash of sugar and milk, took a sip, then said, "So, tell me what you know, about Lachlan, and Kenric, from what you believe is the beginning of all this. Leave nothing out, please."

It took almost an hour to tell the full story. About her mother, the Tudor house in the Kettle Moraine, and the few facts she knew about Shepherd. How she and Leah had escaped the house just minutes before the explosion that destroyed the house and killed everyone inside. About Lachlan's appearance a year later that culminated in an injury that had laid him low, though she knew little of the actual story or details surrounding his injuries.

Fynn didn't interrupt. He absorbed the words and the story and seemed to be trying to make sense of it. With little success, apparently, because he said, "I don't know what any of it means. I knew Kenric had been killed and that Lachlan had come to settle the estate, but I can't imagine what they were entangled in. I do understand that even though he's in a coma, he found a way to communicate with your daughter. Having met her, I understand why. She's gifted, extraordinarily so. May I hold her hand for a minute?"

Dana nodded. "Sure."

He held Leah's hand like a handshake. Dana assumed he was evaluating her psychic abilities just as Lachlan had the year before.

"Yes, I know. She got it from her grandmother. Passed right by me," Dana said, hands clasped in her lap.

Fynn regarded her with a curious expression. "On the contrary.

While your ability is mild compared to your daughter, you do have an ability. You simply haven't recognized your skill and refined it."

Dana wasn't sure she believed him but remembered how resistant her mother had been to the idea. Dana wasn't sure she wanted it either. She was even less happy that Fynn seemed mostly clueless about the situation. In three days, she had mentally inflated him to savior status. The last thing she needed was another inept person bumbling through their lives.

Fynn seemed to sense her discomfiture. "That's a conversation for another time—"

"You know," Dana said, curtly. "Lachlan promised to keep me informed. I never heard from him again."

Fynn eyed her guardedly. "So where is Lachlan now?"

"He's in a facility about a hundred miles from here," Dana said. Looking at Leah, he said, "Have you talked to him since?"

"No. Just the one time."

"How did he talk to you?"

"I called out to him, in my head. He answered, and told me to call you," Leah said. "He said he needs you. To help him wake up."

Fynn sipped his tea. "I don't quite understand, but we should visit him. I hope my purpose here will become clear then."

Dana locked eyes with Fynn. "I'm not sure I want her involved. Whatever they were involved in was dangerous."

"I think she already is," he said gently. "That's why Lachlan spoke to her."

Leah clasped her hands in her lap and nodded her head. "That's what I told her."

"Whatever Lachlan has in mind, he wouldn't endanger your daughter. I'm certain of that."

Dana hadn't expected this at all. She assumed they would talk and Fynn would leave. Then she considered the situation. Having had to leave their house and move at a moment's notice. The attempt on Leah's life. They were in it whether she wanted to be or not. She had been preparing for this moment for months, the martial arts, the weapons training. She was as ready as she could be. "I'm not happy about that, but I guess we're involved regardless."

"Quite. Shall we go then?"

"Now?"

"I sense time is of the essence. Are you available?"

Dana could think of many reasons they shouldn't go but decided it was the only option. "Sure. Give me fifteen minutes to pack an overnight bag—just in case."

They departed thirty minutes later, Dana driving her Jeep Wrangler, Fynn following in his rental car, headed north to Auburn, Wisconsin.

A place that held only bad memories for Dana.

Eight

Lachlan Hayward drifted in limbo.

Lost in suspended animation—minimally aware of light, sound, and touch—his remaining consciousness felt like a gnome hidden deep within his dormant brain. So little energy remained; it took most of it to maintain this minimal awareness. His brain injury was healing too slowly, and he knew it would never fully heal without specialized care.

He had managed to speak to the child, Leah MacKenzie. She understood the message and repeated it back to him.

Had she and her mother followed through? No way to know. Talking with Leah had drained him considerably and he hadn't tried contacting her again. She hadn't attempted to reach out, either—though he might be simply too weak to hear her now.

Willow visited often, which gave him comfort. He could hear her speaking in the distance; Kiera as well on occasion. She sounded more distant than Willow—though that was logical. He had a deeper spiritual connection with Willow due to their shared abilities. Still, he had been unable to communicate directly with her. That he could connect with

Leah at a distance spoke mostly to Leah's exceptional gift. She had been close to Kenric Shepherd when he died. Had she somehow absorbed some of his considerable psychic energies? He had known that to happen.

Lachlan had also attempted to send Willow a message through her Tarot cards but didn't know if the gesture was successful.

If Fynn Alden was on his way, he had no sense of it.

He was certain of only one thing. He had failed.

In a wild gamble, he had attempted to defeat the darkness that killed his friend, Kenric Shepherd, and so many others. He'd risked his life and the lives of others to no avail. Instead, the darkness lived on and had just attempted to kill Leah MacKenzie. He was certain of it and uselessly trapped inside his own head with the knowledge.

No recourse remained.

The darkness was loose, and nothing stood in its path. People weren't even aware the danger existed. It was growing stronger and bolder, and the MacKenzie girl lacked the knowledge and the tools to protect herself.

Though he had few regrets in life, he felt pangs of remorse now. He had once been a sorcerer of considerable skill and wasn't accustomed to failure. Especially one of this magnitude.

Lives were still at risk, possibly many lives, and there was nothing he could do. Had Kenric felt this way when his efforts had come to naught? They had both clearly underestimated the darkness. Why? What had they missed? How had that one woman, Anna Flecher, unleashed so much havoc five hundred years ago?

He wasn't normally prone to depression, but he had slipped into melancholy and lacked the energy to counteract it, to seek and maintain mindfulness. His circumstances bore similarities to *locked-in syn-*

drome, a medical condition in which mentally lucid people couldn't communicate with the world. Perhaps the people in this *vegetative state* experienced the same reality. Indeed, he could live a long time yet and, trapped like this, face a fate worse than death.

Once before, he had fallen ill like this—a head injury that rendered him unconscious for weeks. Kenric had nursed him back to health over three days. It required amulets and very specific procedures. He didn't know if this situation even aligned with Fynn's skill set, though if it didn't, Fynn could summon someone who would know. It would be a start.

If he was coming.

Meanwhile, he performed low-level maintenance, doing what he could to stave off physical decline and disability. He couldn't reach consciousness, but he ran a daily internal routine, maintaining his muscles by directing nutrients to them. Exercising his reflexes with impulses to the nerves in his arms, legs, and torso. Tweaking the reflexes and eliciting minute muscle contractions, keeping them from atrophy.

One thing kept him sane. A strange, ephemeral awareness. He sensed the spirit of Kenric here with him at times, urging him on, offering reassurance. Lachlan didn't know if it was real, a hallucination, a mirage, or some facet of his damaged mind. Nevertheless, he welcomed the presence, the sense of camaraderie.

It was the only thing that gave him hope.

Nine

Smile—don't engage.

Tatiana Palkowski—Tat to her friends—wore her smile like a mask while the old white-haired shitbag went off on her.

"...and finally, this romaine lettuce is limper than my dead husband. Two stars. That's all you get." She tapped her phone screen with an exaggerated gesture and a grimace. "I'll ask for someone else next time."

Smile—don't engage.

"And while I'm at it, why don't you get out in the sun more? With that pale skin and black hair, you look like a goddamn ghost."

Snap!

Tatiana caught the closing door with her hip, snapped a pic with her phone while flipping the woman off with the other hand, and hissed, "Fuck you, you old shitbag!"

Slamming the screen door, she turned and stomped toward her car, spinning one last time to flip the lady off. The old woman just stood there, mouth agape. Good! She had taken way too much crap from that salty old twat.

Boomers. She hated them all.

Tat yanked on the door of her black Kia Soul, resisting the urge to punch the glass right out of the fucking door. Then sat until her blood pressure and anger settled a bit. She marked herself *off-duty* on the FoodBuddy app and drove to her favorite wine bar on the east side of Green Bay. That bitch would rue the day she screwed with Tatiana Palkowski. A personal shopper, her rating on the FoodBuddy app was almost five full stars—well, it had been until today.

The place was empty. Good. She ordered a California cabernet and drank it far too fast.

Just as she signaled for another, her phone pinged.

Oh, great. It was Rob, the regional manager. She was going to get reamed out. Rob was such a dick.

But it was much simpler than that. Two words: *You're fired!*

Shit!

Tat held a fist over her mouth, afraid she would cry. She loved that job. Her clients loved her. Again, her temper had gotten the best of her and now it had cost her the only job she had ever truly liked. Good luck finding another job with *fired!* on her resume. Ric would tell her it's okay, but it wasn't. She was given to melancholy and black moods, especially when she was out of work. That would start up again and Tat dreaded it.

She sat rigid, fighting back the tears, and finished her second cabernet, contemplating ways to get even with the evil old bitch.

★ ★ ★

Tatiana and her boyfriend Ric lived in an older subdivision on the east side of Green Bay, in a plain ranch-style house with white siding. Tat hated it, but it wasn't hers. Ric had bought it years before they met, and he didn't want to move. It was small to boot, with an open-plan living room that segued into a kitchen-dining area. There were two bedrooms and a bathroom down a hallway. That was it.

He was banging around in the kitchen when she walked in the door. Making dinner, hopefully. She was starving and buzzed from the wine.

"Hey, Tat. How was your day?"

"Fucking awful. The worst." She walked into the kitchen and threw her handbag on the brown Formica counter.

Ric was tall, lanky, and good looking in an unremarkable way with mousy brown hair, brown eyes, and angular features. He raised an eyebrow. "How come?"

She briefly recounted her run-in with the mean old shitbag, the two-star review, and losing her job.

"Oh, shit. What are you gonna do?" Ric said, rooting around in the freezer drawer.

"Kill the bitch," Tat said with menace.

"Seriously?"

"Metaphorically, yes."

Ric stopped digging and turned, his interest clearly piqued. "What'd you have in mind?"

"I haven't decided yet. A binding spell? A flat-out revenge spell? I don't know if I'm that good yet."

He pushed his hair behind his ear. "She sounds like a complete bitch. Let her have it, babe."

"Oh, I will. But I need to chill out first. Casting a spell in this mood could come back on me," Tatiana said, flopping into a chair at the maple dinner table.

"How so?"

"Some sects hold that whatever energy you put into the world is returned three-fold. It's called the Rule of Three. It's like Karma. I'm not sure I buy it," Tat said dismissively. "Still, I think it would be wise to chill first. How was your day?"

"Same old, same old."

His answer never varied. A tool and die maker, his job sounded unspeakably boring.

He held up a frozen pizza. "Pizza okay?"

"Sure, just jazz it up, okay?" Tatiana reached for her laptop while Ric preheated the oven and sliced onions and peppers for the pizza.

Tat clicked on the Tor browser and logged on to a site on the dark web frequented by practitioners of witchcraft, or magick as some called it. There were roughly fifteen regulars plus visitors who rotated in and out of the group. Among the regulars, there were three serious practitioners of the dark arts, genuinely spooky people who were clearly talented. Tatiana was happy to learn from them but also glad they were far, far away from her.

She observed the conversation for five minutes until the others acknowledged her presence and welcomed her into chat. It never ceased to feel odd, this ritual, the banal pleasantries upon arrival followed by discussions on how to harm and spite people.

Her stomach growled as the aroma of baking pizza filled the room. Ric set a bottle of beer in front of her.

She posted a request for a revenge curse, a binding spell of some sort. Four separate posts with suggestions quickly appeared on her screen. She copied them to a file, thanked the group, and chatted for a while before signing off.

Ric sat and handed her a plate of pizza slices. "You in the coven?"

She nodded.

"What'd you find out?"

"I grabbed a couple of useful spells. I'm going to sit on them until my anger is gone. Then I'll do something." Tatiana pointed to a world map and a yardstick taking up more than half the kitchen table. "What's going on here?"

"I'm still trying to understand energy vortexes. You might find this interesting too," he said. "You could use energy vortexes to strengthen your magic."

"What's an energy vortex? And the plural is vortices."

He rolled his eyes; he didn't like being corrected. "They're spots on the Earth that contain concentrated swirls of energy. They're also called nodal points and they can be positive or negative. Some people consider the positive nodes to be sacred. The negative nodal points are another story and quite a dark subject. That's where ley lines come in. The nodal points are usually found at the intersections of ley lines."

She put a hand up in a *stop* gesture. "Hold it. What are ley lines?"

"Ley lines are straight lines or alignments between historic places or prominent landmarks."

"Like what?"

"Stonehenge, Machu Picchu, Mt. Shasta, Sedona in Arizona." He pointed to random-looking pencil lines on the map. "The connecting lines between those places are called ley lines."

"So what'd you discover?"

"Not much so far."

"So, the nearest energy vortex is Sedona?" Tat asked.

He nodded as he chomped on his pizza.

"That's kinda far to drive to cast a spell."

"Yeah, but Sedona is just one of the famous places. Like I said, other points exist and are often found at intersecting ley lines. I just started working on this, so I haven't found anything yet, but I will. Something closer than Sedona."

The concept sounded interesting. Ric was an intelligent guy. He'd even had a Mensa membership, though he'd let it lapse. After one meeting, he decided they were a bunch of boring nerds. He had just taken the test to see how high he could score. She, too, was smart and he liked that, so Tat wondered why he'd never gone to college. Ric said he hated school, but if school was boring, wasn't making tools and dies even more boring? It sounded tedious. But Ric said he liked the work, liked working with his hands. She wasn't sure what the job entailed and didn't really care to know.

His real name was Corey, not Ric. When they started hanging out, he wanted a cooler name, something edgier than Corey, and after a long, dramatic search, decided on *Amalric*, or "great leader." She quickly clipped it to Ric, which sounded less pretentious than Amalric. Ric had been pretty vanilla then and had gotten edgier hanging out with her.

She had also chosen a name, *Asleif*, taken from Norse mythology, but somehow, Tat was the name that stuck. Tatiana had been her father's idea. He was a blue collar steam-fitter named George who fancied himself a Communist and loved all things Russian. At least that's what her mother said. He left when she was five and they hadn't spoken since. Tat wished he was stuck in Siberia, freezing his miserable ass off instead of living ten miles away with an ugly bitch named Olga.

Looking at the cold leftover pizza, she had an idea. Scabs, pus, gross stuff. The old bag was vain. It would be her worst nightmare. An idea for a spell was coming to her. Something that would make the old woman miserable. But how would she know if her spell worked? Didn't matter. Just doing something was a start.

Suddenly, she felt better than she had in days.

Ten

Dana felt her anxiety and blood pressure rising.

She last made this journey two years ago, the day before Thanksgiving, and had vowed to never make it again. Then, her mother, father, and aunt had died on a wintry night that she remembered mostly in her dreams and nightmares. As they drove through Milwaukee, she realized her hands were shaking with a fine tremor.

Leah noticed as well. "You okay, Mom?"

"Not really." She stole a glance at Leah in the rearview mirror, saw nothing but concern. "I don't want to go back there. You know why."

"There's nothing bad there anymore."

"You're sure?"

Leah nodded and gave her a confident smile in the mirror that belied her tender age.

Dana relaxed a bit and tried to follow her mother's mantra about mindfulness: push the anxieties away, breathe, focus on the present. Two years had passed but she still missed her mom with a keening ache that never seemed to lessen, an ache she feared would never go away. Dana missed her smile, her casual laugh, her cogent advice. She didn't want to forget any part of her; she just wanted the gut-sucking pain of her loss to ease.

She missed her father as well, but his memory was tainted by the stranger he became in the end: an unbalanced man who cheated on her mother and then tried to kill her. She knew the house had changed him, turned him against them. They had planned to leave the area until her father snatched Leah, forcing her mother back to the house one last time. If not for that, her mother would still be alive.

It was a disturbing, violent story.

Her father had once been the coolest guy she knew. Now he was only a dark and bloody memory.

In the end, the house perished in a violent explosion. She felt certain her mother had destroyed the house and did so believing that she was protecting Dana and Leah. Dana was sure her mother had done the right thing and that whatever haunted the house had been eliminated.

Lachlan's appearance last year shook that conviction. Now, the attempt on Leah's life had shaken her faith further.

It meant things weren't over and that her mother may have died in vain.

The frictions and dissensions that might have driven others crazy were constants with Leah in her life. The girl had a gift she could barely comprehend, a gift that impressed these older men. Who were they? She didn't know but had vague memories of Shepherd performing powerful rituals in the house. She intended to find out, though.

Her mother had the gift as well. What a remarkable woman she had been. She had faced down ghosts. Fought off a homicidal husband. Made the ultimate sacrifice to save her family. When Dana looked in the mirror, she found herself wanting. Lacking the steely resolve of her mother. The wisdom, the grace. Laura MacKenzie had been good at everything she ever tried.

Still, Dana held it all together for one reason: Leah.

Driving to Auburn to help Lachlan was part of the solution. How did she know that? Mother's intuition? Her own sixth sense? She had never had the faintest inkling she possessed such a skill. If she did, next to her mother, next to Leah, hers paled in comparison. Nonetheless, she felt certain this was the right thing to do. Nothing else made sense. Somehow, Lachlan and Fynn were that answer.

Maybe I do have Mom's gift after all.

A darker thought intruded: *Or I'm losing my mind.*

She looked in the rearview mirror as she made the last turn toward Auburn. Fynn was still behind her, a solemn look on his face.

Her anxiety returned. Nothing good had ever happened here.

Nothing.

Dana pulled into the large, nearly empty parking lot.

The Elmwood Rehabilitation Center lay just past a sign marking the Auburn city limits. A bland one-story brick building, it sprawled across the tract of land, the windows adorned with fall décor: stickers of colorful leaves, jack-o'-lanterns, and smiling ghosts. The festive veneer couldn't mask the purpose behind the walls as a warehouse for the chronically and terminally ill. Her uncle Nate had spent months in one of these places, and she grew to hate it.

Without a word, Fynn joined them carrying a satchel, and they walked indoors to the front desk. The receptionist was a perky teen trying to hide an obsession with an iPhone clumsily hidden beneath paperwork. Her head popped up. "Hi!"

Dana said, "We'd like to see Lachlan..." Then she realized she had forgotten his last name.

"Hayward," Fynn said. "Lachlan Hayward."

"Oh, he's popular today! Room 122. Down the right hallway."

Dana was curious about who else might have visited. She didn't imagine Lachlan knowing anyone here but was surprised to find two women in animated conversation at a table in the room which was densely populated with plants and flowers. The women, both later thirties or early forties, were attractive. The blonde had a hippie vibe. They stopped talking and looked surprised to see them. Were they family?

Fynn ignored them and walked to the bedside, placing his fingertips on Lachlan's temple, and closed his eyes.

He nodded a moment later and turned to the women. "Are you friends of Lachlan's?"

The blonde spoke, serious now, challenging. "Yes, we are. I'm Willow. This is Kiera. And you are?"

"Fynn Alden. Lachlan and I are old friends. He asked for my help."

Willow stood, staring Fynn down, eye to eye. "He asked you?" The suspicion in her tone, her raised eyebrows quite clear.

"Yes. He did, via this young lady," Fynn said, pointing to Leah, who nodded with a knowing smile. "I know that sounds odd, but you of all people should understand."

Dana couldn't imagine what he meant, but the woman named Willow look puzzled for a moment before her eyes widened in recognition. Dana noticed that Kiera shared her befuddled understanding of the situation.

"She *talked* to Lachlan?"

Fynn nodded.

"He's still in there somewhere?" Willow asked.

Fynn nodded. "Barely. He needs my help and possibly hers," he said, pointing to Leah. "She's the only person who's been able to communicate with him."

Willow clapped her hands excitedly. "I knew it!"

As Fynn reached for his satchel, Willow said, "Oh, that's just like Lachlan's."

"Identical, I should imagine." Fynn pulled a small silver amulet from it, placed it on Lachlan's forehead, and spoke a few words that sounded vaguely Germanic. Then he said, "Let's find a place to sit and talk."

A few minutes later, they sat in the generic cafeteria at a corner table with a reasonable amount of privacy. Fynn seemed to have assumed control of things and no one appeared to mind. He radiated the sense of calm and confidence of a professional, though it was unclear what his profession might be.

"Introductions seem in order here." He looked at each of them. "I'm Fynn Alden. I've known Lachlan Hayward for more years than I care to remember. That you know Lachlan means you probably know that we're an odd bunch, to say the least. We have a complementary set of skills we've used over time to help our friends and our neighbors. Leah shares that gift with us. Willow, I sense, has well-developed psychic skills as well."

Willow nodded with an expression of growing understanding.

Dana was curious to see how these women fit into this puzzle, though she suspected it related to the sinkhole and tornado that struck near here last year. The connection felt definite, but she was only guessing. Or was she? Fynn had her questioning everything. Was it an astute deduction? Or evidence of psychic skill? No wonder her mother didn't like this.

"Dana has told me what she can about this business. I suspect we should share our stories so we go forward with as much information as possible," Fynn said. "Dana, if you wouldn't mind filling the others in?"

At first, Dana felt self-conscious but soon fell into the story that had brought them here. The Tudor house in the Kettle Moraine that her parents inherited. The initial subtle haunting that seemed harmless but grew more ominous after her uncle nearly died in a suspicious accident. The changes in her father and the last few days when Sally died and Leah was injured. And finally, the details of the day her parents and Shepherd died, and the house destroyed by an explosion likely triggered by her mother.

Dana concluded, "I adopted Leah—she was my late brother's daughter. As Fynn said, she has quite a psychic gift, something she shared with her grandmother. Last week, a car careened across our lawn and crashed into a tree. We think Leah was the target. That night, Leah had a dream in which Lachlan spoke to her and asked her to call Fynn. So here we are."

There was a brief hubbub of startled surprise and comments. All eyes turned to Willow and Kiera.

Kiera was an attractive woman with brown hair and intelligent eyes. She said, "I'm Kiera O'Donnell and this is Willow Monroe. We've been friends since the third grade. Last spring, my boyfriend and I bought an old tavern, renovated the building, and opened a very successful business called Quinlan's Tavern, named after the original owner. We discovered a tunnel beneath the bar which led to a cavern, a cavern that contained a complete Viking longship and ceremonial drawings that depicted a meeting between the Vikings and Native Americans. It was mind-blowing, improbable, and possibly the greatest archeological find in a century. We also discovered—Willow did anyway—that the cavern was a *thin place*."

So Dana had surmised correctly about Kiera and Willow. They had been involved with the tornado and sinkhole. Fynn nodded in understanding, but Dana felt confused about the significance of the cavern. "I don't understand. What's a thin place?"

Willow raised a hand. "It's a spiritual thing. A place where the *walls*"—she made air quotes—"between this world and the spirit world are thinner. In a thin place, the spiritual realm is more accessible, closer at hand. People often experience deep spiritual connections in such places."

Dana felt only vaguely enlightened. More paranormal stuff. She had never heard of such a thing.

"That's where Lachlan came in," Kiera said. "He walked into the tavern one night and quickly made it clear that he was searching for something. Something dangerous."

Dana now had a sense where this story was going and felt her insides clench in apprehension.

"He explained that he was chasing something that he believed had originated in your house," Willow said, looking to Dana. "He thought—"

Dana stood abruptly and walked to the window, wanting to stop the narrative, stop the truth from being spoken—that her mother had died for nothing. That she had given her life for her family, and they remained in danger. That the best and brightest minds had been brought to bear and failed. Shepherd failed. Dynamite had failed. Lachlan failed. She felt bereft. She tried to hold her feelings, but a sob escaped anyway and she broke down. She didn't know what the others might be thinking and she didn't care. At some point, Leah came over and silently held her hand.

A few minutes later, she excused herself and walked to the bathroom. She stood at the sink, ran cold water, and splashed it on her face until she could feel a semblance of calm returning. Dana then attempted to put her mother aside. As distraught as she felt, she wanted to believe some good might come from this meeting, that maybe this meeting really was a beginning of the end. Leah walked in and closed the door.

"You okay, Mom?"

Dana nodded. She couldn't speak.

After another minute of deep breathing, she and Leah returned to the table. "I'm sorry. If this *thing* is still out there, my mother died for nothing."

Fynn spoke, gently. "I understand why you might feel that way and you have my deepest sympathies. I suspect your mother wounded this *thing*, seriously, and diminished it. Slowed it down, gave Lachlan some room to face it. I can't know that for sure until he wakes, but I sense it to be true. In turn, it's likely Lachlan bought us more time to regroup, to mount a successful defense and to eliminate this *thing*—as you call it—once and for all. Regardless, your mother played a large and courageous part in all of this and most likely kept it from coming after Leah, until now. We are all deeply in her debt."

True or not, Fynn's words gave Dana some solace.

"You think Lachlan will wake again?" Kiera asked. "The doctors have written him off, say he's in a persistent vegetative state."

"I'm hopeful. That's all I can say now," Fynn said. "That he contacted Leah suggests a lingering and meaningful consciousness, even if it's not outwardly evident. With my help, we can begin healing the damaged area of his brain. Only time will tell."

"What can we do?" Willow asked.

"For now, nothing. Pray if you feel it might help. I'll sit with him and apply several healing and strengthening techniques and hope they don't toss me out of here." He reached for his satchel and ferreted through it. "You're welcome to sit and wait but I'll need absolute silence."

"Do you pray?" Willow asked.

Fynn nodded. "But not to any Gods you know."

And Dana was again reminded just how strange this world she'd entered truly was.

Eleven

Kiera sat, staring at Fynn.

It was two in the morning and mostly dark, a little wash of light coming from the hallway into Lachlan's room. Her neck felt kinked from sleeping in the chair.

Fynn was a faint silhouette next to Lachlan, standing as he had for eight hours straight, touching Lachlan's temples, occasionally touching his arms and legs, speaking in a whisper.

She, Willow, and Dana had taken shifts sitting here, providing moral support. Dana and Leah also had a room at the Auburn Inn.

Nothing had changed. Lachlan remained still and unmoving, his position changing only when the nurses came in to move him to prevent bedsores. At first, the nurses seemed mildly amused by the attention Lachlan was receiving. Then it became clear the disruptions bothered them, and late in the evening, a nurse said the neurologist would stop by to *evaluate* the situation in the morning.

Kiera thought this was well and good—a noble effort—but knew Lachlan's diagnosis was a grim one and generally irreversible. On the other hand, nothing about Lachlan was normal. While Fynn refused to speculate on an outcome, Willow was hopeful he would wake soon. Kiera smiled. Her situation was a bit surreal. Willow had a thing for Lachlan even though she fiercely denied it. Something had happened in the cavern last year and she was besotted. It was a little sad, really. A relationship that would never happen.

Willow relieved her at four, and Kiera caught a few hours of sleep at home before showering and driving back to the facility. Everyone met in the cafeteria at eight for breakfast. The neurologist was due at nine and they were anxious to hear what he had to say.

Kiera looked at Fynn and said, "You've been with him for about fourteen hours, talking, doing things. What's happening?"

"So far, nothing that I can detect. Deeper down, I think he's healing," Fynn said. "I'm rather hoping he'll communicate with Leah or myself at some point soon."

Leah, sitting next to Dana, shook her head. "Nothing so far."

"It's likely the treatment has induced a coma in his remaining internal consciousness while his brain heals. Kenric did this once before with Lachlan and he responded well. I'm also working with his muscles and reflexes, trying to prepare them for when he wakes," Fynn said—spoken like a foregone conclusion.

Dana said, "So, who are you guys, anyway?"

Kiera said, "Yes, who are you guys? How do you know Lachlan? And who was Shepherd?"

Fynn looked reflective for a moment, rubbing his chin, perhaps wondering how much to tell.

At length, he said, "The three of us formed the core of a group called the Aeldo, an Old English word for *elder*. There are others, but we have always been the most active practitioners of our skills. We—"

"Which are?" Dana asked.

"It gets strange from here, I'm afraid. There was a time when much of the world was ruled by magic, and that remains my specialty. Lachlan had been planning to retire, and Kenric Shepherd had reinvented himself as some sort of modern-day tech warrior; he was quite successful at it, I gather. Lachlan and I never understood it, but Kenric had an exceptional mind. It was a shock when he died. Lachlan only came to the States to settle Kenric's estate and somehow, he was drawn into this mess regardless. I'm only beginning to comprehend the greater story here, but until Lachlan awakes, I am in the dark about many things."

"So what's behind this?" Dana asked.

"I don't know."

"You must have some idea," Kiera said.

"Are you aware of the concept of Right-Hand Path versus Left-Hand Path?"

Willow said, "I am. Basically, it comes down to good versus evil."

"Sort of. The concept is more involved, more esoteric. Suffice it to say, the three of us have generally followed the Right-Hand Path. Occasionally, we resorted to aspects of the Left-Hand Path to achieve a greater goal, thus a 'good versus evil' rationale is rather simplistic. As in all things, others mostly followed the Left-Hand Path. In your terminology, they were evil. We've battled them for centuries. However, I am not aware of any entity as powerful as this one seems to be—the darkness—whatever you call it. We need Lachlan to wake for those answers."

A nurse walked in and informed them that the neurologist had arrived. They all crowded into Lachlan's room to hear him speak. A short, balding man in his fifties, he performed a perfunctory exam and spent several minutes paging through the chart. Finally, he turned and said, "Are you all family?"

Everyone nodded, claiming some distant relationship or other. Everyone except Fynn, who announced he was Lachlan's spiritual adviser. Smart, Kiera decided. As such, they couldn't make him leave.

The neurologist pursed his lips, raised his eyebrows, and said, "I'm not sure about the sudden interest in this case and Mr. Hayward's wellbeing, but there have been no substantial changes in the past month. Mr. Hayward is in a persistent vegetative state. He has minimal higher brain function. That's unlikely to change. The nurses have reported ceremonies of some sort in here. I have no problem with that as long as you don't interfere with the staff and prevent them from seeing to Mr. Hayward's care. I'm sorry, but I have nothing optimistic to report."

Kiera alternately watched the neurologist and Fynn while the doctor talked. Fynn shook his head almost imperceptibly, buying none of it. What did he know? What could he know? Or was it misplaced optimism? What could he do to overcome the steely hard facts of medicine?

But she knew the answer to that.

Fynn and Lachlan weren't ordinary men. Wizards? Sorcerers? It sounded ridiculous—except for everything she had seen since Lachlan walked into Quinlan's Tavern last year.

The bunch of them arrayed around the bed were an odd group. Fynn, quiet Dana, and adorable but slightly spooky Leah, who talked like a tween even though she was only five. Spooky only because Fynn and Willow treated her like some kind of prodigy. Whatever it was these people had, she didn't have it. They were uniquely gifted in ways Kiera only vaguely understood. Maybe *she* needed more faith. She just didn't want to revisit the darkness and mayhem that had nearly ended her life last summer.

After the doctor left, Fynn returned to his place next to Lachlan and continued the quiet chants and touching rituals he had been performing since yesterday afternoon.

They resumed shifts and morning morphed into afternoon. The sun went down, and they gathered in the cafeteria for a communal dinner. Conversation was sparse and Kiera decided to go home and shower after her shift. Leah looked tired and bored while Dana looked nervous and hypervigilant. Willow dealt Tarot cards for no apparent reason and spent thirty minutes on the phone with her daughter.

It had the feel of a wake.

Kiera sat her shift until midnight and drove home in a depressed state. This reminded her of last year, of all they had lost. That Josh was still gone. The tavern destroyed. She had just been finding contentment in her life when that disaster swept through their lives.

Walking into the house, Ghost, her black retriever-border collie mix and best buddy, dispelled her funk with an enthusiastic welcome. Her neighbor had been watching him, but Ghost clearly missed Mom. Playfully grabbing her sleeve, he yanked on it until she dropped to the ground and acknowledged him face to face. He grabbed a ball and dropped it on the floor. After ten minutes of ball play, he seemed satisfied.

Pouring a glass of chardonnay, she sat and checked her email. Kiera then took a long hot shower, decompressing, enjoying the strong spray as it massaged her skin, feeling the tension drain from her body.

She decided to sleep in tomorrow. Willow had the late shift and Dana was on at six. Another day or two, she would beg off. Lachlan wasn't coming back. It was sad, tragic even, but the neurologist had been unequivocal. She had read exhaustively about the condition, and the prognosis was grim. If Fynn's magic hadn't worked by then, she doubted it would.

Or maybe she needed to have more faith. Maybe she was too tired to feel optimism.

Kiera slipped into comfy pajamas, sat in bed, and sipped wine while doing a crossword, soon achieving the desired state, complete fatigue. She turned the lights off and quickly fell asleep.

Twelve

"Hey, look at this," Ric said, sounding excited.

Tatiana lay, sprawled out on the sofa, binging the second season of *Supernatural*. She didn't want to move. Hadn't moved much since she lost her job. "Can't you bring it here?"

"No, I can't bring it. You have to look at the map."

"All right," Tat said with a whiny tone. She rolled off the sofa and meandered over to the kitchen table.

"Look!" Excited, Ric pointed out the lines he had drawn on the map.

Tat stared for a moment, seeing nothing of interest, then shrugged. "I give up. What?"

Ric pointed to three lines drawn from Europe to California. "These are ley lines between vortex points in the British Isles and Mt. Shasta. The middle line connects with Lough Derg, the most spiritual site in Ireland. The flanking lines are drawn from Stonehenge and Rosslyn Chapel in Edinburgh. They enhance the center line."

He then pointed to a line drawn on roughly a north-northwest to south-southeast bearing. "This is the kicker. I drew this line at exactly ninety degrees to the Lough Derg to Shasta line." He paused for effect.

She stood expressionless, waiting for the big reveal. God, he was such a dumbass sometimes. "What does that mean?"

"That circumferential line connects a sacred site in Peru, Chan Chan, with the tip of Door County."

"So?"

"Look at the exact crossing point." Ric pointed to a tiny name on the map.

"Porte des Morts? What's that?"

"This is the cool part, babe. It's French for Death's Door. It's a place of extraordinary tragedy: shipwrecks, several Native American battles. It's where Door County got its name."

Now her interest was piqued. It sounded fascinatingly dark. "Is that one of those vortex thingies?"

"Yes. I think it's a strong negative energy node. If you cast a spell there, it should be greatly amplified."

"You know this for sure?"

Ric frowned. "Well, no. But I'd bet I'm right."

"At least we don't have to go to Shasta or Sedona."

"Right?"

"Holy shit," she said quietly. She had chilled out after her run-in with the old shitbag and her subsequent firing. Tat felt ready to do something. "So, when are we going?"

"How about tomorrow? I've got a couple of days of PTO to burn."

"Done."

Thirteen

Zoie Andolino dropped anchor with a splash.

Seven o'clock, well after sunset, the night was cool and calm, the sky lit by the stars and a waxing gibbous moon.

She had parked Dad's Starweld Fusion Pro about one hundred yards from the rocky bluff in front of the lighthouse. With her in the boat were the other members of the Door County Paranormal Society. Jordan Kemp, sitting in the other front seat, was a thirtyish personal trainer and gaming geek. Tall with olive skin, wavy dark hair, brown eyes, and a small port wine birthmark on his neck, he wasn't bad-looking, but he kept hitting on her, annoyingly so at times. He wasn't her type and seemed the least committed to ghost hunting.

Jordan was best buds with Greg Abbott, a bearded IT specialist sitting directly behind her. Nearing forty, the guy tended to be pushy at meetings and ghost hunts even though she founded the group. Greg was the only married member of the bunch and seemed to have an interest in the fourth member, Tess Patterson, seated behind Jordan. A quirky thirty-something law clerk, Zoie had privately nominated Tess as the most likely to be a crazy cat lady. And she was a vegan.

Ugh. She was quite attractive, though, with pale skin, shoulder-length copper hair and green eyes.

Zoie's plan had evolved from setting up a camera by the lighthouse to this impromptu visit after exchanging excited texts with the others about her sighting two days before. The group had seen little activity in the past six months, so it may have been simple boredom that brought everyone out.

On a list of cool haunted places to investigate, few could rival an old lighthouse, especially one overlooking Death's Door, the strait between Door County and Washington Island. The site of hundreds of shipwrecks, it had a long history of suitable events for hauntings. They had been here before but had always returned home disappointed.

They sat, their faces lit by the screens of their phones, and waited, a low buzz of adrenaline keeping them all a little on edge, fidgety, with frequent hopeful glances toward the lighthouse. Zoie silently prayed for something, another flash, anything. She had made the call and felt the pressure to deliver, and so she'd take anything, even a little St. Elmo's Fire.

The adrenaline slowly burned off as they sat, and disappointment settled in. At ten-thirty, Greg said, "Wrap it?"

Bummed murmurs passed through the group. Zoie gave him an irritated side-glance. The annoying ass was always trying to run things.

She started the engine and took a final look at the lighthouse, willing it to do something.

Anything.

She thought she saw a vague glow in the beacon glass.

Naw.

Wishful thinking. She blinked and it looked a little brighter. *What?*

Tess said, "Holy shit!"

Now Zoie was certain it was growing brighter, suddenly speeding up and rising to a brilliant flash before going dark. But it wasn't a flash of white light. It was a brilliant flash of black, like shiny obsidian. Was that even possible?

The boat exploded with excited conversation.

Greg spoke loudly over the rabble. "Anyone get that?"

Jordan flicked through his phone and triumphantly held it up. "Got it!"

It was an Amityville moment for them all, the excitement palpable.

As Zoie came down from the high of the moment, she worried they were reading too much into it. Maybe the Coast Guard had plans to recommission the lighthouse and this had been some sort of test. She hadn't noticed the ramp-up in the light last time, but that had been in daylight and she hadn't been looking for it. She switched the engine off and asked the others to quiet down, then explained her concerns.

Greg jumped in. "We need to research this thoroughly. Find out if it's changed hands, if there are any plans to recommission the light, or to convert it to a private residence."

Zoie was thinking the same. She should have spoken first. "Yep, good idea."

The others nodded in agreement.

"In the meantime, we should tell no one, post nothing. Especially that pic. Right?"

"Yes, sir," Zoie said sarcastically.

"Seriously, people. Or next time, there'll be twenty boats out here."

"Thanks for your input, Greg," Zoie said, reining in her irritation. "I'm off tomorrow. I'll do the research."

"There may be twenty boats anyway," Jordan said. "We probably weren't the only people who saw the flash."

Greg nodded. "Unfortunately true."

"Any thoughts on the weird color of the light?" Zoie asked.

Jordan scratched his fuzzy chin. "A new type of Fresnel lens? Demons from Hell?"

"Demons would be nice," Zoie said. "Catch a beer at Joey's?"

"Yep!" Greg and Jordan replied. Tess nodded.

As they pulled away, Zoie looked back at the lighthouse, a tall black monolith against the stars and moon in the east. A faint shiver passed down her spine.

This was the real deal.

Fourteen

Kiera was dreaming about Josh.

And the tavern.

They were together again, tending bar, running Quinlan's as a couple in love. Kiera knew it was a dream, but she reveled in it. It made her feel good and whole. This Josh was so much better than real-life Josh, who changed his phone number and moved away without leaving a forwarding address. The tavern phone rang and she reached for it, but it slipped away from her and continued sliding, out of reach, until she realized *her* phone was ringing.

She opened her eyes. Ghost was standing over her, pawing her shoulder.

Willow!

She grabbed the phone and sat up. Sleepily, she mumbled, "What?"

"He's awake, Kiera! He's awake!" Willow was almost shouting. Kiera pulled the phone away from her ear.

The notion burrowed slowly into her brain. "Lachlan?"

"Why else would I call you at two in the morning? Get over here!"

"On my way." But Willow had already hung up.

Kiera jumped into jeans and a sweatshirt. Brushed her teeth and opted for a ponytail rather than messing with her hair. She knelt down and smooched the top of Ghost's head and said, "I'll be back, buddy."

Driving too fast, Kiera pulled into the parking lot twenty minutes later, ran through the front door and down the hallway to Lachlan's room. Dana, Leah, Willow, and Fynn were clustered around the bed.

Lachlan was sitting up, looking little worse for wear, even after months in a coma. A finely featured, handsome older man with striking blue eyes, those eyes lit up when he saw her enter the room.

"Glad you could make it, my dear. Now my day's complete."

"It's the middle of the night, Lachlan."

"A minor detail. You look well," he said.

"Thank you. You look…miraculous."

Voices and footsteps cut through the moment. The neurologist strode in and stopped, clearly stunned, seeing Lachlan awake and sitting up. The man looked disheveled, as if he, too, had been roused from sleep.

"Mr. Hayward. This is remarkable. Welcome back. Everyone, please, give me some room." He shooed them away from the bed with a clipboard.

Lachlan smiled. "I've surprised you, haven't I?"

"An understatement, Mr. Hayward. How do you feel?"

"Hungry."

The doctor smiled. The first Kiera had seen from him. "I imagine you are. Quite a fast you've had."

The doctor asked a series of questions to evaluate Lachlan's mental state. Name. Birth date. Current year. The current president. When he asked Lachlan where he was, he said, "Haven't the foggiest. I was in a coma when I arrived."

"Fair enough," the doctor said with a chuckle. He then examined Lachlan's eyes and ran a set of reflexive tests; the look of shock and wonder never left his face.

"Really unbelievable. Without precedent in my considerable experience."

"The power of faith," Fynn said with mirth in his eyes. The doctor eyed him curiously.

If he only knew, Kiera thought.

"I can go then?" Lachlan said with an impish grin.

The doctor laughed. "Hardly. You'll need physical therapy—"

Without warning, Lachlan swung his legs out and stood, a tad unsteadily. Startled, the doctor lunged and grabbed Lachlan's shoulders in a protective gesture. After a moment, it was obvious Lachlan needed no help. The doctor slowly eased his grip and let go, keeping his hands at the ready. Lachlan stood ramrod straight, then bent and touched his toes.

The doctor stared, more in awe—if that was possible. Keeping his arms at the ready, he took a step back and said, "Take a step, please."

Lachlan did so without hesitation.

"Remarkable! But slow down. I'd like to keep you for at least twenty-four hours, for observation. Just to make sure we're not missing something. And we need to pull your G-tube—a minor procedure. Would that be acceptable?"

"Certainly. I'd prefer to leave with a clean bill of health."

Kiera felt stunned. Again, Lachlan had upended the science she had put so much faith in. Sudden remissions in vegetative states were rare. Even then, the patient usually faced months of rehabilitation and almost never regained full function. Lachlan looked like he had just risen from a nap. Something powerful had passed between Lachlan and Fynn, something beyond science.

Kiera knew how gifted Lachlan was. If Fynn's abilities were even close—and it seemed they were—she was thrilled and relieved to have them on their side. She could take a back seat this time. Whatever these guys needed to do to protect Leah, they certainly didn't need her.

Still, she worried. Whatever lay ahead, she hoped they were truly up to the challenge.

Fifteen

Tatiana loved Door County.

The quaint towns and villages, the shops, the bars, the restaurants; the atmosphere felt artsy, so unlike Green Bay which was shitty and boring.

The day was exceptional for early November, the sky cloudless, a few trees loath to lose their leaves still vivid with reds and yellows. After checking into the Angler's Inn in Fish Creek, they continued up Hwy 42 through Ellison Bay to the tip of the peninsula and Porte des Morts Park, a small picnic area with a perfect view of Death's Door strait.

People knew hundreds of years ago that this place was special, and Tatiana felt it as soon as she stepped out of the car. A vibe, a flow of energy, a dark sensation.

"You feel that?" she asked.

"What?" Ric replied.

"The energy here. It's quite intense."

"No, I'm not nearly as perceptive to that stuff as you are. I'll take your word for it."

She sometimes wondered if he was mocking her with such comments. But his expression remained neutral and he sounded sincere. They walked through the park, a typical county park with a picnic table and a grill, then walked down a metal staircase to the water. Despite the fearsome reputation, the view was serene, the water nearly calm, nearby Plum and Washington Islands clearly visible straight out from the rocky beach. Pilot Island, the site of three shipwrecks, lay farther to the east.

It was perfect.

When she looked west along the shoreline, she saw a sight that sent a powerful vibration through her. The rocky shoreline ran into the blunt edge of a stony cliff, the cliff forming one side of a bluff that jutted out into the lake. At the end of the promontory sat an old stone lighthouse, at least fifty feet above the waterline. The lighthouse spoke to her, called to her.

She grabbed Ric's arm and pointed. "Dude. Look."

"I saw it. It's awesome!"

"It is. That's where we're going."

"Now?"

"Yes, now," she said. They couldn't get there along the shoreline, though. The cliff looked steep and treacherous. Instead, she dragged him back up the stairs and they plunged into the woods west of the park, a twisted landscape of wind-gnarled branches and weathered roots clinging to the bluff, overlooking the water. This was the ideal approach. They could sneak up to the lighthouse unseen. But what if someone was there? Lighthouses didn't have keepers anymore, did they? Everything was automated now—at least she hoped that was the case.

They reached a rough cliff face that rose about twenty feet to the top of the bluff. Tat saw it was easily scalable, with a slight slope and plenty of foot and hand holds. She was in excellent shape and did a yoga routine daily.

Leaving Ric to his own devices, she scaled the cliff in a minute and sat on the ledge, smiling, watching Ric struggle. He was a lazy ass and needed to work out more.

Together, they pushed through the brush and, fifteen feet in, ran into a chain link fence marked with a sign:

WARNING
Property of US COAST GUARD
Trespassers will be prosecuted

The grounds looked unkempt and deserted. No one had been here in some time. Perfect!

Tat said, "Now what?"

Ric, still huffing from the climb, said, "I've got bolt cutters in the truck."

She raised an eyebrow. "What don't you have in the truck?"

"Right?"

"So what are waiting for?"

His shoulders slumped. "Jesus, Tat, I just got up here."

She rolled her eyes. He was a whiner too.

"Hey, you get me in there and I'll let you do me in the shadow of the lighthouse right there on that rock." Tat pointed to a table-shaped limestone outcrop. Ric disappeared without another word. She smirked. She needed no witchcraft to wield power over him. Men were such simple creatures, really.

The lighthouse was an amazing structure, the circular tower built with limestone blocks. The attached keeper's house—two stories tall—

had been constructed with smaller limestone blocks and a slate roof. It had weathered well. Too bad it sat here, mostly hidden from view.

A few minutes later, she heard Ric grunting as he scaled the cliff and stumbled through the underbrush, swearing.

As he emerged from the bushes, he said, "Step aside, babe. Men at work."

Tatiana sighed, annoyed by the exaggerated guy routine, and watched him snip the chain link two feet straight up in a zig-zag line. He pulled the cut edge aside. "Ladies first."

She crawled through the opening, stood, and strolled to the lighthouse. Touched the stone wall and felt the energy of the vortex flowing through it, an awesome sensation.

Ric walked to the door, examined the padlock, and took a pic with his phone. He then slithered up next to her, grabbing her ass.

She elbowed him away. "Can we get in?"

"Not today. I'll bring my lock gear next time."

"All right." She pointed to the flat slab of limestone to the right of the lighthouse and said, "That's where we'll do it."

"Now?" He reached for her waist.

She slid out of reach and said, "Down, boy. Later. After my ceremony. Let's go have dinner and a couple glasses of wine."

★ ★ ★

It was after eight when they returned. Ric killed the lights and crept up the nearly invisible access road to Porte des Morts park. The night had cooled into the fifties, so Tatiana slipped into a fleece and grabbed her witch bag, tossing the bedroll to Ric. "Here, make yourself useful."

Actually, he'd been a pain in the ass ever since she mentioned sex by the lighthouse. He was no better than a horny dog at times, though the same was true of every other guy she had ever dated. The curse of being female.

The night was still, alive with the sound of crickets, owls calling, and the gentle lapping of water on the rocks below. The air smelled vaguely fishy. A patch of clouds hid the moon as they climbed the rock face, the remainder of the sky clear, a bejeweled masterpiece of stars and planets.

That beauty stood in stark contrast to the negative energy from the vortex. Tat reveled in the negativity, bathed in it, a stunning sensation she had never experienced before. When they reached the rock, she grabbed the bedroll, unzipped it, and spread it over the cool limestone.

She grabbed her witch bag, a black denim satchel that contained all of her magick gear—candles, amulets, herbs, oils and jewelry—and pulled out a black candle.

"Back up a bit." She drew an imaginary circle with her finger and shooed him outside it, then lit the candle. With little wind, it burned brightly, casting flickering yellow light upon them.

Tat slipped a carnelian pendant around her neck and warmed it in her hand while she imagined it glowing with energy—her energy. The orange gemstone would give her spell more power. With her focus solely on the candle, Ric and the surrounding trees faded to black.

She chanted quietly, "May a pox defile your skin. May a pox defile your skin."

The curse would be a nightmare for the woman. For the shriveled-up creature she was, she was surprisingly vain. Bragged about it.

Ha! Karma's coming, you old shitbag.

Letting the carnelian amulet slide between her breasts, she wrote the words of the chant on a square of parchment. Ten lines across, ten lines down. She rolled the paper into a thin tube and held it over the flame while holding the carnelian in her right hand. The parchment flamed and burned to ash.

Tat pulled a small sachet filled with asafetida and sniffed the pungent herb, also known as devil's dung. A banishing herb, asafetida was used for reversing hexes and jinxing enemies. In this case, Tat sought the latter properties, and sniffing the sachet further enhanced her powers. She would carry it with her for a few days to maintain the vitality of this spell.

Focusing her inner eye on the old lady, she imagined her skin breaking out in pustules.

For five minutes, she continued to chant and then pulled a photograph from her bag. As angry as she had been, she'd had the presence of mind to snap a quick pic of the woman before she stormed away. Tat knew she would need it.

With a pin, she poked her left forefinger and drew an X in blood on the photograph. Set it alight and watched it burn to ash.

At that moment, a brilliant shooting star blazed across the sky.

"Holy fuck!" Ric said. "That was amazeballs! Talk about timing!"

Tatiana smiled. It was incredible timing. She set her things aside and zipped herself into the bag. Ric just sat and watched.

"What? You need an invitation?"

Sixteen

Zoie spent the day researching the lighthouse.

Then she called an emergency meeting of the Society at her house in Sister Bay. It wasn't actually her house but her parents' summer cottage. They lived in St. Petersburg, Florida seven months of the year and were happy to let Zoie house-sit the rest of the year. It was beautiful, a Cape Cod design, more of a house than a cottage really with three bedrooms, two baths, hardwood floors, a remodeled kitchen with high-end appliances. Most of the decor was nautically themed with many photos of Dad's greatest catches and his fishing excursions with Zoie. The wall colors were all Florida pastels.

Zoie had discovered the Coast Guard still owned the lighthouse and had no plans to recommission the light, and it wasn't listed with a realtor. So no official reason for whatever was happening there. She also checked the local news and social media for reports that other people had noticed the lighthouse flashing.

Nothing.

Yet Zoie had now seen it flash twice. Was it speaking to her? Her father swore it had spoken to him. The idea seemed far-fetched and a little arrogant, but appealing.

Jordan arrived first—early, she was certain—so he could act vaguely creepy and bother her.

"Hey, Zo, how's it going?"

"Just fine," Zoie said, coolly. "Beer?"

"Sure. Whatever you're having, sexy chica."

Zoe rolled her eyes and walked to the fridge. He wasn't bad-looking, but he was just too skeazy for her. Her last relationship had been with a woman, but she could be happy either way. She had no intention of letting Jordan or Greg know that. Men got super creepy about the idea of two women together.

Greg and Tess arrived together a moment later. Zoie wondered what his wife thought about that. Tess was quite attractive, but too old for Zoe. She came off as pretty straight anyway. But Tess and Greg? She wondered.

Zoie grabbed beers for the others. Pizza and breadsticks arrived five minutes later, all paid out of a kitty the group maintained to cover the cost of the meetings.

Setting the food on the dining room table, a chunk of oak surrounded by captain's chairs, she explained what she had learned, and the group broke into excited conversation. After forty minutes of discussion, they agreed on a plan. They would investigate the lighthouse despite the risk of being caught trespassing on Coast Guard property.

"We can't get to it by water," Greg said.

"Agreed." Jordan was playing on his laptop trying to plot a discreet course to the lighthouse fence. They all slid their chairs around him to observe. Pointing to a road west of the lighthouse, Jordan said, "If we park here, we could come at it from the woods."

Greg said, "Zoom in."

Jordan did so and pointed. "We could use this fire road. It looks disused and would put us about two hundred feet from the fence."

"What about the fence?" Zoie asked.

"I'll bring pliers and a wire snips," Greg said. "If we cut the chain link from the ground up, we can easily swing it open and closed. Whoever maintains the property probably won't even notice the cut."

Zoie said, "I don't think anyone does. The grounds are mostly grown over."

"What about the padlock?" Greg asked.

"It's a Master Lock. I can pick it in a minute or two," Jordan said, referring to the pictures Zoie had taken. "I don't know why anyone uses them anymore."

"What gear should I bring?" Zoie asked.

Greg said, "Bring it all. Who knows what we'll run into."

"For once, can't we just do this the old-fashioned way?" Tess said with a vaguely whiny tone.

"Why can't we do both?" Zoie turned and stared Tess down. She was sick of this stupid insistence on tradition. Zoie wanted the group to stay abreast of all the latest techniques in ghost hunting. Over time, they had acquired an EVP Recorder for capturing voice and aural phenomena, a REM-Pod for detecting changes in EM fields and temperature aberrations, and a spirit box for communicating with any ghosts they encountered. The spirit box was a recent addition and one they hadn't tried yet. Tess was a Ouija and séance aficionado and didn't like the gadgets. Tess stared back but stayed silent.

"When?" Greg asked.

"How about tomorrow morning?" Zoie said. "Everybody free?"

The others nodded. It was a Saturday.

"Should we meet there?"

"Three or four cars will draw too much attention. Let's all go in my truck," Greg said. "Can we meet here, Zo?"

"Sure, here's fine, say ten?" Zoie was happy to let Greg drive so her truck wasn't seen anywhere near the lighthouse.

"Yup."

Jordan grinned and looked at Zoie. "Remember asking about the color of the light?"

"Yeah?"

"The verdict's in," he said, adopting a creepy face and gruff voice. "It's demons from Hell."

Seventeen

Tatiana was lying on the sofa when she felt it.

Still binging *Supernatural*, something slid beneath her, a vague rumble. Not under the sofa, not even in the room, but somewhere way down in the earth. It felt dark and immensely powerful. She sat up straight, stunned. "Did you feel that?"

Ric looked up from his map and ley lines. "What?"

"I don't know, but it was freaky, dude."

"Like what? Sometimes, you're a little obtuse."

She threw him a *screw-you* glare and said, "It felt dark. Heavy. And it just slid right under us."

He shrugged. "I didn't feel anything."

Her phone vibrated. Bode, a friend from FoodBuddy.

"Hey, Tat, how ya doing?"

"Okay, Bode. What's up?"

"You know the bitch who got you fired over on Hazelwood?"

"Yeah. What about her?"

"You're gonna love this. I got stuck with her order today. The whole time I'm walking her bags in, she's whining about how she woke up with shingles and how awful they are, and I'm thinking, 'Ha! serves you right, you old bat.'" He snickered. "Anyway, I just thought you might enjoy hearing that."

Tatiana was glad he couldn't see the wide smile on her face. It worked! Holy shit! It worked!

She gabbed for a few minutes and then said she had to run. Ending the call, she burst out laughing.

Ric looked up, curious, "What?"

"It worked! The revenge curse worked! That old shitbag has a bad case of shingles."

"That's pretty spooky," he said, suddenly somber.

"What? Why?"

"You're getting really damn good. I better not piss you off." He looked a little nervous even.

She laughed a wicked laugh. "You're safe—for now."

Actually, she wasn't yet certain that she was truly a witch. Maybe the old bag had just happened to get shingles, though if she did, it was a hell of a coincidence. She had to try again, to see what happened. She had a few scores to settle yet.

"We've got to go back," Tat said. "I want to try it again. This time, inside the lighthouse. Bring your lock gear."

"Sure. Love to look around in there. When?"

"Tonight."

They left Green Bay late in the afternoon and stopped for dinner in Sister Bay. As the moon rose, they continued north to Porte des Morts.

Eighteen

Zoie felt a thrill when she spotted the lighthouse.

Greg located the disused fire lane and parked in a small turnout so they weren't visible from the road. The day was warm, sunlight filtering through the trees. Everyone piled out of the truck and grabbed the gear from the bed of the truck: flashlights, cameras including GoPros, various tools, and Zoie's bag of ghost hunting gear. While the others looked around nervously, evidently worried about the possibility of discovery and arrest, Zoie nonchalantly waited at the edge of the woods for them. After spraying themselves down with oodles of bug spray, Greg led the way into the trees in the general direction of the lighthouse.

Trudging through the underbrush, Zoie now felt anxious. They would be trespassing on federal land. She didn't know what the penalties were, but she felt certain they were severe. Nevertheless, she was undeterred. This felt like the best ghost hunting lead of her life.

Greg accidentally let a branch slip that swung back and smacked Jordan in the face.

"Jesus, Greg. Watch it!" Jordan barked.

Tess slapped his shoulder. "Keep it down."

Even with the bug spray, the mosquitoes and deer flies seemed hardly perturbed and swarmed around them. Zoie ignored them, but Tess freaked out and swept her arms out wildly, trying to shoo them away. A pointless exercise.

It was a slow walk, a thick carpet of mushy leaves and soft loam beneath their feet, fallen branches to trip over, and spiky hawthorns to tear at their arms and clothing. It smelled damp and earthy and Zoie loved it.

They had to be close, but the tree canopy was thick and she couldn't see the lighthouse. Jordan stepped down and the ground resonated with a quality peculiar to sheet metal.

They all stopped. Jordan jumped up and down, the ground beneath his feet resonating with the same metallic sound.

"What do you think it is?" Jordan asked.

"Sewer or utility cover probably," Greg said.

Tess said tersely, "Let's keep going. I don't want to get caught here and you're making too much noise."

A few minutes of pushing through the brush brought them to the fence. Even from here, the lighthouse was barely visible, so overgrown was the property on this side. A sign admonished:

WARNING
Property of US COAST GUARD
Trespassers will be prosecuted

Tess looked at Zoie. "Are you sure we should be doing this?"

"No," Zoie said. "So let's not get caught, okay?"

The chain link fence was ten feet high with three strands of barbed wire angled outward at the top. Greg pulled out his wire snips and grimaced as he leaned into the fence and tried to cut the metal. Repositioned. Grunted and groaned, but the snips failed to cut the heavy wire link.

"Damn it!" he said. "These won't cut it. I need bolt cutters."

Jordan said, "Shit. Now what?"

"We'll have to come back," Greg said. "Sorry. I wasn't expecting such heavy gauge wire."

After a requisite amount of grumbling, they retraced their steps through the woods until Zoie stepped on the metal plate Jordan had discovered earlier. She felt a slight spring when she jumped on it. "Hold up a sec. We should check this out."

Sewer covers were usually solid chunks of cast iron. This felt more like sheet steel. She slid yard gloves on and dug through the cover of leaves, twigs, and dirt. Digging down six inches, her fingers found the rusty metal surface.

"Help me clear this off."

They all knelt and cleared away the debris covering the panel.

"What are you thinking, chica?" Jordan asked.

"I'm not sure, but this isn't a sewer cover," Zoie said.

"Might be a storm shelter or some utility thing," Greg said. "Or maybe, it's a way into the lighthouse."

"Like a secret passage?" Tess said, excited now.

"Exactly."

After ten minutes of digging and shifting the mounds of soil and leaves, they cleared a three-by-four-foot area, exposing the outlines of the metal. While there was no visible lock or hasp, it was a door, hinged on the left. Greg pulled a pry-bar from his backpack and opened the hatch with a screech of rusty metal.

Beneath it lay a six-foot-deep rectangular hole with maybe enough room for two people to stand. Five iron rungs led the way down, the hole festooned with cobwebs, the floor a murky-looking mess. The others looked at Zoie doubtfully. She wasn't thrilled with the idea of climbing down there either, but wanted to lead the way to keep Greg from managing everything.

She grabbed a branch, cleared the cobwebs, and climbed down. The floor, a thin layer of dirt over stone, wasn't as mucky as she had expected. The passage angled down three more steps and then led toward the lighthouse. The passage was five feet high at most, carved out of the limestone bluff the lighthouse sat upon.

"There's a passage that goes toward the lighthouse but it's narrow. We'll have to go in crouched down—there's no head room, except maybe for me."

Tess said, "Do you think we should?"

"No cold feet now, Tessy," Jordan said. "We're well hidden. No one can see us."

Greg said, "I think it's freaking perfect."

"So do I," Zoie said. She pointed her flashlight down the tunnel, clipped a GoPro on her lapel, and stepped forward. Bent slightly, she led the way down the dark, dank passage, clearing the cobwebs with the branch. She couldn't see very far, but the passage looked long enough to reach the lighthouse.

Greg followed at a half-crouch. The others climbed down behind him.

Not normally given to claustrophobia, Zoie felt confined regardless and anxious about being caught. Evidently, the others felt it too. Zoie could hear Tess somewhere behind, mumbling to herself about the tunnel and the police. Jordan evidently bumped into Greg, who barked, "Back off, dude! Give me some room."

It was creepy and buggy, the furry remnants of dead animals here and there. Zoie bumped against the ceiling and something mossy fell into her hair from a cranny above. She freaked and brushed her hair madly while Greg laughed at her.

Annoying ass.

After walking about one hundred feet, Zoie saw the vague outline of a door ahead. Built with heavy wooden planks, it looked solid and she feared it was locked. She approached and wrenched on the rusty iron ring of a handle, but the door refused to budge.

Greg said, "Here, let me—"

But she planted her feet, leaned back, pulled with her full weight, and yanked it open.

She huffed, "Cool! We're in!"

The door opened to a narrow passage that led to a small basement under the keeper's house, an unusual feature in Door County where the limestone bedrock made digging a basement an expensive and difficult process. The room was empty, cobwebby, and mostly dark, a little light coming through a dirty casement window. Stone stairs without a handrail led to the first floor. It was a suitably grim entrance to what she hoped was a very haunted building. In the opposite corner, a small cistern sat behind an old-fashioned water pump with a long handle and a spigot.

When everyone had emerged from the tunnel, they stood in a circle, looking to Zoie with anticipation.

Zoie said, "You guys ready for this?"

"Yep."

"Who's filming?" Greg asked.

Zoie tapped her GoPro. "I got it. I'm switching the EVP on as well."

Tess rolled her eyes and said, "I'll film with my phone. Come on, let's go."

Greg led the way up the stairs to the first floor.

Zoie stopped and stared, feeling disappointed, uncertain what she'd expected. One large empty room, perhaps twenty by thirty, it was underwhelming and dusty. The far corner had once been a kitchenette, judging by the cast iron sink and broken cabinetry. A staircase to the left led upstairs and a door on the back wall probably led to the lighthouse proper. In a word, not creepy. Not spooky. Maybe at night it might feel more conducive to ghosts.

"Not much, is it," Tess said.

"Nope. Maybe we need to come back at night," Jordan said.

"That would be awesome." Zoie kneeled and set up the REM-Pod. Short, round, and black with a short antenna, the device beeped if it detected any variations in temperature or the nearby electro-magnetic fields.

Greg said, "Let's scope it out and come back after dark. We'll want some tarps or something to cover the windows too, so we don't give ourselves away."

"Good idea," Jordan said. "Maybe something to sit on as well."

The rear door did open to the tower.

It was quite bright, sunlight filtering down from the windows atop the lighthouse. A narrow cast iron spiral staircase led up to the lantern room with a handrail attached to the wall, leaving a daunting drop down the center of the tower. Their voices and footsteps echoed as they made their way up to the lantern room, a circular space with a cast iron floor.

The lantern and lens for the lighthouse were gone, probably taken long ago. The Fresnel lenses were popular items for small museums. Its absence created another question, though. Since the lantern had been removed, what caused the flash they had all seen?

Demons from Hell?

Zoie chuckled quietly but nervously.

They tried to be cautious, staying away from the windows as they looked out over Lake Michigan and Washington Island to the north. The view was breathtaking with an almost spiritual feel to the setting.

Zoie stood for a moment to absorb the feeling; then Tess said, "I think we should have a séance right here after dark."

"That's a little clichéd," Jordan said dismissively.

"I'm not sold on a séance," Greg said, "but you have the right idea about coming back at night."

Tess seemed undeterred. "I'll have one myself then."

After another five minutes of staring out over the water, they split up and wandered around the lighthouse for one last look.

Zoie walked a quick loop on the second floor of the keeper's house. Just three empty rooms—probably bedrooms. Nothing of interest. She walked another loop around the lantern room and stepped slowly down the stairs, eyeing the walls and the architecture. It must have been a grim place to live in. There were no bathrooms, and Zoie assumed they had used an outhouse.

Ugh.

★ ★ ★

Jordan darted back up the steps to the second floor. In one of the bedrooms, he'd noticed a deep, narrow crevice in the far corner. It looked more like a building error than an intentional nook or cranny, but he had peeked and saw a glint of gold-colored metal within. Something that may have been forgotten and left behind—though if it *were* gold, who would forget such a thing?

Trying to be discreet, he slipped into the room and pointed the flashlight into the crevice. It bent back at an odd angle, making it hard to see much. Twisting his head into the wall for a better view, the light again flashed on something metallic. He still couldn't see what it was.

Jordan squeezed his hand and phone into the crevice and snapped a quick pic. Pulled it out for a look.

"Fuck!"

He slapped a hand over his mouth. It was a freaking sword! It looked like forged steel with a gold inlay. There were gem-like stones inlaid into the handle.

Holy crap! Someone was coming!

He rushed out of the room and walked down the stairs behind Zoie, trying to look nonchalant, hoping no one would be tempted to look into the corner of that room.

Luckily, they were gathering by the basement stairs, ready to leave and talking about coming back.

As he approached, Greg said, "Tonight?"

"I can't," Tess said. "Tomorrow?"

"I'm in," Jordan said.

The others nodded.

Good!

He was coming back later tonight and grabbing that sword.

Nineteen

Kiera lit her fire table.

A wistful flame played over broken blue glass.

Given the weather—a rare, warmish evening in early November—Kiera decided everyone would sit outside, arrayed around the patio. The patio was large, built with sage-green pavers in an open design beyond double sliding doors off the kitchen. The patio wrapped to the right, to a sitting area covered by a large timbered pergola. There, Kiera had centered the fire table and lit two glass tube heaters. With no wind to speak of, it was very comfortable.

Lachlan had been discharged and the group would converge on Kiera's house shortly.

Night was falling—the sun set before six now—so she flicked the lights on, a set of accent lamps arrayed along the edge of the patio. Kiera and Willow had prepared a table of appetizers, chips and dip, a cheese board with various Cheddars, Gouda, and Muenster, meatballs, a taco salad, and mini pulled pork sandwiches. Kiera had dressed in jeans and a black long-sleeved V-neck top, while Willow made a rare appearance in jeans with a cute summery top in teal. She was charged with serving drinks.

They sat under the pergola drinking chardonnay and chatting while they waited for their guests.

Fynn and Lachlan arrived first, and by prior arrangement, Kiera had cans of Guinness Stout on hand for them. When Dana and Leah arrived, Dana took a glass of white wine and Leah asked for lemonade.

While it was understood why they were all there, they danced around the subject at first and engaged in small talk while Ghost wandered around seeking handouts.

Once everyone had settled in and snacked, Kiera stood and raised her glass, calling for a toast. As much as anything, this was a celebration of Lachlan's reawakening.

"To our dear friend, Lachlan. We're thrilled to have you back!"

After they had all clicked glasses, Lachlan stood. "Thank you all for your good wishes and your support."

Pointing to Leah, he said, "A special word of thanks to you, young lady. For hearing my call and bringing my friend, Fynn Alden, all the way from Mongolia to my rescue."

Leah stood and bowed in an adorable manner.

"Lovely. The young lass gets all the credit?" Fynn said, though he was clearly jesting.

Lachlan said with a smirk, "For those who don't know him, Fynn Alden here has an ego the size of the Hindenburg—and it's nearly as fragile."

Everyone laughed and relaxed a little more. There was a good-natured camaraderie between Fynn and Lachlan, and Kiera enjoyed the banter.

Lachlan brought the group down to earth. "We all know why we're here—besides toasting my good health, of course."

"I'm a bit fuzzy on the details, mate," Fynn said. "Perhaps you could enlighten us?"

There were general murmurs of agreement.

The group went silent as he rose again to speak. Watching him, Kiera could scarcely believe the change from just two days ago. He looked healthy and hale, not like a man who had just risen Rip Van Winkle-like from a year-long coma or vegetative state.

He spoke quietly. "But for Fynn, we've all had an encounter with this thing, this *darkness*, and we know how dangerous it is. Kenric tried to destroy it and failed. I tried with the assistance of Kiera and Willow, and sadly, it seems we too failed, given the recent attempt on Leah's life."

Kiera watched Willow, who stared at Lachlan with rapt affection, her chin resting on her palm. It was amusing. Willow denied having a thing for Lachlan, saying he was too old and all that, but her demeanor radiated smitten, regardless.

"Too many people have lost their lives already," Lachlan said, scanning the group on the patio. "I'm convinced it intends to make another attempt on Leah and Dana's lives before seeking to cause wider mayhem in the world. That said, my first question is for Dana, but also for Leah."

While Kiera knew this conversation was coming, she wasn't ready for it, and had little stomach for any of the awful situations they had faced in the cavern. In fact, she felt a little nauseated. Dana seemed to be fretting, wringing her hands, her forehead furrowed with worry. Fynn was unreadable. If he played poker, he was probably very good at it. Crickets chirping in the yard and the mesmerizing flame on the fire table provided an odd backdrop to the serious conversation.

Turning to Dana, Lachlan said, "I sense your anxiety regarding

Leah. Fynn and I have firm rules about not using or involving children in our endeavors. Still, she is a target *and* she's extraordinarily gifted. We may have to reconsider our long-standing rule. Of course, we will respect your wishes in the matter. What are your feelings, Dana?"

Now the center of attention, Dana looked uncomfortable. She put a finger up, signaling that she needed a moment to collect her thoughts. Finally, she said, "Leah and I have talked at length about this possibility. I'll let her speak for herself. She's an exceptional child."

"Fynn and I are in full agreement on that."

Dana nodded and continued. "I don't personally feel knowledgeable enough to help in any way. I was an observer at the house outside Lost Arrow. What I saw scared the hell out of me. I saw things beyond what I could even imagine were possible. I'd be lying if I said I was happy to be involved in this mess. I fear this thing may be indestructible. On the other hand, I don't want to feel that Leah and I are targets for the rest of our lives." She spread her hands, palms up, with an expression of ambivalence.

Leah swept her long blond hair behind her ear. She smiled self-consciously and put her hand over her heart. "I'm just a kid, but this thing you're talking about? It tried to hurt me, twice. I want to help and I think I can. Until it goes away, I won't feel safe. Whether I help or not, I won't feel safe."

Fynn glanced at Dana. "And you're okay with that?"

"I am—reluctantly."

Kiera had to admire their courage, though she wondered if Leah truly understood what she was getting into.

"Okay, so everyone is committed to working on this together?"

Everyone nodded, including Kiera, who wanted to shake her head and run away instead.

Lachlan sat and set his elbows on his knees. "The next issue is this: before we can deal with the darkness, we need to find it. Where is it? How will we find it? We know it remains a powerful force given the attempt on Leah's life. We know it can travel through the bedrock beneath our feet, so it could be anywhere in that arc of limestone between Illinois and Niagara Falls—a vast area. The method I used last year was very slow. Too slow."

"Sniffing it out?" Fynn asked, tapping his temple. "Is that what you were doing?"

"Yes, it was—sniffing being a relative term for detecting disturbances in the energies. Even with both of us searching, it would take forever—and it's far too subtle a technique to teach to Leah and Willow on short notice. We know it traveled to Illinois, a week ago. From what I can determine, it barely moved after the confrontation with Kenric at the MacKenzie house. Evidently, Kenric and Laura MacKenzie inflicted substantial damage and it took a long time to recover before moving to the cavern. Now, it seems quite mobile."

"Indeed, the attack on Leah suggests the darkness has grown stronger again," Fynn said. "But will it travel far? It seems determined to kill the remaining MacKenzies—that appears to be its raison d'être from what you've told me. But has it found a haven like the cavern where it can bounce back?"

"Logic suggests it shouldn't be far away," Lachlan said. "Though thus far, there has been no coherent rhyme or reason to its movements."

"I don't think we can assign any logic to its motives." Fynn paced slowly in a tight pattern, staring at the sky, looking contemplative. "From Kenric's translation, we know that Anna Flecher cast a powerful invocation over the family, but we don't know exactly how she bound them. Did she bind the family herself? Was she that powerful? Or did she invoke some other entity, and if so, whom did she invoke?"

Lachlan nodded. "I hadn't thought of it that way. You may be on to something. I assumed Anna Flecher was the agent—she was evidently a powerful sorceress in her own right. Based on Kenric's translation of her diary, I'm certain Kenric felt the same. He mentioned no other spirit or proxy and she mentioned nothing in her diary."

"Doesn't mean she didn't invoke one," Fynn said. He took a long pull from his glass of Guinness. "Given that the original incantation has endured for so long, become so strong, and morphed into something that has become nearly indestructible, suggests another, more potent agency at work. She may have omitted the name intentionally."

"Good point. To foil anyone attempting to undo the spell." Lachlan nodded appreciatively. "That is why it's good to have fresh eyes and minds on the problem. I didn't consider that she might have invoked a spirit, but it makes sense. We should assume it's so."

Kiera grew confused by the conversation. "Who she invoked? What does that mean? And who's Anna Flecher?"

"Oh, shit!" Dana suddenly blurted.

Everyone turned toward her including Leah, who said, "Mom!"

There was a look of dawning horror on Dana's face. "Anna Flecher? She wrote the book my dad found in the house, right?"

"I don't know the full story, but I assume so, yes," Lachlan said.

"That book has been the source of nothing but misery for my family," Dana said, shaking her head.

"Indeed it has. At least we have it—or the translation anyway," Lachlan said. "It explains so much."

Before now, Kiera had heard none of this but it sounded fascinating. "How so?"

"Sorry, I should have covered this first. A little background then. Kenric Shepherd translated a diary that belonged to Anna Flecher. In a nutshell, it had a grim ending. Her husband buried her alive because she was a witch. He evidently didn't realize just how powerful she was. She cast a spell before she died that has continued to wreak havoc five hundred years on. We just don't know how."

Fynn said, "In the process, she may have invoked some entity—a spirit—to carry out her wish to bedevil the MacKenzie family. We know Anna is dead, but the spirit she invoked would still be alive. Indeed, it may form the heart of this darkness, as Lachlan calls it."

Fynn paused and gave Lachlan a condescending look. "By the way, the *darkness*? Are you kidding? That name is downright bloody poetic. Have you considered a career in literature?"

"Sod off," Lachlan said tersely, though he was smiling. "I had no idea it was a label I'd be sharing with others."

Kiera said, "Hold it, you two. That sort of thing is really possible? Invoking a spirit and having it perform evil deeds. It sounds ridiculous, like something between the Exorcist and Ghostbusters."

"Accurate really." Fynn pursed his lips into a grimace. "But without the fun bits."

"It helps us draw a more accurate picture of what we're facing."

An owl scolded from somewhere above, the roof perhaps.

Dana raised a hand. "I vaguely remember Shepherd saying the house itself was the problem, not Anna Flecher. Does that help at all?"

Lachlan said, "I think it does. With Fynn's insight that Anna Flecher may have invoked a spirit, that spirit would have been trapped in the tomb when Kenric cast the binding spell. Your family may have inadvertently set it free when they remodeled the house. So it may have been the spirit she invoked and not Anna Flecher that Kenric faced. I can understand he may not have understood that right away. I'm only beginning to understand it myself and I dealt with it head-on in the cavern. So we remain at a disadvantage in not knowing who or what we face."

"Lovely. Barring some bit of serendipity, we're stuck trying to sniff this thing out." Fynn shook his head and sat in a chair by the fire table.

It was silent for a long moment as the enormity of the task settled in. Kiera remembered feeling overwhelmed when they last faced this thing. She couldn't shake the negativity of the moment.

Willow said, "I don't know if this means anything, but I had a recurrence of The Tower in one of my Tarot deals. In fact, while you were still in a coma, Lachlan, I dealt out six cards and three of them were The Tower."

Fynn furrowed his brow. "From the same deck?"

Willow nodded.

Kiera said, "She did. I saw it."

"I thought you were trying to tell me something," Willow said, looking at Lachlan.

He said, "I was, the best I was able—"

Leah, who had been resting against Dana, suddenly popped her head up, her eyes open wide.

In a rush she said, "The tower! I know what the tower is!"

Twenty

Ric parked the truck in the corner near the trees.

In the dark, the black Silverado was almost invisible. Tat grabbed her witch bag and Ric grabbed a bottle of cabernet, the bedroll, and a small tool sack. The moon was near full and lit the way to the cliff. The lake was calm, just a gentle lapping of small waves rolling in. The fishy smell was stronger this time. Through breaks in the foliage, Tat saw the running lights of a fairly large ship heading toward Green Bay.

Atop the bluff, Ric slid a rod out of the fence. The rod held the links together, so it was less obvious the fencing had been cut. He pulled the fabric aside and Tat crawled through. He followed.

The light tower and house were iridescent grey in the moonlight. Tat loved it, the visual, the slightly haunted look of the limestone in this light. A lone bird called out—a raven, she mused. They walked a circuit of the lighthouse and returned to the front door where a sign warned of dire consequences for anyone caught trespassing.

Tat watched as Ric pulled a clump of picks and jigglers from his pocket and worked in silent concentration on the large lock, though he'd told her the size was irrelevant. Bigger locks were no harder to pick. He had watched a YouTube video of a guy picking this very lock. He tried the jigglers first without success. After three minutes with the picks, the lock snapped open. The door itself wasn't locked and opened with an appropriately eerie squeal from a dry hinge. It was awesome.

They walked a quick circuit of the keeper's house, skipping the basement. Basements were grim, and Tat was far more interested in the lighthouse tower and lantern room. There were several sets of fresh footprints in the dust that gave Tat pause. Who else had been here? Why?

But she was too preoccupied to care. Tat wanted to do a ceremony in the lantern room and couldn't wait to get started.

She had waited a long time to settle this particular debt.

They stepped onto the spiral staircase from the second floor and Tat ran to the top, spinning around and around, taking in the view: the moonlit water, the vague shadows of the islands to the north. It looked idyllic, but Tat knew better. This was the center of a negative node, a vortex of contrary energy, and she was about to summon it to do her bidding. It sounded so…medieval.

Ric opened and laid out the bedroll on the iron floor, and Tat sat, staging the area ceremony, placing a black candle and two red candles in the center.

"So, who are you cursing tonight?" Ric asked with a shrug. "Anyone I know?"

"Nope. This is about something that happened fifteen years ago, back in high school." Tat added with venom, "Ben fucking Pruitt to be exact."

"Who's Ben fucking Pruitt?"

"Ben fucking Pruitt was a senior, I was a sophomore, and he was pretty good looking. He was rumored to have a whopper."

"A whopper?"

"A big dick, sweetie," Tat said with a condescending smile. "So I finally got with him, but it was just so-so. Strictly a one-timer."

"So-so?" Ric looked confused. "The sex or—?"

"Both. Anyway, I found out a week later that he taped us doing it and showed it to half the guys at school. I never lived it down." For a moment, Tatiana felt the same rush of shame she'd felt when the rumors, looks, and leers started at school. It helped harden her resolve now.

"That fucking bastard." Ric looked genuinely horrified.

"Yep." Tat shook her head. "He did it to two other girls before we all got wise to him."

"So, where is he now?

"He's still in Green Bay. I see him now and then." She pulled the carnelian amulet from her bag and rubbed it in her palm, warming it.

"So, what are you going to do?"

"I'm going to cast a binding spell to make him eat."

Ric wrinkled his nose into a frown. "Huh?"

"He was addicted to sex, even then. Porn, the tapes, all that stuff. I'm going to focus his addiction to sex on food instead. All he'll want to do is eat."

"Whoa, that's sounds nasty."

"That's the idea," Tat said. "Sooner or later, he'll become a big fat pig—a whopper. Just not the kind of whopper he wants to be."

"Can you do that?" Ric gave her a wide-eyed, wary glance.

"We're about to find out."

Ben Pruitt was a far bigger story than she would ever tell, even to Ric. A part of her history he didn't know. The damage hadn't ended at school. Her mother heard the story and threw all of Tat's belongings into the garage and told her to move out. It was a non-negotiable demand.

Her last words to Tat were, "You slut! You're worthless, just like your father!"

With that, she slammed and locked the door.

Her mother became a born-again Pentecostal freak soon after Dad walked out and preached it incessantly when Tat was younger. She grew to hate religion and loved to rile her mother by plastering her room with death-metal band posters and pentagrams. Then Tat saw the movie *The Craft* and fell in love with magick. She transformed herself into a goth girl. She already had the pale complexion and black hair. Soon, every stitch of clothing she owned was black. And she studied, trying to learn every facet of witchcraft.

Mommy dearest never relented, never let her come home. Tat stayed with friends for a few weeks, then dropped out of school after landing a gig as an exotic dancer. Soon, she was sleeping with the club owner. He treated her badly and tried to pass her off to one of his friends. When she fought back, he punched her and threw her out. A series of meaningless jobs and boyfriends followed.

Ric was the first guy who treated her like an equal. They met at a Metallica concert, Ric fascinated by her Goth vibe and interest in witchcraft—and her ass. She moved in a week later. He soon adopted the name Amalric and started dressing in black too.

She had tried to curse Ben Pruitt several times, but nothing ever happened to the miserable bastard.

Until now.

Tat decided if this spell worked, dear old Mom was next.

"Save some of that wine for me." Tat gave Ric a gentle push toward the wall and motioned for him to sit.

She lit the red and black candles and slipped the carnelian pendant over her neck. In her hand, she felt it warm and respond to her energy and the vortex. She quietly chanted, "Ben Pruitt. I bind you to food, forever and ever. I bind you."

Sliding the amulet between her breasts and over her heart, she wrote the words of her spell on a square of parchment while she continued to chant, "Ben Pruitt, I bind you. I bind you to food, forever and ever."

Tat wrote ten lines of the chant in all four directions on the paper, then rolled it into a thin tube and bound it with black lace. She held it over the flame while holding the carnelian in her right hand, until the parchment flamed and burnt to ashes.

"I bind you, Ben Pruitt. I bind you to food, forever and ever."

Tat pulled a small sachet filled with asafetida and sniffed the pungent herb, focusing her ire on Ben Pruitt, imagining him eating. Gobbling mounds of burgers and fries. Shoving globs of food into his mouth. Gnawing on slabs of bacon and stacks of ribs. Visions of sheer gluttony.

Grabbing a pin, she poked her left forefinger and drew a circle and an X in blood on his photograph. Stared at it for a moment, set it alight, and watched it burn to ash.

There was no dazzling shooting star tonight, but she felt the same dark feeling she'd felt earlier at home. The sense of something living and breathing, lurking deep underground, working with her, doing her bidding. She suspected Ben Pruitt would soon grow very, very hungry.

She sat in silence for a while, caught somewhere between righteous vengeance and the horror and shame of a shattered sixteen-year-old girl.

Tat blew out the candles, pushed them into a nook by the wall, and summoned Ric with a sexy finger.

Twenty-One

Lachlan stared at Leah.

Finally, he said, "What? The card?"

"No. The tower! It's a lighthouse! The darkness is hiding under a lighthouse!"

"How could you possibly know that?" Fynn asked.

"I had a dream. I didn't remember it until Willow talked about her cards."

Lachlan said, "*Which* lighthouse? Do you know that?"

Leah shook her head. "No. I only know what it looks like."

Kiera grabbed her laptop and did a quick search. "Oh, great, there are a hundred and two lighthouses on Lake Michigan alone."

"Are you certain?" Lachlan asked.

Leah nodded.

"Good enough for me," he said. "We'd better get started, then."

A gentle breeze had blown up and clouds slid across the moon. Kiera set her laptop on the edge of the fire table and Leah plopped into the chair next to her. Lachlan and Fynn peered over her shoulder. She searched the lighthouses in Illinois and Indiana first, the last known location of the darkness. It was a short list, only eleven of them, and Leah shook her head after looking at each picture.

Wisconsin seemed like the next best bet, and the list was long. Leah shook her head or said *nope* thirty-eight times before jumping up and yelling, "That's it! That's the lighthouse in my dream."

"Lovely," Fynn said, looking over her shoulder. "Porte des Morts. Seems apropos. The Door of Death."

"What?" Kiera asked, befuddled. She had never heard of it.

"Oh, sure," Willow said. "Don't you know your Door County history? They named the county after that place."

"Do enlighten us," Fynn said.

Willow sipped her wine and leaned forward, clearly enjoying the spotlight. Lachlan momentarily felt an odd sensation in his chest and then realized what it was. He was infatuated. Willow was a beautiful woman and they had shared a deeply traumatic and spiritual moment in the cavern last year. They had a special connection even though he recognized the absurdity of it. He was old, too old to be thinking this way. When he glanced at her again, she was staring at him, smiling. Blimey! She felt it too. He would have to nip this in the bud.

Willow scanned the group and said, "The basis of the legend was a battle between the Winnebago and Potawatomi tribes. On that day, the weather was relatively calm, but by the time the Potawatomi warriors were mid-channel, coming from the islands to the north, a stiff wind set in. They pressed on, confident they could safely land by the signal fire set by a scout—but the scout had been captured and killed.

"When they arrived, the Winnebago attacked, raining destruction from above. The Potawatomi couldn't land, and the strong wind and waves prevented them from fleeing. Their canoes capsized and were dashed against the rocks. A few Potawatomi managed to climb to a ledge above the waves. The Winnebago jumped down to the ledge and fighting continued there until a large wave took them all to their deaths in the lake.

"After the battle at the bluff, the Winnebago waited for the return of their second party. But the wind and waves that had prevented the Potawatomi from fleeing also caught their party, and they were never seen again. The Winnebago took it as an omen they shouldn't try to cross the strait again. They decided it was a doorway to death. When the French arrived, they adopted the name and it stuck. Hundreds of shipwrecks followed and cemented the reputation."

Lachlan had to admit she was articulate *and* breathtaking.

Willow looked thoughtful for a moment and said, "You know, that place might be a vortex—isn't that what they're called?"

"That's an interesting idea," Fynn said. "A node or an energy vortex? Let me consult my map."

Fynn pulled a roll of rough beige fabric from his satchel. It was ancient and Lachlan had one just like it, somewhere. Fynn rolled it out along the edge of the fire table.

It was a crudely drawn map of the world, criss-crossed with lines of black ink. Someone had drawn red circles where several intersecting lines crossed. Fynn pointed to the red circle over the Wisconsin area as they conferred in hushed tones.

Finally Fynn said, "We suspect that area is home to a strong energy node. It lies at the intersection of several important focal lines. The Porte des Morts strait and lighthouse fall dead center of those lines."

"It's perfect, the logical choice," Lachlan said. "The darkness would seek such a place to recharge after the events of last year when it was severely weakened. It may still be weak. If we locate it soon enough, defeating it shouldn't be too difficult. If it has time to recover—recharge if you like—it will become formidable and difficult to defeat."

"That's what I saw in my dream!" Leah said. "It was recharging, like a phone."

"That's a good analogy, lassie," Fynn said.

"What's an energy node?" Kiera asked.

Lachlan spoke. "Nodes are concentrated foci of energy—flows of earth energies and telluric currents—and the energy can flow either into or away from these places, so they can be positive or negative. A great deal of energy can pass through these nodes—or vortices, as some call them. The darkness would be drawn to one of these places."

"Then we need to make haste, go there at once and assess," Fynn said. "Agreed?"

The nods and murmurs of agreement were unanimous.

Lachlan had just woken from a year-long coma after his last encounter with the darkness. He knew the stakes, knew what they were up against.

He had considerably stronger support this time.

And still he felt a twinge of fear.

Twenty-Two

Jordan Kemp flicked the headlights off.

The moon was near full, providing plenty of ghostly light to guide the way along the fire road. He pulled into the turnout, certain his Acura ILX was invisible from the road—though it was after midnight and traffic had been nonexistent.

Grabbing his backpack, he flicked the penlight on and kept it pointed to the ground. He walked into the woods feeling like a spy, dressed all in black right down to his gloves and dark face paint. Deathly afraid of getting caught trespassing on federal property, he had more than once pictured himself behind bars. But he couldn't ignore the sword and wasn't turning back despite his galloping anxiety. Jordan worried far more about arrest than he did about finding ghosts in the lighthouse. While he had a genuine interest in the paranormal, his greater interest was getting into Zoie's pants, and he felt, given sufficient time and effort, that he would succeed.

While the sword was likely some ceremonial Coast Guard junk, if it had been here for fifty or sixty years, it still might be worth serious cash, and he had no intention of sharing it. He knew if Greg or Zoie found it, they would insist upon leaving it. Their virtuous natures were tiresome.

With good directional instincts, he found the entrance quickly, even in the dark.

Jordan swept the leaves and branches away, pulled the door open, and dropped into the tunnel, easing the hatch down behind him. He switched to a flashlight, crouched, and sidled clumsily like an ape, his knuckles nearly scraping the ground. At least he felt safe from discovery now.

He reached the old wooden door and yanked it open. In the wash of the flashlight, the basement looked like a primitive cave, the beam casting long shadows. Now he worried less about arrest and more about meeting something in the dark, spooky building. As in all things, location was everything.

Jordan started up the steps slowly, then ran to get clear of the staircase, feeling anxious. The moonlight cast pale rectangles on the floor, and he felt the skin at the nape of his neck tingle. When he imagined this trip, he had been a lot braver.

The room smelled faintly of some scent. Candles and perfume?

Naw.

It didn't matter. He was here on a mission: get in, grab the sword, and get out. He walked straight to the second-floor bedroom. Stopped cold in the doorway.

He thought he heard something. A voice. It spoke one word.

Jordan.

Holding his breath, his hands, arms, and spine tingling with anxiety, he listened intently.

Nothing.

He blew out a long breath. He was freaking himself out.

Stupid asshole.

The room grew darker as clouds overran the moon. Jordan thought he saw lightning flash through the window.

Reaching his hand carefully into the narrow opening, he hoped a rat or bats hadn't nested within. Buried his arm up to his shoulder. It was so tight, he worried about getting stuck. He clawed around until his fingers connected with something solid. He stretched harder and managed to wrap two fingers around it. Pulled it out and shone his light upon it.

"Jesus Christ!"

The sword was the most amazing weapon he had ever seen. It had to be a fake. The blade was steel with a thin inlay of gold metal. The handle was adorned with gems, which were almost certainly glass. He examined the gold strip closely. It looked real, but how would he know? He was no expert.

There were small markings on the handle, squiggly lines that formed no actual letters. It had to be an older Coast Guard ceremonial or service sword. Regardless, he assumed it was valuable, even if the gems were fake.

He pursed his lips in a smug grin.

Success! Awesome!

He would look for something similar on eBay to determine its value. He let his imagination run to two, maybe five, even ten thousand dollars for a final sale price—though it felt so amazing in his hand, he felt conflicted about selling it.

Another flash briefly lit the room.

Lightning.

Jordan couldn't think of a cooler place to watch a thunderstorm than from the top of a lighthouse.

He walked up the spiral staircase, sword in hand. He wasn't letting go of it for even a second.

The view was amazing. The storm lay just to the west, over the Bay of Green Bay. It appeared quite intense, evidenced by the vivid display of in-cloud and cloud-to-water lightning. He pulled his phone out and started snapping pics, hoping to capture some of the lightning bolts striking the water and drawing beautiful reflections on the Bay. The wind picked up and the trees around the lighthouse bent and swayed in a weird strobed motion synced to the frequent bolts of lightning.

Jordan then noticed something eerie.

The ceiling of the lantern room was glowing with a faint, iridescent blue light. He wasn't sure what it was, but his skin crawled and seemed to shrink inside his clothes. It was spookier than shit. His apprehension grew but he was frozen in place, mesmerized by the storm, the bluish glow, and the arcs of lightning.

Was he safe this high in the lighthouse?

But then he realized the blue glow was probably a buildup of static electricity. Of course it was safe. The lighthouse had stood here for a hundred and fifty years!

A vivid forked bolt struck Pilot Island and Plum Island. Three seconds later, a deafening volley of thunder shook the lighthouse. It was simply the most amazing thing he had ever seen!

And he couldn't tell anyone about it because *he wasn't supposed to be here!*

"Damn it!"

He'd figure some way to post his pics without getting busted.

As he walked back and forth, watching the storm, he glanced down to the fire road.

Holy shit!

His Acura seemed to be sinking into the ground!

What the fuck?

Quicksand? Sink hole?

He needed to move but stood, unable to move. Transfixed.

The blue light was now spreading across the iron floor and steps and up the walls, enveloping the sword leaning against the wall. It was beautiful, amazing and frightening at the same time. He almost peed himself. Is this what they meant by frozen in fear?

Jordan broke the spell and forced himself to move. Pocketed his phone and grabbed the sword. As he did so, a charge surged up his arm, good and bad all in the same breath.

For a moment, he saw something in the room that was so dark it might have been a black hole. Only with this blackness came a mournful choir of voices. A profound sense of terror paralyzed him, rigid and mute.

His arm began to glow blue.

In his last microseconds of consciousness, a vivid flash lit the sky, turning night to day as a lightning superbolt struck the tower and coursed through the sword, his body, and the iron staircase beneath his feet at the speed of light.

Twenty-Three

Kiera laid the groundwork for the trip.

Finding the lighthouse on Google maps, she discovered it was situated on Coast Guard property and surrounded by a chain link fence. There was a cliff to the east that looked forbidding and an access road to the front gate. Seeking the best approach, she worried that parking by the gate would be too obvious, too risky if someone called the police on them. To the west, a narrow fire road extended partway toward the lighthouse. They would have to walk a hundred yards through the woods to the gate, but they wouldn't be visible from the road. In the end, that was the route they chose.

It was a cool sunny day. Flat cumulus drifted idly over the idyllic Door County landscape, a mix of farmsteads and stands of trees. Quaint towns and villages dotted the highway, each with an intriguing mix of shops, antique stores, art galleries, restaurants, and taverns.

Willow found them rooms at Tanner's, a lovely bed-and-breakfast in Sister Bay, twelve miles from the lighthouse. Perhaps once the home of a well-to-do landowner, it had been subdivided into four lovely suites dressed up with Victorian furniture, billowy curtains, and ornate duvets on the beds. The main floor featured an expansive sitting area with a lovely fireplace and an equally large dining room, the décor a mix of Victorian and shabby chic. The woodwork was dark and heavy. In a quieter time, Kiera could imagine sitting by the fireplace, reading an Agatha Christie novel.

The tourists and day trippers had gone for the season, and the rooms were available as long as they needed them. If the owner was curious about the odd bunch who checked into her inn, she didn't show it, though Kiera suspected there would be plenty of questions at meal times. As it happened, the owners were circumspect at dinner that evening.

They had driven up to Door County in Willow's Tahoe, the only vehicle large enough to carry everyone comfortably. For the first exploratory visit, they approached after dark to minimize the chances of being spotted trespassing. Dana and Leah stayed at the inn while Kiera, Willow, Lachlan, and Fynn drove to the lighthouse, parked on the fire road—hidden in a small turnout—and walked through the trees to the front gate.

Lachlan and Fynn led the way. They had the only flashlights, pointed at the ground at all times so the group was less conspicuous. In the poor light, they all tripped multiple times navigating the dark woods. The air was cool and damp, the ground and fallen leaves wet with dew. With the cloud cover, it seemed especially dark, and the lighthouse tower was a dim black monolith against the near-black sky as they broke through the trees.

Lachlan reached the gate first and examined the lock. He mumbled a few words, blew on the lock, and it fell open.

Fynn laughed. "That silly old spell still works?"

Lachlan handed him the padlock and said dryly, "Evidently. You have something better?"

Fynn shrugged. "Nah. I just wanted to note that you're fecking old, mate."

Lachlan said, "þu hæmest sylfum!"

"My, my. Lovely."

"What'd he say?" Kiera asked.

"He told me to—to shag myself. In Mercian. Sorry, ma'am, you did ask."

Kiera laughed. "I can handle it."

Lachlan stood, silent, head up as he stared at the lighthouse. The night seemed preternaturally quiet.

Finally, Lachlan said, "It's been here, or passed through, but it's not here now."

"Agreed," Fynn said. "Let's go in then. I've got this."

He reached for the padlock and it flipped open.

"Nice trick," Lachlan said.

"No trick. It was already unlocked," Fynn said. "I wonder what that means?"

"Trouble ahead, I suspect. We should post a lookout." Lachlan turned to Kiera and raised his eyebrows.

"Sure. I'll wait here."

The others filed through the door of the keeper's house and Kiera could hear them clomping around inside on the plank flooring. The moon popped through occasional breaks in the cloud deck, casting an eerie light on the overgrown yard and the lighthouse tower. At one point, the light reflected off the glass above, and it looked like the lighthouse was still sending out a beacon. Normally, Kiera would have been curious about the house and eager to explore it, but not tonight. The thing they were chasing was almost too frightening to imagine.

And while Lachlan and Fynn—supposedly the two greatest sorcerers on the planet—were in attendance, that they even needed them spoke to the absurdity of the situation.

No, if they wanted her to wait outside, that was just fine.

★ ★ ★

Lachlan closed his eyes and absorbed the energies passing through the lighthouse and the limestone bluff it sat upon. It looked solid and safe, a symbol, a beacon, but Lachlan sensed something amiss. He could feel the negative energy of the vortex that swirled in the Porte des Morts strait and swept over the lighthouse here and the range light on nearby Plum Island. He could discern nothing else. The darkness was nowhere in evidence. Could it be present and yet concealed in some way?

"Fynn?"

Reading his mind, Fynn said, "Nothing. But I don't trust the feeling."

"Neither do I. A quick tour today, then. We'll come fully prepared tomorrow."

"Right you are."

"Look at all the bloody footprints in the dust," Lachlan said. "It looks like Paddington Station. I wonder who else has been here."

"That would be good to know. A lot of them seem to originate in the cellar. We should look."

He and Fynn filed down the stone steps.

The cellar was a grim affair, a smaller room, carved out of the native rock. A well with a hand pump for drawing water and a small cistern sat off to the left. He noticed a nook in the far back corner. He peeked around the sharp edge and saw a door.

"Come here."

Fynn walked over and pushed it open, revealing a tunnel. "Interesting. I wonder where that pops out?"

Lachlan shone a light down the passage but couldn't see a clear ending. "Somewhere in the woods, I expect. We probably walked right by it."

"Something to investigate next time."

They meandered around the first floor one more time, then the second floor, carefully scanning the energies in each room. The only problem with coming at night was the visibility, everything all shadowy and indistinct, except in the direct beam of a torch, or flashlight as the Yanks called them.

In one of the bedrooms, Lachlan sensed something amiss, the lingering trace of something familiar?

He couldn't define it, but the sword of Stikla came to mind and he wondered what became of it. He assumed it had been lost in the cavern beneath Miller's Crossing.

Lachlan found Willow, staring up the spiral staircase.

"Willow, what happened to the sword of Stikla? Did Rachel bring it out? Does she have it?" Rachel was a teenager who had helped them last year in the cavern.

"No." Willow stared for a moment more and turned. "She left it behind when she and Kiera pulled you out of the cavern. It was buried when the tunnel collapsed. She was heartbroken."

Hmm. Some residue the darkness carried with it? Perhaps, but he didn't like the explanation nor the feeling that the sword remained, somewhere nearby.

He and Fynn scaled the narrow iron staircase next.

When they reached the lantern room, Lachlan saw the candles tucked in the nook at once. A separate but equally disturbing feeling pressed on his temples. The candles were trying to tell him something, but he wasn't sure what.

"Those likely explain the open lock and the footprints," Fynn said, pointing to the candles. "Looks like someone has been practicing a little magick here."

"I suspect you're right. But was it recent, or sometime in the past?"

"Why would that matter?" Willow asked as she reached the top of the stairs.

"Just wondering if they've interacted with the darkness."

"Good thought," Fynn said, looking pensive. "Though it wouldn't likely be a good thing for them."

"I'm just not feeling anything."

Fynn said, "Nor am I."

They looked out over the water. The view was beautiful and serene—but misleading. Though the lines of the energies were invisible in visible wavelengths of light, Lachlan sensed them rotating in a great circle and spiraling into the earth right over the lighthouse and the water of the Porte des Morts strait. He knew Fynn sensed it too. The flux created a negative energy sink that affected everything here, including the weather. No wonder this passage had such a checkered past.

When he closed his eyes, they appeared in his inner vision. No evidence of any major disturbances, just a few minor ripples of undetermined origin.

Still, it felt right. If the darkness wasn't here already, it soon would be.

"We should go. It's likely we're being sized up as well."

"Indeed." With that, they headed for the door.

Leaving felt a little anti-climactic and that worried him greatly. What were they missing?

Twenty-Four

Zoie eyed Tess nervously.

Somehow, her house had become the preferred meeting place for the group. Tess had arrived a few minutes before, but they decided to delay any conversation so they could discuss Jordan as a group. She then stared out the front window at the streetlights.

Just after nine, Greg knocked and walked in. "Hey, Zoie, Tess. Any word?"

"Nothing," Tess said. "He didn't show up for his appointments at the gym and his parents haven't heard from him."

"I don't know anything either," Greg said. "He always tells me what he's into. I've heard zip."

"So what are we going to do?" Zoie asked. She wanted to go to the lighthouse, badly.

"Go anyway," Tess said. "It's Jordan's fault he's not here. We don't know how long this possession will last."

"Haunting," Greg said. "Places aren't possessed. Only people."

Tess looked at Greg dismissively. "Whatever. Shall we?"

"You guys aren't worried about Jordan?" Zoie added jokingly,

"Maybe the lighthouse got him."

Greg side-glanced at Zoie and shook his head. Tess looked vaguely alarmed. They shuffled out the door, piled into Greg's pickup, and drove the twelve miles to the lighthouse with no real plan of action once they arrived.

As they approached, the moon peeked through a window in the clouds and lit the lighthouse ghostly grey for a few seconds before the landscape plunged back into darkness. It looked like the opening scene from an old black-and-white movie. The only thing missing was the creepy music.

Parked out of sight on the fire road, they walked to the metal hatch. Zoie was glad she wore a fleece. A front had come through and the night was cold.

Greg stopped and hissed, "Crap! Someone else has been in here."

The branches they had used to conceal the hatch had been tossed aside, the metal exposed.

A look of fear crossed Tess's face. "What if it *was* Jordan?"

Greg said, "No way. He would have covered it up when he left."

"What if he didn't leave?" Tess said.

"That's silly," Zoie said, but a shadow of doubt unnerved her. Was there a danger here? She had been doing this for years and never encountered anything remotely dangerous. Sure, hauntings were creepy, but not dangerous—or were they? She thought of poltergeists moving things and throwing them around. Still she had never heard of a single instance of injury or death caused by a haunting.

She looked at Tess. "I'm going in. Coming?"

Tess shrugged with a reluctant nod. Greg pulled the hatch open, climbed down, and led the way to the basement, his flashlight casting eerie shadows on the walls and low ceiling. Zoie eased into the passage next, feeling jumpy and nervous, and heard Tess drop down and close the hatch behind them.

When they reached the basement, nothing had changed. Old and dingy, it looked vaguely creepy, but Zoie suspected there was little to fear here.

Sadly.

"Cameras on?" Greg asked.

In unison, Tess and Zoie said, "Yep."

Greg took one step up the stairs and froze when the keeper's house rang with a resonating *clang*, a noise somewhere between a giant bell and a gong.

Tess yelped. "What the hell was that?"

Zoie stood at the base of the stairs, wide-eyed. "No idea, but that was freaky, dude."

The ringing slowly subsided.

Greg said, "With the weather growing colder, the cast-iron staircase must be contracting."

Skeptical, Zoie said, "That's a thing?"

"Absolutely. Big structures like bridges and such do the same thing."

Reassured by the explanation, Zoie continued up the stairs into the living area, flicked her lantern on and set it down. She swung around, allowing her GoPro to film the room for later reference.

Tess looked to her. "Tower next?"

"Yep. Hang on a sec," Zoie said. She pulled the REM-Pod from her backpack and set it up on the floor. Turned it on and set it to zero as Greg walked toward the door.

The door shuddered abruptly.

As Greg turned the handle, the door blew open and an icy wind blasted into the room. A mad flurry of snowflakes followed, rushing down the tower and through the door in a mini-blizzard. The wind and snow blew harder and harder until it pushed Greg back into Tess and knocked Zoie off her feet. The REM-Pod went crazy, beeping and flashing in manic warning.

Seconds later, it was over. Tess stood rigid like a statue, her face a rictus of fear. Greg looked stunned. Zoie couldn't even ascribe a word to what she felt. Greg reached and pulled Zoie to her feet.

Looking at the REM-Pod, Tess yelled, "Turn that damned thing off!"

Zoie slapped the switch and sat for a moment, stunned. Then she burst out laughing. "Jesus, dudes! That was amazing!"

Her unbridled enthusiasm seemed to shake the others back to the present.

Zoie said, "Don't you get it? This place is haunted! It's the real deal!"

Still, Zoie was concerned. Vaporous specters were one thing; this had been a physical assault, even if it was just wind and snow. She just hoped the GoPro had caught it.

Greg shook his head. "Hard to argue with."

"I don't know," Tess said, still looking spooked. "Anything else and I'm out of here."

Greg nodded. "Yeah, I'm a little freaked out too."

Only Zoie seemed energized by the strange phenomenon. Then she thought, was it paranormal, though? What if a window in the tower was broken and it was snowing? That wouldn't be quite so strange, or supernatural. Except that it was above freezing outdoors, and no snow had been forecast.

"Let's go up and check the tower," Zoie said, grabbing her lantern. "Maybe there's a broken window."

"Don't be a killjoy," Greg said. "That was a freaking ghost and you know it."

Zoie shrugged and slowly stepped up to the top platform, wary of the wet metal steps. Her hands were black from touching the handrail along the wall. The floor appeared to be covered in a thin layer of soot. None of the windows were broken but Zoie saw a grouping of black and red candles in a cranny by the wall. Pointing, she said, "Somebody else has been here. That might explain why the trapdoor wasn't covered."

"What's with the candles?" Tess asked.

Zoie said, "Red and black? Black magic, witchcraft—"

"Shut up."

Zoie stood and put a hand on her hip. "Seriously. I know a little about the Craft."

"The Craft? The movie? Are you serious?" Tess said.

"I am. And no, not the movie. That's what adherents of witchcraft call it, the Craft."

"You're missing the point," Greg said. "Somebody else knows about this. They've been in here and clearly,"—he waved towards the candles—"they know something's going on."

"Witches?" Tess said. "You guys trying to pull one on me? Is Jordan going to jump out next and go 'boo!'?"

"No. But I'm worried," Greg said with a frown. "I want this to be our story."

"I'm with Greg," Zoie said. "What should we do now?"

Greg shrugged.

"A séance! Let's see what happens," Tess said. Without waiting for an answer, she pulled a Ouija board and a blanket from her backpack, spread the blanket on the floor, and set the board in the center of it.

"We haven't done Ouija before," Zoie said. "We don't know what we're doing."

"I do," Tess said. "Greg, you in?"

Though Greg looked skeptical, he said, "Sure. Why not."

"Okay. Let's sit in a circle. Greg here and Zoie right there." Tess grabbed two of the black candles, set them next to the board, and lit them with a lighter. "Black candles, perfect!"

Greg sat rather close to Tess and Zoie rolled her eyes in what she hoped was an obvious gesture. Still, the candlelit lantern room did look suitably creepy.

"Okay. We all hold hands. I'll be the medium."

Greg's hand was warm and sweaty; Tess's cold and clammy. *Seems about right*, Zoie thought.

Tess spoke. "Spirit, speak to us. Speak through me."

"Repeat after me," Tess coaxed. "Spirit, speak to us. Spirit, join us here."

Greg jumped in and finally, reluctantly, Zoie joined them. "Spirit, speak to us. Spirit, join us here."

Time passed, Zoie wasn't certain how much. The chanting was lulling her to sleep and the more she fought it, the more the lure of sleep beckoned. She was almost gone when the staircase again rang with a resounding clang.

Her eyes snapped open. The others looked similarly startled. It was likely a coincidence, but the candlelight, the atmosphere of the séance, the power of suggestion made it feel like they were no longer alone. The spiral staircase seemed to hum slightly and the metal platform they sat upon shook with a minute but persistent vibration.

This is genuinely creepy, Zoie thought.

"Spirit, speak to us. Speak through me," Tess said. She looked into space in awe, then spoke in a low voice. "Someone's here."

The planchette quivered and moved to the letter C. They were still holding hands. No one was touching it, though it occurred to Zoie that perhaps Tess could manipulate it somehow. She was about to call foul when the planchette moved again, first to R followed by O and M.

"Nice, Tess," Zoie said with snark, smelling a rat.

"I'm not doing it. Honest!"

"Yeah, right. It's a magnet, right?"

Zoie listened but kept her eyes on the board and noticed Greg was doing the same.

The planchette continued to move, spelling C...R...U...A...C...H.

Zoie started to protest. "Yo, guys—"

The board and planchette suddenly flew across the floor and clattered down the stairs, followed by Tess's backpack. The black candles continued to burn unperturbed.

"I didn't do that!" Tess protested.

"Bullshit!" Zoie said.

Greg, still staring at the spot where the board had been sitting, looked up. "I believe her. I don't think she was messing with it."

Zoie felt aggrieved regardless. "You're in on it too? Pretty childish if you ask me."

"Shut up, Zoie."

Stung, she said, "Fuck you, Greg. I thought we were serious about this."

He looked at Zoie, taken aback. "Sorry, Zo. I am, but I don't think Tess faked it."

"I didn't do anything! To be honest, I'm a little freaked out." Tess started down the stairs in a huff and picked up her board. "Let's go. I have to work tomorrow."

Zoie didn't feel the séance was legit and wished the REM-Pod and spirit box had been operating. That would have been proof Zoie could get behind. She felt certain Tess manipulated the session somehow and that Greg had been tricked by her misdirection.

She had to come back. Do her own thing if need be. And she thought Jordan was the flaky one? Tess was cray-cray.

Tess finally broke the silence. "Are we coming back? Tomorrow night?"

"I'm in," Greg said. "Zoie?"

"I suppose. No more Ouija nonsense, though."

"I didn't do anything!" Tess protested.

"Whatever."

As Zoie stepped up out of the passage, she took one last look at the lighthouse. Imposing, blotting out the stars behind it, it looked like a dark and dangerous obelisk. A shiver ran through her midsection, a feeling that didn't leave her until halfway back to Sister Bay. Tess had faked the Ouija sitting, she was sure of it. Some trick to validate her stupid insistence on tradition. She planned to look up CROMCRUACH to find out what that meant—if it meant anything at all.

Regardless, the snow and the wind earlier *had* been real. A genuine, haunted moment; one that hadn't been faked.

She shivered.

What *were* they getting into?

Twenty-Five

Tat reached the base of the cliff.

The distinct feeling she was being watched made her glance back across the gnarled landscape of the woods. But it was deserted, the day grey, raw, and inhospitable. Pulling herself onto the ledge, she reached and helped Ric climb the last few steps. They walked to the fence where Ric fiddled, unwinding the rod that held the chain link together.

The feeling of eyes watching persisted.

Tat had a different plan today. While doing magic at night by the light of the moon was a time-honored method, she had just read of a newer, counter-intuitive approach. That casting spells during the day might be more powerful, more effective. When the sun was shining, more energy flowed through the atmosphere, energy she could tap for magick. And the vortex would only enhance her powers.

Tat ran to the door, unhooked the lock, and slipped inside. The keeper's house felt like home today. Comfortable, inviting, even if it was cool, darkish, and damp. It smelled faintly of some unidentifiable herb. Ric slipped an arm around her waist and then grabbed her ass.

She stifled an irritable comment and said, "Later, dude. Patience."

He moaned like a petulant child. Sometimes, she wondered what she saw in him and sensed the shine fading from the relationship. But he was a typical guy and no matter who she got with, she'd be dealing with a grabby dude. Sometimes, she wished she liked women. They were more subtle in just about everything.

They climbed the spiral steps up the tower to the lantern room. As Ric spread out the bedroll, he said, "Look at this. Looks like soot."

He ran a finger across the metal floor and held it up. It was black. "Odd, don't you think?"

She shrugged. It was an abandoned lighthouse. What did he expect?

"Who are we cursing today?" Ric asked.

"No one. I want to see what spirits I can invoke."

"Whoa. That sounds freaky."

Tat said, "Relax. We're not talking the Exorcist or anything like that."

"If your head starts spinning, I'm out of here," he said with a nervous laugh.

"Just sit quietly over there and drink your beer. I'm going to sit and call the corners and then leave myself open to—whatever. Don't disturb me until I'm done and you'll get what you want, okay?"

"Whatever." He grabbed a beer from a small cooler, twisted the top off, and leaned against the wall, playing with his phone.

Tuning him out, Tatiana listened to the faint sounds of the water below and the wind in the trees. The last time here, she had sensed a presence in or beneath the lighthouse, a presence that seemed ready and willing to work with her. The idea was exciting, but she tried to temper her excitement to become more receptive to whatever resided here. She needed to relax.

Tat closed her eyes and cleared her mind.

When she felt fully at ease and in tune with the lighthouse, she spoke. "Spirits of the Tower, I invoke thee."

Silence.

She repeated the words, softly.

The atmosphere felt solemn. Only her faint heartbeat was audible. She took a deep breath and spoke with a confident voice, chanting:

"Hail to the Master of the West. Poseidon, God of Water, Ruler of the Deep, I invoke thee. Be here now!

"Hail to the Master of the North. Cernunnos, God of Earth, Ruler of Life, I invoke thee. Be here now!

"Hail to the Master of the East. Quetzalcoatl, God of Air, Ruler of Wisdom, I invoke thee. Be here now!

"Hail to the Master of the South. Apollo, God of Fire, Ruler of Inspiration, I invoke thee. Be here now!"

As she chanted the words in a steady drone, she fell into a trance. Ric and the room slipped away. She loved this feeling, thought of it as an astral high as her mind seemed to disconnect from her body and float above it.

Tat lost any sense of physical self. A transcendent feeling, and she soon realized she was no longer alone. Someone or something had joined her—the presence she had previously sensed beneath the lighthouse was in the lantern room, invisible but fully evident.

She felt paralyzed but didn't fight it.

Then it spoke: *Welcome, Tatiana.*

Holy shit!

She had expected something preternatural. But it wasn't a disembodied voice. Wasn't deep, eerie, or haunting. Nor was it plaintive. Instead, it was a simple statement spoken in her inner voice. She wasn't even thinking the words. Someone or something had put the words there, in her head. Was that possible? Or was she imagining it?

Had she finally invoked a spirit? The spirit of the tower? It was surreal. She spoke in her head: *Who are you?*

Crom Cruach.

She felt equal parts excited and afraid. Who or what was Crom Cruach? It—he sounded...ancient.

Again, it spoke in her voice, reading her mind.

I am Crom Cruach, the spirit of the lighthouse. We are kindred spirits. I have carried out your request and bound Mr. Pruitt to a strong desire for food.

Tat sat, frozen in ecstasy. This was some heavy, heavy shit. She was communing with a ghost!

She thought: *Thank you.*

Soon, I will make a request of you. I will ask for your help.

Tat couldn't imagine why.

There are those who seek to destroy this place. They envy my power.

Giddy, she *knew* she wasn't imagining this, wasn't dreaming, but she didn't know what to say or what to ask. Soon, it became clear she didn't need to. This Crom Cruach did all the talking.

We must turn them away. Help me and I will show you the path to a full understanding of magick.

Her mind froze for a moment. She felt overwhelmed.

You need not speak. I know your answer. Tomorrow night. Come very late. You will stay here and your training will begin.

She wondered about Ric.

Bring the man as well. Tatiana, you are very gifted. I will make you stronger and more dangerous than you can imagine...

Enthralled, Tat felt a tingling sensation not unlike an orgasm wash over her.

She had no idea how long they communed, but when she emerged from her trance, Ric said she had been unresponsive for an hour, time that now felt like a dream. Except that she remembered every word of it. She had to make preparations, had to get ready; she had important work to do.

She lay back and allowed Ric to have his way with her while she planned and plotted. By the time he was finished, she wondered just how much longer she wanted him hanging around.

By mid-afternoon, they were making their way back down the cliff face.

Tat took a final look at the lighthouse, feeling transformed.

At long last, her moment had arrived.

Twenty-Six

Kiera woke early.

She walked down to the dining room and poured a cup of coffee into her travel mug. Sunlight peeked through the trees to the east, so she grabbed a fleece and wandered around the center of town, peeking into the windows of clothing stores, a cheese shop, an antique store, plus several interesting restaurants, one with a living roof covered entirely in sod.

After enjoying a large breakfast at the Inn, including fruit, eggs made to order, fresh bread, pancakes, waffles, and various breakfast meats, Willow drove the full group to the lighthouse, parking in the nearby Porte des Morts park. Cloudy and cool, a damp wind blew off the lake from the northeast. There was one other vehicle parked in the lot, a black Silverado pickup. Fynn wanted to investigate both approaches to the lighthouse, from the east and the west, by exploring the terrain around the base of the bluff. He wondered about alternate routes just in case they ever needed to make a multi-pronged assault on the lighthouse. Lachlan thought he was being overly dramatic.

They all donned sweatshirts or fleeces and started toward the trees west of the park. Fynn's arms shot out suddenly and stopped everyone in their tracks. He nodded ahead and put a finger to his lips. A man and a woman were walking through the woods toward the bluff and the lighthouse. The woman had striking raven-black hair. Moments later, they disappeared into the trees and brush.

Kiera whispered, "Stay here."

She ran thirty feet in, near silent by avoiding branches and twigs, dodging behind trees, and watched them approach a cliff. They were going to the lighthouse. She ran back and rushed the others into Tahoe.

"Let's go! Hurry!"

Willow said, "Where?"

"The other side," Kiera said. "Let's see if we can figure out what they're doing."

Willow spun the wheel and gunned the engine, racing back to the highway.

"I think that explains the open lock on the door and the candles," Lachlan said. "I wonder what they're up to?"

"The guy had a bedroll," Kiera said. "A little nooky?"

"A little cold for afternoon delight," Willow said.

"No. It's something else," Leah said.

Fynn and Lachlan looked at her in surprise.

"I'm not dumb," Leah said defensively.

Dana reddened a bit and Kiera stifled a laugh.

"So, what's your feeling?" Fynn asked.

"She felt—dark," Leah said. "That's it. Sorry."

Kiera hopped out first. "Stay here. I'll check it out."

She ran a quick, silent path to just short of the fence.

The couple were crouched directly opposite as the man unwound something from the fence. He pulled the fence back and the woman slid through; the man followed. They looked around furtively and beelined for the door. Kiera walked back to the Tahoe.

"They went inside. Not much we can do until they leave."

They drove the various roads around the lighthouse to become more familiar with the terrain, then took the ferry to Washington Island in the afternoon, catching perfect views of the lighthouse from the water and the island. Having fully explored the terrain around the lighthouse, they returned to Tanner's B&B.

★ ★ ★

The group enjoyed a lovely dinner of roast beef, potatoes, and green beans, and Willow then drove the group to the lighthouse. After confirming the parking lot at Porte des Morts Park was empty, she pulled into the fire road.

The sky overcast, the woods were dark as they picked their way through the trees to the front gate. Kiera felt less anxious with one uneventful trip under their belts.

Lachlan worked his magic, pulling the lock and leading the way to the lighthouse. Even with the flashlights, the interior of the keeper's house seemed unusually dark, as if the walls were stealing light from their lamps. Lachlan and Fynn stood in the center of the large room on the first floor, Lachlan with eyes closed and Fynn chin up as if sniffing the air. Dana and Leah walked over to the crumbling kitchenette in the corner and snooped around.

Finally, Fynn said, "Very strange. I sense something and yet, I sense nothing."

"Likewise," Lachlan said. He looked concerned, nervous. "The energy fields are disrupted, frozen in some way. They tell me nothing. We may be in trouble, old friend."

"I agree."

Oh shit! Kiera felt her insides tighten. "What trouble?"

Before anyone could answer, there was a thump on the ceiling, the sound of something heavy landing on the floor overhead, almost like a bowling ball hitting the alley.

Everyone looked up, except Dana, who yelped and backed toward the front door, a protective arm around Leah. "Crap! There's something wrong with the walls!"

Kiera trained her Maglite on the nearest wall, startled that it seemed alive. "Spiders!"

Willow let out a girly "Eek!" and backed to the center of the room. Kiera sidestepped over to her.

Dana yelped again and froze in place, hugging Leah close to her.

The door was crawling with spiders too.

Fynn edged toward the wall, head slightly atilt, with a curious expression.

Kiera felt a cringing shudder pass through her as he reached and ran his hand along the wall. It seemed to smear, but no spiders fell or clambered up his arm.

"Relax. It's a trick. An illusion."

"A bit of a worrying sign, though," Lachlan said. "The darkness is here, and I feel nothing. Like it's invisible."

"Cloaked."

"Of course. An ominous development," Lachlan said in an unnerving tone.

"Why?" Kiera asked, trying to relax after the walls had stopped crawling.

Lachlan reached into his satchel and retrieved several small items—it looked like a clutch of gold amulets in his hand. He said, "The darkness is growing stronger more quickly than we anticipated."

Fynn added, "I agree. It's drawing more energy from the vortex—"

A loud droning noise from the tower itself spooked Kiera, and the faces of the others reflected the feeling. Voice rising, she said, "What is that?"

Lachlan took one step toward the tower when a black cloud of enraged wasps exploded from the open doorway and swarmed over him. They appeared real and stung him repeatedly. He dropped, curled up, and yelled, "Fynn! Blue! Hurry!"

Fynn yanked a shaker from his satchel and blasted the swarm with blue powder from a shaker. The wasps seemed to pause momentarily. Shocked? Frozen—? No time to consider, though Kiera noticed that Lachlan had at least a dozen red welts already.

Fynn and Kiera grabbed Lachlan by the arms, helped him up, and yanked him toward the outer door while Willow ran outside behind Dana and Leah. Kiera stopped, shaken and afraid, the adrenaline in her system running amok.

Fynn pushed from behind. "Keep moving! Everyone, keep moving! We're not safe here."

They ran, stumbling through the woods to the Tahoe only to be greeted by a fresh horror.

All four tires were flat.

"Oh Jesus! Wait—I've got Onstar," Willow said, sliding into the Tahoe. A moment later she said, "Shit! The battery's dead too."

"Bloody hell," Lachlan said, hand on head, in shock and anger. "Outsmarted at every turn and sent running with our tails tucked."

Fynn shook blue powder in a circle around the group and the truck. "We might as well settle in until help arrives."

"Can't you two geniuses do some magic thingy?" Dana said tartly, with a dismissive wave of her hand.

Fynn winced and looked at Lachlan. "We deserve that, old chap."

Indeed you do, Kiera thought, still shaking from the experience. She was used to Lachlan taking command of a situation. Right now, he and Fynn looked like bumblers.

Lachlan nodded and said, "We can repair the damage to the tires, but we can't reinflate them. Not quickly anyway."

"Someone will be here in an hour." Willow tapped her phone screen.

Lachlan appeared to be in some pain with welts on his face and neck. Fynn had been stung as well.

Willow examined them and said, "I have a first aid kit in the truck."

Moments later she was ministering to them in nurse mode.

"We can recharge the battery as well," Fynn said. "This mess is our fault. We should've protected the vehicle."

"Indeed," Lachlan said. "Nothing like a big fat *bugger off!* from our friend in the lighthouse."

"What are we going to do now—about this thing?" Kiera asked.

Lachlan held a finger up. "Not discuss it here, for one. We can't risk revealing any strategy."

"I'll run back and lock up. We don't want to draw undo attention to the lighthouse." Fynn grabbed the shaker of blue stuff and a Celtic cross and ran into the woods.

"What's the blue powder?" Kiera asked.

"Sorcerer's blue. It provides some spatial protection with certain amulets and talismans," Lachlan said.

"I'm impressed," Kiera said with sarcasm. The powder had seemed mostly useless to her.

Lachlan shrugged and remained silent. Evidently he had no answer. Nervously, they settled in to wait.

Twenty-Seven

They met at Zoie's just after nine.

Tess looked perturbed, Greg impatient.

Zoie was fuming. She had done a quick search and learned that *Crom Cruach* was a pagan god of the Irish. According to Google, he was into human sacrifice and his worship had been ended by Saint Patrick. What a lame bunch of crap. Did Tess really think she was that dumb? Sure, Greg couldn't see it. He was all gaga over the bitch. Still, she held her tongue—for now.

"Any word yet on Jordan?" Zoie asked.

"Not a word," Greg said. "Nothing from his folks or his sister. His boss called looking for him."

"Think this has anything to do with the lighthouse?" Zoie asked.

Greg said, "No."

Tess shook her head less convincingly.

With some sarcasm, Greg said, "He's off doing something. Or he's met a woman. He's done it before. Come on, let's go."

Greg drove and parked in the turnout on the fire road. The night was cold and raw, just above freezing, a brisk wind blowing off the water. When they reached the hatch, it remained hidden by the branches they had covered it with the night before. Zoie still wondered if Jordan had been in the lighthouse. His disappearance felt odd but maybe Greg was right, that he had just hooked up with somebody. Still, a nagging suspicion gnawed at her. Then she sighed. Maybe she was just grasping at paranormal straws because she really wanted this lighthouse to be super haunted.

Greg opened the door after clearing the branches and dropped into the passageway. Taking control again like he was a frigging boss. When they got inside, she was going to lead the show tonight. Greg and Tess would just have to deal with it.

Zoie followed Greg into the basement and up the stairs. He paused on the first floor and she bounded up the spiral staircase to the lantern room. She spread a brown blanket in the center of the room and, on a whim, grabbed a red candle and two black candles, setting them in the center of the blanket.

Greg reached the top of the stairs. "What are you doing?"

"Lighting candles."

"Why?"

"Creating a little atmosphere," Zoie said. Why not? The candles were a nice, spooky touch even though she usually preferred the modern approach to ghost hunting. It was cold in the lighthouse, though. She could see her breath.

Tess, huffing from the climb, said tersely, "So, what are we doing tonight?"

"Let's start with a standard séance and our devices. Nothing to manipulate," Zoie said, giving Tess a stink eye. "By the way. I looked up Crom Cruach—are you kidding? You couldn't do any better than that?"

Tess stared her down. "I have no idea what you're talking about."

Zoie wasn't sure why she was growing to dislike Tess. The thing with Greg? Her prissy attitude and the insistence on tradition? Sometimes, she wanted to boot Tess out of the group, but then Greg would probably leave and she'd be stuck with Jordan. Ugh.

Zoie returned the glare. "The Ouija letters? They spelled out Crom Cruach, some medieval demon."

Tess rolled her eyes. "Really? You still think I faked that?"

"Yep." Zoie lit the candles and she motioned for the others to sit, facing the candles, equally spaced in a circle. She hoped something cool would happen and set the devices off to validate her approach.

The candles blew out.

"Now who's playing games," Tess said.

Zoie relit them. They blew out a moment later.

Well, this isn't going well, she thought.

She tried one more time, but they refused to light. Finally Zoie said, "Fuck it."

She set the candles aside and pulled a small camping lantern from her backpack, placing it in the center of the blanket. "Give me your lanterns. We need three altogether."

"Why?"

Zoie was growing annoyed with Tess's skepticism. "The ritual calls for three. You know that."

"Three candles," Tess said with a disapproving frown.

Zoie arranged the lights and pulled two fresh rolls from her backpack and split them open, setting them to the side—the customary food offering. Zoie switched her phone to airplane mode and reminded the others to do the same.

Placing the EVP recorder to her right, she set the REM-Pod on the left and raised the antenna, switching it on and setting it to zero. Set the spirit box front and center. Switched it to scan at a quiet volume. Zoie then put her hands out and motioned the others to do the same so they were holding hands in a circle.

Tess seemed to be fighting the atmosphere. "This feels like a cheap horror movie. I thought we were just going to observe."

"We could. But we have a better chance of seeing something if we summon it," Zoie said. "How is this different from your Ouija board?"

"It's not, I guess." Tess shot Zoie a dismissive glance. "But the gadgets are dumb."

"Whatever."

"If you two don't settle down, you're going to scare the ghosts away," Greg said.

Zoie and Tess glared at each other, and then Tess broke eye contact.

Zoie chanted, "Spirit of the lighthouse, move among us."

For a few minutes it was quiet except for the blips of radio stations the spirit box captured as it scanned the frequencies. The REM-pod sat mute.

"Spirit of the lighthouse, move among us."

Tess tittered. Greg shushed her.

"Spirit of the lighthouse, move among us."

A low moan, faint at first, filtered through the tower. It sounded a bit like a voice with a metallic edge. It was weird, not coming from the spirit box but the tower itself. Then the spirit box burped out something in a low voice, "I'm—"

At least that's what Zoie thought she heard.

The REM-Pod started flashing, and the indicator light closest to the stairs flashed, suggesting a paranormal disturbance in that direction.

Tess jumped up. "This is bullshit."

Zoie looked at Greg. "You doing anything?"

He shrugged and shook his head. "No. You?"

Zoie rolled her eyes toward Greg, who did the same. "You still in?"

"Yep."

"I'm going to wander around," Tess said.

Good riddance, Zoie thought.

★ ★ ★

Tess tried to shut out the noise of the gadgets as she wandered down the stairs. Trying to absorb the ambiance of the old lighthouse. Listening, feeling, leaving herself open to connect with whatever spirits might inhabit the building. Doing it the right way even if Zoie thought she was old-fashioned. Sometimes, the old ways were best, and she'd had just about enough of Zoie, her gadgets, her new agey vibe, and know-it-all attitude.

She was here mostly for the ghost hunting, but she also wanted Greg in the worst way. He was decisive and strong, and good-looking in a woodsy manner. And funny. She liked that in a man. She loved to watch Zoie struggle to maintain the upper hand with him, just because it was *her* ghost club.

In the minus column, he was married. She had met his wife, though, and she was short, snarky, and fat. Yuk.

As yet, Greg had been nice but had given her no sign of personal interest. She had to play it cool. In enough time he would *notice* her. In reality, she felt he already had. Always offering to pick her up and such.

She focused on the wall.

Tess could concentrate to a fine degree and the sounds from above slowly faded from her consciousness. She tuned into the faint creaks from the iron staircase, the waves rolling in on the shore below, the wind in the trees. Soon, she felt at one with the lighthouse and sensed a subtle presence watching her.

Yes!

This was the experience she sought. Connecting to the spirit plane in her head, one-on-one with the souls living here.

It was a high, a feeling almost like a line of coke or a tab of Oxy.

Suddenly, she felt cold. Some buzzer or alarm above went off, breaking the spell, severing her contact with the tower—

Except that someone or something was still here with her. Tess felt a cool sensation on her skin and an odd change in the light just down the stairs from her.

For the briefest moment, she was fascinated.

Then terrified.

The light in the space in front of her was disappearing. Leaking away. Resolving to black.

Something was sucking the light out of the room.

Tess stepped back. She wanted to shout, to warn them, but her mouth wouldn't work. Her feet tangled and she lost her balance. The subtlest touch—almost like the wind—pushed her off the stairs.

She fell sideways with a yelp and threw a defensive hand out as she hit the floor.

★ ★ ★

Zoie heard a burp of static and a garbled word that sounded like *Crom* from the spirit box.

Was she imagining it? Power of suggestion from Tess's Ouija nonsense?

A nanosecond later, she heard a stifled cry. Zoie looked down and saw Tess tumble off the staircase and fall fifteen feet to the stone floor. Tess let out a horrifying scream. Greg dashed down the stairs with Zoie on his heels.

Tess was sitting, arm tucked in and cradled by her opposing hand. Even so, Zoie could see her forearm was messed up. Clearly, both bones were broken given the impossible angle between her wrist and her elbow.

"Oh, that arm doesn't look good. Anything else hurt?" Greg asked.

"Oh Jesus, I don't know. My hip maybe?" She was in tears and considerable pain. "Call an ambulance!"

Greg paused for a moment and said, "We can't."

"What?" Tess fairly well screamed at him. "Call a fucking ambulance!"

"Seriously, we can't. We're trespassing and we'll probably end up in jail instead. If you can stand and walk, I'll get you there faster."

Tess seemed to consider. "You're probably right. Help me up. Don't touch my arm."

As Greg carefully helped Tess to her feet, Zoie ran up the stairs and collected her gear and backpack. They walked her down through the tunnel and out to the pickup truck. They strapped her in the back seat and Zoie sat with her. Tess was still in considerable pain but more composed. Greg drove fast and sure down Hwy 57 toward the medical center in Sturgeon Bay. For want of anything better to say, Zoie asked, "What happened, Tess?"

"I saw something. Then I was pushed."

Greg tapped the brakes and stared at Tess in the rearview mirror. "What?"

"Something pushed me off the stairs. I'm not going back there," Tess said with a look of fear.

Zoie said, "Are you sure?"

"Yes, I'm fucking sure! Tess yelled. "Oh Jesus, this hurts! How far yet?"

"Twenty-five miles."

"Hurry!"

A moment later, Tess passed out.

Twenty-Eight

Lachlan woke at daybreak.

The sky was overcast, sunrise a muted affair. He felt barely rested after lying awake most of the night—time spent considering every possible angle in their efforts to bring down the darkness. He called the other rooms to rouse everyone and walked down to the dining room.

After breakfast, the group met in his room. Lachlan sprinkled a small amount of blue powder in each corner of the room, placing an amulet at each location. He then poured a cup of tea while Fynn added a splash of whiskey to his black coffee, and they made themselves comfortable in armchairs by the window. Willow, Kiera, and Dana brought in the fixings for mimosas while Leah had orange juice. The women sat, arrayed around the room. Leah plopped down on the floor.

"Well then," Lachlan said. "I lay awake half the night thinking about this."

"As did I," Fynn said, sipping his coffee.

"The darkness is considerably stronger than we anticipated." Lachlan leaned forward and said, "That it strengthened so quickly, feeding off the energy node, has thrown a spanner in the works. Most critically, we're running out of time to deal with it before it becomes unmanageable. We need to formulate a plan and we need to implement it tomorrow."

"It's too dangerous to set foot inside the lighthouse again," Fynn said. "We need a ritual that we can perform outside the lighthouse. The darkness clearly controls the space within, but the three of us are strong enough to face it down from outside the lighthouse."

"Agreed. What are you thinking?"

Fynn stood and walked to the center of the room. "The three of us—you, Willow, and myself—will set up outside the lighthouse and perform a binding ritual first. If we can bind the darkness within the lighthouse, we can wear it down and move in for the kill. Leah and Dana can join us when it's safe to do so. The four of us should then be able to crush it."

"That will take considerable time and effort," Lachlan said. They had used this approach successfully once before, but it had taken almost twenty-four hours to bind their opponent.

"How much? How long?" Willow asked.

"Many hours. Possibly a full day."

"A *day* of continuous effort?" Willow asked, looking incredulous.

"Yes. It will be exhausting," Lachlan said. "We'll need to be rested and well nourished. I suggest we devise a firm strategy and practice it, looking for any weaknesses. Then have a hearty dinner and off to bed early so we're all in prime form."

Lachlan knew Fynn understood the difficulties ahead, but he sensed alarm in the others. What they were attempting would be grueling and difficult. He knew Willow, Fynn, and Kiera were up to the task. But Leah and Dana? They had no experience in this type of ceremony.

He didn't want to mislead them or have them go in with unrealistic expectations. Leah was an unknown. While her powers were unquestioned, without time to train her, they could be placing her in danger. He preferred to keep her a safe distance away. She and Dana might be bored but boredom seldom proved fatal.

In the afternoon, Lachlan and Fynn drove to Porte des Morts Park to observe the lighthouse from a distance. The day was cool and grey, the wind off the water like a knife. They walked down the metal stairs to the narrow shoreline and stood, trying to measure the strength of the darkness, assessing for any potential weaknesses. The darkness was clearly present and seemed significantly stronger than it had last year in the cavern.

Fynn pulled a thin cigar from his pocket and lit it. He then said, "Not making any attempt to hide itself now, is it?"

"No. It's taunting us. Acting smug. Waiting for us to step forward and confront it—"

"So it can dropkick us off the bluff again?"

"Indeed." Lachlan pondered the situation. "Think we can do this?"

"There was a time you wouldn't have asked that question," Fynn said. "Though I don't know the answer either."

"One of the pitfalls of advancing age, I guess."

Lachlan worked to conceal his thoughts but worried their ideas were exposed here. "It would be safer if we left and plotted at the Inn."

Fynn nodded. "Agreed."

"Better to come tomorrow, fully prepared, and fully rested."

They needed to get this right. Thus far, he and Fynn had looked more like hapless twits than the gifted sorcerers they were. They were losing Dana's trust—and risked losing Leah if Dana decided she was no longer safe. He sensed disappointment in Kiera as well.

Lachlan and Fynn returned to the Inn and discussed the necessary preparations. They drew up a list and checked their satchels to ensure they were bringing every tool at their disposal, then discussed several tricks from their extensive repertoire. Once they had defined a strong binding spell, they rehearsed it with Willow until they felt like a finely tuned machine. After supper, they discussed how to safely integrate Leah into the plan, working at a distance in the Tahoe.

They were ready, but Lachlan continued to feel a vague anxiety, an apprehension that the preparation and plan might not be enough.

That the darkness was already too strong, and their efforts would be for nought.

★ ★ ★

In the morning, they left Tanner's just after nine.

As Willow eased the Tahoe into the nook at the end of the fire road, Lachlan silently recited the words of a protective invocation. He stepped out and walked a circuit around the Tahoe, sprinkling a barrier of sorcerer's blue before setting an amulet on the hood and another on the dashboard. This time, the truck would be safe.

The day was suitably dreary with low clouds and intermittent drizzle. Lachlan leaned in the car door. "Fynn, Willow, and I will go first just as we planned. Willow will call when it's safe—if we need you."

"We'll be ready," Leah said. Sitting in back, she was playing on a tablet, looking angelic.

Dana didn't seem to agree—she looked tense and frazzled—but gave them a quick nod anyway. Kiera also stayed behind, ready to drive everyone out in a hurry if need be.

Lachlan and Fynn grabbed their satchels and Willow followed them through the woods to the front gate. Lachlan handled the lock, closing the gate behind them, leaving it slightly ajar just in case.

He had developed a new anxiety overnight. What if the darkness, instead of fighting, slipped away and hid in a new location, growing stronger while they fumbled around trying to find it? He had tried to clear his mind of the toxic thought with little success. They would know soon enough, though he sensed the darkness actually welcomed the fight.

The disturbance in the energies around the lighthouse were minimal. He prayed the darkness had stayed and was toying with them, mocking them, attempting to lull them into complacency. If so, it wouldn't work. They were proceeding on the assumption that the darkness was present no matter what they felt.

Fynn defined the places where they would stand by stomping the grass down in each spot and outlining them with sorcerer's blue. The positions formed an equilateral triangle facing the lighthouse, aligned precisely along the focal line between Mt. Shasta and Lough Derg in Ireland. The position gave them the greatest access to vortex energy as they pressured the darkness.

He and Fynn stood in long grass while Willow held the center position behind them, in a stand of trees. They felt confident their combined energies would be more than enough to overwhelm the darkness. No underestimating the risks this time. No embarrassing retreat. It was time to end this, once and for all.

As they faced the lighthouse, the wind picked up and the drizzle morphed into a steady rain. They were wearing ponchos, but the wind cut through the thin plastic and the sweatshirt Lachlan wore beneath his poncho. It was a miserable day to be outdoors, and it promised to be a long one. No matter. He had endured worse.

They chanted in Mercian, reciting an age-old spell to bind the darkness, to render it harmless and leave it vulnerable. Then they would close in and destroy it. Behind them, Willow acted like a reflecting lens, focusing their binding words like a magnifying glass concentrates sunlight into a beam capable of burning anything in its path.

Then Lachlan detected the darkness within.

Excellent!

It had stayed to fight. By this time tomorrow, this long nightmare would be over.

Slowly, Lachlan felt the energies bending to their collective wills, transforming the power of their words into an incredibly potent force. They fell into a groove, like a tight-knit orchestra, their efforts working in perfect rhythm. He and Fynn had a long history together and each knew exactly what to do. That was the ingredient missing last year in the cavern: the synergy of a trusted partner.

He felt confident. They were on the right track with this ritual.

The energies gradually aligned and bowed inward, compressing the lines of force passing through the lighthouse, constricting the darkness between them. Though his eyes were closed, Lachlan saw the flux of energy lines in his mind. For hours they pressed on, tightening the noose as they choked the darkness into submission. Lachlan lost track of time and had no reference with the sun lost beyond dark clouds and rain.

Their progress was tangible. Enough energy was now flowing through the lighthouse to power a small city.

He took a moment to probe the lighthouse. *Yes!* The darkness was still there, deeply stressed by the pressure they were exerting.

It seemed easy, but that idea struck a discordant note. He had expected more resistance.

It was almost too easy.

Until the moment it wasn't.

As he realized it, he felt a similar note of alarm from Fynn. The energies were distorting, backing up and bunching vertically as if encountering an immovable obstacle. He pushed harder, clenching his fists and jaw. Fynn was doing the same. Willow remained steadfast behind them.

What was happening? But he feared the answer.

The lines of force were bending into loops now and the harder they pushed, the more the energies compressed into a mangled mess between their position and the lighthouse.

Suddenly, order returned, only the flux of energies had been reversed and reflected back at them. The darkness was countering the binding, opposing them and doing so with little evident effort, beating them at their own game. His connection to Willow and Fynn broke down.

Fucking hell!

They had lost control of the situation.

He feared they had only moments to live.

Twenty-Nine

Zoie's phone buzzed.

She hopped up and slid into the driver's seat of the F-150 after a tiring day at work and peeked at her screen.

Greg.

Since Tess's fall, he had been acting strangely, talking obsessively about the lighthouse. Kept on about Tess being pushed. Zoie didn't buy it. The woman wasn't terribly graceful and given to dramatics.

Zoie thought about letting the call go to voicemail but changed her mind. "Hey, Greg, what's up?"

After a brief silence, he said, "Tess is dead."

She almost dropped the phone, her mind stuck somewhere between incomprehension and disbelief. "Not funny, Greg."

"I'm not joking. She's dead. She called me earlier and said she wasn't feeling well. She was having trouble breathing." Greg sounded shaken, breathing audibly and talking too fast. She could tell he was driving.

Stunned, she couldn't speak. Like her brain had frozen and needed a reboot.

"Zo?"

"How?"

"They think it was an embolism. A clot from her fracture."

"Fuck me." Zoie's thoughts careened around in her head. The lighthouse. The fall. Tess claiming she was pushed.

Greg said, "I know. Fricking unbelievable. The doctors were shocked. She went downhill in a matter of hours."

Still struggling for words, she said, "What about her family?"

"They're on their way. They live in Eau Claire. I didn't want to be there when they arrived."

"Ugh, I don't blame you. Do you want to meet somewhere?"

"Sure."

"Meet me at Joey's in twenty."

Zoie felt a shock she couldn't get her mind around, a cross between fear and morbid fascination. It was weird enough that Tess had fallen and claimed she was pushed. Zoie assumed she was just embarrassed and had told a lie to cover her ass.

Now she was dead.

Beyond the physical injury Tess had suffered, was the lighthouse somehow responsible for her death? Was that even possible?

She shook her head. She didn't believe it. Ghosts didn't act at a distance. She had been hunting and reading about ghosts long enough to avoid reading too much into a likely coincidence. There wasn't one documented case of such a thing.

Still, Zoie had never been involved in a haunting of this magnitude. They'd had some fun times and had encountered ghosts before, but they had all been harmless. It was an unwritten rule that all ghosts were harmless.

Or was it? Was it an actual rule? Or just her rule?

Jordan was still missing, and now Tess was dead. Dying abruptly of a blood clot seemed unbelievable.

Coincidence or not, it was too easy to draw ominous conclusions. Her worried mind said they shouldn't go back, shouldn't even think about it. And yet, a dark, primordial curiosity beckoned her anyway. She was an unabashed horror junkie. She had read stacks of scary books and watched every horror movie ever made, but the lighthouse was *so* much better. The Porte des Morts lighthouse was the real deal.

Joey's, halfway between Ephraim and Sister Bay, was an upscale bar and very popular. They had remodeled recently, replacing the pool tables with tall bar tables and chairs. The bar was long and dark, the ceiling low with exposed timbers. It was quiet, the only other patrons a couple of guys sitting at the bar. They had a small kitchen, so the atmosphere smelled of fried food and beer in a pleasant mix.

Greg was waiting when she walked in, sitting at a table in the far corner. She ordered a raspberry White Claw and joined him. Drinking a beer, he looked anxious and frazzled.

"Hey, Zo. Freaky, huh?"

"I'd say. This is getting weird. First Jordan disappears and then Tess ends up dead."

"Jordan's probably just shacked up somewhere. He'll surface in a day or two—"

"Saying it doesn't make it true, Greg," Zoie said, tersely. "It's been four days. His voicemail is full. And now Tess—"

"Tess was a freak accident. You were there." His expression firm, he didn't appear interested in alternative explanations.

"You don't suspect the lighthouse, even a little?"

"Not really. Do you?" Greg said, giving her a patronizing glance.

"No. Yes. I don't know." But she was beginning to believe it. "I'm just freaked out about Tess. You don't think her death is connected to the lighthouse?"

Greg shook his head. "No. Just because something's going on there doesn't mean Tess's death is connected."

Greg took a long draw from his beer.

Zoie eyed him curiously. "I'm surprised you're not more broken up about Tess."

He eyed her with genuine surprise. "What? Why?"

"Weren't you guys becoming a thing?" Spoken with a flourish of hands and a conspiratorial tone.

"With Tess?" Greg laughed, then cut it short. "Sorry, I shouldn't laugh. Tess is dead. But she wasn't my type, and I'm married."

"Oops. Sorry for assuming." But she didn't buy it. A brief look of guilt flashed in his eyes when he said *I'm married*. It was an awkward moment.

They sipped on their drinks in silence. Zoie should feel bad about Tess, but she didn't. They weren't really friends, just members of the same group. Then she felt bad that she didn't feel bad. Maybe she was just in shock. Really, all she could think about was the lighthouse, despite the aura of danger.

"So, we're going back, right?" Greg was insistent, his eyes boring into her.

Zoie hesitated for a second. Despite what she'd said, she felt conflicted, disturbed that Tess had died and Jordan was missing.

"Right?" More insistent, bordering on cray-cray.

"Yes, but you're getting a little pushy."

"Sorry." He put his palms up in apology. "I just know something is going on there and I don't want to miss it. It may just stop. If we can document this, we could sell it, who knows?"

"I guess. I just want to remind you the club was my idea."

"I know. Sorry. I get carried away sometimes," Greg said. "So, when are we going back?"

"I gotta check my schedule. I'll call you later. I gotta run."

When Zoie jumped into the truck, she felt momentarily disoriented.

Was she excited? Afraid?

She couldn't tell.

But she liked the feeling.

Thirty

Lachlan felt intense pressure on his chest.

Not only had the energies defied their commands, the original spell had been hijacked and pointed back at them, using the lighthouse as a giant mirror. By the time Lachlan realized what was happening and tried to signal to Fynn to break off, it was too late.

The darkness had bound them with their own spell.

Lachlan was frozen, unable to move. He sensed similar distress from Fynn and Willow, though he couldn't turn his head to look and confirm the feeling. The lines of energy were relentless, pressing and squeezing, trapping them with the very method by which they had hoped to cripple the darkness. Lachlan couldn't speak, not even a moan or a whisper.

The binding quickly grew so tight, he couldn't breathe. The compression on his rib cage was such that he was unable to inhale or exhale. Every invocation and spell he recited mentally to counteract the binding had no effect.

He had only moments to live. He tried to signal Fynn and Leah, but their telepathic connection had been blocked and was now useless.

Lachlan sensed people approaching, a fuzzy image in his panicked mind. With his head locked in one position, he saw them only in his peripheral vision. A man and a woman—a woman with raven-black hair, dressed entirely in black—the woman they had seen in the woods the other day. They both carried guns and seemed to be arguing as they emerged more into his line of sight. The man then tossed his pistol on the ground with an angry gesture.

It made no sense to him, though he knew they were coming to kill them. Doing the bidding of the darkness? Was it testing them? Why? They would be dead soon anyway—though perhaps the darkness intended to make doubly sure they were dead before sending the assassins to kill Leah and Dana.

As the man turned around, the woman jammed her pistol into his chest and fired one round through his heart without missing a step. A ruthless act with no apparent qualms. She turned toward the group, her face set in fierce determination.

Fucking hell!

They were next. Nothing could save them now.

As the woman raised her pistol toward Fynn, it flew from her hand.

What the—?

And Lachlan was released from the binding spell.

Confusion reigned. The woman looked at her empty gun hand in shock, then turned and fled.

Lachlan sucked in a huge breath of cool fresh air and he heard Willow and Fynn do the same. He spun around, trying to assess the situation, and saw Leah and Dana emerge from the woods outside the fence. Of course! Leah must have broken the binding. Had she recognized the risk and come to help? Perhaps she had sensed their fear and read their minds at a distance.

There was no time to consider further. He sensed the darkness nearby, formidable and preparing to strike, off-balance perhaps at the failed attempt on their lives.

"Run! Everyone, run! Now!" Thank God he hadn't locked the gate!

He pushed Fynn ahead of him and grabbed Willow's arm to hurry her along. They had to flee far from here before the darkness struck again. Thankfully, he could feel Leah working, holding the darkness at bay while they made their escape. He ran sure-footed through the woods, prodding the others along until they reached the Tahoe, which remained unharmed. So there was that.

"We need to leave, now! Hurry!"

They piled in and Willow slammed the last door shut. "Go! Go!"

Kiera hit reverse with a spinning of tires and backed down the fire road at a high rate of speed. She spun the wheel and the truck skidded into the turn, then shifted and sped down the road. Her driving was superb. Then he remembered she chased tornadoes. For fun.

For a few minutes the only sounds were their ragged breathing, the roar of the engine, and the tires on the road. Lachlan began to relax once they passed through Ellison Bay and Kiera slowed to a saner speed.

Willow, sitting in front, still pale with wind-tossed hair, turned and said, "What just happened back there?"

Lachlan was still trying to parse that very question.

"The darkness anticipated our play," Fynn said, his elbows on his knees, his hands clasped. "We were ambushed. And it has a human ally, a witch or a medium, I'd guess."

At length, Lachlan said, "I have to agree. She seemed modestly powerful. I don't really understand why she shot the man, though that distraction probably saved our lives."

"I had a better view," Fynn said. "They were arguing. I don't think he wanted to be involved and tried to back out."

Lachlan shook his head, discouraged by this unexpected and chilling turn of events. "So who broke the binding?"

From the far back seat, a little voice spoke. "I did."

Lachlan spun around to Leah. "Did you now? How did you know what to do?"

With a coy smile, she said, "Fynn told me."

"I'm glad you heard me," Fynn said. "I only had time to send the one message before the binding paralysis set in."

"How did you read the situation so quickly?" Lachlan looked over to Fynn.

"You know me, sensitive to the fine details. I detected a subtle disturbance just before the energies started to pile up. I made a judgement call and sent a message to Leah first. By the time I went to warn you, we were irrevocably bound."

"Not the first time your attention to detail saved us."

"We were damned lucky, my friend." Gesturing at Leah, Fynn said, "That young lady has a powerful gift, perhaps equal to Kenric's."

They had been lucky, Lachlan thought. He suddenly felt weary and ill-suited to the current conflict. He had been a fearsome warrior in the cavern last year and had acquitted himself well, but it had taken a toll. The ensuing coma had exacerbated the wear on his faculties. And while he'd won that battle, it now felt like they were losing the war. A five-year-old had saved his bacon. And for a second time, this very dangerous opponent had outsmarted and outplayed them; forced them to tuck tail and run. He chided himself for this moment of self-pity. It wasn't his style. Still, maybe he was simply too old for this nonsense.

It didn't matter. Too old, too weary, too jaded, he had no choice. The darkness had to be eliminated.

Somehow, Kenric Shepherd had set this disaster in motion and it fell to them to end it. It was part of their code of honor. But it wasn't a judgement against their friend. He felt certain Kenric had no hand in killing Anna Flecher and couldn't have anticipated this outcome. Regardless, when one of them erred—even unintentionally—they all felt obligated to rectify matters.

It was no longer a question of acting before the darkness grew too strong. They were too late—that had already happened. The plan today would have worked in any other situation. It had been a good plan. Or so they thought.

They needed a fresh approach, something different, radical. At best, they had one more crack at this, before the darkness destroyed them all and went on to create havoc elsewhere. The last time an entity this powerful had gotten loose in the world was 1933 in Berlin, Germany, starting with the Reichstag fire and everything that followed. The outcome had been horrific.

Leah was the key. She was young and raw, but her powers were significant. Long ago, the three of them—Kenric, Fynn, and Lachlan—had been a tremendous force to be reckoned with. Now Kenric was gone and somehow, Leah appeared to fill the missing link between Fynn and himself. He wondered if Dana would allow her closer to the front lines? But just the thought of it was an affront to their principles. Children were off limits, never used as pawns or shills, never exploited.

Still, this was a unique situation, one he had never encountered before. If they didn't destroy the darkness, its avowed goal was to kill Leah and Dana. Their survival depended on Leah's ability to assist and help them bury the darkness once and for all. Either way, she was in danger. He didn't think they could overcome the darkness without her.

"Awfully quiet there, old boy," Fynn said. "Though I understand after having our hats handed to us a second time."

"Indeed. It's clear we need an entirely novel approach."

"I want you to know that I'm not terribly impressed with you guys," Dana said, pointing a finger. "I had hoped you'd be protecting my daughter, not the other way around."

Lachlan, feeling humbled, sighed and shook his head. "I wouldn't be impressed either. We've performed miserably thus far. You have every right to be upset, especially since your daughter was the only one of us who met the challenge today."

"This is a far more complex situation than we realized," Fynn said. "That woman, the woman in black if you like, is clearly a force in her own right—"

"She was empowered by the darkness," Lachlan said sullenly. "We don't really know how powerful she is."

"Quite. Regardless, your darkness has an ally."

"But now we know. We can plan for it."

The ride was quiet thereafter. Thinking about the near-miss. The fact that three of them had almost died.

Finally, Lachlan said, "I need to go back to Milwaukee to pick up some additional gear and such from Kenric's basement."

"A short break would be good," Fynn said. "I have matters to attend to as well."

"I'd like to go home, change clothes, repack," Willow said.

"Me too," Kiera said. She turned to Dana. "Why don't you and Leah stay with me? I have plenty of room."

Dana nodded. She looked shell-shocked.

"I think we need to be far away from here to devise a new plan, well beyond the reach of the darkness," Fynn said.

As they pulled into the bed-and-breakfast, Willow said, "My place, tomorrow?"

Nods all around.

Lachlan sat fretting in the Tahoe long after the others had gone to their rooms to pack. Feeling stupid and melancholy.

They had only one more shot at this.

If that.

Thirty-One

Tatiana stood naked in the basement.

In the keeper's house, using water pumped from the well, she was removing blood spatter from her hands, arms, and face. The water was cold but clear and odorless. Tat had thrown her coat in the corner. Bloody and ruined, it had spared her clothes the worst of the blowback from shooting Ric. After fetching a change of clothes from the truck, she would burn all the bloody clothing.

Tat couldn't quite determine what she was feeling until she realized she felt nothing. Nada. Shooting Ric had been like taking out the garbage. Just walk it out and forget about it. She couldn't even remember a specific thought accompanying the urge to kill him, but when he chickened out, she saw red and knew he was of no further use to them. The relationship had run its full arc. Shooting him had certainly simplified the process. No messy breakup, no drama.

Just bang. Goodbye.

And evidently, her new mentor, Crom Cruach, had literally taken the garbage out. Ric's body was gone. She didn't know where. It didn't matter because she didn't care. She had tried talking to Crom about it, but he wasn't listening. He was either gone or resting after the excitement earlier.

No matter. Without a doubt, this had been the most exciting day of her life. Exciting, dramatic, surreal—with the promise of so much more to come.

The people trying to destroy the lighthouse were an odd bunch, though. A couple of old wizards, a psychic, and a little kid. Who knew such a world even existed? It was fascinating, almost unbelievable. Now she had a teacher who would show her everything. The crazy thing? Somehow, today had ended in a draw, though she didn't know why. They would be back, and she couldn't wait.

After dark, Tat climbed down the cliff and walked through the woods to Ric's truck. Then she drove to the house in Green Bay.

On the way, she compiled a mental list of things she needed to do or remember.

Ric's truck?

Dump it in the water somewhere. Lake, pond...

Easy enough. Pick a spot and dump it late at night.

The house?

Stay there for a week or two and then leave.

Tat figured she had time before people asked questions about Ric. Work would call. She'd call work and say he'd be gone for a week, a death in the family or something like that. No rush to move out.

His mom? She might call, but it was doubtful. Ric had family in the Valley, around Appleton, but none of them liked her. They all thought Ric had lost it, morphing from a normal guy into a weird goth dude in a matter of months, and they blamed her. Often, he didn't hear from his family for months, so it probably wasn't an issue.

To be safe, she would come and go at night only. Slowly remove her stuff. Erase any evidence she had stayed at the house recently. Claim they broke up when someone started looking.

As she thought these things, answers just popped into her head, almost like a conversation. But was it Crom talking, or were the ideas hers? The voice was hers. Could he follow her? She found it confusing and wanted clarity on those questions. They needed to talk.

For now, no problem existed that she couldn't deal with. Then Tat realized she was over-thinking everything.

Like where to live? It was obvious.

The lighthouse.

Leave the truck in a busy parking lot somewhere. Call no one. Take money but don't clean out the accounts. Grab her clothes and a few belongings and leave everything else. She would essentially disappear. They broke up. Beyond that, she knew nothing about Ric if anyone asked.

Settled.

While she felt nothing at Ric's death, she marveled at how deeply she had embraced this world, how natural it felt.

Tat didn't see it as light and dark, or even good versus evil. If her mother had taught her one thing, it was that things were relative and not always as they seemed. What appeared good could be evil, and from evil, good sometimes followed. Her mother, for all her praying and virtuous talk, was an evil bitch. Who throws their daughter out like that? She had never asked Tat how she felt, never acknowledged the pain and shame she felt. All because of her crazy religion and a God who seemed indifferent to the pain and suffering on the planet. An evil bastard who had sanctioned the Crusades, the Inquisition, and the death of millions throughout history.

If she and Crom Cruach killed a few people to preserve the lighthouse, it seemed a reasonable price to pay.

Still, that she felt nothing after killing Ric gave her pause. Was she trading a piece of her soul for this power she was being given? Did she even have a soul? Until today, she would have said no—not in the religious sense anyway. But the world was far more strange than she imagined, even as a witch. If all these weird things really existed, a soul no longer seemed like an improbability.

Despite those conflicted feelings, the allure of the power Crom Cruach promised was intoxicating. Power that would lift her above mortal laws and consequences. Who would say no to that? Still, she could resolve to use such power wisely. Then she realized that virtuous idea was simply a justification—a good one, though.

Strangely, armed with such power, she no longer felt the need to get even with her mother. She might even let Ben Pruitt off after he had suffered sufficiently.

All she had to do was kill these meddlesome wizards. It was clearly a worthy cause.

Her preparations would take a few days. She would take care of the truck late tonight, then keep her car hidden in the garage until she left. Clean up and pack tomorrow, and in a few days, she would be living in the lighthouse. The possessions they owned jointly would stay behind. She had no interest in material things. Just her clothes and some sleep gear.

She couldn't wait to be there.

Forever.

Thirty-Two

Willow shuffled the cards.

She sat at the table in the study where she dealt Tarot cards, prepared daily horoscopes, and studied the numbers in her life. The oak was ornately engraved and inlaid with brass symbols for the planets and the twelve constellations of the zodiac, the centerpiece a six-inch crystal ball. She never used the glass but loved the way it looked on the table. The soft light of candles lit the four corners of the room.

The room was shadowy, painted dark red—almost burgundy—the windows covered by thick velvet drapes. A contractor had removed all the electrical wiring from the room, and she allowed no electronic devices within, not even her phone. At the rear of the house, it was quiet, her relaxed breathing and the shuffling of the cards the only audible sounds.

Her clients came to this room and sat for readings: Tarot, palmistry, and horoscopes. She had a small but loyal clientele and also made money from her weekly blog posts on a variety of paranormal topics. The latter had become her most lucrative channel in the last year. The time spent with Lachlan last year had improved her knowledge and skills immeasurably.

Willow shuffled her Tarot deck for over a minute, then laid the deck on the table, face down, and spread them in a long straight line. Without looking, she selected five cards, shuffled those, and laid them side by side, also face down, a formation she viewed as her *I need advice* spread. The first two cards were ho-hum and not terribly illuminating.

She hesitated before reaching for the third, the card that represented the obstacles ahead. Taking a deep breath, she flipped it.

The Tower.

The fucking Tower.

Willow shoved the cards away. She was growing to hate that card. But now she knew exactly why. It had come to represent a dangerous lighthouse on the aptly named Door of Death.

The others would arrive soon to discuss strategy. She had offered her house, feeling that a change of venue might help them strategize with fresh ideas, and the others had agreed.

Kiera arrived first. Willow felt somber when she opened the door and gave Kiera a small nod instead of her usual flamboyant greeting.

They sat at the kitchen table, sipping wine, picking at the edges of their anxieties. The oak table was an antique, part of her shabby-chic theme, the walls pastel blue, the room decorated with baskets and vintage floral paintings, ruffled curtains, and ceramic canisters on the quartz countertops.

Making full eye contact, Kiera said, "We should get out while we can."

Willow nodded. "I know. I know."

"So?"

"I can't leave Lachlan high and dry, and I've taken a liking to Fynn as well."

"I know, I feel the same way. You scared?"

"Hell yeah!" Her voice inflected sharply upward along with her eyebrows. Yes, she was scared. Terrified even, but she tried not to dwell on it. She would do whatever Lachlan asked, go wherever he went. She felt compelled to with no choice in the matter.

The doorbell rang. Dana and Leah joined them, and they moved the gathering to the living room. The shabby-chic theme extended to this area, a room stuffed with plush sofas and armchairs in sage green, Tiffany lamps, and oak end-tables. The floors were random-width pine, with a brown and burgundy center throw rug. Dana looked distracted, nervous, and kept fidgeting with her wine glass. Leah wandered around the room, looking at Willow's wall art and decor.

Fynn and Lachlan arrived separately but just minutes apart. They, too, looked weighted down by the fiasco yesterday at the lighthouse.

Then Willow glanced at Leah as she examined a deck of Tarot cards and remembered the stakes. They couldn't be higher: lives of her friends; the life of that amazing child, above all. That was the cause, and it was a good one—even if it felt like a lost cause.

Fynn and Lachlan both passed on tea. Lachlan held up a small cooler. "I've brought Guinness."

Willow had bought a four-pack of Guinness for Lachlan but said nothing. When Kiera quizzed her about Lachlan, she denied any romantic feelings for him but knew in her heart she was smitten. Found herself strongly attracted to him, a feeling she couldn't fully explain, given his age. She tried to see him as a father figure but tingled in all the wrong places when she did think of him. It was beyond silly, but what could she do? Feelings were feelings.

Fynn held up a small silver flask. "I'm all set, ma'am. Thank you. Shall we get started?"

Lachlan stood near the entry arch, pacing. "Indeed. Starting with the obvious, nothing we've done so far has worked. Kenric sent it spiraling out a window with some very powerful magick. Willow and I drove it into the ground in the cavern with considerable energy. We've weakened it, but thus far, we've failed to destroy it. We must do something different. The standard playbook is out."

Smiling, Willow said, "Sounds like you're planning for a big game."

"A figure of speech. Everything we do must be fresh, new, unexpected. We continue to underestimate our opponent. We failed to recognize how quickly it would strengthen by interacting with the negative node. We've almost run out of time to deal with it. We need to come up with a plan and we must do it soon or lose any chance to overcome the darkness."

"Well, thank you for that rehash of the obvious, coach." Fynn plopped into a comfy armchair and said, "Do you have any actual ideas or just quotable adages?"

Lachlan put a finger to his lips and shot a look of disapproval at Fynn.

After a long pause, he looked around the room and said, "We should think of the lighthouse as a fortress, a castle if you like. Tall, strong, impenetrable. A direct assault is doomed to failure. This was proven time and time again in the Middle Ages. Indeed, it was demonstrated again yesterday. A siege is the surest way to bring down a fortress."

"That's all well and good, but we don't have bloody months to do this," Fynn said. "We have a few days, at best."

For the first time, Willow sensed tension between Lachlan and Fynn, a feeling they were growing frustrated and grumpy because of the continual setbacks.

Lachlan threw him a dismissive glance. "Have some vision, Fynn. I'm not suggesting a physical siege. I'm talking about a psychic siege."

Everyone was silent for a moment. There were a multitude of emotions on display. Anger, fear, frustration, a hint of desperation.

Suddenly, a light bulb lit up in her head. Willow said, "I get it. We'll cut it off from the vortex, starve it of energy."

"Exactly."

"Might work," Fynn said, nodding with eyebrows raised. "But we won't destroy it. Only weaken it of course."

"That's my intention. We weaken it substantially and then go in." He sipped from his glass of dark stout. "I'm not sure of the exact approach yet. Through the front gate? Maybe we'll use that underground passageway."

Kiera groaned. "Oh God. Underground again? I hate it underground."

Willow couldn't agree more. The claustrophobia in the cavern had been almost unbearable, especially once the collapse had started.

Fynn said, "I don't know that we'll need you—"

"We need her," Lachlan said firmly. "She was a veritable warrior in our last encounter."

"I'd worry the passage might be a trap," Willow said. "Like in the tunnel last year."

"I've thought about that too. We'll need to be careful."

Fynn sat forward and said, "Right, then. What's your plan?"

"We should assume the darkness and,"—Lachlan raised his fingers in air-quotes—" 'the woman in black' have set up a defensive perimeter around the lighthouse. We'll set up outside that." Lachlan turned to Willow. "Did you print the maps I asked for?"

"Yes. Right here."

Willow produced several pages taped into a square and laid them on the coffee table in the center of the room. Together, they formed a high resolution map of the northern tip of Door County.

Looking at it, Lachlan said, "First, we'll need a boat."

"Just like that? We need a boat?" Fynn added in a grandiose tone, "Planning an assault by sea, Admiral Nelson?"

"Shush, you irritating git."

"Not much for a lead-in—"

"Shut up and listen," Lachlan barked. But Willow thought she detected the hint of a smile.

Fynn stood to attention and saluted. "Aye aye, sir."

Willow imagined that Fynn and Lachlan were a hoot at parties. She hoped they lived to enjoy that experience.

"We need to triangulate the lighthouse by putting people here, here, and here," he said, standing over the table, pointing at Table Bluff to the west, Isle View Park to the southeast, and Plum Island to the northeast, a mile offshore.

"I have a friend who'll lend me his boat," Willow said. "We aren't going to wreck it, are we?"

She felt it was a valid question given the trail of destruction behind them, including an irreplaceable Viking longship and Kiera's tavern.

"I fervently hope not," Lachlan said. He eyed them in turn. "Okay then. Willow, you will go to the island, Fynn to Table Bluff, and Dana? I'd suggest you and Leah go to Isle View Park. That's the safest of the three locations."

"How safe?" Dana asked.

"Very safe. You'll be a mile from the lighthouse. Until we've tamed the darkness."

"You plan to be nearby, eating bon-bons?" Fynn said.

"*Hwaet!*" Lachlan barked with an irritated scowl. He wasn't joking.

"Touchy, touchy." Fynn patted him on the back, looking suitably contrite. "Carry on."

"I will be nearby, with Kiera. If you would, love?"

Kiera nodded.

"I will combine our collective energies into an impregnable shield, what we call a *sídrand*. As soon as we're able, we'll go in—probably through that passage to the cellar and maintain the siege until everyone arrives to finish it." Lachlan added, "That will be the moment of greatest danger."

"Why?" Kiera asked.

"It'll be difficult for everyone to move to the lighthouse *and* hold fast on the siege."

Willow wondered how they would pull that off. Then she asked, "What about the girl with the gun—the woman in black?"

"An unknown quantity. We left too quickly for me to get a read on her," Fynn said.

"I suspect she fancies herself a witch and the darkness is using her to its best advantage," Lachlan said. "If we can weaken the darkness, she should lose most of her power."

"You sure about that?" Kiera asked.

Lachlan rubbed his chin and shrugged. "Not even a little. We'll assume the worst. At least we know she's there this time."

"It feels like we're rushing this," Dana said.

"We have to. We dare not delay," Lachlan said. "The darkness is growing stronger quickly. Your safety depends on quick, decisive action."

"How's the weather look the day after tomorrow, Kiera?" Fynn asked.

Scowling at her laptop, Kiera said, "Rainy. Windy. Cold. Otherwise not too bad."

They then spent an hour compiling a lengthy list of supplies, and Kiera ran to the nearest Lowes to buy them.

It took several hours to fine tune the plan, finalize the exact locations, and perform the calculations needed to confirm the plan would work. They practiced until midnight and planned to rehearse again in the morning. All day if necessary.

Willow suspected she should be more afraid than she was. She had spent her entire life with one foot in the paranormal world and had been ridiculed and mocked for it. Many people perceived her as a flaky, dumb blonde when she was anything but. The experience in the cavern last year had validated her beliefs in the paranormal. Further, these people respected and appreciated her talents. They needed her skills. Yes, the plan was dangerous, but she couldn't imagine dying. They would get through this, somehow. They would prevail.

But for all that bravado, her annoying contrary voice whispered: *In two days, bitch, you'll be dead.*

Would she?

Thirty-Three

Tat stared out at the grey sky.

She had just put the finishing touches on her new home in the lantern room of the lighthouse.

Along the wall, she built a sleeping area with two bedrolls and her pillows. In the center of the room, she laid out her round Ouija rug laden with candles, amulets, and talismans. She had brought a backpack full of food and snacks: almonds, pistachios, granola bars, dried fruit. She had also brought a case of bottled water and four bottles of her favorite cabernet.

Two nights before, she had dumped Ric's Silverado in a truck stop parking lot and walked to the house. Packed the clothes she wanted in two suitcases and bagged the rest to drop at Goodwill. Soaked the blood-soaked clothing in gasoline and burned them in the fire pit. After the ashes cooled, she dug them out and dumped the bag of ash in a random dumpster.

Next, she packed her amulets, pendants, jewelry, and candles into two cardboard legal boxes. Went to the bank, took some cash from their joint account, and closed her accounts. Cleaned the house and shredded any paperwork bearing her information. Called Ric in sick, then wrote a goodbye note to Ric and left it on the table next to his maps. Hopefully, it would look like they broke up. Then she closed her phone account and tossed her iPhone into the Fox River. She had watched enough *CSI* to be very careful about what she took and what she left behind.

Tat had no clue how Crom Cruach disposed of Ric's body, but given his power, she assumed it was simply gone. Disappeared. And with luck, she would never need to answer the question: *Where's Ric?*

Driving back to Porte des Morts, Tat found a secluded spot to hide her car in the woods near the lighthouse.

Now she was simply gone too.

Off the grid.

From the lantern room, the view was monochrome. Grey sky, grey lake. In the murky light, even the pines looked grey. The sunset was muted, just graduated shades of drab until fog settled in and obscured everything. Tat opened a bottle of wine and lit black candles arranged near the center of the rug. Sitting in Lotus position, she sipped her wine until the glass was empty, then closed her eyes, leaving herself wide open to the spirit plane and the presence inhabiting the lighthouse with her.

With the intriguing name of Crom Cruach, he was dark and powerful and had promised to make her equally dark and powerful. Give her the ability to slip in and out of the plane of the living. To travel underground. To command forces of nature she hadn't even known existed. She called Crom *him*. He sounded male, and his vibe was male. She assumed he was male but didn't know for sure.

Slowly, she felt him slide into her. Into her nostrils in wispy tendrils. Through her skin. Into her mind. She gave herself over to him as they talked and plotted.

People were coming to kill them. They had to be ready. Probably tomorrow.

She thought about the blonde child and it gave her pause. She couldn't kill a kid. If it became necessary, Crom would have to do that. She understood the need to kill, and in this case, she considered any killing to protect the lighthouse to be self-defense, but kids were out. Or did he already know? Did he read her mind? Know her every thought?

I'll take care of it.

Perfect. She felt her shoulders relax. Situation resolved.

Tat didn't know exactly why these people were trying to kill them but understood it was Crom and the lighthouse they were after. For allying with him and helping him, he promised to teach her all the secrets of his world. She simply needed to reinforce his powers and guard his flanks.

Giddy with her newfound powers and influence, she couldn't imagine any human who could be as powerful as Crom. She gave herself over to him completely and promised to do her best.

After several hours, Tat had no idea how long, she slid sideways to a prone position and descended into a deep, dreamless sleep. Crom Cruach was there with her, watching over her and scanning the landscape around the lighthouse. Waiting. He would handle the child—would just neutralize her—not kill her. She was certain he didn't believe in killing children either.

Much later, when she awoke, she knew.

Today was the day.

Thirty-Four

They called him the darkness.

Fitting but inaccurate. His name was Crom Cruach and he was ageless, as old as time itself—*he* being a relative term. *It* might be more appropriate since he had no actual sex or gender. A male human was simply the form he adopted when he moved among people. Devious and cunning, he once held sway over large populations of Celts in Europe. Alas, he came to a sticky end at the hand of St. Patrick, who banished him at the Geata de Ifreann—literally the Gate of Hell—in Lough Derg, Ireland.

He was given a second life after being invoked by a particularly powerful witch named Anna Flecher in 16th century England. Unfortunately, Anna had aroused the ire of even more powerful people who had buried her alive in a brick tomb. Her final invocation to him, one of the deities of the underworld, gave Anna Flecher the retribution she craved as thirst and hunger took her human life.

Once he answered her summons, he was obligated to carry out her wishes. He was also trapped in the brick tomb hidden within the Tudor mansion of Edward MacCoinnich, secured there by a fearsome binding spell neither he nor Anna had been able to break. Despite that binding spell, Crom Cruach had followed Edward and his family, followed his descendants as the family name evolved to MacKenzie, killing them one by one and bringing misery into their lives.

He traveled across the Atlantic and halfway across this continent to fulfill his obligation and had done so by invoking other, lesser spirits to do the dirty work. It had been difficult, hobbled as he was by imprisonment in the brick tomb, and yet, he had slowly neared completion of the task: killing every descendant of Edward and his second wife.

Then a veritable miracle occurred. Nate MacKenzie discovered and opened the sealed brick tomb, breaking the binding spell and setting him free. In a way, Crom Cruach owed Nate his life but wouldn't hesitate to kill the man when the time came. And while it took time to recover after five hundred years of captivity, it should have been so easy to fulfill his obligation to Anna. Every remaining MacKenzie but one was living in the house with him!

He had been playing an enjoyable game with them when Kenric Shepherd, author of the original binding spell, came after him. How had he known? Crom Cruach didn't know but it should have been a bonus, killing the man who had bound him within the brick tomb. Instead, Shepherd nearly destroyed him. The wily old bastard put up a spirited fight, but in the end, he outsmarted Shepherd with a classic feint: pretending to fall in defeat before bouncing back and striking hard, giving the senile old wizard the surprise of his life.

Shepherd died, but he had anticipated the need to destroy the house and brought the necessary supplies. In an astonishing scene, Shepherd passed his scheme to the MacKenzie woman telepathically. To his utter amazement, she carried it out, destroying the house with brimstone and fire, killing herself in the process.

The confrontation and the explosion had left him grievously wounded. He slithered away, down through a breach in the bedrock, and had lain hidden, trying to mend the injuries they had inflicted upon him.

A year passed, mere seconds in the grand scheme of things, but he had healed little. For him, it took more than time. He needed the right environment.

Then he stumbled upon the cavern—an amazing location—home to a thin place, an interface of spiritual light and a Geata de Ifreann, a passage to the dark side of the spirit world. It was like a healing spa, a luxuriant mix of light and darkness, good and evil, yin and yang.

Just as he began to regain his strength, another wizard arrived, angered by the death of his friend, Shepherd. They clashed in the cavern in a titanic battle of wills and Lachlan Hayward, working with a medium, proved to be a potent and creative opponent who nearly destroyed him. With a final desperate effort, Crom Cruach had plunged deep within the limestone and collapsed the cave and tunnels as he fled, killing some of his tormentors and sending the rest scurrying to the surface like rats before they could finish him off.

He had suffered more dreadful injuries and nearly succumbed to the wounds.

Still, the dim-witted wizards had been unable to destroy him. Another lesson learned. He began to feel invincible. But he needed to recharge, restore. Repair the wounds he had suffered. So he had wandered through the layers of limestone, searching for sustenance and energy, seeking the perfect place.

Then Crom Cruach made a serious error in judgement. He attempted to kill the MacKenzie child, a rash impulse, driven by anger.

He feared her the most. Though young and untrained, she possessed powerful skills and had become his greatest remaining enemy. Killing her would have been a master stroke and left only two, weaker MacKenzies to deal with. Instead, she had seen him coming and escaped death.

It was his second attempt on her life. The first had been in the MacKenzie house, and the two failures weighed on him. They felt like an omen, and in the second effort, he had not only failed but alerted the doddering old fools of the Aeldo as well. Now another one had arrived, and he would face two of them.

They were an annoying distraction. His first priority was to kill the remaining MacKenzies. Then his obligation to Anna Flecher would be fulfilled and he would truly be free. As a reminder of his debt, he still carried the essence of Anna Flecher with him, a small nucleus of pure, depraved hatred that felt like a burr in his side. Crom Cruach hoped that too would disappear when the slate was cleared.

Knowing he had erred and exposed his position, he traveled north to put some distance between himself and the attack on the girl. Continued to follow the fissures, caverns, and natural tunnels within the natural strata.

Then he sensed an area of warmth ahead. The *warmth* had little to do with temperature; rather, it represented a concentrated flux of energy, the kind of energy that would restore him to full lethality so he could finish the mission he had been taxed with five hundred years before.

This energy node had been a fortuitous find with an auspicious name: The Door of Death.

Perfect.

The energy available here was even greater than that available in the cavern. Lying here, bathing himself in that energy, his recovery had been quick, and now, he was a fearsome force to be reckoned with. A few details to handle and he would be free. He had so much to make up for since his banishment at Lough Derg.

The attack would come today. Four of them. The two sorcerers, a medium, and the child, who resonated with the same energy as the old men. Things would be different this time. He had proven himself superior in every way and dominated in his early encounters with them.

He had an additional advantage. The woman. Tat, while modest in ability, gave his power more focus. She was also useful as a soldier, to guard his flanks, and ready to kill anyone who slipped through his defenses. She awaited his summons, armed with the sword of Stikla—a fortuitous grab in his retreat from the cavern last year. Tat was much more effective with the sword in her hands, but she had qualms about killing children. Indeed, Tat was still raw and in need of additional training. She would come around; they always did.

The bumbling wizards were coming for him, and he was ready. Charged and refreshed, he felt immensely powerful. The two fools and their hapless accomplices would soon be dead. While he hadn't been able to divine the nature of their plot, the details seemed unimportant.

Today, he would end the Aeldo and kill two of the remaining three MacKenzies.

It would be a magnificent coup.

He was stronger than them. Smarter. Better in every way.

Invincible.

Thirty-Five

Three in the morning.

Kiera shut off her alarm and shuffled to the kitchen to make a large pot of coffee.

She had slept fitfully, knowing she had to be up early, daunted by what they faced. Ghost didn't even bother to stir beyond a brief look of irritation aimed in her direction.

Her gut buzzed with a steady pulse of anxiety. An adrenaline junkie, she thrived on risk and danger, but this undertaking today was entirely out of her wheelhouse. She had faced this thing once before in the most frightening event of her life and had barely survived.

Kiera had no illusions about today. She might not make it and had made concrete final arrangements in case her worst fears came to pass. Updated her will. Penned a letter to a sister she mostly despised. Arranged for Jack, her neighbor—who loved Ghost dearly—to take him in if needed. She had been suitably vague about the dangers, but Jack knew her penchant for risk. In a different life, she could imagine them together, but Jack was gay, so a relationship wasn't an option.

One by one, the others surfaced and shuffled toward the coffeepot, except Lachlan who brewed tea, and Leah who asked for orange juice. She and Willow cooked up a hearty meal of scrambled eggs, toast, bacon, and sausages, probably the last warm meal they would have today, maybe even tomorrow. Kiera fired up her laptop for a weather update while the others discussed the fine details and potential problems with their plan.

With one look, Kiera started in alarm. "We've got another problem."

"The rain?" Fynn asked.

"Worse." She turned her laptop around to show the others. "This low over southeast Colorado is heading our way and deepening rapidly, what we weather geeks call a *bomb-cyclone*. It didn't look this bad yesterday, but the weather models changed overnight. With a forecast central pressure of 962 millibars, we could be dealing with storm-force or hurricane-force winds. The trip back from Plum Island is going to be very dangerous, near impossible. This system could be more intense than the storm that sank the *Edmund Fitzgerald*."

"When?"

"By midnight tonight. Gale and storm warnings likely by five or six o'clock. Can you handle a rough return from the island, Willow?"

"I think so. I've been caught in thunderstorms a few times. It was pretty hairy, but I made it. It's only a mile to Plum Island."

They left in the dark, just after four, in a convoy of three vehicles: Willow in her Tahoe, pulling the boat, Kiera, Fynn, and Lachlan in the RAV4, and Dana and Leah in her Jeep Wrangler. Everything had been packed the night before: high-quality rain gear, goggles, changes of clothing, snack nuts and power bars, waterproof boots, flashlights, walkie-talkies, Lachlan and Fynn's satchels, and a box of gear from the basement of Kenric's house.

The trip would take nearly three hours. Kiera led, using her radar detector to push their speed over eighty when possible. They set up a conference call via FaceTime to talk, prepare, and begin developing the mindset they would need to execute the plan. As they drove, the sky grew lighter in the east, a dull grey sky filled with low scuddy clouds pushed to the northwest by strong winds aloft.

Just after seven o'clock, they reached Gill's Rock and went their separate ways. Fynn drove to Table Bluff in the RAV. Dana and Leah drove the roundabout route to Isle View Park to the southeast as there was no direct road between the park and the lighthouse.

Lachlan, Kiera, and Willow headed to the east shore. They ignored the nearest boat landing at Gills Rock to shorten the trip on the water to Plum Island. Willow chose to improvise the launch and backed out onto the beach at Northport. The Washington Island ferry had shut down and the landing was deserted. She slipped into waders and walked the boat out twenty feet from the shore, climbed the stern ladder, and started the engine, waving as she took off for Plum Island.

★ ★ ★

Lachlan was the critical hub of this siege.

He would direct the incoming energies from the others in a tight ring, a sídrand around the lighthouse, and starve the darkness of fuel.

Kiera, driving the Tahoe, parked out of sight on the road near the front gate of the lighthouse, and they waited for the others to get into position. Lachlan sensed a defensive perimeter in place around the lighthouse, set by the darkness and the mysterious woman in black. He had expected as much. They needed to be alert to any deviations or unexpected strategies from the darkness. They couldn't fail this time. Fynn was the best suited to the task with his preternatural attention to detail, and Lachlan trusted him to alert them to any changes in or around the lighthouse.

Fynn came on line first—on line being a relative term. They would communicate telepathically as they bent the energies into a barrier around the lighthouse. Their minds would work like tools in the hands of a blacksmith, molding and shaping the energies into an ironclad ring.

Leah was next. The wave she sent was strong and clear and devoid of any fear or anxiety. She was five years old! The depth of her gift still astounded Lachlan. When this was over, he planned to seek Dana's permission to guide her development, just as his mentor, Godric, had guided him so many years ago.

Fifteen minutes later, Willow joined them. They were ready.

Lachlan closed his eyes and brought his mind to bear on the task, focusing the efforts of Fynn, Willow, and Leah into a powerful energy field. He pictured it in his mind, the confluence of all those lines of energy forming a sphere around the lighthouse, an impregnable shield, the sídrand.

He held a gold amulet bearing the face of Wōden in his left hand, an ancient piece given to him by a Romany sorcerer, with a *cargástriftr*—literally *ghost-scythe*—an athamé or ceremonial blade, in his right. He shimmied in the leather seat until he felt perfectly comfortable. He would need to sit like this for hours.

Over the next thirty minutes, the energy flowing from the vortex to the lighthouse slowed to a trickle and then ceased altogether.

Excellent.

Phase one was complete. The darkness was isolated.

Now, they would need to concentrate to hold this siege for as long as it took. This had gone so well, Lachlan hoped they would be ready for the second phase by nightfall.

He sensed the defensive perimeter beginning to degrade and leak energy in places. Concentrating on those defects, he picked at them like holes in a dike, turning them into torrents, until they were bleeding and choking the darkness at the same time. This was where he had erred last year in the cavern. He hadn't weakened the darkness sufficiently first. Hadn't severed all the energy sources, allowing the darkness to tap into the Geata de Ifreann to effect an escape as the cavern collapsed. He couldn't have known. He had been winging it.

No winging it this time. They had a coherent strategy, the resources to execute it, and he had enormous talent and energy arrayed on his side. The only wild card was the woman in black. If she was somewhere inside, she was undetectable, likely shielded by the darkness—which was making no attempt to conceal itself. Indeed, it was fully evident and bristling with malignant energy, fighting the sídrand with a massive push-back of energy. But they were stronger, holding it in check. Fighting them, the darkness was slowly depleting its energy reserves.

Lachlan still had no sense of the central nature of the darkness. Who or what was it? He liked Fynn's idea that Anna Flecher had summoned someone to carry out her invocation. It made sense. She knew she would die, but also knew whoever she summoned would carry out her wishes—for centuries if necessary.

Was it simply a malignant force? He didn't think so. It responded intelligently and creatively to their attacks. It was a being of some sort. He just wished they knew more about it.

Time passed. The steady tick of a clock. Subtle changes in the light occurred as the sun, hidden by the clouds, tracked low across the sky. As Kiera promised, the rain grew heavier, the winds ramped up, and the swaying trees bent farther, the sky accented by occasional bursts of lightning.

Their combined efforts held firm while Lachlan drained more and more energy from the lighthouse and the darkness. Soon, he and Kiera would go in and somehow, they would hold the darkness at bay until the others arrived to breach the lighthouse and destroy this beast once and for all. That would be the most fallible phase of the plan. Their guard would invariably slip, and the darkness would have a small window to recharge and regroup.

Sitting in the driver's seat, Kiera had disassembled and reassembled her Sig Sauer and another, smaller handgun. She monitored the weather on a series of maps and charts but had otherwise remained silent, respecting the process and his request for no distractions. Fynn, Leah, and Willow were a finely tuned unit, working flawlessly, though Willow—cold and wet and exposed to the worst of the weather—was suffering on Plum Island.

He could only offer encouragement but marveled at her tenacity.

Time ticked away relentlessly. Hours of it. The storm grew ever more intense, whipping the trees into a frenzy. The rain became a driving downpour and thunder rumbled in volleys overhead. The scene was disturbing and violent; reminiscent of hurricanes he'd experienced in the past.

Glancing at Kiera's computer screen, he noticed the low pressure center was rotating in the same direction as the vortex: counterclockwise. It was an "aha" moment. The two motions naturally enhanced each other and suddenly, he understood the dangerous currents here and the long history of shipwrecks. This synergy had occurred many times in the past.

He sat, reclined, and tried to relax, doing all the work in his head and his heart. It was an antiquated notion, the idea that the heart was anything but the pump that kept all creatures alive. He understood the science but had a romantic notion of the heart as the seat of so much more, of courage and valor, of love and friendship, the list was long. The idea warmed him.

Though he never actually saw the sun, it sank just after four-thirty and the landscape descended into stormy darkness, a night as black as he could recall.

By seven o'clock, Lachlan believed they had bled the darkness sufficiently, and he called to Willow, summoning her back to shore. Even if they hadn't reached this level of control, the winds were intense and he worried about her making the trip back from Plum Island. He would do his best to protect her, though he needed most of his energy focused here. It was a conflicted effort, given his personal feelings for her. As insurance, he would keep Fynn and Leah in position until Willow was ashore.

He sat and waited for word from Willow.

Until now, he had felt calm and in control. Everything seemed to be following the script they had written, but now, his calm was replaced by the low-level buzz of anxiety. Over Willow making it back to shore. Coming face to face with the darkness. Putting the others at risk, especially Leah.

The battle in the cavern last year had been monumental. This felt bigger, the stakes even higher, the risks enormous.

Lachlan heard a cry for help from the northeast.

Damn!

Willow was in trouble!

Thirty-Six

Willow braced herself as the boat crested another wave.

The trip to Plum Island was rough but no worse than any other stormy weather she had navigated in the past. Mike, her ex-husband, had gotten her into boating but walked off with the boat in the divorce. She had wanted a boat, but the desire never rose to a priority where she actually shopped for one. Most of her subsequent boyfriends owned boats so there was little pressure to buy one.

This boat, a twenty-one-foot Alumacraft fish-and-ski, belonged to Nick, who was still a friend after a recent and amicable breakup. He gladly lent her the boat for research; she told him she was investigating a possible paranormal event on Plum Island. He didn't question it further. He knew her interests.

With the canvas cover snapped in place, it was dry and tolerably cold on board, but bumpy as hell running into the wind and across the waves. Good thing she was an old salt and immune to seasickness.

The wind, while blustery, was not yet gale-force. Rain fell in intermittent patches, and it was cold. Forty degrees. She was glad she had worn Cuddle Duds beneath her clothing and felt perfectly comfortable.

Willow pulled the boat in on the south shore of the island at a rock-and-sand beach. The small cove would protect the boat from the waves and the worst of the winds blowing off the island. She secured the aft with an anchor and tied the bow line to the nearest tree.

Grabbing her backpack, she walked past the front range light, a short metal tower with a red beacon. She continued north for a quarter of a mile along a path to the rear range light, a much taller white gantry with a round center support. It looked more like a water tower and was also fitted with a stationary red lamp.

The island was some sort of wildlife sanctuary and otherwise uninhabited. An abandoned keeper's house stood a bit inland from the light, but they had boarded it up and she couldn't get inside. Willow settled in the southwest side of the house on a foam gardening kneeler, out of the wind and most of the rain. Reasonably comfortable now, she wondered how she would feel in a few hours. She had no cell service but felt confident Lachlan could communicate with her well enough telepathically that it wouldn't be an issue. If all else failed, she had the walkie-talkie.

Once in place and organized, she joined the others and completed the ring, establishing the blockade and cutting the darkness off from the vortex. She couldn't really describe the sensation, but it was a physical feeling, like a firm set of handshakes in her head.

How long would they have to do this? Hours for sure, but for how many? She dreaded the idea of spending the night out in the elements on this island, regardless of how well she had dressed. No matter. She knew she would stay as long as they needed her, would do whatever Lachlan asked of her. And when this was over, she would tell him how she felt. The thought made her nervous. What if he thought she was crazy? Or too young? Wouldn't that be ironic?

Time dragged by, slowly. So slowly, it almost droned in her head as a steady *tick, tock, tick, tock*. The rain and cold worked at the edges of her clothing. Eventually, even her Cuddle Duds felt damp. They weren't, but they no longer kept her warm either.

While she was tempted to play with her phone, she knew the plan required total concentration. But alone, focused on the single task, boredom and fatigue set in. She had brought snacks just in case, but by mid-afternoon they were gone. Concentration grew ever more difficult and elusive. She received encouragement from the others, especially Lachlan, from their warm, dry places.

Willow grew resentful. Why had she taken this spot? Why wasn't Kiera out here suffering with her?

The wind picked up significantly throughout the afternoon. Waves started breaking over the shoreline and foamy sprays, pushed by the wind, lashed the island. The sun set in a dull fade to black.

Then it was just her, the violent din of the storm, and the red glow of the range light. Could this place grow any more inhospitable?

She fretted about getting off the island. Talk had been cheap in the comfort of a warm house, but she wouldn't survive the night here. Hypothermia would kill her.

Finally, the message came.

Come as fast as conditions permit. The others are ready.

Oh, thank God!

She didn't have to be told twice. She was more than ready to leave this god-forsaken rock.

The wind blew fiercely as she walked to the boat, pushing and shoving at her back like a persistent, ornery beast. Despite the layers of clothing and the rain poncho, she was cold and wet, felt saturated to her core. What the hell was she doing here? She could be home by a fire in comfy clothes, but *no*, she had to come out here and be a hero. According to Lachlan and Fynn, they were saving the world. At the very least, she hoped they were saving a five-year-old girl.

But she was here, willingly, in part because of her deep affection for Lachlan forged months before in the cavern. She couldn't say no and wouldn't. Grumbling about it made her feel better, though.

The boat held fast in the cove. Just beyond, the water looked like a boiling cauldron, the tops of the waves whipped into a frenzy by the wind, imperfectly lit by her flashlight. The nightmarish scene was beyond anything she had ever experienced.

Lachlan must have sensed the danger and anxiety. He spoke to her, *I'll help guide the way.*

But she wasn't worried about finding her way—the boat was equipped with an expensive Garman GPS unit. No, she was worried about surviving the horrendous waves and the wind crossing one of the most dangerous passages on the Great Lakes.

The wind was fierce, even in the cove. She untied the rope and walked through the water in waders that were soaked and near useless. Pushing the boat out a bit, she climbed up the stern ladder and into the boat. She unsnapped the cover in the back corner, pulled the anchor, and quickly snapped the cover shut again. She didn't have to worry about grounding before she started the engine. The wind pushed her to the southeast, out into the raging waters of the Porte des Morts passage.

She smiled a tight-lipped smile as the motor roared to life.

Willow spun the wheel and steered southwest toward Northport and the ferry landing. As she left the shore behind, the waves grew taller, whipped into spray and foam by the storm-force winds. The first big wave almost took her out. The boat rose fast and canted thirty degrees sideways as she rode the wave and then tipped the other way as the boat fell over the crest, the motor roaring as the prop momentarily broke clear of the water.

It was a wild roller coaster ride. She quickly learned to anticipate as each wave heaved her skyward and crashed over the bow in a blinding explosion of water. She fought to stay on a firm heading, the wind and waves constantly pushing the bow around to the south.

Thank God for the GPS! She wouldn't have even attempted this crossing without it.

Virtually nothing was visible through the windows, and the wipers were useless. Several times, the boat flopped over the crest of a wave and corrected so sharply, she thought they were going over. She tried to lean her weight into the waves, but the gesture seemed futile in the heavy surf.

Slowly, she closed the distance to Northport but had trouble steering toward the invisible gap in the breakwater. Marker lights normally framed the gap, but she couldn't see them. The wild surf was blocking her view.

Then lightning flashed overhead. Willow saw the gap—briefly.

The boat canted as the next giant wave crashed over her.

This time, the boat rolled and capsized.

Thirty-Seven

Zoe arrived first.

They met at Joey's for lunch to discuss a plan. The location was convenient and neutral—important because Greg's wife had started to complain about the late nights and the time he spent at the lighthouse, but mostly, she suspected, the time he spent with her.

Zoie had wanted to visit the lighthouse yesterday, but Greg had worked late—mandatory overtime on a job the company was rushing to finish. She almost went there herself but realized she didn't have the nerve. With Tess's death and Jordan still missing, this felt more real, more dangerous than any ghost hunt in the past. Greg might be a pain in the ass, but she welcomed his company.

"Can you think of a better time to go with this storm?" Greg said with a conspiratorial smile. "One, incredible atmosphere. Two, no one will be watching. Little chance we'll be disturbed."

"They're talking about one of those bomb-cyclone thingies," Zoie said with a note of concern.

"So what? That lighthouse has stood for a hundred and fifty years. It's built like a fortress. We're probably safer there than anywhere else."

It was true, she decided, sipping her White Claw. "I'm in. Tonight? After work?"

"Yep. Six sharp."

"What about your wife?"

"We're not talking so I'd say she's against the idea," he said, giving Zoie a side-glance and an eye roll. "I'm not missing this. She'll get over it."

Zoie nodded. She might appreciate his company on the hunt, but she was liking him less and less as a person. Then, remembering the news clip that had freaked her out this morning, she grabbed her phone, scrolled to the article, and set it down. "Did you see this?"

Boaters Missing in Porte des Morts Passage

"Two boats have gone missing without a trace in the last twenty-four hours!" Zoie said in a rush. "It's like the Bermuda Triangle."

"Holy shit!" Greg looked genuinely shocked. "That seems more than coincidental."

"Right? Downright spooky."

"Losing your nerve?"

It was a toss-up. She was scared and thrilled in equal measure, but fear would not stop her. "Hell no!"

He emptied his beer in one swallow. "See you later."

★ ★ ★

Greg pulled in the driveway just after six and honked.

Zoie had assembled the gear into two backpacks: cameras, lights, the REM-Pod, EVP recorder, and spirit box, plus her rain gear. She ran out, tossed her stuff in the back seat, and hopped into the truck. The storm was fierce, the rain driven down the road by a strong northeast wind, the wires and near-empty branches whistling and moaning an eerie dirge.

Zoie loved it. They were going to a haunted lighthouse in this weather—literally a dark and stormy night. She smiled at the thought.

"Ready?" Greg said.

"Hell yes. The weather's perfect."

"I told you. This is going to be so freaking cool."

Small branches littered the road when Greg pulled out. The trees thrashed back and forth and made her nervous. Out on the highway, Greg had to steer around two larger branches. How much worse would this get?

They rode in silence, Zoie imagining the weird and wonderful things they might encounter tonight. She had developed an impromptu theory that the storm would energize the spirits or whatever inhabited the lighthouse. She tried not to think about Jordan and Tess lest her mind made disturbing connections as it was prone to do. She was already turning the missing boats into something paranormal—or extraterrestrial—even though the bad weather was the most likely cause. After all, they disappeared in the Port des Morts passage. It had always been dangerous. What were those people thinking?

She wondered what Greg's wife thought about him running off into the night with a strange woman, looking for ghosts. If they weren't talking, it couldn't be good.

They had never met, and Zoie had no idea what she was like. Greg said he loved her but seemed mostly indifferent to her feelings.

She'll get over it. Hmm. Zoie had never met the woman but already sympathized with her.

It took almost thirty minutes to reach the turnoff. Zoie saw a Tahoe pull out of the road leading to the lighthouse but gave it little thought, focused only on the hunt. Besides, they were leaving. Greg turned and slid into the indent that kept the truck hidden from the road.

The wind at the top of the bluff was wild, sweeping right off the lake, tossing the trees violently back and forth.

"Dude. Is the truck safe here?"

"Probably. It's ten years old and at worst, a branch may fall on it. I have insurance—"

"What if we need to bail in a hurry?"

He shrugged. "Relax, Zo. We'll be fine."

Only slightly reassured, she shoved a backpack at Greg and slipped the other over her shoulders and set off into the woods.

The storm was a full-on assault of wind and water. Zoie was glad she'd worn her heavy parka with the hood. Even so, her face was soon dripping wet. Greg plowed ahead, his flashlight leading the way, striding quickly toward the trapdoor and shelter. He tossed the branches aside and pulled the door open. Then jumped down, reached for Zoie's backpack, and put a hand out for Zoie. As soon as her feet hit the floor, he pulled the door shut, cutting off the rain.

"That was fun," she said sardonically.

With a nod, he motioned with his flashlight. "After you."

"That's okay, you've got the light. Go."

Zoie felt alive, excited, and appropriately afraid. The weather, the late hour, the dark lighthouse left her tingling with anticipation. Tonight would be the ultimate experience in the paranormal. She hoped to see ghosts and spirits and who knew what else.

She couldn't even imagine.

Thirty-Eight

"Back to the ferry landing! Willow's in trouble!"

Lachlan spoke too loudly. Panic crept into his best efforts at calm. Willow was in mortal danger.

Kiera threw the truck into reverse and spit gravel everywhere as she backed up, cranked the wheel hard, and gunned it, turning a sharp left onto the highway.

Lachlan saw headlights to the right but gave them no further thought. He felt his worst nightmares coming to pass.

The most important part of the plan—to encircle the lighthouse and deprive the darkness of energy—had been successful. The darkness had been trapped for hours and had further weakened itself fighting to regain access to the vortex. Lachlan and Fynn felt that as long as they moved in measured steps, they wouldn't be temporarily powerless, nor would they allow the darkness much opportunity to recharge. So he pulled Willow in first because of the deteriorating weather.

Now, she was in trouble and unable to support the sídrand. Having to leave his place at the critical hub position, the sphere was further weakened, perhaps broken. He only hoped Fynn could coach Leah sufficiently to carry the slack now that he needed to concentrate on bringing Willow in safely.

Even the best laid plans...

Fynn remained rock-solid and Leah was sending a strong signal from a mile south of his position, indicating she was safe.

How long could they hold the fort?

They were asking a great deal of Leah. He admired her inner strength, but she was a child and he felt guilty for imposing so much upon her. He sent another message of encouragement—as they had all been doing since their arrival. He couldn't even imagine the stress Dana was operating under. Watching her child take on something so dangerous and unable to offer more than moral support? He feared she might hate them when this was over. And if anything happened to Leah, no one would hate him more than he himself.

There was also the question of the woman in black. She was still nowhere in evidence. They had to assume she was lurking inside or somewhere nearby, protected by the darkness. She would be unaffected by the sídrand, though Lachlan wondered how much power she possessed on her own.

Nevertheless, she was a wild card and he imagined that was the intent. Using her as a medium to focus its powers and as a spoiler. A guerrilla to attack their flanks and keep them off balance. Exactly what he would do. As an adherent of *The Art of War* by Sun Tzu, he saw this encounter as a military engagement and sensed equal intent and purpose in their opponent. Despite the strategy they had laid out, they would now need to go forward on the fly, precisely what he had hoped to avoid.

The truck bumped when they hit a branch in the road.

"Sorry," Kiera mumbled.

While worrying whether they could hold this all together, he was already thinking about breaching the lighthouse defenses, getting inside and coming face to face with the darkness. With the sídrand in jeopardy, he felt the need to develop a feint. A distraction to keep the darkness off balance once Willow was safe and Fynn and Leah moved closer to the lighthouse.

There were only two ways in: bursting through the front door or through the underground passage in the woods.

The passage seemed like an obvious choice, but it also represented a bottleneck and might be set as a trap. Were the tables reversed, he would anticipate an attack through the tunnel. Forcing their way through the door would be bold, unexpected. There was a brute but elegant appeal to bashing in the front gate in a big, noisy display of power. Ramming the gate with Willow's Tahoe, lights blazing, horn blaring.

He remembered Kenric's ruse against Lord Alington. Creating imaginary fighters out of thin air to confuse their opponent. The tactic ultimately led to the defeat of Alington in a battle in which they were vastly outnumbered. If he could get things in order, the tactic felt right. And if Kiera was willing, he wanted her to slip into the passage during the ruse as an additional diversion; she could also perform recon in preparation for the final confrontation.

The truck bounced as Kiera left the road and drove out onto the beach. The waters of the lake looked black, violent, and forbidding.

Deadly.

There was so much to do, to think about. It felt overwhelming.

First, he had to pull Willow out of the water.

She had only minutes before hypothermia killed her.

Thirty-Nine

Willow was blind.

The lights and the engine failed when the boat flipped. It took a moment to realize the boat had capsized, that she was lying on the canvas cover and that the floor lay somewhere overhead. Water sprayed in along the edges of the canvas and was colder than anything she could imagine, so cold it felt like jaws of ice biting into her flesh.

In that instant, she knew she was dead. The end. The boat would fill with water, sink, and take her down with it to a freezing, watery grave. Even if some air remained, trapped in the hull, hypothermia would kill her in ten or fifteen minutes, maybe less.

She felt little sense of panic, perhaps still in shock from being flipped over, or already numb from the cold. Her life did flash by in random bits, but most were the moments spent with her daughter. She would never see her again. And with the realization, an immense sadness washed over her.

Still, some part of her struggled in denial against the imminent death sentence. She squirmed, trying to orient herself, but the darkness and wild wave motions made any concerted effort futile.

Rising with a swell, the boat suddenly flipped again. The cover tore and the momentum propelled her out of the boat and into the water. Already cold and wet, the frigid water was scarcely a shock. For a moment she was totally confused, lost and uncertain whether she was oriented up or down, but then realized her head was above water. When she focused, Willow saw a light on the shore, maybe three hundred feet away.

A wave crashed over her but she kept her eyes on that light and glimpsed the Northport breakwater to her left.

She could make it!

The marker lights at the entrance to the breakwater were dark and had evidently failed. No wonder she had difficulty seeing it before. She swam hard, fighting the waves and the wind. It was brutal. The cold, the wind, the spray. Even with her head above water, it felt like she was drowning as she gasped raggedly for air.

She made slow, steady progress. The light followed her as something else, an outside force, pushed her, mentally and physically, toward shore.

Lachlan!

Two minutes more and she reached the stone breakwater. Exhausted, her arms frozen and rubbery, she reached for a rock but couldn't pull herself up. Then she tapped a last reserve of energy and climbed atop the wall of stacked boulders.

Fierce wind gusts nudged her over to the more protected side of the breakwater where she collapsed, gasping for breath.

Intense cold soon overrode the fatigue, and Willow sidled along the seemingly endless rock wall seeking safety and warmth. The breakwater ended sixty feet from the shore and the wind and knee-deep water were just as fierce there as she struggled the final steps to the beach.

Lachlan met her at the water's edge and gave her soaking wet body a huge hug, his clothing protected by his parka. "Thank God you made it. I feared the trip would be too much."

Willow couldn't speak. She choked a sob and buried her head into his shoulder. He held her for a moment and then wrapped a protective arm around her as they walked to the Tahoe idling twenty feet away.

"Get in!" he yelled. "We have to get you warm before hypothermia sets in."

She felt quite warm now, almost hot, and then remembered that was a cardinal sign of hypothermia. He directed her toward the rear door of the truck and Willow struggled to push the door open against the wind. The heat was blasting and almost felt like fire on her skin at first.

Kiera clambered from the front into the back seat, grabbed Willow, and hugged her. "Thank God you're safe! When Lachlan said you were in trouble, I feared the worst."

Willow, still shaking from fear, cold, and fatigue, said, "I thought I was a goner. Lachlan saved my ass."

Sliding into the front passenger seat, Lachlan said, "Get those wet things off now. I shan't look."

Kiera moved back to the front seat as Willow peeled off wet layer after layer. "Go ahead, look. Be my guest. I'm so happy you guided me in, you're welcome to a freebie."

Kiera looked genuinely shocked. "Willow!"

"Not in my nature," he said primly, looking resolutely forward.

"In fact, if we make it out of this alive, I plan on shagging your brains out—if you want to."

Kiera pointed a forefinger with a smug expression. "I knew it!"

"You don't see our age difference as an issue?" Lachlan asked.

"Twelve hundred years? No big deal. Do you?"

He didn't answer but she thought she saw him smiling in the dim lights of the dashboard.

Willow dug into her backpack and pulled out her dry clothes and dressed quickly. She felt strangely energized.

Kiera turned to Lachlan. "What now?"

"Fynn and Leah have managed to hold the darkness back from the vortex this far. Barely. With us offline, so to speak, they're struggling, and things will grow more dangerous from here, especially once they try to move in."

The brief moment of wistful sanity was over. She could feel the darkness trying to break out of their perimeter and making progress. They needed to get back to the lighthouse.

Perhaps reading her mind, Lachlan said, "I rather fear that was the easy part. If you're ready, we need to get back into the fray, now!"

The look of anxiety on his face was unnerving.

He was an ancient wizard.

If he was worried, things were about to get ugly.

Forty

Zoie clipped a GoPro to her front pocket.

Following Greg by about five feet, the passage seemed unusually dark, even with the lantern. Maybe the battery was fading. No matter. She had a lantern, a decent flashlight, and two electric candles. Good luck blowing those out, Mr. Ghost.

But as she thought it, the fine hairs at the back of her neck shimmered as an icy wave rushed down her spine. This was the real deal. Two nights they had been here and two nights they had experienced events that were clear evidence of haunting. The weather was wild, providing the perfect atmosphere. Even down here, she could hear the wind in the trees. It sounded like a hurricane—or a monster loose in the world.

Again she mused, *'Twas a dark and stormy night...*

Greg grabbed the handle and pulled the door open with two grunted yanks.

"Sticky. Must be the humidity."

As the door banged against the passage wall, his lantern quit and they were temporarily plunged into darkness. Zoie fumbled in her backpack, pulled out her lantern, and flicked it on. "Whew! That's better."

"Yep, thanks."

They emerged into the basement and again, the light seemed dimmer, the shadows longer, the air humming with the faint crackle of static electricity. An effect of the storm, she decided, but it was freaky and surreal, regardless. It felt like stepping on to a movie set with creatures lurking in the shadows, every nook and cranny a lair for dangerous, evil things.

Greg evidently sensed it too. "Dude, the air feels electric."

"I was just thinking the same thing."

"Still in?"

"Hell yeah! What are we waiting for?" Tonight, though, she happily followed Greg instead of charging ahead. Simple self-preservation. Just in case a monster decided to show up and smite somebody. It was always the person leading the group.

Except when it was the straggler, Zoie mused ruefully. She glanced over her shoulder into the darkness.

Nothing.

Stepping onto the main floor of the keeper's house, the storm sounded farther away. The building creaked and groaned an odd assortment of sounds as the wind assailed the stone structure and tree branches scraped against the walls. The few windows were pitch black, not the slightest evidence of light outdoors, except for occasional vague, grey flashes of lightning.

It was like an old black and white movie. Eerie. Beyond spooky.

Her heart pounded in her chest, her hands clenched, her breaths shallow.

When Greg opened the door to the tower, the sounds of the storm assailed them in full force. The structure itself occasionally groaned, as if the heavy limestone blocks themselves were shifting. Probably just her imagination, but she was sensitive to every sound and the slightest variation in light or atmosphere. Her palms were damp with sweat. If someone had said *boo!* at that moment, she would have jumped a mile.

The iron spiral staircase hummed faintly, a resonant sound in sync with the wind gusts. Occasional bursts of lightning lit the staircase in stark black and white.

"Cool," Zoie said.

"Turn the light off," Greg said.

Zoie complied and the tower went dark. Wind lashed the building, and rain slapped the windows above in the lantern room. Lightning flashed, brilliant grey light, filling the tower with strobe-like flashes.

Just for an instant, Zoie thought she saw something up there.

A woman.

An image so dark and ethereal, she doubted it was real. A strange shadow like a charcoal drawing on the wall. She tried to shake off the fingers of fear gripping her insides. She tried to speak but nothing came out, her mouth bone dry. She slowed her step as everything suddenly set off her anxiety. This was far scarier than any Halloween haunted house. Would the GoPro capture this atmosphere? She feared not. Reaching for the EVP recorder, she clicked it on. When they got up the stairs, the spirit box was coming out. Zoie knew she was wound up and could no longer discern real from her overactive imagination.

Greg seemed unfazed and charged ahead as he was apt to do, clomping up the iron stairs.

Zoie felt that it was a bad idea, but maybe she was just freaking out, and who wouldn't be in this place? Jesus! This was the scariest movie ever, only it wasn't a movie, and that nebulous impression of someone up above—

Another blast of lightning struck. Zoie looked up at the lantern room, and this time, she saw a woman, armed with a sword.

Ridiculous! It couldn't be real, except that the vague image was now burned on her retina.

What the fuck—?

The tower went dark for a moment.

Zoie blurted, "Greg!"

When lightning flashed again, Greg had half turned toward her as the woman, brandishing the sword, jumped and landed on the stairs half a dozen steps above him. She looked like a creation of CGI: impossibly agile, completely black but for her pale face and hands.

Zoie's mind froze for a second, startled into paralysis, while adrenaline left her jittery and nauseated—until she forced herself to move.

Everything then seemed to click forward in slow motion, her mouth opening to shout a warning as her arm brought her lantern up, the woman jabbing with an exaggerated flourish and the blade of the sword piercing Greg's side, mid-flank. A microsecond later, he vaporized in a cloud of fine dust. His expression never changed. His face didn't even register the blade piercing his torso before he disappeared.

She blinked, but he was still gone.

Zoie wanted to scream and maybe a squeak escaped, but she locked eyes with the woman and saw nothing but pure cold malice.

Dropping the backpack, Zoie turned and ran, flicking her light ahead to guide the way. She ran like a gazelle, her footsteps fleet and sure, down the stairs, headlong into the basement, pivoting right and slamming her palm into the passageway door, shoving it open, never once looking back.

Forty-One

"What now?" Kiera asked.

She pulled the Tahoe to the side of the road leading to the front gate at Lachlan's direction. The lighthouse was just out of sight. The truck was warm but smelled of Willow's wet, fishy clothing.

For a moment, Lachlan said nothing, his eyes closed in concentration, face dimly lit by the dash lights. He then said, "Fynn and Leah are struggling to hold the sídrand in place. Willow, when you're ready, please help them hold the fort?"

She put a hand on his shoulder. "No problem."

"I'm assigning some consciousness to assist them as well."

Kiera looked at him in awe. "You can do that?"

"Oh, yes. It's a skill, not easily—" He frowned, as if losing a train of thought, before continuing. "We need to retrench and regroup before we can go in. I plan to create a feint, a diversion so the others can move up and we can commence with the second phase of the operation."

"And me?"

He put a hand on Kiera's arm and trained a serious eye on her. "Would you be willing to go into the underground passage to investigate? Check for traps? See if you can get into the basement of the lighthouse. Our distraction should assist you as well."

"I can do that."

"We can then decide on the best path into the lighthouse, the passage or the front door," Lachlan said. He locked eyes with her again. "It will be dangerous. Be wary. Especially of the woman in black. I don't know where she is."

Kiera nodded, trying to remember how and when she volunteered for hazardous duty in what amounted to a war zone. Really, she hadn't. She had been press-ganged into service by Willow. She was an adrenaline junkie, but this was ridiculous. Still, while she was taut and anxious, she wasn't terrified. Maybe she should be.

"What's your plan?" Willow asked.

Lachlan said. "I'm developing an idea. I'll create the diversion while you maintain the siege and allow Fynn and Leah to move in. We're going to mount a full-frontal assault on the lighthouse. Lights on, horn blaring—we might scratch your truck, my dear."

Willow shook her head dismissively. "No big deal. I already owe my friend a new boat."

Kiera caught her nonchalant expression and broke out laughing. She might have been talking about a broken wine glass. A moment later, Lachlan laughed and Willow joined in. Willow's expression had been priceless. Kiera would never forget it.

It seemed absurd to be laughing just now. Or maybe they were blowing off steam in the face of an absurd existential threat. Whatever. It felt good.

When Lachlan regained his composure, he said, "My dear friend Kenric once created a fake army and used it to defeat an evil man named Alington. I intend to do the same."

"How?" Willow asked.

"Using whatever I have at hand. You'll see." Lachlan grabbed his satchel and looked at Willow. "I need you to continue working with Fynn and Leah. You know what to do."

Willow nodded.

He reached into his satchel and handed Kiera a Celtic cross. He maintained a gentle grip on her hand. "You know what to do with this and you have your guns. You are a fearsome woman, Kiera O'Donnell. Go slowly and be vigilant. As soon as I can, I'll send Fynn to assist."

Kiera nodded. She slid the Kimber Micro 9 into the small of her back, the cross and the Sig into her right pocket.

"While you're making your approach, I'm going to conjure up an army. I'll have Fynn watch over you as well."

Kiera pulled the hood over her head and took a deep breath, steeling herself. "Ready?"

Lachlan nodded and Kiera noticed bushes moving in from the woods, lining up behind them as she jumped out of the Tahoe into the roaring wind and rain. Kiera ran with her powerful Maglite leading the way. She almost wished she could stay and watch, but knew her mission was equally important. She liked the way Lachlan appealed to her vanity by putting her *in charge*. Uh-huh. Fynn would *assist*.

These crazy dudes were out of her league. These magicians, or sorcerers—whatever—stood in incredible contradiction to her scientific background and training. The beliefs these men held were considered pseudoscience, the world they inhabited a superstitious myth to most people in the modern era. Yet it existed, an invisible niche in the natural world, invisible to scientific instruments or perhaps hiding in plain sight. As a result, the world had never looked the same to Kiera after her experience in the cavern last year.

By the time Kiera reached the trapdoor, her anxiety had run amok, imagining all manner of threats in the passage. She knelt down and listened, but it was a useless gesture with the storm.

Kiera pulled the metal door open with a shaky hand and flashed her light around. When she was satisfied it was safe, she dropped down and closed the hatch behind her, shutting out the noise above but leaving her feeling confined and claustrophobic. The flashlight revealed a shadowy, damp tunnel carved out of the native limestone, leading to the lighthouse. There were no traps or hazards visible in the tunnel.

So far, so good.

Then Kiera thought she heard heavy footsteps running somewhere in the lighthouse but could have been mistaken given the racket outdoors. She shook her head, trying to reassure herself that it was nothing.

Inching forward, she bent her back to clear the low ceiling. The weight of the Sig Sauer in her pocket felt reassuring, as did the Celtic cross gripped in her right hand.

Kiera spotted a door ahead, an old plank door.

As she reached for the handle—an iron ring—the door flew open, narrowly missing her as it slammed into the wall.

Someone or something crashed through the opening, sending Kiera's light flying. In a backwash of light, it looked like a small woman as she plowed into her, screaming and yelling, "Get out of my way! Get the fuck out of my way!"

Kiera held the cross up in a death grip, ready to strike before she realized, with a flash of insight and recognition, that the woman wasn't a threat. Instead, some danger lay just beyond the door. She lowered her arm and quickly grabbed the arm of the stranger trying to force her way through and slammed the door with her foot.

"Stop!" Kiera bellowed and the woman stopped dead in her tracks, her eyes open impossibly wide. Kiera added, "I'm not going to hurt you."

The woman stared at her. Short, cute, with a dark pixie cut, she seemed to believe the words and relaxed a little. Then she said, "Maybe you won't but there's a woman behind me with a sword and she just killed my friend. We have to get out of here!"

"A sword?" A bad feeling ran through Kiera. A sword? Like the one Rachel had last year in the cavern? The sword that turned people into dust?

She wasn't waiting to find out and decided the woman was right. They had to get out now.

"Go!" Kiera yelled.

The woman ran ahead, and Kiera followed close behind. Bursting through the trapdoor, the woman sprinted toward the fire road.

The woman was sure-footed, but Kiera snagged a fallen branch and fell face first into the dead leaves on the forest floor. When she caught up, the woman was staring at an empty pickup truck with four flat tires. Kiera was certain the battery was dead as well. She gently took hold of the woman's arm and said, "Come. Come sit with us. You'll be safe."

She looked at Kiera. "Who are you people? The government?"

Kiera uttered the first words that popped into her head.

"No. We're way cooler than that."

Forty-Two

Tat stood in the basement, panting.

That had been the most exhilarating two minutes of her life, bar none. Better than sex. Crom Cruach had guided her to the sword, and what an impressive weapon it was. With a forged steel blade, inlaid with gold, the hilt adorned with gems, it felt absurdly light in her hand. When she impaled the man with the sword, a surge of energy had coursed up her arm and through her body, an orgasmic sensation she wanted to feel again and again. She chased the girl, who proved to be surprisingly fast, but Crom Cruach had warned her to stay within the lighthouse to maintain her powers, so Tat had let her go.

Still, more intruders were coming.

She needed to be patient, but it was hard. Having advanced from casting silly little spells to mind-blowing powers in a few short days, she couldn't wait to use them.

Tat looked around the basement and, satisfied that it was empty, climbed the stairs and continued up the tower into the lantern room. She had no light and didn't need one. Her senses were enhanced; even the darkest corners were clearly visible to her.

Sitting on her Ouija rug, Tat lit the black candles and absorbed their dark energy. In this room, she was protected, invisible to the wizards.

There was so much to do, to learn. And she needed to be ready for the intruders. Foiling their efforts, dispatching them as readily as she did the first: stabbing him and turning him to dust in one fell swoop.

Ha! Amazing!

She had no idea this much psychic energy existed—energy she could bend to her will once she knew the secrets. Crom Cruach was teaching her and she grew ever stronger. Tat felt near invincible now.

That such incredible power was available to her—a mere mortal—convinced Tat of something she had long suspected: religions were pure fiction. Every one of them. There was no all-powerful *God*, no supreme being, and no consequences if she chose the left-hand path. There seemed to be no virtue in goodness. The best things in life went to those who were free of such silly beliefs. Religion was for weak-minded people and zealots like her mother who were afflicted with what Tat considered a mental illness.

She still wavered between ignoring her mother and killing her in some awful way. Most of the time, the bitch hardly seemed worth the effort. Wasn't living well the best revenge? Though at the very least, she liked the idea of conjuring some demon to scare the bejesus out of the woman.

At times, Tat imagined herself going out into the world, armed with that sword like some kind of deadly vigilante, killing rapists and child molesters. It sounded vaguely virtuous, though. Performing good deeds, protecting the innocent? Maybe she just needed to redefine her ideas of good and evil. Tat saw no contradiction in committing the murders, though. With that kind of power, wouldn't it be wrong *not* to kill those sorts of people?

She communed with Crom Cruach in an altered state of consciousness, giving her access to his moods and a pathway to communicate beyond words. He seemed to be feeling the strain of the siege on the lighthouse. Nevertheless, he was managing and wanted Tat to wait until he summoned her, though he didn't say why. Who was she to question his plan? She closed her eyes, ready to fall into a trance. The astral states she experienced here were much deeper than any she'd had before and allowed her to soar. Time stood still. They were heavenly.

But a call from Crom Cruach interrupted and brought her back to earth. Some of the intruders were planning an assault on the lighthouse.

She jumped up and grabbed the sword, ready to meet them. Crom Cruach was busy dealing with the others and fighting for access to the vortex.

A smile spread across her face. She was more than happy to accept the challenge.

A window broke somewhere below.

Oh, they would pay for that!

Feeling like a superhero, she flew down the stairs.

Forty-Three

The preparations were hurried but elaborate.

Like conducting an orchestra, Lachlan made deliberate gestures with his arms, pointing and directing the elements of the faux army: brush, bushes, broken branches, bundles of fallen leaves, big clumps of grass. These creations wouldn't stand the light of day but became a formidable-looking force in the dark, almost frightening in the staccato flashes of lightning.

He thanked Wōden for the companionship of the others fighting with him. Willow, a gifted medium *and* a goddess. Fynn. Along with Kenric, they had always formed the core of the Aeldo. Leah was a prodigy. And Kiera. He had never met a more fearless woman. Together, they were genuinely formidable.

Focusing on the lighthouse, he saw the darkness plainly; indeed, it was now trapped. With the loss of energy from the vortex, it could no longer conceal itself.

Lachlan felt a momentary thrill. The plan was working.

But he detected a discordant note, something else in play—the woman in black? He couldn't get a read on her, her intent, her motives.

Then another wrinkle. Someone had just died in the lighthouse and it wasn't Kiera. He didn't understand what that was about. Who else was inside? Why?

Then he detected Kiera, emerging from the passage. She was okay. No time to probe further. Too much going on in his head already.

With Willow holding the sídrand in place, Lachlan felt they were ready to mount the diversion. He signaled to Fynn and Leah to move closer to their next assigned positions.

Lachlan revved the engine while holding the brake pedal, hit the flashers and laid on the horn. Pulling his foot off the brake, the Tahoe lurched forward as the tires spit gravel, fish-tailing and blasting through the front gate. The gate panels flew inward, the hinges on the right side breaking, sending the gate crashing into the trees. He screeched to a halt and threw the truck into reverse, rolling back and stopping about twenty feet outside the fence.

Lifting his hands and pushing upward, as if raising a beach ball, Lachlan watched as his army of trees, brush, and grass marched forward, lobbing rocks and boulders, shouting an ancient chant. Lachlan was thrilled. It was a fearsome sight!

Windows broke and glass clattered to the ground as the rocks bombarded the keeper's house.

Still, there was no response as the army closed on the front door. The darkness wasn't taking the bait.

The woman in black was moving, though—

Another disturbance. Leah had some sort of problem.

A moment later, Fynn broke away from the siege.

Bollocks!

The door to the keeper's house flew open. The woman in black rushed out and began hacking through his faux army with a sword or a machete—he couldn't tell in the poor light—vaporizing everything in her path. The only blade with that kind of power was the sword of Stikla. But that weapon lay buried under tons of rock, didn't it? Then he remembered detecting a hint of it here on their first visit. What other surprises awaited them?

They were losing control of the situation—again.

He tried to warn the others of the danger but felt isolated, his messages trapped in the ether. What looked like a great plan moments ago was disintegrating.

His attempted warning shook Willow out of her trance. She gave him a startled glance. "Crap! What are we going to do?"

"Watch me!" He stomped on the accelerator and they bolted forward as the woman made quick work of his army and retreated toward the lighthouse door. He couldn't let the darkness win another round.

Grabbing the cargástriftr, his ghost-knife, Lachlan jumped out and gave chase, hoping to prolong the battle, to give the others more time.

She reached the doorway. If he could take her out now—

Lachlan threw the knife in a last-ditch attempt to stop her.

But she slipped through the opening and slammed the door. The knife struck and held, the tip embedded into the wood. When Lachlan grabbed the door handle, it wouldn't move. Both the handle and door felt rigid and impenetrable, like the steel door to a bank vault.

Bloody hell!

Lachlan had known she was there; he just hadn't expected her to be so powerful, so effective. While she was busy hacking the bush-soldiers to bits, she had glared at Lachlan with one of the most piercing, evil looks he had ever witnessed. She could be the reincarnation of Anna Flecher herself.

Willow yelled, "Shit! What do we do?"

Lachlan grabbed his knife. "Retreat, of course."

Lachlan slid into the Tahoe and threw the truck in reverse, backing out of sight of the lighthouse, gripping the steering wheel like his life depended upon it.

His stellar plan had come unraveled.

Forty-Four

Leah struggled to stay awake.

They were parked south of the lighthouse at Isle View Park, a small picnic area that had been otherwise deserted all day. Mom had brought plenty of snacks and soda, but then she had to pee, and Mom had to hold an umbrella while she went behind a tree.

The wind had been gusty all day, but in the last hour, it had grown stronger and whipped the trees back and forth in wild, frenzied motions. It was spooky and she sensed Mom felt nervous as well. It would be a relief when the call to move came.

She had been sitting in the Jeep for hours, trying to focus her mind on the single task at hand. It was hard. There were so many distractions. The storm, the lighthouse, the incessant questions that kept popping up, driven by her curiosity.

What were they fighting? It was the monster of her dreams, but she couldn't see it; she could only feel it. Why was that?

Why did it hate her? Why did people hate at all? She didn't hate *anyone*, so she couldn't understand the feeling. All the energy they were wasting fighting this thing was energy that could be used for better things. She understood the idea of evil, but it wasn't a fully formed concept in her mind and she knew it. Why were things evil? She didn't understand why people couldn't just be nice and treat each other with kindness. What was so bad about fairy tale endings? And while she understood fairy tales were stories and fantasies, she also saw them as ways of life to aspire to.

Leah also felt a degree of wonder. The forces here were very powerful. They seemed bigger than life, like looking into an extra dimension or deep into space. But she was also afraid. She had seen what this monster could do, and it was bad. People had died, including Grandma Laura. While she had no vivid memories of the old house and the final night there, she had impressions of noises and smells that filled her with great anxiety. The sense of a giant whirlwind in the room created by a stranger who had come to help, a whirlwind he had sent rushing out the window. She also remembered falling through the floor of her room into the kitchen and being hurt. The monster had done that too.

Throughout the day she struggled to keep all of those conflicting feelings under control.

Lachlan and Fynn kept sending messages of encouragement and *thank-yous* for all her hard work. She knew what they were doing, appreciated it, and felt better knowing they were there. Leah knew they were unhappy involving her and despite her fears, she wanted to help—needed to know this would be over once and for all. Not only for herself, but for Mom and Uncle Nate too. This monster wanted to kill them all.

So Leah was excited, anxious, afraid—a whole host of feelings—and she was wasting energy hiding them from the group. She didn't want to fail Mom or the others and she worried about upsetting everyone. On it went: questions, feelings, few answers, and the steady tick of anxiety. Then she sensed Willow was in trouble and that Lachlan had gone to help. Fynn continued sending her encouraging thoughts.

The worst part? No one said *when* this would be over.

She sensed the monster they were fighting was growing stronger again. That wasn't supposed to be happening. Then two smallish branches fell out of the sky near them and Mom jumped.

Finally, Lachlan told her to move closer to the second position by the ferry landing.

"Lachlan says—"

At that moment, she heard a loud crack and a tree fell on the hood, crushing the front of the Jeep, tipping them sharply forward. Mom flopped into the steering wheel, but Leah flew forward and smacked her head on the windshield. Her brain felt temporarily scrambled, but when she got her bearings, she felt okay. Leah stared, wide-eyed.

Holy crap!

The tree trunk looked enormous.

Mom twisted her head in a frantic gesture. "Leah! Are you okay?"

"I'm fine, Mom. Lachlan says it's time." She shook her head, still feeling a little off-balance. The windshield looked like a big spiderweb and the tree seemed bigger than a house. "We're going to have to walk, aren't we?"

Mom looked thoughtful for a moment, nodded, and said, "Yes. We should walk by the water, it's much shorter—"

"I know. It's two miles by road and less than one mile on the beach."

"Less dangerous, too. No falling trees."

"It's going to be hard in the wind and the rain," Leah said.

"I know. Are you up to it?"

She nodded. Mom looked scared. Leah had a bad feeling, but she said nothing.

A fear that overpowered all her other feelings. That mile would be filled with many dangers. It might be the longest mile ever.

Forty-Five

Fynn nodded in agreement.

A pointless gesture really. Lachlan was talking in his head, not standing anywhere nearby.

Thus far, he had contributed his part from the comfortable interior of Kiera's RAV4 on Table Bluff. Now, he needed to venture into the elements and wasn't looking forward to it. Warm and dry, fortified by a skosh of Irish whiskey, he watched the trees bending, assailed by the wind as rain pelted the vehicle like attacking locusts. No sane soul would consider leaving this sanctuary.

Fynn pulled into the fire road, noted a pickup truck with flat tires parked in their customary spot, and pulled to the other side of the gravel track. He grabbed his satchel wrapped in oilskin but hoped he wouldn't need to resort to any of the tools or tricks within. Zipping his poncho and bracing himself, Fynn stepped into the maelstrom. The wind was fierce, driving the rain like shrapnel, stinging any exposed flesh.

Lovely. It was even worse than he imagined.

He walked into the trees, located the fence line, and tracked due north along it to the bluff head. He would now stand in a direct line with the lighthouse and Leah—once she was in position—that would give them the best leverage against the darkness.

The situation made him uneasy, an unfamiliar feeling given the crazy things he had stared down in Northern Mongolia. Unlike Lachlan or Kenric, Fynn had kept himself grounded firmly in the realms of magick and hermetics. He'd spent most of the past three years fighting a cult of black shamans in Mongolia, the word *black* referring to their worship of evil spirits rather than their race.

He knew how powerful Kenric had been in his prime. When he died, it had shaken him to the core. Fynn rationalized that Kenric had lost his edge when he decided to forgo magick for the modern realm of hacking. Technology? What a bunch of boring tripe. Geeks, computers, and CPUs? He understood none of it—though he did like the mobile phone in his pocket. Still, it hadn't done him much bloody good in Mongolia when the nearest tower was often fifty kilometers miles away.

Then Lachlan had been laid low. He hadn't known until the little girl called him, and he only understood the situation to be critical because the girl had recited their call to action to him: *Oft sceall eorl monig anes willan wræc adreogan.*

Often, when one man follows his own will, many are hurt.

It was a line from *Beowulf*, the great Old English epic poem. To them, it was about the value of teamwork and a code phrase employed when one of them needed help. It was never invoked lightly. So here he was.

Fynn emerged from the trees near the edge of the bluff into the full force of the gale. The fence went right to the cliff edge and he was grateful for that, the heavy chain link as solid as a brick wall. Fynn put his left shoulder into the fence and turned to the south to keep his face out of the wind and rain, then closed his eyes and tried to connect with Leah. She had done a remarkable job holding the darkness back from the vortex, and now he would reinforce the sídrand again.

That child amazed him. He had never seen the gift manifest so strongly at such a young age. But he had a theory. She had been present when Kenric died and Fynn believed she had absorbed some of his energy. Plus, the grandmother had the gift. With training, there were no bounds to what she might accomplish, and the Aeldo needed new blood even if she didn't look much like an Elder. He knew Lachlan had plans for her.

Leah did not answer. She must still be moving. No matter. He would contribute on his own until she was ready.

Another message from Lachlan: *Keep an eye on Kiera.*

Fecking hell! How many people did Lachlan think he was?

Nevertheless, he fell into a trance within minutes, tightening the ring around the lighthouse, giving Lachlan and Willow an opportunity to get inside and start the process of crushing the darkness out of existence. For now, Kiera seemed fine.

His eyes closed, shutting out the wind and the rain. He almost missed the faint disturbance in the energies.

Something to his right—

Fynn snapped his eyes open just in time to see a grey wolf snarl and leap at him, canines bared. He had the wherewithal to react by flipping his satchel wrapped in oilskin up to deflect the lunging bite. He nearly went off the bluff—as did the wolf, which slid perilously close to the edge. Fynn stepped to kick the creature off the rim of the cliff but it rolled, leapt to its feet, looped, and charged back at him.

"Jesus, Joseph, and Mary," he yelled, frightened and off-balance.

Using the satchel as a shield, he deflected another lunge as he pushed inland, away from the edge, and tried to grab his cargástriftr to defend himself. The wolf might be real, controlled by the darkness, or simply a manifestation of the darkness, but he had to assume it was real and just as deadly. Unless he gained the upper hand and soon, the beast would kill him.

He broke the link with the sídrand and locked eyes with the wolf, fierce amber eyes that were cold, calculating, and decidedly real.

The wolf took a step into a stance, ready to pounce. Time slowed to almost naught. Fynn took a step back, dropped the satchel, and unlocked his knees, ready to drop when the wolf came at him, never breaking eye contact.

The wolf leapt and Fynn dropped to a half-crouch, using his powerful quads to hold a ready stance.

Time slowed further and he parsed the trajectory of the wolf which, once set in motion, was fixed and unchangeable. Fynn had an uncanny knack for detail and could imagine vividly the wolf's position in minute increments.

As that fearsome mouth and sharp canines flew towards him, Fynn dropped a little farther—out of reach of those teeth—and grabbed the creature above the elbows on the upper shanks, heaving with all his might, sending the beast flying into the void beyond the edge of the bluff and hurtling to the angry waters below.

He collapsed, huffing from the effort. He had hated hiking around the mountains in Northern Mongolia but, as a result, he now had the tough quads of a climber. All that walking had just saved his life.

He sat and tried to reconnect with Lachlan when he felt a further disturbance nearby.

What now?

The figure of a man resolved out of the dark near the trees, and Fynn knew exactly what it was. A Draug. A reanimated dead person. A drone. It walked with purpose, but the black bullet hole in its chest and the ring of old, dark red blood were a dead giveaway. He almost snickered at his pun.

He lunged for his satchel.

Fynn closed his hand around a Celtic cross, yanked it out, and, as he stabbed it hard into the black hole in its chest, he yelled, "Fecking Christ!"

Boom!

He felt a microsecond of relief before the Draug's forward momentum propelled them both over the edge of the bluff.

Forty-Six

Kiera stared in shock.

As she and the woman emerged from the woods by the front gate, they watched the Tahoe accelerate backwards out of sight.

What the hell were they doing? This was supposed to be the big offensive. Instead, the drive was covered in branches and clumps of grass and leaves. So much for Lachlan's phantom army.

Shit!

Not a good sign, and the truck leaving looked like a retreat. The sword business was freaking her out, and she knew nothing about the woman next to her, though discovering a probable ghost hunter in the lighthouse gave her pause. How many people knew? Kiera wanted her full story, but first, they had to get out of the weather.

Thank God they'd brought walkie-talkies since she was the only non-psychic dimwit here—at least she felt like a dimwit around the others.

She hit the talk button and yelled, "Willow! What the hell are you doing?"

Kiera waited, watching the frightened woman. She looked catatonic. Thirty seconds later, Willow said, "Sorry! We had to bail. Walk to the road. We're sitting there."

Kiera took the woman's arm. "Come with me."

A minute later, they jumped into the back seat of the Tahoe. Willow and Lachlan stared in shock and confusion at them.

"I stumbled on her in the tunnel," Kiera said. "Actually, she almost ran me over."

★ ★ ★

Lachlan eyed the woman seated next to Kiera with skepticism.

Small and attractive, she looked frightened beyond belief, shell-shocked, but he worried this was some sort of ruse. He gave her a moment to catch her breath and sent a calming wave in her direction. He spoke gently. "What's your name?"

Sitting rigidly, she eyed him with suspicion and hostility, her mouth a tight line. The calming wave took hold, and she drew a deep breath. Her shoulders relaxed. She hitched a sob and drew a hand across her wet face. Willow handed her a small towel.

"I'm Zoie. Who are you guys?"

Lachlan pursed his lips. What to say? "Researchers."

Zoie looked puzzled. "Are you guys ghostbusters or something?"

Lachlan nodded. "I assume you were also…ghost hunting?"

She nodded and started shaking again. "We got way more than we bargained for—and now—and now my friend is dead."

Zoie choked back a sob and spent a moment trying to compose herself, lost somewhere between tears and panic. She looked in the direction of the lighthouse nervously. "Are we safe here?"

"For now, you're safe with us." *Well, somewhat,* he thought. What had she seen that frightened her so badly? What happened to her friend? Was that the person who died in the lighthouse?

He gave the woman a moment as the calming wave continued to relax her. Finally he said, "What happened?"

A violent gust shook the Tahoe, followed by a heavy pelting of rain. Lightning struck somewhere nearby. Zoie nearly jumped through the roof.

"We noticed stuff happening here for a couple weeks," Zoie said. She rubbed her hands and hugged herself. "The light flashed first, even though the lighthouse had been decommissioned. We could feel things getting more intense. We were convinced tonight was the night to be here with the storm and stuff. I had turned my lantern off and we were climbing up the spiral stairway because the lightning was so cool—"

Her eyes grew wide as she recalled the moment. "All of a sudden, this—woman—she jumped off the top landing and stabbed Greg! No warning, nothing! She stabbed him with a sword, and then—and then—he disappeared in a cloud of dust!"

Zoie bent forward and broke into sobs. Kiera leaned in and put her arm around her.

Lachlan had sensed some imbalance in the energies and now he knew what it was. The sword of Stikla. The woman in black had been using the sword of Stikla. Somehow the darkness had concealed that from him as well. He didn't like it. The darkness continued to play from strength to strength and always seemed to be one step ahead of them.

Still, the darkness was no longer cloaked. Their efforts seemed to be paying off. Lachlan realized this woman may have saved Kiera's life. Without her warning, the woman in black may have been able to surprise Kiera. They couldn't afford to lose a soul. Without their combined efforts, Lachlan doubted they could defeat the darkness. But the sword of Stikla added a new and more dangerous wrinkle to their plan—as if things weren't dangerous enough. How had it gotten here? Had the darkness gone back into the cavern after it? No matter. It was here now, though knowing the sword was in play, they could adjust their strategy accordingly.

He felt the woman in black, a witch, growing powerful in her own right. She was being trained well by the darkness. Another fear raised its head: that the woman in black could tip the balance of power just enough to make the darkness almost invincible. They needed to act even bolder going forward.

Trying to shrug off his dark thoughts, Lachlan said, "How'd you get here?"

"My friend drove," Zoie said.

"Her truck is on the fire road with four flat tires," Kiera said. "No one's going to come out to fix it in this weather."

"It's not my truck. It's my friend's. Now he's dead. What am I gonna tell people?" She looked lost. Close to tears again.

Lachlan didn't know how to handle her and had neither the time nor the inclination to continue this conversation. Every second was critical. He gave Kiera a look and hoped she understood. They didn't need this diversion.

Kiera said, "You're welcome to sit with us for now, but we need to get back to work."

Lachlan messaged Leah but received no answer. He sensed an issue with her moments ago; now he couldn't find her. She and Dana should have reached the next assigned position. Then he found them, still moving, out by the water. He didn't understand. For some reason, they were deviating from the plan.

Fynn had simply disappeared. Lachlan assumed that Fynn had found it necessary to break contact while he moved. Still, it shouldn't be taking this long. He signaled Fynn to get into position and hoped the message found its target.

"Willow, I need everything that you have. Now!" He focused all his attention on the sídrand. Willow pulsed with energy in the passenger seat; her concentration was exceptional. He tried to push her offer of intimacy aside. It was a needless distraction. He wasn't entirely successful and worried about Leah and Fynn. They should be in the assigned positions. He wasn't a fan of the *no news is good news* adage.

For five minutes, he and Willow applied extraordinary pressure to restore the sídrand.

Zoie must have gotten curious. "You guys aren't doing anything—"

Kiera said. "They are. You just can't see it."

After a long pause, Zoie said, "Holy crap! They're psychic?"

Lachlan shushed her and Kiera said, "They need absolute silence."

"That's so cool!"

Kiera whispered, "Yes, it is. Shh."

She seemed to be recovering quickly from the loss of her friend—apparently, he wasn't *that* great a friend. With no evident understanding of the word *absolute*, she whispered back, "Are they talking to the ghosts?"

Lachlan barked, "Silence, please!"

When he glanced in the rearview mirror, she had clapped a hand over her mouth. Good. His anxiety was rising. Still no word from Fynn or Leah. He understood they might be dealing with issues of their own, but this was taking far too long. And now he had this added distraction.

Without a doubt, they were now entering the most dangerous phase of their plan.

They should have been strong, united, and firmly in control.

Instead, it felt like everything was coming unglued.

Forty-Seven

Dana's anxiety deepened.

It looked like a hurricane outside the damaged Jeep. It seemed counterintuitive to abandon the warm vehicle, but the engine was smashed and they wouldn't be warm for long. Worse, another falling tree might crush them. No, they were probably safer on the beach.

Leah reached over and gripped her hand. "It'll be okay, Mom. I love you."

"Love you too, sweetheart."

If Leah was afraid, she didn't show it. Dana did her best to protect Leah from the elements by checking and rechecking every button, flap, or snap.

"Can you talk to Lachlan yet?"

"No. He seems busy. He's not answering."

Dana checked her own rain gear, grabbed a flashlight, and stepped out, walking around to help Leah out. The wind was fierce, the rain stinging her face as it blew in almost horizontal waves and swirled around the trees. The night was deeply black, the flashlight beam a hazy cone cutting through the storm. Dana felt ready for most any possibility with the Beretta stowed in her right pocket, a Taser in the left, and a six-inch hunting knife sheathed to her belt next to the walkie-talkie.

"Come, hurry, before another tree blows down."

Leah hopped out and grimaced when the rain and wind hit her.

They leaned into the wind and walked the short distance to the rocky shore. As they left the shelter of the trees, they staggered as the full force of the storm slammed them. They had to bend farther to make any progress walking straight into gale.

The stony beach was treacherous, a mix of pebbles and larger stones smoothed by wave action, wet and slick and difficult to walk over. The surf was violent and loud, running parallel to the shore, thankfully, minimizing the spray. It mattered little as the rain was so heavy and unrelenting that it penetrated every crack and crevice in her clothing. The light revealed nothing but the driving rain in a nightmarish hellscape.

Dana flashed back to the night two years before, when she was lost in a blizzard on the road by the house, carrying Leah in her arms, running from her father. It had been the longest, loneliest trek of her life, and she never imagined having to do it again, even in her worst nightmares.

Yet, here they were, doing the same thing. Would they ever be safe? Would they even survive the night?

The weather had been threatening then, perhaps more so than this. They survived that walk and she had to believe they would survive this too. Dana wasn't a quitter. She had proven it then and had no intention of quitting now. If necessary, she would walk on hot coals for this child.

In places, they traversed stretches of sand, and the beach was wider than when they first explored this area. Then Dana realized the wind was pushing water away from shore and made the walk a little easier. Leah said nothing. Just gripped her hand, head down, and kept stride with Dana.

On they walked. Time seemed meaningless. In the storm, Dana had no sense of progress, no sense that they were any closer to the ferry landing. The wind and the flashlight had a way of turning swirls of rain into the faces and bodies of various beasts rushing down the beach at them.

Leah suddenly gripped her hand tighter and a second later, lightning struck a tree a few dozen yards away.

The flash lit the beach in garish light, illuminating the hurricane-like storm and the raging waters just offshore. So close that Dana marveled grimly that they hadn't been shocked, then realized Leah had sensed it coming.

Then another bolt struck the same tree.

They were being targeted! Leah must have felt it too, clutching Dana's hand ever tighter. In turn, Dana held her gun in a death grip—as if that would be any use against a lightning bolt.

Then the flashlight quit.

As Dana wondered how to escape this, Leah screamed—loud enough to be heard over the storm. "Lachlan!"

Dana wasn't waiting for Lachlan.

She tugged Leah's arm and they ran.

Forty-Eight

Fynn grabbed for the rocky ledge.

Too late.

His momentum combined with the wet surface allowed no purchase and he plummeted toward the water and near-certain death.

As he fell, he felt remarkably lucid and composed. He had been near death many times and those moments always assumed this detached mode rather than blind panic. Time slowed and his senses heightened. He had lived many, many years and given his vocation, sooner or later, this outcome was inevitable.

In one second, Fynn knew he had fallen about thirty feet and had about a second to live. The odds seemed stacked firmly against him. If the fall didn't kill him, the waves would.

In the dark, he didn't see the tree growing out of the cliff until he hit it.

Again, his attention to detail saved him. He felt the three-inch trunk scrape his thigh and reflexively locked his arm around the tree, managing to hang on as it bent under his weight.

For an instant, he thought the bough would break. It held and he remained suspended, bouncing precariously as the tree rebounded while his inner arm screamed in pain from the impact. The dead man that had attacked him hit the water with a dull wet thud suggesting that the water wasn't very deep just below him.

"Jesus, Joseph, and Mary," he mumbled into the wind, shaking his head at the vagaries of fate and life. He wasn't a Christian but enjoyed playing the part of a good Irishman.

Still, he wasn't out of danger. He was hanging about thirty feet above the rocky shore and could hear the waves crashing against it. Big, violent waves. He couldn't imagine climbing up the sheer rock face and if he climbed down or fell, he would be beaten to death by the angry waters. The rain fell at an angle into the cliff in buckets, rushing across his face in a torrent, and breaching every crevice in his clothing. It was almost overwhelming.

He messaged Lachlan, though he had no idea what Lachlan could possibly do to fish him out of this mess.

Disturbingly, he heard nothing. Lachlan wasn't ignoring him; he simply wasn't there. Leah had disappeared as well. Same for Willow.

Bloody fecking hell!

Despite all their planning and preparation, they were clearly losing. The darkness had either cut him off from the others or had already killed them. His satchel with his tools, amulets, and talismans lay somewhere above, far out of reach.

Death lay below.

He managed to find a narrow ledge with his foot, a little purchase to support his weight. With a firm grip on the tree, Fynn thought he could hold out for twenty minutes, maybe thirty. If he didn't get help by then, he would come to one of three sticky ends: death by hypothermia, pounded to bloody bits below, or drowning in the rain and water pouring down the cliff face.

This was yet a stranger twist. He had lucked on to the tree and now, he was left hanging there, likely to die regardless. This wasn't even the worst pickle he'd ever found himself in. There was the time an arrow had knocked him off his horse. He'd tangled his foot in the stirrup and had been dragged for several hundred yards before he convinced the horse to stop.

Falling ill with smallpox. That wasn't the least bit fun.

Or the time Shamus O'Henry caught him in the stable with his youngest daughter. The crazy man had chased him on foot forever.

He found some comfort in these distractions. They only proved the gods weren't always logical or even sensible.

Fie! The gods be damned.

He tried to summon Lachlan again.

Nothing.

He would just have to keep trying.

Huddled into the cliff face, he yelled into the raging storm.

"Lachlan!"

Forty-Nine

Lachlan tensed. "Something's wrong."

Fynn had been in some sort of trouble and then simply disappeared. The siege was breaking down. He tried to warn Leah to stop where they were. To go back to the Jeep and lock the doors but she had gone silent as well. Wind and rain lashed the Tahoe.

There were things afoot in the woods. Dangerous, deadly things. Draugen and other creatures animated by the darkness. They were losing their grip on the sídrand.

Willow opened her mouth to speak.

"Willow, stay focused," he said gravely.

A moment later, he received a fragmented message from Fynn. *Help...fell...tree...*

Where are you?

Fynn had to repeat the message twice before Lachlan understood. The man was in deep trouble.

He locked eyes with Kiera in the rearview mirror. "You need to help Fynn. He's hanging from a tree halfway down the bluff."

"What?" She stared at him for a moment, uncomprehending, and then said, "What can I do?"

"Willow, you brought rope, right?"

"Yep. Back of the Tahoe."

"Walk north along the west fence line," Lachlan said. "He's straight down from that edge."

"Do you think I can pull him up by myself?" Kiera asked with a puzzled, unfocused gaze.

Even though she was tough and fit, Lachlan doubted it was possible. In this weather, it would be a challenge for two people. He shook his head. "I don't know."

Zoie leaned forward. "Can I help?"

"No." Lachlan had no intention of endangering anyone else and the woman was small—though she looked wiry. "You're welcome to stay here with us but I'm not willing to put your life at risk. What Kiera needs to do is quite dangerous."

"I've already dealt with the ghosts in the lighthouse. How bad can this be?" She crossed her arms, her jaw set resolutely.

It was false bravado. Lachlan could tell, though he admired her pluck. She was fighting her fears, not giving in to them. Good for her.

Kiera said, "I could use—"

"Right now, ghosts are the least of your worries," Lachlan said, feeling distracted by the problems rushing at him. Where the hell was Leah? He focused on Zoie. "There's something far worse than a ghost in the lighthouse."

"Worse than that crazy bitch with the sword?"

"Really, I could—" Kiera began.

"Much worse. You're welcome to stay here in the truck until we leave. Even here, I can't promise you it'll be safe."

Zoie sat, her expression blank until the corner of her mouth turned up ever so slightly. She seemed to have formed an attachment to Kiera. "If it's not safe here, I'm going with her."

Kiera grabbed his arm. "Lachlan! If she wants to help, let her help. We need all the help we can get!"

Lachlan forced himself to take a deep breath. To relax. To be mindful. The truth was, the woman was in danger no matter what they did now. If she wanted to help, it would be foolish to say no.

"If you insist, yes, please. A man's life depends on the two of you." To Kiera, he said, "I'll assist from here if I can. Hurry!"

They zipped and buttoned up, grabbed the rope, and headed out into the storm. Lachlan stood in awe at their courage and willingness to put themselves in danger. Watching them disappear into the dark, swirling rain, he also marveled at the way his mind worked. He hadn't known *why* they needed rope when he added it to the list, just that they would need it.

There was no time to muse further. Every disruption weakened the sídrand around the lighthouse, allowed the darkness to recharge. It seemed to be cloaked again—an ominous development—and he had no fix on the woman in black.

He continued trying to message Leah. Were they still moving? Or had the darkness blocked their communications? Why had they diverted from the plan? Anxiety ticked in his stomach. So much to worry about.

There was nothing to do but wait and retighten the noose around the darkness. He and Willow worked together to reestablish the sídrand. It was a déjà vu moment. Here he was, facing down the darkness, barely in control, feeling the early advantage slipping away yet again. He had barely escaped with his life in the cavern last year and feared he might not be as lucky this time. But he couldn't give in to dark thoughts. Too many people depended upon him.

Soon, they began to regain control. Fynn came back on line even as he hung from the face of the bluff and gave them some support. He had no idea how Fynn got into that fix, but imagined being regaled with a colorful story at some future date. He stifled a smirk and focused on the lighthouse, locking his thoughts on the sídrand and increasing the pressure on the darkness while seeking out the woman in black.

At the same time, he offered what support he could to Kiera and Zoie, who had reached the edge of the cliff. He was finely focused on every detail. He called it concentration. Now people called it multitasking.

He tried again to connect with Leah. They'd had plenty of time to reach the ferry landing. They really needed her help to fortify the siege while Fynn was otherwise occupied.

Nothing.

The connection to her was broken. He began to fear the worst. A momentary lapse was common and understood.

This was something else, and with Fynn hanging from a cliff, he couldn't investigate himself.

"Willow?"

Lost in a trance, she took a moment to respond. "Problem?"

"Are you in touch with Leah?"

"Not consciously." She closed her eyes for a moment. "No. She's not there. Try the walkie-talkie."

He shuffled around on the dash and found it. "Dana? Leah? Can you hear me?"

He waited twenty seconds and tried again. Silence.

Bloody hell!

His worst fears were coming to pass.

A creeping dread that he had failed Leah and Dana MacKenzie.

Fifty

Kiera found the spot in minutes.

Crouched down, they were full into the weather here: hurricane-force winds, rain lashing the bluff, the noise at once horrendous and mournful. Kiera viewed the wet, rocky ledge with abject fear. One false move and she would be swept off into that abyss. Then she looked at Zoie, a complete stranger, feeling unhappily responsible for the woman even though she was grateful for the help.

Pointing to the ledge, she handed the light to Zoie and lay down on her belly.

Kiera crawled to the edge and looked over. A series of lightning flashes obliged, and she saw Fynn, arms wrapped around a small tree that had found purchase in the rock. He must have sensed her presence. He looked up and waved congenially as if meeting her for lunch. It was the most surreal moment yet of this long day.

After tying one end of the rope around a tree, she let the other end dangle down the cliff face until she felt Fynn tug on it. She didn't know if he would climb it or need help, but decided to provide as much assistance as they could.

She shouted down to him, "We'll pull you up!"

There was no response—or if there was, she couldn't hear it. The storm was simply too loud.

Kiera sent him a message.

We'll pull you up.

She wasn't psychic, but Fynn was. But how would she know if he heard it? A moment later, she felt a double tug on the rope. Okay then.

She yelled to Zoie, whose face was dripping with rain, "Step back. Let's try pulling him up!"

Zoie nodded.

They sat in a tug-of-war position, Zoie behind Kiera. Kiera dug her heels into a crevice in the rock and pulled with everything she had. Zoie, despite being small, proved to be surprisingly strong. Two minutes later, a hand appeared. They continued pulling as Fynn crawled onto the ledge, one hand still clinging to the rope. He scampered to safety and fell into the wet grass, gasping for breath. A sharp red line, like a scratch from a talon, ran down his face. It had been washed clean by the rain.

Kiera knelt. "You okay?"

He nodded but held up a finger, looking too winded to speak.

A moment later, he inhaled deeply and rolled onto his feet.

"We need to go! We're needed now!" Fynn yelled over the storm. Then he looked at Zoie. "Who's this?"

Kiera yelled, "Zoie, a ghost hunter we ran into. She wants to help."

"We'll take all the help we can get!" Fynn went to tip his cap and realized it was gone.

He grabbed his satchel and Kiera led the way along the fence.

Fynn stopped and grabbed her arm. "Lachlan says to come in through the basement—carefully. Do you know what that means?"

Kiera nodded. "Follow me!"

They single-filed through the woods until they reached the door. Kiera flipped it open and played the light across every corner. She hung her head down, looking along the passage for the woman with the sword, then dropped down and waved. "All clear!"

When they were all in, Fynn pulled the door closed.

It was surprisingly quiet after the mayhem of the storm above. Fynn, crouching, leaned against the stone wall with his eyes closed. A moment later, he said, "Lachlan wants us to wait here but be ready. He's working on some big offensive, and apparently, Leah's in trouble."

Kiera started and felt her belly clench. "Oh no! Is she okay?"

"He doesn't know yet."

Looking from Kiera to Fynn, Zoie said, "You better tell him about the crazy bitch with the sword."

"You saw her, you tell him."

And she did; Fynn's eyes grew wide as she related the details.

When she finished, Fynn said, "Feck! What else can this wretched beast throw at us?"

Kiera feared that the answer was darker than she could imagine.

Fifty-One

There was no time.

Lachlan knew it with certainty. He had finally located Leah and understood the problem.

A tree had crushed the Jeep. Now, Leah and Dana were running along the beach, assailed by lightning bolts. He couldn't reach them and couldn't offer sufficient protection from here before the darkness finished them off. Kiera was busy hoisting Fynn up a cliff. Willow lacked the skills to take on the darkness alone.

He couldn't be in two places at once and was certain the darkness wanted him to save Leah, wanted to goad him away from the lighthouse. Then it could recharge further, become stronger again—perhaps invincible in synergy with the woman in black. It was within reach of its avowed goal: the elimination of the entire MacKenzie line. Worse events would follow. He pictured the Reichstag. That could never be allowed to happen again. They needed to be brazen and daring. No plan. Just guts, brawn, and sorcery.

They needed another, more dramatic distraction. One that would force the darkness to ignore Leah and deal with the immediate threat to the lighthouse.

He looked at Willow. "Do you know what I'm thinking?"

"Yeah, we're going in. Now." Her tresses had mostly dried and framed her face in waves. She looked like a goddess in the light from the dashboard.

"We're going to scratch your truck a bit more."

She flashed him an evil smile. "I'm driving, then. You can't have all the fun."

"Fair enough."

"Do you have a plan?" Willow looked at him expectantly.

He shrugged. There was no sugar-coating this. "No."

"What are we waiting for?"

They switched positions. Willow then waited for Lachlan to buckle in and gunned the engine, spinning the tires and spewing gravel as the Tahoe fishtailed and roared forward. Her jaw set, she wore a fierce look of determination on her face. She was enjoying this!

"Hit the door at an angle," he said. He had the glimmer of an idea and messaged Fynn.

Willow sped toward the keeper's house and swerved at the last second, the right side of the bumper and quarter-panel slamming into the front door, blowing it off the hinges and sending it flying far into the house.

The time for finesse was over. Willow backed up as Lachlan grabbed his satchel and dug around inside. He was heartened to realize the darkness hadn't been able to recharge as much as he feared. There had been no attempt to stop them. The darkness was also juggling too many balls, it seemed.

Lachlan felt confident the four of them could finally destroy it for the first time today. Fynn and Kiera were on their way and would soon enter the house through the cellar.

The lightning around Leah and Dana had stopped. He sent her a message.

A moment later, she replied, *On our way. Thank you!*

The distractions and interference with their communications suddenly felt more like a last-ditch effort by the darkness to save itself and less like domination.

The wild card remained the woman in black, but now he knew where she was. No longer shielded, she was in the lantern room of the tower. They could manage her too. But now, there was something else here. He couldn't put his finger on it and dared not give it too much thought. Another distraction he didn't need—though he couldn't dismiss it either. They ignored any details at their own peril. Fynn would soon join them. He'd figure it out.

"Now what?" Willow asked.

He handed her a gold Celtic cross. "Follow my lead. We're about to step on its neck."

With that, they jumped out and ran into the keeper's house.

Fifty-Two

Kiera watched Fynn curiously.

His head cocked, he looked like a dog listening to his owner as they stood crammed into the space beneath the steel door.

"Okay, here we go," he said finally. "Lachlan has a plan. I need to join them. He says the woman in black is in the lantern room. Eventually, she'll come after us. You two need to stop her."

"Us two?" Kiera felt blindsided. Zoie was an unknown quantity at best, a hazard at worst. "That sounds like a bad idea."

"Why?" Zoie looked shocked. She spoke, her voice rising as she pointed at Fynn. "I just helped you save him."

"This is way more dangerous than pulling Fynn up a cliff," Kiera said dismissively. The woman had no clue how ugly this might get. "I'll handle it."

Zoie grabbed Kiera's arm. "Hey. The way I see it, I saved your ass. You were just gonna charge in there earlier."

Kiera had to admit she might be right. And she was feisty, but how far would feisty get her? Then she thought about Rachel, who had helped them last year. Sixteen years old, she had been amazing.

Zoie locked her hands on her hips. "Earlier, you said 'we need all the help we can get.' I don't see much has changed."

"I did." Kiera acquiesced, realizing she might be useful in a secondary role. "Okay, you're in. Don't tell me I didn't warn you."

Pivoting to face Kiera, Zoie said, "So, how are we going to deal with that sword?"

Kiera reached into her pockets and showed her the Sig Sauer and the Kimber. "These will help. Beyond that, I have no clue."

But she considered several ideas as she followed Fynn along the passage. As they emerged into the basement, she heard a tremendous impact, like a vehicle crashing into a wall, followed by a loud bang overhead as something crashed to the floor.

Kiera ducked involuntarily. "Jesus!"

"Lachlan always did like to make the big entrance," Fynn said, raising his eyebrows, smirking. He charged up the stairs to the main floor while Kiera and Zoie followed at a more cautious pace. For a moment, her nose wrinkled at a vague, unpleasant odor that reminded her of the cavern last year. Kiera shrugged and shook it off. As they topped the stairs, Lachlan and Willow burst through the remains of the doorway, the jamb broken and askew, the door itself lying in the center of the room.

Lachlan tossed a flashlight to Fynn and barked orders, sounding like a drill sergeant. "Fynn! Set up protection! Willow! Sídrand! Set your flashlights on the floor!"

As Fynn dug through his satchel, Lachlan started around the room with the shaker of sorcerer's blue and a fistful of amulets.

"Fynn! Scan the lighthouse and the cellar. There's something else at work here."

Kiera dawdled, wanting to delay going into the tower, mostly wanting just to watch these two work.

Finally, she walked toward the tower, inched the last few feet to the open door, and looked up, running the beam of her Maglite slowly up the spiral stairs to the top. Zoie eased up next to her and whispered, "Anything?"

"Not yet. But I have an idea." *A few rough ones anyway,* she thought. It seemed silly to worry about this woman and her sword. As soon as she showed her face, Kiera would simply shoot her. Bang. Dead. End of story.

Except with this stuff—the darkness and all the craziness around it—she could assume nothing.

Kiera thought about the guys in the cavern last year, dead people somehow animated by the darkness and sent to kill her. Back then, Lachlan had handed her two Celtic crosses and said, "Use these. Your gun is worthless here."

It was true, she had shot one of them several times. Didn't even slow it down. She had been forced to stab them with the crosses, a memory that sent a wave of revulsion and nausea through her, even now, a year later.

Your gun is worthless here.

She clenched her fists and tensed at the thought. Would she face similar horrors this time?

"What's your idea?" Zoie asked, looking nervous now, biting her lip and rubbing the back of her neck.

"We should assume the worst here, that this woman may be difficult to stop." And by stop, she meant kill. "You sure you're up for this?"

"I wouldn't miss it for anything."

Zoie had no clue what she had gotten into and Kiera had precious little time to explain it. "We'll have to kill her."

"I hope so. She killed my friend," Zoie said with an angry edge. "Aren't you just going to shoot her?"

"I don't know. I don't want to tip our hand too soon, and I'm not certain shooting her will be...effective."

Zoie looked confused, her nose wrinkling. "What? A gun won't work?"

Kiera shook her head. "Maybe. Maybe not. Sorry, there's no time to explain."

"That's cray—"

"We may end up dead, too."

"I'm still not leaving," Zoie said resolutely, hands on hips, but with a strong air of anxiety about her.

Kiera looked at her, surprised. Most people would flee in these circumstances, but this woman wanted to stay and fight. How did Lachlan keep lucking upon all these amazing people? Was he a catalyst who somehow inspired everyone around him?

"All right. You stand here, in the doorway." Kiera took her by the shoulders and positioned her a foot into the tower with a clear view up the stairs. Actually, if her plan worked, the danger to Zoie was minimal. "When she starts down the stairs, I want her to see you. Keep your flashlight on."

Zoie nodded. "Ah, I'm the bait."

"Yep. I'll be up there on the second floor." Kiera pointed to a closed door, the doorway to the second floor of the keeper's house. "As she passes that door and walks down to you, I'll slip out behind her and shoot her."

Kiera held up the Sig and a Celtic cross. "You ready for this?"

Zoie gave her a nervous nod.

After giving her a hug, Kiera looped back and climbed the stairs in the keeper's house, out of sight of the lantern room. She waited, ready for every possibility with two guns and a Celtic cross in her pockets.

Then thought: *Who am I kidding?*

She had no clue what *every possibility* might be.

Fifty-Three

Leah and Mom ran like hell.

Lachlan hadn't answered her plea and Mom decided the only course was to run and keep running. The lightning bolts continued to crash down in a blinding, deafening display that followed them and drew nearer as they ran. Ahead, the beach narrowed, and Leah feared the lightning would catch them there and kill them. Or they might be forced into the frigid, angry waters—though Leah began to think the darkness had lousy aim. They were still alive. The bolts were only coming to frighten them. She imagined pushing the lightning away with her mind. The next bolt crashed farther afield.

Yes!

Leah did a little fist pump like they did on TV.

Suddenly, the lightning stopped. It ended so abruptly that she and Mom slowed to a walk.

The storm, while still fierce, seemed quieter than before. Rain dripped from her face and had blown into the neck of her poncho. She was cold and wet.

Lachlan spoke in her head. *Leah, come quickly. We need you in position!*

Certain Lachlan had somehow stopped the lightning, she thought, *On our way. Thank you!*

She squeezed her mother's hand and yelled, "Lachlan's back! He stopped the lightning. We need to get to the next spot, quickly."

While the flashlight had quit, her eyes had acclimatized to the dim light, a vague and nightmarish black and white scene like a scary movie.

Mom abruptly yanked Leah away from the water's edge as a rogue wave washed over the spot where they'd stood a moment before.

Yikes!

Clearly, they weren't safe until they were off this beach and closer to the others. The relief she felt a moment ago evaporated.

Grabbing Mom's hand, they ran, watching the skies and the waters for unexpected dangers. A couple minutes later, they saw the dark outline of the Northport breakwater.

Almost there!

The highway lay just ahead. A hundred feet of beach to go. Her heart leapt and Leah wanted to run to the road, but she was out of energy. She slowed to a walk as her mother stopped and put her hands on her knees to catch her breath. Leah tried to imagine how she would do her part now. They were supposed to park at the landing and work with Fynn from there. She couldn't imagine concentrating on that stuff outside in the wind and rain.

Leah tugged on her mother's arm and yelled, "We're supposed to stop at the landing. Where are we going to sit?"

Rain dripped from Dana's face. "I don't know. There's a little shelter by the landing. Or the visitor's center. Maybe we can get inside."

She felt better. Of course Mom had an answer. She always did. Leah might have the telepathy thingy, but her mom knew so many other things. It boggled her mind that one person could know so much stuff.

Leah shivered deeply. She didn't know if they were more exposed to the wind here, but suddenly, it felt very cold. Winter cold. Her next step seemed to catch in the sand. She had to jerk her foot free to take another step.

The wind cut through her like an icicle. The rain changed to snow in an eyeblink. The beach and water disappeared and now, they were lost in a blizzard. Mom tightened her grip and Leah could read her mind. She was remembering another walk like this in a blizzard—

The next step was her last. Her foot stuck, frozen in the rapidly freezing sand.

Leah yelled, "Mom! I'm stuck!"

"Me too! Can't you do something?"

She looked at her feet and willed them to come free as the wind shrank her cold skin until it felt like flimsy paper beneath her clothes.

The frozen sand was unyielding.

Leah yelled at the top of her lungs, "Lachlan!"

Fifty-Four

Lachlan scanned the room and barked orders.

"Fynn! Set up protection! Willow! Sídrand! Set your flashlights on the floor!"

He felt great pressure to throw up a defensive perimeter quickly. They were established in the keeper's house and needed to capitalize on the brief advantage.

With half the windows broken, it sounded like the wind, the pelting rain, and thunder were invading the room. Fortunately, most of the broken windows faced south and were sheltered from the worst of it. It was cold, though. Bone-chilling dampness that penetrated his clothing and thin skin. The flashlights on the floor provided sufficient light to work by.

Running to the right front corner on the main floor, Lachlan sprinkled sorcerer's blue around his feet and placed four equally spaced amulets in the powder. It wasn't armor but nearly as effective, particularly against binding spells and other hurled threats.

He sprinkled a path to the center of the room. Handed Willow the shaker and four amulets and pointed to the left front corner. "Stand there."

Then, nodding to his corner, he said, "Sprinkle this around you and place the amulets just like I did. Be ready with the cross."

Across the room, Fynn stepped into position and performed a similar operation with the powder and two gold talismans. He held a cargástriftr in his right hand.

He and Fynn didn't need to speak. They were reverting to the original plan and knew instinctively what to do. The darkness lay somewhere beneath and seemed to be locked in a holding pattern, watching, waiting, trying to reach maximum strength before they cut it off from the vortex for the last time. Lachlan could feel it preparing for a face-off while the woman in black waited in the lantern room. The darkness was holding her back as an ace in the hole, but they knew exactly where she was. There would be no more surprises. An hour ago, it had seemed all hope might be lost, but Lachlan felt his confidence returning.

With the three of them in place, a strange calm settled upon the room despite the storm outside. This space now belonged to them.

Nevertheless, things would soon get ugly.

He and Fynn reinforced the sídrand, giving Willow a chance to finish positioning herself. Something felt askew, but he couldn't put his finger on it.

Lachlan held up his cargástriftr with both hands in preparation for the ceremony. "Willow, hold your cross up like this."

Just as everything was falling into place, the odd recurring disturbance returned. He sensed Fynn trying to parse the details. Something was going on in the cellar.

"Fynn! What is it?"

"Draugen! Two or three of them! I can hold them for a little bit."

No surprise, really. The darkness was animating dead people to assist in the fight. In Anglo-Saxon mythology, they were called Draug—or Draugen, the Old English plural of Draug—but they were no myth. At one time, medieval villagers were so afraid of the dead rising from their graves, they mutilated their bodies or smashed the skeletons to pieces before burying them. They also resorted to burying bodies upside down, covering them with rocks, or cutting their heads off—all to prevent them from returning as Draugen.

Lachlan considered them to be little more than a parlor trick, but they were dangerous nonetheless.

He thought about sending Kiera after them, but no, she needed to guard against the threat from the tower.

Then he heard Leah yell, *Lachlan!*

Damn! She and Dana were in trouble again. The darkness had literally frozen them *in situ* on the beach. They would soon freeze to death. That settled the issue.

"Kiera! We need your help!"

Kiera appeared a moment later on the stairs leading to the second floor and gave him a challenging look. "We're waiting for the woman in black."

"Leah's in trouble!" He pointed to the doorway and yelled, "Take the Tahoe and drive to the ferry landing, hurry! Leah and Dana are there. Get them back here safely. Quickly!"

Kiera pulled Zoie away from the open doorway. "Come with me."

Lachlan broke from the siege just long enough to send a protective binding spell at Dana and Leah. A spell to banish the cold and to prevent the darkness from harming them further until Kiera could bring them to the relative safety of the lighthouse.

As he thought it, he realized how ridiculous that sounded. This had to be one of the most dangerous places on earth right now.

Fynn then blurted out two words that sent a deep chill down his spine.

He sensed Willow faltering and yelled, "Hold steady!"

A minute later, Willow screamed and ran out of the lighthouse.

Fifty-Five

Willow scrambled to her corner.

Sprinkling the powder around her feet, she placed the amulets precisely ninety degrees apart. She could feel the buzz of energy flowing through the lighthouse and applied her psychic skills to help maintain the siege.

Then Lachlan instructed her to hold the cross upright.

She hesitated. It felt weird. While not an atheist, she wasn't a Christian either. Raised Catholic, she had come to view the Church as a dark and evil empire. She had toyed briefly with Wicca but found the ceremonies silly. Holding the cross seemed melodramatic even though Lachlan had explained the Celtic cross had no religious significance. He and his friend Kenric had tested dozens of shapes and the Celtic cross was simply the most efficient device for controlling the *energies*, electromagnetic fields passing through the earth. It was a matter of physics. Maybe the ancients had understood the effect since the cross was so widely used in religion and paganism. Still, she had seen enough bad horror movies for this moment to feel like a cliché.

She raised it regardless as Fynn and Lachlan held their ghost knives up, the tips pointed skyward. Willow couldn't wait until this was over and her training began in earnest. Lachlan had promised to teach her what he could. She would teach him a few things too, she thought with a smirk.

Right now, she needed to concentrate. She closed her eyes and shut everything out. Concentrated on focusing the energy flowing from Fynn and Lachlan into the sídrand.

The pushback from the darkness was immediate and intense, humming in her head like an electronic buzz while Lachlan and Fynn talked about something she didn't understand—something in the basement.

In her mind, the lighthouse was now transparent, and she could see lines of force revolving over the nearby strait. Was it real or imagined? Willow didn't know, but she saw the vortex rotating majestically, absorbing lines flowing from above and the surrounding countryside. From it, lines descended into the water. Near the lighthouse, they were blocked by a diffuse sphere of energy—the sídrand—that resolved to a more robust feature as they reinforced it.

The darkness struggled against that sphere, but also seemed to be pushing especially hard in her direction.

She found the effort needed to resist the pressure almost more than she could handle—like the darkness was boring right through her brain. Migraine-like pain pressed on her temples and behind her eyeballs—it felt as though they were being pried from her skull. There were so many opposing energies, emotions, and contexts in the room, her mind was spinning out of control. She feared she might pass out.

Willow grew more and more alarmed. Fear rose within her like a corrosive wave of acid. She needed help. Willow opened her eyes, looking for Lachlan, ready to cry out in pain and fear—

Lachlan and the room were gone!

She blinked, but they were still gone, and she was lost in a swirling fog. Willow felt restrained, frozen in place, unable to breathe, just like she felt during the ceremony outside the lighthouse a few days before.

The fog began to clear, a strange iridescent blue light shining through the gaps. She recognized the place. The cavern under the bar! How could that be? It had collapsed over a year ago! But the Viking longship was gone, the walls wiped clean of the vivid drawings of Native American and Viking ceremonies. It was barren and cold.

A man stepped out of the wall, walking toward her. Willow squinted and revulsion cramped her insides into a twisted knot.

He was dead, his body rotting, strips of flesh hanging from his arms, his clothing covered in burial dirt. The smell hit her like a bulldozer and nausea overwhelmed her. Willow retched, but her stomach was empty and nothing came up. Her body convulsed in a wave of spasms, a visceral response to her pain and terror as the face of the man resolved into a person she knew.

Her father!

She hadn't seen him in thirty years. Not since he tried to crawl into her bed one night, she remembered grimly. She'd punched him in the face and her mother had kicked him out.

Willow feared she had died. Was this Hell?

But if she was dead, what were these horrible feelings? The panic? The dread?

The scream building within her was like a nascent explosion, rising, expanding—it would blow her to pieces when it finally escaped. Willow hardened her resolve and pushed back with all of her will, trying to escape the cavern and the visage of her dead father. Seeking the keeper's house and Lachlan. This had to be a trick.

She startled when Leah screamed *Lachlan!* somewhere in her head.

He was here somewhere—but then Kiera ran out the door—?

Fynn said something that upset Lachlan.

Crumb Cruiser?

It was all nonsense, but she couldn't force it away. She thought she heard someone say, "Willow? Are you okay?"

Fynn?

Her dead father stepped closer and reached for her with a rotting hand.

The confusion and disconnect were unbearable.

"Hold steady!" Lachlan yelled from a faraway place.

It was no use. The dam burst and her scream gushed out, loud and shrill.

The grip holding Willow in place let loose and she ran blindly from the lighthouse and her dead father.

Fifty-Six

Fynn dashed to his position.

Taking the corner opposite Lachlan, he sprinkled sorcerer's blue around his feet. In lieu of amulets, he laid a gold talisman on each side of him.

He held the cargástriftr, the tip pointed skyward. The lines of energies then flowed through both knives and reinforced the siege that Willow had managed, just barely, to hold in place. He and Lachlan were equally matched, equally powerful, Willow less so. Placing Leah opposite to Willow would balance the fields. Clearly, Lachlan had thought this through, anticipated much of it ahead of time.

With the four of them in place, they would invoke the corners as the first step to crushing this darkness, whatever it was. He still had no clear conception of what they were facing. Maybe that was part of the problem. He recalled a line from *The Art of War* by Sun-Tzu: *If you know yourself but not the enemy, for every victory gained you will also suffer a defeat.*

Truer words had never been spoken.

Why could he discern nothing about this beast Lachlan called the darkness?

He settled in and cleared his mind, connecting deeply with Willow and Lachlan, allowing all stray thoughts to vaporize and disappear. In precisely allotted divisions, Fynn assigned his consciousness to three tasks: contributing to the sídrand, trying to define the darkness, and scanning the lighthouse for the faint disturbance that Lachlan was feeling.

With the support he was receiving from the others, he could probe deep into the keeper's house and the darkness, more so than Kenric or Lachlan were capable of. Indeed, it may have been far too dangerous for them to do so on their own. This acuity was one of his strengths, a talent to discern the small and hidden details that weren't evident to others—what kids these days liked to call a superpower.

Slowly, Fynn isolated the wrinkle that was disturbing Lachlan to the cellar.

Draugen! Dead things like the drone that had tried to kill him on the bluff.

"Fynn! What is it?"

"Draugen! Two or three of them! In the cellar. I can hold them for a little bit."

He aimed a binding spell down the stairs and focused further on the darkness.

While most of his energy assisted the siege, he slowly focused deeply and intently on the darkness for the first time and decided the name was appropriate—the darkness was actually *visible* to him as an absence of light rather than in any physical form. Pure black. A black hole sucking the light out of the surrounding space.

As he probed every nook and cranny of it, he first detected the tiny remnant of Anna Flecher.

Then he had a flash of insight.

"Bloody fecking hell!" he muttered. Fynn knew exactly who Anna had invoked to carry out her retribution.

A name he knew well. A name well known to all adherents of pagan religions.

Crom Cruach.

He was also known as Crom Dubh, or the *crouching darkness*, so Lachlan's moniker for the beast wasn't so far-fetched after all.

According to the legends, Crom Cruach was a wizened deity who had lived atop a mountain, hidden by perpetual mists. He had been worshiped since time immemorial, a ghoul appeased by human sacrifice, his followers offering up their firstborn child in return for a plentiful harvest in the coming year. In a horrific rite, the children were killed by smashing their heads on the stone idol representing Crom Cruach, and their blood sprinkled around the base.

He was a mercurial and vengeful sort, though. The Irish high king, Tigernmas, died along with three quarters of his army while worshipping Crom Cruach on Samhain Eve, murdered for some slight to the deity, real or imagined. Despite that bloody event, worship of the beast continued until St. Patrick ended the cult. He destroyed the stone idol by beating it with his crozier and then banished Crom Cruach to Hell.

Fynn had never tangled with him—Crom Cruach had lived long before his time—but his mentor, Godric, had and described him as a murderously irredeemable bastard.

Lachlan sensed his consternation and sent the mental equivalent of a question mark. At the same time, he felt Willow losing her grip.

"Crom Cruach! She invoked Crom Cruach!" Fynn yelled.

"Bloody hell!"

Without breaking concentration, he called, "Willow? Are you okay?"

At that moment, Willow screamed and ran out of the lighthouse.

Fifty-Seven

Kiera ran for the Tahoe.

Zoie trailed, grumbling, but she hopped in the truck without hesitation. Kiera spun the wheel, performing a sloppy U-turn, and tore down the drive. The damaged fender rattled as it scraped against the tire, and the alignment was messed up. Between that and the wind, she struggled to keep the truck on the road. The right headlight pointed into the trees, and the path ahead was a dim blur even with the wipers running flat out. Something metallic screeched as she turned toward the ferry landing.

A moment later, she spotted a large branch lying across the highway, blocking their path. Kiera's foot instinctively went for the brake, but at the last second, she swerved into the ditch, plowing through the smaller branches in the upper part of the fallen limb. The Tahoe bucked wildly but stayed upright while Zoie hung desperately to the overhead strap, her jaw set in a tight clench. They cleared the ditch after narrowly missing a telephone pole.

Roaring down the road, the ferry landing and the dark waters of Lake Michigan loomed ahead. Two people—Dana and Leah—stepped into the wash of the left headlight as she approached. Thank God they were safe!

The truck skidded to a stop and they clambered into the back seat of the truck, their ponchos and faces soaking wet. Leah, shivering, wrapped her arms into herself.

"Thank you," Dana said, putting a hand on Kiera's shoulder. "God, that was a nightmare."

Dana frowned, staring at Zoie in the passenger seat. "Who's this?"

"This is Zoie," Kiera said "She's a ghost hunter. We literally ran into each other in the lighthouse."

Suddenly Leah blurted, "We have to go! Hurry! Trouble at the lighthouse!"

Kiera gunned the engine and swung the wheel, turning in a tight arc toward the lighthouse. "Why are you guys on foot? Where's the Jeep?"

Driving to the lighthouse, Dana made eye contact with Kiera in the mirror and briefly recounted the horrifying details of their journey after a tree fell on the Jeep. Leah's eyes were closed and she seemed calmer than her mother, more relieved to be out of the elements. Dana didn't blink when they plunged into the ditch and drove through the branches. Oh, the stories they would be able to tell after this.

As they turned onto the lighthouse drive, Kiera startled at the sight of Willow running down the access road toward the Tahoe. What the hell—?

"Stop!" Leah yelled.

As Kiera screeched to a halt, Leah jumped out before Dana could react. She ran to Willow and grabbed her arms. Willow fought back at first, but then appeared to realize she was struggling with a child. Leah was talking—seemed to be imploring Willow to listen.

A minute later, Willow nodded in agreement to something Leah said. Leah led her by the hand to the truck.

As they climbed in, Kiera said, "Willow! What happened?"

Willow lay back, panting and crying, her hair wet and bedraggled. Finally, she said, "A nightmare. A dreadful nightmare."

"What?"

Willow drew a deep breath and leaned forward. "The darkness got into my head and sent me on a bad trip—Leah convinced me that's what it was." She was tightly wrapped, hugging herself and rocking back and forth. She looked like an escapee from an asylum. "It felt so real. It scared the bejesus out of me."

Leah said, "Lachlan explained it to her. I was just the medium. We have to get inside, now."

Kiera stared incredulously. Leah was a five-year-old, talking more like an adult than ever. It wasn't natural—though who in this group was?

She hit the accelerator, rolled up to the doorway, and jumped out, helping Willow into the lighthouse. Zoie, Dana, and Leah followed. Willow still looked haunted and fragile after her experience—yet she was going back in. Kiera marveled at her gutsiness but wondered what fresh hells awaited them inside.

Without opening his eyes or moving his head, Lachlan directed Leah to the fourth corner with a couple of hand gestures. She grabbed the shaker of sorcerer's blue and sprinkled it about her, then placed the amulets just as Lachlan had. His gestures were evidently superfluous as Leah knew exactly what to do.

The room seemed to crackle with electricity as invisible and potent energy coursed through the room. Then, the staircase resonated deeply as if a giant hammer had struck it. Kiera felt that same clash of immense forces she had felt in the cavern, the collision of forces beyond her imagination. The thought resonated through her in a confusing combination of wonder and horror. Suddenly, she felt small and insignificant. An existential bug that could be swatted out of existence at any moment.

Lachlan disturbed her gloomy musings. "Kiera! You need to deal with a problem in the cellar. Let Dana handle the woman in black."

She didn't question Lachlan's directive. She trusted his judgement implicitly, so the task of handling the woman in the tower would fall to Dana. She could handle it. They had talked one night, and Dana outlined an impressive set of defensive skills she had mastered to protect Leah.

But what problem awaited her in the basement? She was afraid to ask.

Kiera led Dana to the tower door and took a cautious peek up the stairs before explaining the mission they'd been given, positioning Zoie as bait and then lurking behind the second floor door with her gun to take the woman out.

Dana's eyes grew wide at first and then hooded as she considered the plan. Finally, she said with menace, "Gladly."

Kiera was relieved to have another helping hand. She was about to ask Dana about her weapons when Fynn's voice boomed, "Draugen! Two or three of them! In the cellar—"

Draugen? What?

Kiera had no clue what he meant. Then Lachlan yelled, "You'll need the Celtic crosses!"

She heard a sound, the shuffling of footsteps on the basement stairs and felt a dawning sense of dread, a feeling like hands twisting her insides with a death grip.

Oh God, no!

A wave of fear and nausea engulfed her. That awful sound still prowled her nightmares a year later.

A man shuffled to the top of the stairs.

Kiera started to step back, and she heard Dana gasp.

What the hell—?

The man was an awful mess, his skin nearly black and covered in soot—he looked like a chimney sweep fresh off the job. His flannel shirt and jeans hung in burnt tatters and his feet were bare. Kiera had a bad feeling.

Zoie's face was contorted in wide-eyed shock. "Jordan! Where were—?"

"You know this guy?" Kiera snapped, voice rising in fear.

"He's been missing for a week."

"Oh, Jesus." Kiera knew in that instant just who and what Jordan had become.

She flinched and bellowed, "Lachlan!"

Fifty-Eight

Tat sat in the lantern room.

Comfortable on her Ouija rug, focused on the burning black candles, she was ready to strike, to maim, to kill—whatever was necessary. She could barely stand the suspense. Crom Cruach was struggling with the strain of fighting the siege, battling on multiple fronts and yet, from what she could tell, still holding the upper hand. He wasn't distracted by the feeble attempts of the intruders, or ghost hunters—whatever they were. Their plans were falling apart, especially after she and Crom had repelled their frontal assault.

Seriously, they thought raising an army of bushes and driving an SUV through the gate was a winning play? She snickered. They had no idea how powerful Crom was, how dangerous. They were mere people! How could they? By daybreak tomorrow, they would all be dead.

Crom had killed the dude named Fynn dramatically. Tat was in absolute awe of those moves. He had grabbed a stray dog and transformed it into a killer wolf. Then he zapped Ric into some living-dead creature and sent him to finish the job. It was crazy, crazy stuff.

The kid and her mother were trapped on the beach. Crom had said he would handle that. Would he kill them or just leave them to die? That thought gave her pause—a little anyway—Tat still uncomfortable with the idea of hurting a child.

Had she made a deal with the Devil?

She shook her head.

No. She had entered into a pact with some dark entity. One of many gods or devils, she suspected. The supreme eternal beings of the world's religions were nothing but myth. In reality, a bunch of players, good and bad, ran loose in the world. They were invisible, except to people like her who were perceptive to their presence. Good and bad were relative—though in her mind, good was lame. This was thrilling. Oh, the shit she could do once Crom finished teaching her!

As the intruders tried to move in, the siege weakened and Crom could again tap energy from the vortex. He assured her the time was coming when she would be needed. She would have her own moment of glory.

She couldn't wait.

Then several discordant notes confused her. Somehow, Fynn had survived the fall from the cliff. How? And the kid and her mother were running again! How had these people survived Crom's powerful magic? Had she underestimated them?

This didn't feel like winning.

Her musing was cut short by a revving motor and a deafening crash. They were attacking again. Tat could barely restrain herself now, sitting with her eyes closed, her fists clenched. She wanted to run down the stairs and kill every one of them. But Crom remained silent.

A while later, Tat heard a trenchant scream followed by hard running footsteps somewhere below.

The call came.

Tat opened her eyes.

It was time. The intruders were in and Crom Cruach intended to crush them now. He had other henchmen in the basement, ready to attack. He had grabbed them off the water, building a force for this very moment. All part of the grand scheme Crom had shared with her to fight for the lighthouse. Let them gain access and then crush them, using his and her combined forces to overwhelm them. While Crom destroyed the wizards, she and the others in the basement would kill any stragglers.

He wanted this over once and for all. He had bigger plans and had tired of skirmishing with these fools over the past two years. Once they were gone, her serious training would begin. Then they would go out into the world and...?

She couldn't even imagine.

Right now, Crom wanted her to go down and slash everyone in her path to bits, starting with the two bitches laying a trap for her at the bottom of the stairs.

So stupid.

Did they honestly think there was anything Crom Cruach couldn't know or foresee? She planned to have fun with this. Let them think she was blithely falling into their trap. Then she would pounce and send them screaming into the next life.

She picked up the sword. Holding it infused her with an incredible sense of power and, most of all, a sense of invincibility. Once this was over, she had a few scores of her own to settle, starting with the assholes in Ric's family. She felt a brief twinge of sadness at the thought of losing him but crushed it ruthlessly. She was better off without Ric.

Tiptoeing down the stairs, Tat saw a woman waiting by the door at the bottom of the staircase.

This would be so much fun.

That bitch had seconds to live.

Fifty-Nine

Kiera spun toward Lachlan.

He tossed a Celtic cross to her without looking or skipping a beat.

She caught it and swung it around in a wide arc, stabbing the creature dead center of the chest.

Wham!

Kiera let loose a primordial scream of revulsion and anger as she shoved the body down the stairs and watched it tumble ass over teakettle, landing with a thump at the bottom of the stairs. Jesus! She prayed that was the only one—

Zoie charged and slammed into her, screaming, "Are you fucking nuts? That was my friend!"

"He was dead!"

Zoie hitched a sob, looking at Kiera with a confused look of anger and fear. "Well, he is now!"

Kiera gripped her wrists and looked into her eyes. "He was already dead. That's why he was missing. It's part of what's going on at the lighthouse."

At first, Zoie struggled with Kiera, trying to free her hands, but calmed down as Kiera continued to reassure her. Her expression was a conflicted mess of fear and confusion, as if she couldn't believe the things Kiera was saying. Why should she? It was crazy, insane.

"He was already dead?" Her face had frozen into a mask of disbelief and horror. Zoie looked like she could pass out at any moment.

Kiera nodded. Damn! The woman was falling apart. She knew including her was a mistake. Too late now. They needed every hand. She knew they had reached a critical juncture in taking this thing down, this darkness. Holding Zoie's shoulders, she donned her best firm-but-kind coaching manner and said, "I can't explain it all. I don't have time, but we really, really need your help right now and I know you can do it. When this is over, I'll explain all of it. Can you do that? Please?"

Zoie nodded slowly, sniffling.

Lachlan yelled, "There are two more of them in the basement! Kiera, you need to stop them!"

Freaking hell! She didn't know if she could face them. Didn't like what she was becoming, some sort of ghoulish monster slayer. She felt adrift and disconnected from reality. Was this what incipient insanity felt like? Lachlan brought her briefly back to earth.

"Kiera!" He tossed her another cross. Kiera grabbed it out of midair and gently pushed Zoie toward the tower, remembering she had a second cross in her pocket.

"Dana!" As she walked over, Kiera pulled her close. "Did you bring your gun?"

Dana produced a pistol and a Taser.

"Oh, awesome! Why don't you give Zoie the Taser?" Kiera said, hoping Zoie might feel more empowered with a weapon in her hand.

Dana handed it to Zoie and explained its simple operation. Hopefully, she wouldn't accidentally tase one of them instead.

"Okay, you guys understand the plan?"

Dana and Zoie nodded convincingly. Kiera turned and walked reluctantly to the basement stairs, hemming and hawing, trying to talk herself into this awful task. Eyeing the front doorway, she considered running. This wasn't a reasonable ask. It was a nightmare—

Lachlan spoke gently, "Kiera, we're all counting on you. You can do it."

She felt a wave pass through her, a calming wave from Lachlan, she was sure. She sighed. Again, he would find a way to get her through this. But where had these awful things been hiding? The basement had been empty when they came through earlier. Then she remembered the odd odor on the stairs. Maybe they had been lurking in the cistern. No matter. They were here now.

Steeling herself, parsing her next move, she thought about waiting on the stairs but decided it was too dangerous to face them on the narrow steps.

Kiera inched down slowly, step by step, acutely sensitive to her surroundings, tuning out all other sounds. The storm and the sounds in the large room above faded, but the staircase wasn't silent. Her heart pounded and blood seemed to rush through her ears. A faint electrical hum replaced the sounds outside. The air smelled musty and dead, filled with the all too familiar smells of rotting flesh. The stench turned her stomach, but it was empty. She eyed the stairwell, hewn from the native rock, while keeping an eye on the body below, alert for even the slightest change around her.

Zoie's friend Jordan lay at the base of the stairs. She couldn't imagine what lay ahead and dreaded finding out. Thinking about it almost paralyzed her with fear, her arms and legs tense, her gait clunky, her insides jittery and awash in adrenaline.

The smell grew more intense. She couldn't hold back any longer and doubled over, retching up a thin stream of bile.

Kiera stopped on the last step, watching the body at her feet, listening intently for any sounds from the basement. Lachlan said there were two more dead things down here, and she had long ago learned to trust him implicitly.

Silence. So they were lying in wait for her.

What had Fynn called them? Draugen? It sounded suitably grim and awful. Kiera envied Dana at that moment. Whatever she was facing, it wasn't as horrific as this promised to be.

She worried most about light. She needed both hands free, but she had to see as well. Holding the Maglite was a liability. In most cases, it could double as a weapon, but not now.

Your gun is worthless here.

So was the damn flashlight. Only the Celtic crosses worked, and they required close-quarter contact. She wanted to hit fast and run.

Best to get rid of the light.

She looked down at Jordan and quickly had an idea followed by another jolt of nausea.

He looked awful close up, his skin burned all over, his eyes yellowed and cloudy, showing signs of decomposition, smelling of some gross combination of roast pork and death.

She gritted her teeth, leaned over, and propped the Maglite between Jordan's chest and his dead arm so it pointed into the room.

Then she heard a shuffle. Kiera jerked back and reached into her pocket. Pulling out a smaller flashlight, she side-armed it into the basement. It clattered across the floor but thankfully stayed lit.

Feet scraped in the basement. With a cross in each hand, she hazarded a look around the corner. Two of them stood, their backs to her, evidently drawn by the light she had tossed. They were well illuminated by the beam of the light propped up on Jordan.

With one silent step, Kiera pivoted and leapt. Bringing the Celtic cross in her right hand swooping down, she buried it in the back of the guy closest to her, a short dude wearing a windbreaker and a rain cap.

He arced his back in reaction to the cross plunging deep into his back. Kiera hesitated, fearing she'd made a mistake and killed a living person, but then he collapsed in a heap, just like the others. No blood. No final gasp. He was already dead.

The moment of hesitation proved nearly fatal. The other Draugen—a tall, heavy guy in fishing gear—swiveled in a lightning fast move and grabbed her by the neck as he mumbled, "Not so fast, bitch!"

Sixty

Dana understood perfectly.

Kiera's plan was simplicity itself. Zoie would stand by the door between the first floor and the tower. She was essentially bait but Kiera had instructed her to back away before the woman drew too close. Dana would hide behind the tower door on the second floor, ready to slip down the stairs behind the woman, primed to disarm or kill her, whatever the situation demanded. Thank God the builders had put a door on each level, giving them the option of surprise. Any other approach would have been too dangerous if the story about the sword was true.

Zoie was already in position, but Dana worried her nerve would fail, having just watched Kiera jam a cross into her friend's chest and shove him down the stairs. How could the woman process such insanity? Zoie was either too stunned to react or had a resilient nature. They would find out which soon enough.

Hell, Dana was struggling to process it. She should have felt more shocked, but she had seen something like it before. How awful was that? She was becoming accustomed to the horror. She flashed back to the last night at her parents' house two years before. One of the few things she remembered was her Aunt Ashley rising from the dead like this Jordan dude, a vision that continued to be a source of many of her worst nightmares. Then again, maybe the nightmares meant she wasn't becoming inured after all.

Dana was just thrilled to have a chance to strike back. She had trained tirelessly for this moment. Until now, she had been merely an observer, unable to make a meaningful contribution to the effort. Little more than a bodyguard to Leah. This thing—whatever they called it—had cost her so much: her mother, her father, her aunt. She had never imagined having the opportunity to exact revenge and she was fully down with wreaking some good old-fashioned vengeance on it.

Dana heard a faint ping as the iron frame of the spiral stairs shifted under the weight of somebody stepping on them.

"Thank God," she whispered, relieved she didn't have to wait long. No chance for her mind to descend into runaway anxiety. Though armed and trained in self-defense, was she skilled enough to deal with a woman wielding some kind of supernatural sword? Sweet Jesus, when would this nightmare be over? For two years she had lived under the shadow of this *thing*. So while she was nervous, Dana was also supremely angry. Leah had been in danger far too many times. Her mother had fought to the bitter end and died for them. If need be, she would do the same for Leah. Zoie had just lost her friend here. Hopefully, she was angry too. Anger was a great motivator.

Thus far, Zoie was holding steadfast.

The door ajar, Dana peered through the narrow crack, watching, waiting to act. Even with the storm outside, she could hear a faint creak in the ironwork every time the woman took a step. Kiera had only a minute to explain the plan but had made one thing clear: Dana should assume the worst, that the woman couldn't easily be killed.

The woman slithered past her door and down the last flight of stairs, the sword aimed forward, without a glance toward the door, a confident walk like nothing could stop her.

Dana let her take another three or four steps. Slipping through the door, she moved like a cat across the landing and down the first few stairs in stockinged feet, stepping in sync with the woman ahead of her. Her Beretta led the way.

The woman didn't hesitate, gave no indication she suspected any presence at all.

Dana felt coiled tight like a clock spring. She should just kill her now, but Dana didn't really know what she was dealing with. The woman looked so normal—beyond the sword in her hand. She hesitated, feeling that with the element of surprise on her side, maybe she could take the woman by non-fatal means. Punching her in the face sounded far more satisfying than shooting her in the back—though perhaps she was waffling because she had never killed anyone and wasn't sure she could do it now.

She was about to find out.

These thoughts rushed through her brain in a microsecond while she stopped, set a stance, and tightened her grip on the Beretta.

Dana was about to speak—to demand the woman stop—when the plan went awry.

Sixty-One

Kiera couldn't breathe.

She could scarcely move. The Draug was taller and had perfect leverage on her neck with a single-handed ironclad grip.

In a minute, she would be dead.

She had dropped the second cross when the thing grabbed her. With her neck in the vice-like hold, she couldn't swivel her head to search for it and couldn't reach down and grope for it.

She tried not to give in to despair.

Think! Think! Think!

There had to be something.

Your gun is worthless here.

Like hell it was!

Kiera grabbed the Sig from her pocket, slammed it against the underside of the creature's arm and fired. The blast was deafening and spattered her with dead tissue. She slid the barrel a bit, closed her eyes, and fired. The creature did not respond. She moved the gun a bit more and fired.

The death-grip on her neck let loose, the creature's wrist and hand now a useless appendage, hanging by the threads of tissue that had survived the bullets.

Kiera spotted the Celtic cross.

Ha!

As she fell sideways to grab it, the Draugen grabbed her with its good hand. Their combined momentum sent them sprawling to the ground. The creature fell on her as her hand closed around the cross, the dead weight trapping her face down on the floor.

Kiera groaned as the air rushed from her lungs. The body had to weigh three hundred pounds, maybe more. Unable to move, one arm wedged beneath her, the creature's shoulder pressed against the other arm. In that position, the cross in her hand was useless.

No matter how hard she struggled and squirmed, Kiera couldn't budge the heavy body lying on top of her. Almost as if the beast had decided trapping her was sufficient, that no further effort was required.

If it was simply dead again, then even the cross was useless. She tried to call out, but she was having trouble breathing and only squeezed out a raspy whisper.

Kiera could move her head a bit and spied a crevice in the stone floor. Turning the cross, she stabbed the point into the crevice. It sank almost to the hilt.

Yes!

She squeezed the cross and pulled with all her might, feeling the cross cutting into her hand.

Nothing. Still no leverage.

But half her right leg was free. She flailed it about, looking for leverage.

A wasted effort.

The thing remained inert and she was irrevocably trapped. It smelled foul and something dripped from its head into her hair. Convinced it had died again—an insane thought since this person was already dead—nausea welled up and she coughed out a few bubbles of bile that pooled against the cheek squished into the floor, deepening her misery.

She felt an onrushing wave of hysteria. Trapped here like this, she wouldn't last long. The others were fighting something powerful and dangerous and were too preoccupied to sense her plight.

Physical fight, mental bravado, none of it was working.

Never one to quit, she rested for a few seconds and tried to relax, fighting against overwhelming panic to be mindful, willing the situation to change. Upstairs, someone chanted, and she thought she heard yelling, none of it discernable as words. She felt abandoned, but she understood. They had far bigger problems to deal with. Still, she didn't want to die here alone.

Kiera threw every bit of energy she possessed into moving the immovable.

Squirming her body, pulling and yanking her arms, hoping to free them, shoving the free leg every which way, a violent last-ditch effort to save herself. The body atop her wobbled slightly but remained firmly planted, wedging her in place against the floor. It seemed to grow heavier, pressing down harder. The darkness squeezing her with every intention of killing her.

She wasn't psychic, but she had sent a message to Fynn earlier. He heard her then. Would it work again?

The message was simple—she whispered the words as she imagined screaming them.

Fynn! Help me!

Sixty-Two

A subtle shift of the shoulder.

Dana tensed in anticipation—it was a warning. The woman was about to strike.

The next seconds played out like some weird slow-motion film.

Zoie stepped backward through the doorway as Dana carefully aimed her gun, finger on the trigger, and opened her mouth to speak. The door started to close.

While there was no hesitation in the woman's gait, she swiveled abruptly and jumped up three steps in some crazy ninja move, spinning so hard and so fast that Dana startled in response and fired high. The loud gunshot echoed up the tower as the sharp stainless blade scythed inexorably toward her at chest level. Dana snapped her gun to the right in a blocking motion as she ducked.

The sword slammed into the gun barrel, deflecting the blade upward, the impact sending the gun flying and skittering along the floor to the wall, far out of reach.

As forward momentum carried the blade through an arc and safely out of the way, Dana struck back with her own ninja move, twisting and spinning, her leg flying around in a reverse roundhouse kick, the back of her heel making hard and exquisite contact with the woman's head.

She flew sideways and tumbled down the stairs, losing the sword as she fell and slammed her head into the wall. Zoie stood transfixed, staring from the doorway.

Dana leapt to the floor and gave the sword a toe nudge, yelling, "Zoie! Grab it!"

Then she leapt forward to pin the woman. In a surprisingly swift move, the woman rolled at Dana, swinging a solid roundhouse, punching Dana just under the eye and knocking her backward onto the floor. The blow stunned her, her vision a blaze of stars.

As Dana shook her head and spotted the gun, it vaporized into dust.

"Fuck!" Dana recoiled. She was damned lucky the sword hit the gun and not her! Zoie hadn't exaggerated at all!

The woman rolled the other way and tried to grab the sword, but Zoie had snatched it and slammed the door in her face.

As Dana pushed off the wall, the woman ran up the stairs. Dana gave chase, afraid she would take the second floor door and circle back after Zoie.

★ ★ ★

Tat had fucked up.

Badly.

What looked like a simple slash and burn attack had been turned upside down.

The sword was gone. So was the gun, thankfully.

Now she risked being drawn in to hand-to-hand combat with the other woman. Those two women should be dead. Instead, one of them had the sword and the other one appeared to be well-versed in self-defense and martial arts. If Tat only knew her name, she could simply bind her. She called to Crom for an answer, but she also worried she had angered him.

Somehow, she had to turn the tables back in her favor and kill the bitch. And she had to get the sword back.

Tat had gotten off one lucky punch but feared the woman's skills.

Right now, she felt defenseless and insecure. Off-balance with only one option.

Run.

★ ★ ★

The woman ran and Dana leapt, grabbing her ankle, pulling her down. Dana scrambled up, but the woman looked back, lashed out with her foot, and kicked Dana in the face.

Dana fell backward and rolled down two steps while the woman ran up another three or four, past the second floor door. Dana charged hard—she was clearly faster—and yanked the woman's feet from beneath her with a swift forearm sweep as she closed the distance between them.

The woman went down hard, but she was fit and wiry. She looked muscular too—yoga or something. She swung hard but Dana dodged the fist and lunged, then lost her footing and nearly slipped over the edge.

Jesus! The lack of a railing and that drop were a real hazard she had best not ignore again!

The woman was already clambering crablike up the steps. She turned and scrabbled up the remaining steps using her hands and her feet, almost like a dog, and collapsed onto the platform of the lantern room.

As Dana reached the top of the stairs, the woman grabbed something and swung it at her—a wine bottle. Dana ducked but the bottle glanced off the top of her head and sent her sprawling backward down the stairs. She landed a foot from the edge of the steps and a much longer drop.

Whoa!

As Dana leapt to her feet, the woman eyed Dana curiously from the top of the steps.

"Dana, is it?" The woman pushed her hands out in a shoving motion.

Dana's forward progress abruptly slowed to a crawl, as if her body had been encased in heavy water. All her motions were difficult and labored. No matter how hard she struggled against the binding hex, she could barely move, and she certainly couldn't defend herself. The woman walked down slowly toward her, smiling, sliding a thin knife from behind her back, from a pocket or a stealthy sheath, perhaps.

Her smile was evil, devoid of any warmth, the smirk of a psychopath who would slice her up without compunction; so intent on murder, so confident in herself, that killing Dana would be no more consequential than carving a turkey.

The woman fondled the knife and closed in for the kill.

Fully immobile now, there was nothing Dana could do.

She had seconds to live—feared Leah would lose yet another mother.

Dana knew it was her fault. She should have just shot the bitch instead of equivocating.

A regret she would take to the grave.

★ ★ ★

Tat concentrated and the woman's name came to her, sent by Crom.

"Dana is it?" Tat shoved her hands out, palms forward. She felt like she was regaining the upper hand. She concentrated and mentally squeezed Dana in a tight binding spell until she stood, suspended in space, almost like a mannequin.

Tat smiled. Dana's face was rendered in slow motion and gradually twisted into a look of terror and resignation. The bitch knew she was dead. Good! Tat slipped the knife from its sheath and took one slow step after another, relishing the moment.

A head appeared, coming up the stairs, catching Tat by surprise. She had almost forgotten about the little pixie at the door downstairs.

A jolt of fear stabbed through her. What if she had the sword?

But she was holding something smaller in her hand.

Tat heard a *pop* and her body convulsed as the electrodes struck and an electric charge ripped through her.

Her legs failed and she toppled forward.

★ ★ ★

Zoie didn't know it was possible to be so terrified and still able to move. She crept up the stairs, one step at a time, her left hand clinging to the handrail, the right clamped to the Taser in a death grip. She really wanted to run screaming from this awful place, but felt obligated to watch Dana's back. Maybe she could take out the crazy sword lady, too.

As she circled up the stairs, Zoie spied Dana in her peripheral vision. She seemed frozen in place, in a trance. What in the hell was she doing?

Then she saw the bitch who had stabbed Greg stepping toward Dana. The woman slipped a knife from behind her back.

Zoie's eyes narrowed and focused. It was payback time, but her hand was shaking almost uncontrollably. She steadied it with the other hand, and, as the woman looked her way, squeezed the trigger.

Pop!

The woman's eyes flew wide as her body arched rigid and the blade fell from her hand.

Released from her trance, Dana stepped up and punched the woman in the face as she fell. The blow smashed her delicate nose, her body collapsing on the iron stairs with enough diagonal momentum to send her over the edge.

For a moment, Zoie thought she was gone and stared at the empty space in shock and horror.

She then saw a hand clinging to the edge of the step. She automatically jumped forward into a crouch to help, but the woman in black reached up, grabbed her hair, and pulled her down.

Zoie screamed as she pitched forward and stared down the long drop to certain death.

A microsecond later, Dana grabbed her foot and yanked hard, pulling Zoie back onto the steps and into her lap.

Zoie rolled her head and looked up at Dana, who said, "You okay?"

Too shocked to speak, Zoie nodded.

Dana then lashed out with her boot, kicking the hand grasping the step into the abyss, the woman's shrill scream cut short by the thump of her body hitting the stone floor like a wet sack of cement.

Sixty-Three

Kiera finally succumbed to despair.

No one was coming.

She would die here. Her breathing was difficult and shallow, and her vision was growing fuzzy, almost like falling into sleep. She saw Josh in vivid relief, the ex-boyfriend she still pined for, and Ghost, a companion who was so much more than a dog. He had become her emotional support buddy, a better friend than most of her supposed friends. She would never see them again. Tears leaked from her eyes and she cursed her predicament and her weakness. She knew that she might die today—in the abstract at least—but had imagined some stellar moment, a final blaze of glory, not this ignominious death, crushed beneath a big dead guy.

Still, if they prevailed, if they killed this thing, would losing her life be worth it? She didn't know. Would never know the outcome now, but she trusted Lachlan and Fynn to finish it. This would be the only accomplishment she left behind. With no child and no husband, she would leave nothing else, not a single mark beyond some obscure papers in various journals of archeology. Hopefully, someone would give her a decent burial. Her sister could pretend to mourn her...

Her fading consciousness merged into the nightmares that often haunted her sleep. Dead creatures in the cavern, reaching for her, squeezing her breath away.

Her body slumped. The fight left her.

Felt her consciousness fading—

The dead weight atop her suddenly wobbled. The body rolled on its side and flopped on the floor, freeing her.

A smiling Fynn stood above her. He extended his hand. "Come, lassie, we have work to do."

Kiera drew in a deep breath and stood slowly, her body a tangle of aches and kinks from the prolonged time trapped beneath the dead man. She twisted her head and stretched her arms. Nothing was broken, though her ribs felt bruised.

"Thank you—"

Fynn's smile morphed to a grimace as the Draugen grabbed his waistband and threw him against the wall. As it turned and cast its dead gaze upon Kiera, she realized she was still clutching the Celtic cross in her right hand.

No fucking way would she go through that again!

Kiera lunged forward, shoving the Draugen back. It got tangled up in Fynn's legs and fell to the floor. She jumped atop it and swung the cross down, burying the metal stem in the left eye of the beast with an angry grunt.

The Draugen slumped, limp and inert. She pushed away from it and fell to the floor next to Fynn, exhausted by the struggle and her near-death experience just moments before.

Turning his head, Fynn smiled. With a look of admiration, he said, "Lachlan is right. You are a fearsome woman, Kiera O'Donnell."

He stood and held a hand out. "We should probably go up now."

Kiera gave the basement a final nervous glance, drew a deep breath and trudged up the stairs behind Fynn, praying to God this would soon be over.

Sixty-Four

Lachlan held the cargástriftr high.

He sensed Fynn returning to his position and linking up with the sídrand, throwing his considerable energy into the fray. Kiera stood guard by the cellar steps and Dana watched the tower, both armed and ready to deal with unexpected intruders. Finally, the woman in black and the Draugen were gone, eliminated. Outside, the storm raged on. Rain, pushed by stronger gusts, occasionally strayed in through the broken windows. A near-steady rumble of thunder accompanied frequent, vivid lightning.

Facing no distractions, they had now established an ironclad sphere of energies, severing any link between the node and Crom Cruach.

Roughly aligned along the ley lines in the room, Lachlan, Willow, Leah, and Fynn were situated at ninety degrees from each other and seventeen degrees west of due north. Lachlan realized the position of the lighthouse was no accident. Why hadn't he seen it sooner?

The builders might have been aware of the ley lines or, more likely, influenced subliminally by the alignment of the energies around them. They had built not only a signal light for shipping but also a beacon for one of the stronger nodal points in North America. The Native Americans had recognized the significance of this place and given it a fitting name later appropriated by the early French trappers and military.

Having aligned themselves this way, they also drew the maximum power from the vortex, the process further enhanced by the nearby low-pressure center—both rotating counterclockwise in tandem. The energies flowing through the lighthouse were immense, the kinds of energy that could split atoms and power entire cities. Lachlan had never witnessed or imagined anything like it.

★ ★ ★

Willow was in serious pain. From sitting too long on the island; from her misadventures during the trip back; from the enormous effort she was pouring into this siege. The darkness kept trying to creep into her consciousness, but she was more adept at deflecting the attacks with guidance from Lachlan.

This experience was so different from last year when she had acted merely as a mirror. Now she was a full partner, locked into a psychic ring with Lachlan, Fynn, and Leah. She felt a physical connection with them, like a cable linking her brain and consciousness with the others. And via that connection came a deeper sense of the others, of their feelings, their determination.

The connection to Lachlan was the strongest, and through him, she could visualize the lines of the energies around the lighthouse, a glowing wheel, a subset of the vortex rotating over the Porte des Morts passage. Inside that smaller vortex, they had created a sphere, the sídrand. And within that, they had finally confined the darkness and were forcing it up and out of the bedrock—literally dragging it into the light.

The visions were vivid, a transcendent experience, like leaving the earth behind and soaring high into space. And despite the pain, she was fueled by righteous anger at the awful visions Crom Cruach had tormented her with. He would not survive the synergy of their combined efforts.

That's how Lachlan felt, and she trusted him implicitly.

It was just a matter of time.

★ ★ ★

On the brink of success, Lachlan knew they could not lessen their grip, become complacent, or celebrate prematurely. A beast more formidable than any he had ever encountered opposed them. He now understood why Kenric had misread the situation in the MacKenzie house and died. Why he himself had underestimated this opponent last year and had failed to destroy it, nearly losing his life. Wrapped within that darkness, hidden within a layer of protection or cloaking, lay a being both ancient and tyrannically evil.

Anna Flecher hadn't invoked just any demon to carry out her invocation on the MacKenzies. She had invoked one of the most feared deities of the ancient world, a murderous creature who had once demanded gruesome human sacrifices from his adherents. Lachlan was lucky to have survived their encounter last year. But luckier to have so much help now. Crom Cruach had proven to be diabolically versatile in juggling a multifaceted defense, including the Draugen and the woman in black.

A worry lingered. Crom Cruach had demonstrated a remarkable ability to survive on minimal resources, to slip through any gap within the five-dimensional framework of the energies. To escape, survive, and to fight again.

Thus, he had to be captured and caged, worn down and crushed out of existence.

Only then would this be over.

He didn't need to speak to relay this information to the others. They were psychically connected. They understood.

And they were close to success.

Crom Cruach was now trapped within the sídrand. Each of them was extraordinarily focused on maintaining pressure on the darkness with a circular force-field that was as strong as the magnetic field in a particle accelerator—an invisible cage of extraordinary strength that now occupied the center of the room. There, an amorphous shadow about three feet in diameter was visible, the physical form of Crom Cruach, who still resisted them with tremendous tenacity, seeking any escape.

None remained.

Outdoors, the storm seethed. The room was cold and the lights were fading as the batteries wore down.

No matter. They would stand here all night—in the dark if necessary.

As long as it took.

★ ★ ★

Fynn had locked precisely ninety-five percent of his awareness into the sídrand and the remainder into scanning the environment for any changes or intruders that might upend their efforts. He also allowed a little consciousness to wander idly. He bored easily and this tendril of thought helped preserve his sanity during long ceremonies like this. His attentions kept alighting on the face of Kiera O'Donnell. She was a beautiful woman. Intelligent. Incredibly resourceful. She—

Why was he thinking like this?

He was ancient. It was nonsense. Besides, she was besotted by the memory of a daft fellow named Josh who had walked out on her over some minor issue in their life. These thoughts made no sense.

Yet another, small piece of his consciousness probed the sídrand and the shell that contained the darkness within. Crom Cruach had adapted a novel approach in an attempt to survive the unsurvivable, one Fynn had never seen before.

Clearly well versed in alchemy, Crom Cruach had used it to build a lattice around himself composed of carbon. At least Fynn thought it was carbon, and it had interesting properties. As they compressed the lattice, it grew stronger.

With that realization, Fynn felt a twinge of unease. The cage they had built housed a second cage, hidden within the amorphous black cloud.

One that might ultimately prove indestructible.

Sixty-Five

Lachlan sensed the unease.

He dismissed it immediately. They couldn't allow a hint of doubt into their rites, lest it weaken the sídrand.

While Lachlan guided the process, they were a collective and, as such, immensely powerful. Lachlan had never done this before. Generally, they worked in pairs. Rarely they would use a third, but he had never managed to connect four minds into one psychic apparatus—what the modern techies called a hive mind.

It was a monument to the power of three disparate realms: physics, psychic energy, and the human mind. As impressive as any device ever designed by man and yet, one the world at large would never know about. That was one of the central tenets of Aeldo philosophy: to never share their ceremonies, their skills, or any of their formulas. Any of it would be very dangerous in the wrong hands or the hands of unskilled practitioners.

As they compressed the darkness, a great moaning filled the room, a sound like nothing he had ever heard. Perhaps it was the collected pain and sadness of the souls trapped within the darkness all these years. Were they now being set free as they crushed Crom Cruach to zero? Perhaps some vestige of Anna Flecher remained, a bitter spirit crying out as her life's work was destroyed.

He often mused, wondering what would happen when the last of the Aeldo died. It was sad to contemplate, but he now saw a future in Leah. He took a moment to pass a small mental gift to her in case he didn't make it—although that outcome seemed increasingly unlikely.

They were winning.

Slowly, by imperceptible degrees, the confining sphere shrank and, in some improbable way, transitioned to ever darker shades of black. Crom Cruach, until now only visible as an absence of light, was being transformed by the pressure into a physical form.

The moaning voices pitched up to a keening wail. The building shuddered more violently—not from movement in the earth, but from the cosmic streams of energy colliding and crushing the space at the center of the room with incredible pressure. A burgeoning crack appeared in the outer wall of the keeper's house. Something heavy crashed to the floor above with a thunderous racket, perhaps part of the roof. The ground itself shook sporadically with minor tremors.

Sensing alarm from Willow and distraction in Leah, Lachlan admonished, "Concentrate!"

★ ★ ★

Leah wanted to sleep. She could imagine her bed, the soft feeling of the sheets, the warmth. Fynn and Lachlan continued sending waves of encouragement, but she was tired and cold, and struggling to stay awake. Someone or something was trying to worm its way into her brain as well. She pushed back, but the effort was tiring, making it harder to focus with the others.

The probing came from the cloud in the center of the room, a weirdly shaped black fog. The sensation felt like rough fingers or claws, digging, searching for an opening, wanting into her head at any cost.

The lights went out.

Flashes of lightning lit the room and, as her eyes adjusted, it looked like a scary old movie on TV, dark and grainy. Alone and under water, she looked desperately for Mom and the others, then spotted them far above, beyond some barrier like the rippling surface of a pool as seen from beneath. The room had grown impossibly tall. Leah drifted down until her feet settled on a hard surface. Her mind was still tied to the others, but they had no idea she was gone.

Leah tensed as the dim image of a woman resolved out of the dark, her arms out, hair floating in the water. Her back to Leah, she looked familiar. And dead.

Something moved at the murky edges of the room.

A fin?

A shark!

Her body locked rigid with terror.

Without warning, the predator swept in and bit the woman's arm off.

Leah screamed a silent scream.

The shark swam a loop before darting back and attacking the body, biting it in half, leaving a floating arm, two legs, and a head.

Leah could no longer bear to watch, but her head was locked in place, her eyes glued open as so often happened in nightmares. She couldn't make it stop, couldn't scream, couldn't call out as the water turned bloody red.

The floating head slowly turned and, as it did, Leah sucked in a terrified gasp.

Mom!

Her fear and panic were absolute. She prayed to faint, to die, anything to make it stop. As the shark circled around, its cold, dead eyes fell on her. It intended to tear her apart, too.

Frozen in terror as it approached, she screamed bloody murder in her head.

Help!

A voice shouted over her scream: *Leah!*

Mom?

Open your eyes! It's not real!

When she did, she flashed back to reality in the room with the others.

Oh, thank God!

The nightmare was over. But how did Mom know?

An odd, fleeting sensation in her head calmed her nerves. It felt like a gift.

Then Lachlan yelled, "Concentrate!"

★ ★ ★

Lachlan remained focused and resolute.

The minutes and hours ticked by, the storm raged, fatigue set in, but he stood fast, determined to end this tonight.

As they compressed the sphere, the resistance from Crom Cruach grew more intense in what felt like an inverse relationship. More and more energy was needed to continue crushing the darkness. Even with the broken windows, the room was becoming quite warm from the energy fluxing through it. Sweat beaded on Lachlan's forehead. The darkness grew blacker and more solid, now resembling a rough chunk of coal the size of a basketball.

As the sphere shrank further, the crunching sounds of collapsing matter filled the room. The mournful wails grew more sorrowful—if that were possible. Perhaps Crom Cruach himself had joined in.

Lachlan had no idea how long they held that configuration, pushing with steady, inexorable pressure. The orb slowly shrank and changed in state to a glassier material resembling obsidian. The crack in the wall grew longer and wider. The cast iron staircase resonated with a deep hum followed by a resounding *clang*. It collapsed moments later onto the floor of the lighthouse with a massive, noisy crash of metal and stone.

Lachlan heard a frightened yelp from someone. Dana appeared unharmed but she and Zoie bolted away from the tower and nearer to Kiera, who stood alert and steadfast by the cellar stairs.

Time seemed to hang, to stand still. The lights grew ever dimmer.

A further transformation took place and the sphere condensed into a black diamond roughly the size of a golf ball—Lachlan only knew it was a diamond because Fynn scanned it and verified the details. As it collapsed, the entire bluff shuddered, the rock beneath the lighthouse shifting in response to the immense energy flux and the physical changes taking place in the center of the room.

With that, Lachlan and Fynn winced with a collective twinge of fear. The diamond crystal—a tetrahedral lattice of carbon atoms—was the strongest possible atomic structure. There was nothing harder and Crom Cruach was now protected within it.

They could cleave it open—maybe—but that would only release the beast, not end it.

Had they reached a barrier that couldn't be breached, like the speed of light?

Would this be a standoff? A stalemate? No winner, no loser?

Lachlan refused to accept such an outcome, even though it had taken their maximum efforts to reach this stage. Lachlan didn't know what else they could do. They had brought every ounce of energy to bear, but Crom Cruach had not only refused to concede, he had found a way to transform himself into an indestructible object. Lachlan imagined him lurking inside, laughing at their inability to end this yet again!

"Push harder!" he yelled. His hands were clenched in tight fists gripping the cargástriftr, his jaw sore, his back and legs cramping. Lachlan sensed the same supreme level of effort from the others. He imagined they, too, were weary and in pain. Still, he barked, "More pressure! We need more pressure!"

Enormous waves crashed against the bluff and the keeper's house shook with each impact. The wind moaned and screamed like the dead souls in the room. This lighthouse had survived for over a hundred years on a rock that had stood for millions of years. Despite that, Lachlan felt it might crumble at any moment. Then he remembered Stikla and her fearsome weapon.

"Kiera! Bring me the sword!"

She appeared a moment later, looking wild and disheveled, one eye and her neck bruised with various shades of red and purple.

She handed him the sword of Stikla and retreated to the cellar stairs. He slowly lifted and turned it, aligning the blade parallel to the cargástriftr. This further concentrated the energies pressing on Crom Cruach. It was almost as if Stikla herself, the fiercest of all Norse *skjaldmö* or shield-maidens, stood there fighting with them.

Still, the strain was incredible. They couldn't hold this much longer. What if it wasn't enough—?

Lachlan thought he heard a laugh followed by a mocking voice speaking in an old tongue. *Chì mi thu sa bheàrn!*

I'll see you in Hell!

Crom Cruach?

Suddenly, the entire building and the rock they stood upon trembled violently, a quake of considerable magnitude.

The black diamond imploded with a brilliant white flash of light. The instantaneous shock wave stunned Lachlan and threw him backwards into the wall. He dropped the knife and sword as his mind teetered at the edge of consciousness.

The room filled with smoke and the acrid smell of sulfur. For a moment, Lachlan was blind, the flash burned onto his retina like an image of the midday sun.

But it didn't feel like success. Some dark aura hung over the room.

Indeed. He feared they were about to die.

Sixty-Six

Crom Cruach was losing.

The enveloping pressure of the sídrand was crushing him to nothing. Into oblivion. No matter how hard he fought and pushed back, he couldn't escape the encircling forces. Cut off from the vortex, he was bleeding the energy he needed to survive and continue the fight.

As a last resort, he had thrown up a defense, a latticework of carbon that grew progressively stronger as they bore down on him. It was a desperate measure, an attempt to buy time, but ultimately self-defeating. While the cage was indestructible, he couldn't survive much longer within it. Even if he did, he wasn't sure he wanted to. It would become an eternal prison cell. They couldn't breach it, but compressed to this degree, he couldn't escape it either.

Slowly fading, he was out of tricks and ruses. This was the end.

Crom Cruach felt no regret, no sadness. None of those emotions existed in his nature. He was a visceral being, a creature of appetites. What point was there in living if he could no longer satisfy his multitude of desires?

He had enjoyed a glorious run, though. Once the most feared

deity in the medieval world, he had ruled over the pagan Celts of northwestern Europe until St. Patrick banished him. But that was just geography, albeit in five dimensions. Sanctimonious old Patrick had failed to destroy him and Anna Flecher—the only witch powerful enough to call him back—had given him a second life on earth.

He had expected more, craved more, especially after being released from the brick tomb in the old MacKenzie house. He had been so close to breaking away from these meddlesome sorcerers—a bunch of pretentious old bastards with an equally pretentious name: The Elders.

Bah! He silently cursed them in disgust: *Ruith don bheàrn!*

But they were empty words. These sorcerers were crushing him to infinite nothingness. They were winning.

This was a different experience from his loss to St. Patrick, and he would only learn his fate once he left this world—if he wasn't simply annihilated.

He did feel that someday, somewhere in the future, some desperate soul would give him life again. The word *hope* wasn't in his vocabulary. He only cared about certainties, but right now, the physical changes taking place were excruciating. The pressure and pain had grown to a level more unbearable than the exhalation of a fire-breathing dragon. He needed to end it, but not with ignominy. He preferred the grand statement, a blaze of glory.

And if he could kill the wizards? Their deaths would be a bonus.

With a sudden, brilliant flash of insight, he conceived a final maneuver, one transcendent ploy that would give him the last word. An ancient solution to his dilemma. A master stroke of retribution and one they would never see coming.

One they couldn't even *imagine*.

Ironically, the crushing pressure they were exerting would actually facilitate his ultimate revenge. The idea had a certain finesse.

He would employ alchemy, the ancient study of substances in magic and astrology and their interactions. It was also a skill, the practice of changing worthless minerals and ores into valuable metals like gold or silver. He had once been a master alchemist, but it was an imperfect science. The results were unstable and the newly created metals invariably reverted to base substances after a few hours, a day at best. Still, it would last long enough for his purposes.

His stratagem would destroy them in minutes.

And in that time, they could contemplate their impending deaths, knowing there would be no reprieve.

Crom Cruach concentrated and spoke the necessary words, casting an invocation to end all invocations, inverting the molecular structure of the surrounding diamond lattice into a small sphere with incredible destructive power.

This might be the end of him, but they weren't getting out alive, either.

He laughed, a sound his subjects had once described as more awful than the howl of a demented jackal.

As the spell bound him and transformed him into something entirely new, Crom Cruach spoke his final words aloud, a curse to send them to a hell beyond Hell.

"Chì mi thu sa bheàrn!"

Sixty-Seven

Lachlan collapsed to the floor.

Water sprayed in through the broken windows as an enormous wave washed over the bluff and the lighthouse. The building shuddered under the impact of the water but held fast. As the wave receded, the keeper's house grew silent. Even the storm outdoors seemed to have abated. The smells of ozone and sulfur lingered, and Lachlan heard an assortment of moans and groans from around the room.

What in the hell had just happened? Had Crom Cruach escaped yet again?

Slowly, his vision returned. Stunned and exhausted by the enormous day-long effort, he was grateful to be alive. The room seemed brighter, the lights stronger than before. Still, the dark feeling that followed the implosion lingered as he sat up.

An aura of danger.

While things were momentarily quiet, they didn't feel finished. If he had learned one thing, it was to never underestimate this monster. He had no desire to spend the rest of his days wondering if the darkness still lurked somewhere, waiting for an opportunity to kill Leah and

Dana. He wanted proof, but they would have to proceed warily and be vigilant in finding it.

The others looked similarly stunned, varying degrees of shock reflected in their faces.

Fynn had been knocked off his feet and pulled himself slowly to a sitting position with a shake of the head. Willow sat with her head in her hands. Kiera and Zoie were peering from the cellar stairs, perhaps wondering if it was safe to step out as Dana rushed over to her daughter.

Leah appeared to be the least affected. Dana embraced her but Leah didn't lean into her mother's hug. Instead, she stared at the center of the room with peculiar intensity, a quizzical expression on her face.

To Lachlan, the center of the room looked empty. He scratched his head. What was she seeing?

Without looking up, her hands tented over her forehead, Willow said, "Is it over?"

"I don't know." Lachlan tried to follow Leah's line of sight. She was focused on something, but Lachlan saw nothing.

Fynn said, "We must have—"

"No, we didn't," Leah said firmly. She pointed. "Look."

At first, Lachlan saw nothing. He tipped his head slightly, focusing on the center of the room with an unaffected part of his retina. Then he saw it. At least he thought he saw something—a tiny floating black speck, like the dot of an *i*. But was it an object? For all he knew, it could be a hole punched into the three-dimensional fabric of the room. The day had been that strange.

Then Fynn spotted it. Squinting, he said, "Jesus, Joseph, and Mary. What in the hell is that?

"I have no idea," Lachlan said, shaking his head. "And when did you become a ruddy Catholic?"

"I'm not, but I *am* Irish. Almost the same thing."

"Wannabe Irish," Lachlan mumbled derisively. "You were born in Kent!"

Fynn stuck his tongue out dismissively.

Willow stood and admonished them. "Settle down, boys."

Lachlan inched forward, feeling anxious but curious while Willow crept in from her corner, stopping ten feet short of the tiny floating speck. "If I didn't know better, I'd say it's something freaky, like a mini black hole or something."

"That's a crazy leap," Kiera said tersely. Walking over from the stairs, she peered at the orb with a nervous, skeptical eye. "A miniature black hole is highly unlikely."

Willow scanned Kiera's injuries. "Jesus, lady. You look worse than I feel."

Fynn spoke. "Do you know what it is, Kiera?"

Lachlan stopped, noticing a barely perceptible halo around the tiny orb. It appeared to be swirling or fizzing maybe—some atmospheric disturbance near the anomalous speck. Perhaps stray air molecules were being drawn into and reacting with the object. He knew a bit about black holes. He had read the Stephan Hawking books, though he didn't fully understand them. He did understand the intense gravity fields around black holes. But wouldn't they all just get sucked in then?

No, this was something worse. He feared Crom Cruach had found a way to have the final say.

Kiera blew gently toward the black speck, and the halo flared into sparks as her breath interacted with it. The orb slowly drifted away from Kiera and closer to Lachlan.

"I don't know if that was a good idea," Willow said, her eyebrows drawn together in a worried frown.

Kiera remained focused on the dot with a thoughtful expression. Lachlan inched closer still for a better look. "What is it, Kiera?"

She seemed to be performing some mental calculations or searching her memory for a forgotten nugget of knowledge. Finally, she said, "I'm not sure why, but I think that might be something infinitely more dangerous. While mini black holes probably exist, current theories predict that they would evaporate in fractions of a nanosecond."

Lachlan marveled at the depth of knowledge in their head. She and Willow were extraordinary. He had met many memorable people in his long life, but these two would always hold a special place in his heart. Willow in particular.

"Kiera?" Her silence was disconcerting. The others gazed at Kiera with expressions ranging from Fynn's curiosity to Zoie's rapt horror. Fynn edged closer, extending a finger to touch it.

"Don't touch that!" Kiera grabbed his arm and pulled him back. Finally, in almost a whisper, she said, "Antimatter. I think it's antimatter. And if it is, once it touches anything substantial, there will be a massive explosion—I don't know why it hasn't exploded already. In case you haven't noticed, it seems to be falling slowly. We have maybe a minute, before we're all annihilated."

Lachlan felt a sensation like ice water running through his veins. Of course. Suspicion turned to certainty. Crom Cruach had left them a gift. Antimatter or not, Lachlan was certain of one thing. Kiera was right. That tiny object would soon explode and vaporize every last one of them and the rock they stood on.

"No running then?" Fynn asked with surprising composure. Certainly more than Lachlan felt.

Kiera shook her head. "I don't think so."

"We're buggered then?"

"Probably."

Sixty-Eight

Lachlan understood perfectly.

Antimatter was the opposite of matter. When the two collided, both were destroyed in the reaction, releasing massive amounts of energy. Like a nuclear bomb. The Einstein equation in action.

That speck was retribution. Payback. Crom Cruach was wily, talented, and supremely evil. He would have thought about revenge. Losing with no way out—just like Anna Flecher—he had cast a spell and taken a parting shot to get even. Now Lachlan was certain of one thing. That orb was exactly what Kiera suspected it was. He had no alternative theories regardless. Even if it wasn't antimatter, he was convinced it was very dangerous.

Lachlan knew of no spell that would convert matter to antimatter, wasn't sure it even fell within the realm of possibility. Then he considered alchemy. He had toyed with it over the years, but the results had been uniformly poor. The new substance or metal reverted to base substances fairly quickly. He had used the trick himself. Of course, in this case, the material needn't last long. Worse, the reversion to regular matter might be equally deadly. Maybe they had assisted him. By compressing the darkness, they may have provided sufficient energy within the sphere of the sídrand. Given him the boost he needed.

Oh, bitter irony.

Fynn stepped forward and cautiously slid his hand palm up beneath the black orb.

"Don't touch that!" Kiera barked. "Are you nuts?"

"A hunch." Fynn stayed focused and slowly raised his hand. The sphere stopped its lazy descent and slowly rose. He held his other hand palm down above it, but the particle slid sideways to the left.

An impressive intuition, Lachlan thought. He put out his left hand and deflected the speck to the right. When Lachlan raised his right hand, it drifted toward him.

Bloody hell!

He lifted his left hand, palm out, and the orb moved toward Fynn. By continually moving their hands, they were able to hold it in check, just like ping pong—except that they dare not touch the ball.

But for how long? He and Fynn needed to get everyone else out and away from here.

Now.

Leah stepped forward to assist, but Lachlan blocked her path. "No! This is too dangerous. Fynn and I will deal with it!"

Dana quickly pulled her back and swept her into a protective hug. "They're right! We need to get you out of here!"

Then Willow tried to inch closer, but Lachlan shook his head and blocked her with his arm. "No! You—all of you. Get out! Take the Tahoe and drive away. Now!"

Willow attempted to argue, "But we want to—"

"No! This is out of your league." Lachlan had never felt such dreadful anxiety before. It was probably out of his league too.

Fynn said, "He's right. We'll handle this. Go. Let us concentrate. I'll make sure he doesn't muck it up."

Fynn had somehow feigned greater composure. Lachlan sensed Fynn's anxiety and confusion, which were equal to his. Fynn cared little for modern science, and this antimatter stuff would be Greek to him. It was only in the last few years that Lachlan had taken an interest in the subject. They both felt the same disdain for the newer technology—as most old geezers did. Sometimes, Lachlan wondered if they had simply lived too long.

"What about you two?" Willow clasped her hands and held them to her mouth.

"We'll handle this and follow in Kiera's car."

"What are you going to do with the antimatter—?"

Lachlan took her hand. "You two need to get Leah, Dana, and Zoie to safety. We'll manage this. We're wizards, remember?"

Kiera hooked Willow's arm and tugged.

Lachlan wasn't sure being a wizard would matter and knew Willow was thinking with her emotions. Kiera was the more rational of the two. Good. He wanted Willow out and away from here.

Willow gave him a long, lingering hug and said, "You be careful."

"I will. Go, hurry."

As Dana, Leah, Kiera, and Zoie ran out the front door, Willow turned back, fixed her eyes on Lachlan, and said, "I love you."

Those were the absolute last words he expected to hear from her. They almost knocked him on his bum. Windblown and disheveled, she still looked like a goddess.

He pursed his lips, self-conscious in a sudden rush of emotion. Finally, he mumbled, "I love you too. Go!"

Fynn spoke under his breath. "She's very—"

"Not a word!" Lachlan ran a finger across his neck as their footsteps faded into the night.

Lachlan heard the Tahoe start and pull away. Then the only sound was a faint hiss from the orb. The wind outside was easing, the storm spiraling away to the northeast. The silence was ethereal. The room felt like a cathedral nave or some other deeply spiritual place with the ancient gods in attendance.

Fynn said, "What shall we do with this bloody thing?"

Lachlan shook his head. The dot had drifted lazily toward the tower.

Lachlan tried to stop it by blocking with his left hand. It slowed but didn't stop. When Fynn added his hand, the orb stopped but then began falling, slightly faster than before. It seemed the more they blocked or interfered with it, the faster it moved.

Shite! They were running out of time.

He saw Fynn's shoulders slump as he evidently realized they may not make it out alive.

While that might be the case, Lachlan only worried about giving the others time to escape. Leah especially, but also Willow. He was smitten for the first time in many, many years. He could no longer remember how long. No matter. He pulled his mind back to the present and the task at hand. They had to delay the inevitable.

"All we can do is buy them time," Lachlan said. "We may be done for, mate."

As they talked and considered, they played an intricate game of cat and mouse with the tiny ball of antimatter.

"Lovely. Any chance this is something else and not this antimatter stuff?"

Lachlan shrugged with a small head shake. "I have no idea. Anything is possible."

"What if we just cut and run?" Fynn asked, his brow furrowed.

"If this *is* antimatter, we may not make it. I'm worried about the others. I think the course is clear. We need to see this to the end to ensure they're safe."

Lachlan had known this man more than a millennium. Their enduring friendship was deep and marked by considerable mutual respect. Along with Kenric, they had become the backbone of the Aeldo after their mentor, Godric, had passed. He was no longer sure if any others remained—perhaps they were the last of their kind. Lachlan placed a hand on Fynn's shoulder. "We need to make sure Crom Cruach is eliminated once and for all. I'm afraid that's our duty, even if it costs us our lives. Kenric unwittingly set this business in motion and we're obligated to finish it."

Fynn nodded. "Still, I wouldn't mind making it out alive."

"Neither would I. But according to some annoying pop singer, you can't always get what you want."

"Annoying pop singer?" Fynn said incredulously. "It's Jagger, you tosser! That song is fecking brilliant."

"Whatever." This wasn't the time nor the place given their impending fate.

Fynn looked to Lachlan, a hint of resignation in his face. "We've had a good run, my friend."

"Indeed, we have," Lachlan said. An idea began to form in his head. "What if we send it out over the water?"

"I was wondering the same thing."

Fynn tossed a rock through the nearest window facing the water. They heard it splash seconds later. The path was clear.

"Then that's the plan," Lachlan said. "Where's Kiera's vehicle?"

"On the bluff where I started out."

Probably too far to run. "Did Zoie have a car?"

"Yep. All four tires are flat."

"Damn!" Nothing would be easy. Just like last year in the cavern. He had barely escaped with his life then. He didn't fancy the odds this time. It helped having his old friend here even if they were blown to bloody bits.

Fynn tugged on his ear. "You think they're far enough away? Do you think they're safe?"

"We can't know for sure, but I think so." Soon the decision would be out of their hands. The orb was a time bomb—a ticking menace without a timer.

"Best course out of here?" Fynn raised his eyebrows. "What are you thinking?"

"Straight out the front door, down the drive, into the woods. The trees will temper any blast, hopefully. We'll keep running south in a straight line."

Fynn nodded. "Agreed. Think we'll make it?"

"Haven't the foggiest." Lachlan eyed Fynn with a resigned look. "Ready?"

Fynn pulled Lachlan into a hug and said, "Let's roll. Isn't that what the kids say these days?"

Lachlan embraced his friend and nodded.

The shortest path to the water was out a north-facing window. The wind was blowing out of the west-southwest. Given that the keeper's house had been built facing slightly northwest, the wind would help them push the deadly orb out over the water.

"Okay, let's send it to the north with an upward trajectory."

"Agreed."

With some fancy hand and footwork, they focused on the black dot and sent it floating toward the window and the water beyond. They inched away to avoid creating disruptive air currents. When they were certain the antimatter was on a favorable trajectory, Lachlan whispered with a wave of his arm, "Go!"

They ran.

Out the front door.

Ran like the wind.

Sixty-Nine

Kiera led the way.

Looking over her shoulder repeatedly, she dragged Willow along as she rushed out the front door into the dark night. When Lachlan said they had to move quickly, she took him exactly at his word. She hopped into the Tahoe and fired it up as the others piled in. It was the only vehicle left and, having driven it last, she felt the most adept at handling its current idiosyncrasies.

"Everybody in?"

The doors slammed. Willow slapped the dashboard and yelled, "Yep. Go!"

Kiera tore down the drive, skidding as she turned west onto the highway toward Gills Rock. She was deeply worried about Fynn and Lachlan. Whatever they faced was bad and she knew it. She really wanted to stay and help and felt certain Willow did as well. It felt wrong leaving them behind, but they needed to get Leah, Dana, and Zoie away from the lighthouse. That was their responsibility.

"They'll figure it out," Willow said.

Reassuring herself, Kiera suspected. She pursed her lips and gave Willow a tight nod.

The more she thought about the strange orb, the less she believed it was antimatter. Her scientific mind felt compelled to pick at the question from every angle. It made no sense. Antimatter couldn't exist on earth and if it did, it would have reacted immediately and violently with the air in the room. And how would it arise spontaneously in the lighthouse?

Kiera had no answers. Most everything she had seen today defied much of the science she did know. That mysterious little sphere, the Draugen, Crom Cruach, Fynn and Lachlan, the vortex, the sword—all of it incomprehensible scientifically. Nope, she decided those answers were probably written on magic paper taped to the pot of gold at the end of the rainbow.

She snapped back to the present. She had to remain vigilant, watching the road ahead, which was littered with branches of various sizes and occasional pieces of outdoor furniture. Right now, her job was getting these people to safety, Leah first and foremost. When Lachlan said it was out of their league, she believed him. Hell, she knew nothing of their world and whether it extended to the ability to create antimatter. Conversely, she worried that their knowledge didn't extend to antimatter and they would be killed trying to handle it, wizards or not.

She tried not to think that way—that things would go badly—but then the questions, doubts, and fears intruded again, and the entire process started over.

In the passenger seat, Willow sat chewing a nail while tears ran down her cheeks. The others rode silently in back. Leah resting, eyes closed, Dana wearing a worried mom face. Zoie hadn't spoken a word since they killed the woman in black and looked catatonic.

Lost in her thoughts, Kiera almost missed the tree in the road lit by just one wonky headlight.

Kiera stomped her foot on the brake and the Tahoe skewed and slid sideways. A large Colorado spruce had been uprooted and blocked the road. There would be no driving around this obstruction. They had traveled maybe a mile, half the distance to Gills Rock. Had they come far enough?

No way to know. Regardless, they needed to assume the worst and walk to put more distance between them and the lighthouse. It would only take another fifteen minutes or so. There was no other road to Gills Rock—unless they backtracked to the lighthouse.

"We're gonna have to walk," Kiera said. "Hurry!"

Willow nodded and pushed her door open.

"Wait," Leah said, sitting forward.

Willow and Kiera both turned, agape. Kiera said, "What?"

"Give me a minute." Leah closed her eyes. Squeezed them tight. Held a fist to her lips.

A moment later, Willow grabbed Kiera's arm. "Look!"

The left side of the tree was rising, slowly but perceptibly. The road appeared beneath the branches. Soon there was a gap of almost six feet between the road and the upper part of the tree. There was room to squeak through, but was it safe? Of course, how safe were they if they stayed here?

As if reading her mind, Willow yelled, "What are you waiting for? Go! Hit it!"

Kiera cranked the wheel and swerved, barely holding the shoulder of the road as they accelerated under the tree. Safely past it, Kiera peeked in the rearview mirror and saw the tree crash back to earth.

"Good lord, girl. That was amazing!" Kiera said.

Leah just leaned back and closed her eyes, looking pleased with herself.

The rest of the trip was uneventful. They were almost two miles from the lighthouse. Would that be enough? Kiera didn't know but had no desire to drive farther in case Fynn and Lachlan needed help, or a ride.

It was one in the morning and a lone tavern remained open in Gills Rock, neon beer signs beckoning them to warmth and alcohol.

Willow pointed. "Let's wait there."

Kiera pulled in. The doors opened and, as they stepped out, Leah blurted, "They're running! They're out of the lighthouse!"

Willow grabbed Kiera's arm. "We need to go back!"

"We're staying here," Dana said with some mixture of anger and weariness.

"Good idea," Kiera said. "You three stay here. Willow and I will go partway back and see if they need help—or a ride."

Leah said, "Mom, I have to go. That tree's in the way."

Dana sighed heavily and shot Kiera and Willow an ugly look. Finally, she said, "All right."

"We won't get too close," Kiera said. She wasn't happy taking Leah closer to the lighthouse either. Dana looked seriously pissed and she understood why.

As she climbed back into the Tahoe, Kiera noticed that Zoie hadn't moved from her seat. She feared Zoie was broken.

Suddenly, the ground and the truck shuddered as the night sky lit up with a brilliant flash of white light, followed seconds later by the sound of a deafening explosion.

A strong gust front blew through town, and the shock wave rocked the truck as a mushroom cloud rose into the sky. The windshield cracked and the large illuminated bar sign crashed, shattering on the tarmac of the parking lot.

Gradually, the light of the explosion faded, and the dark of night returned while small stones and vegetation rained down. Several people ran out of the bar.

Willow screamed and let out an agonized, drawn out, "No!"

Kiera slid over and tried to console her. "Maybe—"

"Go back! Go back! Go back!" Willow yelled, slamming her fist on the dashboard.

Kiera jumped over, backed up a bit, and threw the wheel all the way to the left as she burned rubber and accelerated back toward the lighthouse. She felt dread rising within, clawing her insides as the shock from the explosion wore off. She feared the worst. Struggling with the wheel and her emotions as she drove, the Tahoe pulled to the left even more than before. She kept a wary eye open for the spruce in the road and feared they were placing Leah in unnecessary danger.

Visibility was bad with one headlight but as they drove east, Kiera saw that more and more of the trees lining the road had been knocked flat. They had fallen parallel to the roadway and were pointing away from the lighthouse. The spruce that had blocked the road earlier had been pushed partway off the road.

Kiera squinted. The road and surrounding landscape looked unusually dark ahead. She took her foot off the gas, then slammed on the brakes when she realized the road ahead was simply gone. They skidded, stopping ten feet short of the jagged edge of the demolished roadbed.

The cloud cover was breaking and the waning gibbous moon peeked from an opening, illuminating an apocalyptic scene. The truck stood at the edge of a crater at least two thousand feet across. The Porte des Morts passage was visible only because everything between them and the water had disappeared.

Vanished. The road, trees, the bluff, and the lighthouse were gone. All of it.

As they all climbed out to look, Willow cried out, "Lachlan!"

Kiera felt gut-punched, stunned by the destruction. Had Lachlan and Fynn escaped? It didn't seem possible.

Leah had said they were running, but they hadn't passed them on the road.

Maybe they had run south?

As if reading her mind, Leah said, "They ran to the south. I'm trying to contact them."

After a moment, Willow said anxiously, "Did you find them?"

"Nothing yet," Leah said with a distracted scowl. "The explosion messed up the energy fields in the area."

Despite the shock of the moment, Kiera was struck by her adult assessment of the situation. They remained standing in the road, watching, waiting. Minutes passed and they all stared at the girl, looking out over the crater, her blonde hair billowing in the breeze.

More time passed. In the distance, they heard the first sirens, red and blue lights reflecting off the low clouds to the west. The wind was fresh and clean. Kiera thought she saw a helicopter approaching from the south, a low flashing light. Then she heard the faint beat of the rotors. Soon, the whole world would be here.

"Did they make it?" Willow clung to Kiera, clutching her arm with both hands.

Kiera looked at Leah, hopeful, fearful, feeling as shell-shocked as the others looked.

Finally, Leah looked up with tears in her eyes.

"No. They didn't. They're gone."

Seventy

Kiera couldn't sleep.

Lying in bed, staring at the ceiling, she was in considerable physical pain from her encounter with the Draugen. The day continued to play out in her brain in disconnected loops. Nearly dying beneath a fat dead man. Almost losing her best friend to the lake. The storm. Fynn on the cliff. The orb. The last glance over her shoulder at Lachlan and Fynn as they fled the lighthouse. The explosion. At that point, she was invariably overcome by grief and sadness, and the tears came again.

Stupid things popped into her mind as well. Willow losing the boat. The Tahoe beaten within an inch of its life. Fynn had left her RAV4 sitting on the bluff. What would she tell the insurance company? Then she would think, *who the hell cares?*

Willow lay on the other bed crying, occasionally sobbing and punching the mattress, mumbling to herself. Kiera occasionally heard Lachlan's name. Willow was inconsolable and had pushed Kiera away when she tried to comfort her. It pained her deeply to watch Willow suffer so.

Hours earlier, they had driven to the bed-and-breakfast in Sister Bay just as the first squad cars and helicopters arrived. Kiera had driven a roundabout route to avoid police, worried about being stopped and questioned.

No one spoke during the trip, and Zoie had wandered away after they parked and shuffled into the Inn. Exhausted and in shock, no one had noticed her leave. Kiera worried about her being alone and spent ten fruitless minutes driving around, looking for her. Maybe she lived in town and had gone home, though really, they knew little about her. If nothing else, they owed Zoie a big *thank you*, though Kiera mostly worried about her mental state.

At four in the morning, certain sleep would never come, Kiera walked to the dining room for coffee. One of the owners was sitting at the table, drinking coffee and watching CNN. Kiera poured a cup of coffee and wandered over.

"Any news?"

"Nothing, so far. Just that there was an explosion." The man was heavy and bald, wearing grey sweats. He looked her up and down and said, "What happened to you?"

"Oh, car accident." Kiera didn't know what else to say. She made a little small talk and retreated to her room.

Just after seven-thirty, the sun rose into a clear blue sky, an ironic bookend to the night before. The air was November crisp and still, the temperature near freezing. Kiera walked around town, astonished by all the activity taking place.

The road was closed just north of the Inn, and it looked like they had cordoned off the entire area. All the side roads were blocked as well, a perimeter manned by the police, various sheriffs, and the National Guard. There was a veritable alphabet soup of government people in the area. FBI, ATF, Homeland Security. Overhead, black helicopters flew back and forth.

The walk did little to relieve her abject sense of gloom, so she roused everyone for breakfast. A meal seemed like a good idea even though she wasn't hungry herself. Or maybe food was just a reflexive human response to stress. Besides, she wanted to leave and get away from here. The sooner, the better. There was no reason to stay, and she didn't want to risk being questioned by the police or the FBI.

They sat silent and sullen at breakfast, picking at their food, eating little of it.

Setting her napkin down, Willow pushed her chair back and said, "I want to go back."

"You can't," Kiera said.

"I don't care. I want to try."

"I want to leave as soon as possible," Dana said curtly.

"So do I," Kiera said. "Willow, the roads are blocked. The FBI is here. We don't want to get caught up in that."

Willow stood and walked away.

At ten o'clock, two sheriff's deputies marched into the bed-and-breakfast and announced that an evacuation was underway. Everyone, including the owners, had one hour to leave town. They recited a vague story about the need to move people out of the danger zone after the explosion. While Kiera suspected there was no danger, the authorities couldn't possibly know what actually happened and wouldn't want people snooping around. Fair enough. Given the size of the blast, they were probably in panic mode.

They discovered the right front tire on the Tahoe was flat after packing and checking out. Kiera, with an assist from Dana, used a tire iron to bend the fender back and changed the tire. As they loaded their things into the Tahoe, two black Chargers arrived, filled with men and women in black suits. More feds, probably. They milled about on the street, supervising the evacuation of the town. Their presence gave Kiera chills. This was becoming a very big deal.

Kiera drove. Willow was in no condition to drive and continued to cry quietly on and off. With the evacuation, chaos reigned. Traffic was a nightmare.

She tried to clear her mind and achieve some level of mindfulness, but she couldn't. The weight of the last twenty-four hours was almost too much to bear. Driving was uncomfortable with her bruised ribs and neck. The emotional toll was worse. She couldn't believe they were gone. Lachlan with his quiet wisdom. Fynn with his flippant attitude about most everything. Their easy camaraderie.

Dana sat in back with her eyes closed, her arms crossed tightly. Leah looked catatonic. Maybe she was sleeping.

It was a long ride, and no one spoke, not a single word all the way to Miller's Crossing.

One thing continued to bother Kiera. She had no idea what the explosion meant. Had Lachlan and Fynn prevailed? Or had the darkness managed to slip away yet again?

With Fynn and Lachlan gone, how would they ever know?

Seventy-One

Kiera clicked the TV off.

Setting the remote aside, she said, "They'll never figure it out."

Dana nodded in agreement. They were sitting at the island in Kiera's kitchen just after seven am. The island, an oak rectangle, was covered with a beautiful piece of dark green granite. The coffee was fresh and hot, their mugs steaming.

The news story, filled with utter fabrications, had gone national. The army claimed that a ship carrying munitions had foundered and broken up in the Porte des Morts strait during the worst Great Lakes storm in living memory. There had been an explosion. They showed a fuzzy photo of debris and warned that a twenty-mile perimeter had been set up until they were certain the area was safe. Sadly, the historic and picturesque Porte des Morts lighthouse had been destroyed in the explosion. Rumors about a nuclear weapons accident or a terrorist incident were false. There were no photos or videos of the explosion itself and the media had been denied access to the area.

Kiera had slept fitfully. Dana said she hadn't slept at all and looked the part, her skin grey and papery. Dark rings lined her eyes. Kiera hadn't looked in the mirror yet, but she knew she looked worse.

Perhaps reading her mind, Dana said, "You look like hell."

Kiera just nodded. Ghost had tucked himself between the island and her stool, and she ran her bare feet lightly over his furry back. He had been incredibly needy since they returned from Door County, permanently glued to her side. Or maybe he sensed her unease and wanted to be supportive. Either way, his presence was soothing.

"How is Leah doing?" Kiera asked.

"She was awake most of the night, but she won't talk to me. Still in shock, I think." Dana cupped her mug in two hands and sipped her coffee. "She's resilient, but she had a special connection with those two—they were the only other people she knew who were like her."

"Oh, jeez. I never thought of it that way," Kiera said.

"I think she's felt lonely at times," Dana said. "Lachlan had offered to work with her. Now I don't know what we'll do."

"Not something you can look up on the internet, is it?" It wasn't really a question.

"Nope." Dana shook her head and sighed.

Kiera ran her finger along the lines in the granite, thinking, wondering. "These guys, Lachlan, Fynn, and Kenric. Do we really know who or what they were?"

Dana said, "They were part of some warrior class of wizards or something, I'm not sure. The whole thing sounds ludicrous—crazy."

Kiera nodded. "It does—except for everything we witnessed at the lighthouse."

Until last year, Kiera had been blissfully unaware of their world, a realm beyond current science, existing on a completely different plane, populated with outlandish characters both good and bad. A world that was invisible without a psychic gift. Still, it wasn't something she could unlearn or forget. She now saw the world through a different lens. Never again would she feel safe in her smug scientific certainties.

She had lived it, experienced it, and it still sounded ridiculous. There was no telling this story. People would lump her with the conspiracy nuts in tin foil hats. It was sad. Those men were two of the most principled people she had ever met. Gallant like knights of old. Charitable. Guided by insanely moral compasses. The world would never know what they had lost. Tragic, really.

Kiera said, "I think we just lost two of the finest men on the planet."

"I think you're right."

There was a deep sadness in her eyes and Kiera thought about Dana's family and all they had lost. Thought of the people who had died last year in Miller's Crossing. Now this. In two years, the death toll had been horrendous. All the consequence of one woman's death five hundred years before in England. The name Anna Flecher should be consigned to infamy as a prolific serial killer, but the world would never know her name.

They sipped at their coffees for five or ten minutes, lost in their thoughts. Dana stared into space.

Kiera wondered where she would go from here. Her entire life had been upended, and she saw no way forward. Besides the fur baby at her feet and the broken friend sleeping nearby, it felt like she had nothing left.

Dana then voiced the fear they both had been avoiding. "We don't even know if it's over. That's the worst part."

"I didn't want to say that. I can't stand thinking it might not be over."

"Me either."

A quiet voice spoke from the doorway. "It's over."

Leah stood there, clutching a blanket in her right hand.

"Are you sure?" Dana knitted her brow. "How can you be sure?"

"You're my mom. You know how." Leah tapped her head with her forefinger. "I just do. It's over."

She walked over and crawled onto Dana's lap.

Five years old, she had seen more, done more, lost more than most people would experience in a lifetime. She shared a powerful gift with Lachlan and Fynn. If Leah said it was over, Kiera believed it was over.

Dana stroked her hair. "Promise?"

Leah snuggled into Dana's embrace. "Promise."

Seventy-Two

Kiera hugged herself and shivered.

The sun shone brightly, but the winter rays were feeble. It was twenty-one degrees below zero and the waters of the Ports des Morts passage were mostly frozen. A raw January wind hailed out of the north. The bluff and beautiful stone lighthouse that once stood to the northwest were gone, reduced to a rocky pile of rubble that rose just above the waterline.

Willow had dressed like a widow all in black, including a black parka. Kiera, Dana, and Leah were heavily bundled in coats, hats, gloves and scarfs. The four of them had come to hold a brief, private ceremony. To pay their last respects.

They stood on the shore at Porte des Morts Park at the base of the steel staircase that had somehow survived the blast. The park was otherwise a wasteland. Every tree had been blown down except for a few scrub trees and some brush. All that remained were the stumps and stacks of timber, cut and ready to be hauled away.

Ceremony was probably the wrong word as no solemn words were spoken. Instead, they told stories about their dear friends, Lachlan and

Fynn, reliving the fonder memories and talking about the enduring sense of friendship between the two men.

It was, in essence, a wake.

They communed with the rocks and the waters of Porte des Morts. Felt warmed by the moment of shared grief. There were no graves to honor. Fynn and Lachlan's bodies were never recovered. No remains had been found in the blast zone itself. Twelve people, all locals who lived just outside that area, were found dead in cabins or homes destroyed by the explosion.

Kiera found Zoie through the website for the Door County Paranormal Society. She seemed upset that Kiera had tracked her down. After a couple of minutes mumbling about some vague and ongoing health issues, she told Kiera, "don't bother calling again" and hung up. Sadly, Kiera understood perfectly.

Willow opened a bottle of thirty-year-old tawny Port. It was Lachlan's favorite *bracer*, as he called it. They weren't sure about Fynn's preference, but Willow thought he would be fine with it.

Willow raised her glass. A tear ran down her cheek. "To Lachlan and Fynn, two of the finest people I've ever known."

They all clinked glasses and drank. Leah toasted with orange juice.

More quietly, Willow said, "To Lachlan, my soulmate. I hope we meet again."

They stood for a minute, heads down, then carefully approached a small hole in the ice. One by one, they each tossed one of the amulets Lachlan had given them into the water.

This place was indeed a door to death, but Kiera hoped that for Lachlan and Fynn, it had also been a doorway to the next life.

Finally, the bitter cold chased them off the beach and Kiera was happy to leave. Just being here raised the persistent anxiety that it wasn't over, that things might start all over again. Kiera wondered if the others felt the same. Dana seemed to be less angry now. That was good. She needed to be there for Leah. Kiera wasn't angry. Just profoundly sad, a feeling that seemed immune to time. And haunted by everything she had seen in an unending parade of nightmares and flashbacks.

As they approached the vehicles, Kiera offered to buy dinner for Dana and Leah, but they declined, anxious to get back to Naperville. Before leaving, they gave each other long hugs—tearful goodbyes with promises to stay in touch and get together sometime.

Would they, she wondered?

Kiera and Willow stopped for dinner in Fish Creek, a quaint but upscale Door County town filled with shops and restaurants, a town that wouldn't look out of place on Cape Cod. O'Dougan's Pub was a mishmash of Irish and British influences, and it seemed a fitting place to stop, to pay their respects to Lachlan and Fynn with a meal in their honor.

Seated in a quiet corner, the booth was wonderfully private. A good thing, as Willow was still weepy after the wake. She was somber and carried the pain of losing Lachlan on her sleeve. She occasionally reverted to her outgoing, fun-loving ways, but Kiera knew it was only a front for the intense sense of loss she felt.

After ordering wine, Kiera put her hand on Willow's. "I love you and I'm here for you."

Willow dabbed her eyes. "I know. I love you too."

"You considered him a soulmate? I've never heard you say that before."

"I do. I can't explain fully, but he was right inside my head. I was right inside his head. It was intimate on a level I can't even describe. I know I'll never feel it again."

A long silence hung over the table. Kiera couldn't imagine knowing someone that well. Being that connected. She felt a little envious.

The wine arrived and the waiter took their order. As he walked away, Kiera tapped Willow's hand and said, "Guess who called me yesterday?"

"No idea."

"Josh."

Willow perked up. "Really? Do tell."

"He wants to give us another chance."

"And are you going to?"

Kiera smiled. "I think I am."

★ ★ ★

Leah decided the time was right.

They would be in the car for another two hours before they got home. She had been putting this off partly because she couldn't think about Lachlan and Fynn without becoming very sad. And because her mother was going to be mad.

Mom was still having trouble dealing with the events at the lighthouse, still feeling lost, angry, sad.

Leah had developed a sense of calm by believing that Lachlan watched over her like a guardian angel. She hadn't seen him, hadn't talked to him, and realized her belief was childish. She didn't care. She was still a child—even if she wasn't a normal child. And she knew that the monster was dead and gone.

"Mom. Lachlan gave me something before we left the lighthouse."

Her mother gave her a startled look. "What?"

"He gave me a book."

"When? Why are you just telling me now?" Her eyes narrowed.

This might not go well.

"During the ceremony in the lighthouse." More quietly, she said, "I knew it would upset you."

"Do you have it with you?"

Leah nodded.

"Show me."

"I can't." She then pointed to her temple. "It's here in my head. He uploaded it to my brain, just like you upload books to your Kindle."

Mom stared straight ahead, her mouth tight. She didn't say another word. She was really mad.

Uh-oh.

She pulled off at the next exit, parked at a gas station, turned and gave Leah her sternest mom-look. "What's it about?"

"It's like a schoolbook."

"What?"

"It's a book," Leah said. "To help me learn how to use my abilities."

"Do you understand it?"

"Most of it. Lachlan wrote it just for me, but maybe it can help you too."

"I doubt it." Mom stared out the windshield for the longest time.

It had started to snow, and flakes drifted lazily to earth. Mom seemed to relax. Finally, she said, "So, what am I thinking right now?"

"I know you're mad at Lachlan."

"Maybe. Truth is, I feel stupid around you sometimes."

"I know. I'm sorry." And she was. Besides, it was silly. Mom was the smartest person she knew. Leah smiled and said, "Okay. So, what am *I* thinking?"

"I don't know. I'm not like you."

"Fynn said you were."

Her mother shook her head. "He was trying to make me feel better."

"Then how did you know I was in trouble that day?"

"I don't know. I just did."

"You talked to me *in my head.*"

"I don't remember that." But Leah knew she wasn't being completely honest.

"So, let's try it again," Leah said. "What am I thinking now?"

Leah concentrated hard, drawing a vivid picture of a red container, filled with french fries.

A minute went by. Then two.

Mom turned her head suddenly with a dawning expression. "You want McDonald's?"

"Very good, Mom." Leah snuggled into her. "See? Fynn was right. You do have it."

Thank you!

Thank you for reading *Hayward's Revenge*. I hope you enjoyed it. As an independently published author, I rely on all of you wonderful readers to spread the word. If you enjoyed *Hayward's Revenge*, please tell your friends and family. I would also sincerely appreciate a brief review on Amazon.

    Again, thank you!
    Cailyn Lloyd
    http://www.cailynlloyd.net

Acknowledgments

Many thanks to Jennie Lloyd who read and critiqued all three drafts and provided many valuable observations.

Thank you to Lucy Snyder and Susanne Lakin for their insightful critiques of the early drafts.

Also, thank you to Sara Kelly who provided editorial guidance and copyedited the final draft.

And lastly, thanks to Katie Lloyd who proofread the completed manuscript.

The Porte des Morts passage is real as are the historical stories and the shipwrecks. Door County, Wisconsin takes its name from this place. With the exception of the lighthouse, the place names are real but used fictitiously. The inns, taverns, and restaurants are fictitious.

Books by Cailyn Lloyd

Shepherd's Warning (2019)
The Elders Book 1

Quinlan's Secret (2020)
The Elders Book 2

Hayward's Revenge (2021)
The Elders Book 3

Made in the USA
Coppell, TX
03 July 2021